HIGHLAND HUNGER

Marsi's breath caught in her throat. Her lips parted.

"Ah, lassie," he said, moving his free hand gently under her veil to the back of her head. "You are as tempting as any woman I've ever met. I believe you'd have tempted Saint Columba, and God kens that I am no such virtuous fellow."

With that, Hawk's fingers laced themselves through her hair and he pulled her closer, bending just enough to touch his lips to hers. At first, she thought he would taste them and tease them as he had before. Instead, he pressed his own hard against hers, demanding a response and holding her in place with the hand at the back of her head, as if he feared that she might try to slip free.

She did not. Every fiber of her body responded to his, and eagerly. She could not have pulled away had she wanted to.

"Scott creates a lovely, complex cast."
—*Publishers Weekly*

BORDER MOONLIGHT

"Features Scott's trademarks: strong-willed women and warrior men, mystery and intrigue, dashes of humor and wit, deep characterization, complex plots, and, above all, historical and geographic accuracy in the days of ancient Scotland." —*Sacramento Bee*

"Fast-paced...An exciting Border romance with plenty of action...A terrific historical gender war."
—*Midwest Book Review*

BORDER LASS

"5 Stars! A thrilling tale, rife with villains and notorious plots...Scott demonstrates again her expertise in the realm of medieval Scotland."
—FallenAngelReviews.com

"4½ Stars! TOP PICK! Readers will be thrilled...a tautly written, deeply emotional love story steeped in the rich history of the Borders." —*RT Book Reviews*

"Scott excels in creating memorable characters."
—FreshFiction.com

OTHER BOOKS BY AMANDA SCOTT

AMANDA SCOTT

Highland Hero

FOREVER

NEW YORK   BOSTON

This book is a work of fiction. Names, characters, places, and incidents are the product of the author's imagination or are used fictitiously. Any resemblance to actual events, locales, or persons, living or dead, is coincidental.

Copyright © 2011 by Lynne Scott-Drennan
Excerpt from *Highland Lover* copyright © 2011 by Lynne Scott-Drennan
All rights reserved. Except as permitted under the U.S. Copyright Act of 1976, no part of this publication may be reproduced, distributed, or transmitted in any form or by any means, or stored in a database or retrieval system, without the prior written permission of the publisher.

Forever
Hachette Book Group
237 Park Avenue
New York, NY 10017

www.HachetteBookGroup.com

Forever is an imprint of Grand Central Publishing.
The Forever name and logo are trademarks of Hachette Book Group, Inc.

The publisher is not responsible for websites (or their content) that are not owned by the publisher.

Printed in the United States of America

First Edition: October 2011
10 9 8 7 6 5 4 3 2 1

To Caitlyn, born 25 August 2010,
endowed with true grit and an indomitable spirit

Rothiemurchus

CAIRNGORMS

Balmoral

HIGHLANDS

Cargill

Dundee

Perth

St. Andrews

Lindores

River Earn

FIFE

MENTEITH

Kincardine

Aberfoyle

Doune

Falkland

Drymen

Dunblane

Firth of Forth

Balloch

Stirling

Dumbarton

Milton

Glasgow

Edinburgh

Firth of Clyde

Ayr

SCOTLAND 1402

Turnberry Castle

1 Loch of Menteith
2 Redmyre Tower
3 Firth of Tay
-- Highland Line

Author's Note———————

For the reader's convenience, the author offers the following guide:

Ivor (hero's name) = EE-ver

Aberuthven = Aber-RIV-en

Behouchie = backside

Clachan = Highland village

Fain = eager

Forbye = besides, furthermore, however

Pawkie = roguish, coquettish

Plaid (great kilt) = all-purpose garment formed from length of wool kilted up with a belt, the excess length then flung over the wearer's shoulder.

Rothesay = ROSS-y

Ruthven = RIV-en

Strath = valley, usually a river valley

Prologue _____

The dying Queen's chamber at Scone Abbey was quiet but for a murmur of conversation between her grace and her husband, the King of Scots.

The couple had been conversing in low tones for some time. Nearby, Walter Traill, Bishop of St. Andrews and thus Primate of Scotland, knelt on a prayer cushion. His lips moved in silent prayer for her grace's soul, soon to take flight.

The only other person there was the youngest of the Queen's ladies. Wearing a demure gray damask gown with a white caul and veil to conceal her hair, she sat on a cushioned seat in the window embrasure. Occasionally, she touched the narrow gold ring on the middle finger of her left hand.

The door to the chamber opened to the sound of muttered expostulation from the arcade outside. A terse but otherwise unintelligible remark followed.

Silence fell when a tall, thin, dark-haired man entered the chamber alone.

Bishop Traill crossed himself and got to his feet.

With a measuring look at the Queen, he said, "My lord duke, 'tis good of you to pay your respects. Recall, though, that her grace's doctors desire her to remain peaceful."

The Duke of Albany, at sixty-one, was the King's younger brother. He also stood third in line for the throne after his grace's sons—twenty-three-year-old Davy Stewart, Duke of Rothesay, and seven-year-old James Stewart, Earl of Carrick.

Silver buttons and lacing leavened Albany's customary black clothing. Silver also streaked his once glossy black hair. His dark eyes glinted with intelligence and with the calculating look that was habitual for him.

Queen Annabella visibly recoiled when he approached her deathbed.

"Sister," he said, "I trust that you feel better today. I come only to see if I might do aught to ease your way."

Annabella shut her eyes, then opened them and said, "Thank you, sir. But I..."

When the pause lengthened and her eyes closed again, the King said, "She has asked that we pray for her. Otherwise, we can do nowt. She must rest now."

The firmness in his voice doubtless startled the others in the chamber, for it was unusual. By nature, Robert III of Scotland was gentle and scholarly.

Unimpressed, Albany said, "I mean only to assure her that she need have no concern about her sons. I'll look after them and see that no harm befalls..."

Here, he paused, because the Queen's agitation was plain to all.

The young woman in the window embrasure behind

the duke stood abruptly. Her lips pressed tightly together, and she hesitated, watching him.

Annabella tried to raise her head, but the King gently laid a hand on her brow, saying, "Nay, my love." A wave of his free hand warned his brother off.

Paying no heed, Albany gazed down at the Queen.

The young woman took a step nearer but stopped when the bishop moved to Albany's side. "You do no good here, my son," Traill said. "Her grace did ask that only her close kin attend her. We must pray that Rothesay arrives before she departs."

"I, too, am close kin, Father. I will stay."

"You will go, because your presence upsets her grace when she should stay calm. I have administered the last rites. So for you to disturb her further," he added on a sterner note, "would be an ungodly—in troth, a *censurable* act, my son."

Albany seemed about to refuse again, but the bishop's pale blue gaze caught and held the duke's darker one.

Despite the sternness in Traill's voice, his demeanor remained serene.

Apparently, Albany saw something else, for with a nod, he turned away.

As he did, he encountered the steady, accusatory gaze of the Queen's lady.

An approving spectator of his banishment, she stared calmly at him without flinching, although the look he gave her ought to have chilled her soul.

Despite his departure, Annabella remained agitated, fiercely clutching her husband's arm. When he bent his head near, she muttered anxiously into his ear.

The King nodded and murmured back to her. The

bishop returned to his prayer cushion and his prayers. And the Queen's lady returned to her silent vigil.

Half an hour after Albany left, Davy Stewart, Duke of Rothesay and heir to the Scottish throne, entered the room. He was just in time to bid his mother farewell.

Chapter 1 _____

Scotland, Turnberry Castle, 19 February 1402

Her bare skin was as smooth as the silky gown she had worn before he'd helped her take it off. His fingertips glided over her, stroking a bare arm, a bare shoulder, its soft hollow, and then the softer rise of a full breast heaving with desire for him.

Cupping its softness, he brushed a thumb across its tip, enjoying her passionate moans and arcing body as he did and feeling the nipple harden.

Part of him had hardened, too. His whole body urged him to conquer the lush beauty in his bed. But, although he was an impatient man, he was also one who liked to take his time with women. Experience—a good deal of it—had taught him that coupling was better for both when he took things slowly.

Neither of them spoke, because he rarely enjoyed conversation with sex. Preferring to relish the sensations, he favored partners who did not chatter.

Stimulating them both with his kisses, he shifted an arm across her to position himself for taking her. As she spread her legs for him, she caressed his body with her hands, fingers, and tongue, sparking sensual responses from every nerve.

He found it increasingly harder to resist simply taking her, dominating her, and teaching her who was master in his bed.

The bed shifted slightly on the thought. He had a fleeting semiawareness that he was dreaming—fleeting because he shoved the half-formed thought away lest, if true, he might waken too soon.

Somehow, in the odd way that dreams have of changing things about, the beauty had got to one side of him. He could no longer see her in the darkness, but ever willing, he shifted to accommodate the new arrangement.

Finding the warm, softly silken skin of her shoulder, he reached for her breasts again, rising onto his elbow and leaning over her as he did. He felt her body stiffen. And when his seeking hand found one soft breast, it seemed smaller than before, albeit just as well formed and soft. Sakes, but the *woman* seemed smaller.

Most oddly, though, he touched real silk instead of bare skin.

Undaunted, he ignored her increasing rigidity and slid his hand down to move the annoying silk out of his way, seeking access to his primary objective.

As he eased his hand along one silken thigh, her body heaved. A gasping cry sounded near his right ear, and in a flurry of movement, she slid from his grasp.

Flying from the bed, she managed on her way to deal him a stunning blow on his cheek with a bare-knuckled fist. He saw only flashes of movement after that, and light. Before he could collect himself enough to know that he was awake and had been toying with an unknown but very enticing female in *his* bed, a sound near the door told him that she was rummaging through the kist there.

Leaping from the bed, he shot toward her. But the door crashed back as he reached for her, hitting his out-stretched fingers and hand hard when it did.

The glow of torchlight in the corridor revealed long, lush, dark-red hair; a drab robe hastily flung over a pink shift that barely concealed long, lovely legs; curving hips; and a tantalizingly small waist as she ran. His aching hand and burning cheek provided excellent reasons to retaliate. But he had no sooner started to give chase than he recalled his own state of naked readiness and collected his wits.

Chasing a nubile young beauty by dead of night in a state such as his might find favor in some masculine establishments. But his grace the King's royal castle of Turnberry was definitely *not* one of them.

⁓

The young woman fleeing up the corridor did not dare look behind her, lest her pursuer know and recognize her. But as she gripped the handle of the royal nursery door, she could not resist glancing back through the veil of her unplaited hair to see with a surge of relief that the dimly lit corridor behind her was empty.

She had been sure that he would pursue her. But what a coil if he had! And worse had he chanced to recognize her or see her well enough to know her later.

Shoving the nursery door open, she whisked herself inside. Quietly shutting the door, she eased the latch hook into place and shot the bolt, giving thanks to God that Hetty had not done so before then.

Feeling safe at last, she noted in the light of the one cresset still burning in the chamber, and the dimmer glow of embers from the banked fire, that Hetty was fast asleep on a pallet near the hearth. In the far corner of the room, the drawn curtains of a cupboard bed warned her to wake Hetty quietly.

Moving to the pallet, listening for sounds from the corridor that might herald a search by the man who had been sleeping in Hetty's bed, she gently shook the plump, middle-aged mistress of the royal nursery.

"Hetty, wake up," she murmured. "Oh, don't screech, but do wake up!"

The woman's eyes flew open, and she sat bolt upright. "My lady!" she exclaimed. Softening her voice, she added, "What be ye doing in here?"

Eighteen-year-old Lady Marsaili Drummond Cargill grimaced. "I could not sleep, Hetty. I went to your room and climbed into your bed as I used to do, but—"

"Och! Ye did nae such thing! Not tonight of all—! What time is it then?"

"I don't know. Midnight I think. Oh, Hetty—"

"Mercy, but his grace's man did say—"

"Someone was *in* your bed, Hetty. A man!"

"Is that no what I was just trying to tell ye? The King's gentleman—"

"It cannot have been Dennison," Marsaili said. "Dennison would never—"

"Whisst now, will ye whisst? I'm trying to tell ye, if ye'll just hearken to me. Bless us, but I thought ye'd learned to curb such foolish, impulsive—"

"Hetty, the man was naked!"

Henrietta Childs, mistress of the royal nursery, grabbed

the lady Marsaili firmly by the shoulders, gave her a shake, and looked into her eyes. "Lady Marsi, have done! Tell me right now, was the man awake?"

"Not at first."

"At first!" Hetty's voice went up on the words. With a swift look at the curtained bed in the corner, she lowered it to a whisper to add, "What did he do?"

"He rolled over and...and...Before I realized that he wasn't you—"

"Ay-de-mi! Did he touch ye?"

Remembering, and instantly feeling the strong, hitherto unfamiliar but most pleasurable sensations that his touch had stirred in her, Marsi swallowed. But Hetty looked fierce. And Hetty had known her from her cradle and was reminding her of that with every word and look. So Marsi said, "He did, aye. But he did not see me, Hetty. I jumped out·of the bed, snatched up my robe, and fled here to you."

"Snatched up your robe, did ye? What more have ye got on under it?"

"My shift. But, Hetty, who is he?"

"I dinna know his name, and I'm no to tell anyone about him."

"Hetty, it's me. Who would I tell? I haven't a friend left in this whole castle except you, and haven't had since Aunt Annabella died." Twisting the ring on her left middle finger as she pictured her beloved aunt, she added, "What's more, they say that Albany may arrive tomorrow! And if not tomorrow, then Tuesday. His grace warned me that Albany wants to see me wedded at once and will *not* wait the year that I *should* wait if I am to mourn Aunt Annabella's death properly."

"My lady, I ken fine that the duke comes soon to Turnberry. Sithee, that is why that man sleeps in my bed now."

"He is *Albany's* man?"

"Nay, he is not." Hetty looked upward, as if seeking guidance. Then, drawing breath and letting it out, she said, "I'll tell ye, then. But only so that ye willna go trying to find out for yourself, as I ken fine ye will if I keep silent. But ye must no breathe a word to anyone else of what I say. Swear to it now."

"You know that I will tell no one," Marsi said. "I keep secrets even better than I ferret them out, Hetty. You know that, too."

"I do, aye, or I'd say nowt of this to ye. Your wee cousin Jamie's future may depend on it, though, so see that ye keep your word. Sithee, his grace did send for that man to take our laddie away from here before Albany arrives."

"Away? But when do they go? And where will he take him?"

"Dennison didna say *where* we will go," Hetty said. "Nor were I so brazen as to ask him. But we may go as soon as tomorrow, for I was to pack for Jamie."

"Aye, sure, his grace *must* want Jamie away at once if Albany is coming. Recall that Albany told dearest Annabella that he would look after Jamie and Davy and keep them safe from harm. But she feared that he meant to take charge of Jamie as soon as he could after she was gone and would use him as a pawn whenever he thought that doing so would serve his own ends, just as he means to use me. Then, if he controls Jamie when the King dies, and aught should happen to Davy..."

"Jamie would be all that stands then between Albany

and the throne," Hetty said. "As ruthless as Albany can be, our laddie's very life might be in danger then."

"But I wish that you need not go, Hetty, either of you."

"I'd liefer we didna have to go, either," Hetty said. "I ken fine that ye'll miss us sorely. But if we stay and Albany does come, he'd likely take charge of ye both if he means to arrange for *your* wedding straightaway. And I doubt that he'd let me accompany either of ye then."

"Faith, I wish he would recall that I am not his ward but the King's," Marsi said. "As set as Albany is on marrying me to his boot-licker Redmyre, and as aware as he must be that Aunt Annabella supported my rejection of the match, I doubt that he'll heed my protests, especially if Jamie eludes his grasp."

"He might have to heed ye, though," Hetty said. "Although he is the King's brother and *much* stronger of will, his grace has stood against him before."

Marsi gave an unladylike snort. "Aye, he has, but rarely. You ken as well as I do that his grace cannot hold out long if Albany gets him alone and says that he must do as Albany wishes. What can I do, Hetty? Albany has threatened me with dire punishment if I do not obey him, and in truth, he frightens me."

"Aye, he frightens most folks with any sense."

"Come with us, Marsi," piped up a third voice. "Wherever we go, it must be a happier place than Turnberry will be whilst my uncle Albany bides here."

Both women turned toward the curtained bed, where the tousled auburn head of Marsi's cousin James Stewart, Earl of Carrick, peeped between the blue curtains.

"Jamie, were you listening to us?" Marsi demanded. "Naughty laddie!"

"I couldna sleep," the dark-eyed boy who stood second in line for the Scottish throne said soberly. As always, he sounded older than his seven and a half years.

Hetty got up and reached for a yellow silk robe that lay across a nearby stool. "I'll warm some milk, sir," she said. "It will settle ye again."

"I don't want milk. Must I command ye tae go with us, Marsi?"

"Oh, Jamie, I wish you could. But your royal ways don't fool me, laddie. You fear your uncle almost as much as I do."

"Aye, sure, but he canna find either of us if we be else-where," James pointed out. "When he leaves Turnberry, we can come back and be comfortable again with my royal sire. Do come with us, Marsi. Ye make me laugh, and Hetty does not."

Marsi hesitated, absently twisting the gold ring that her aunt Annabella had given her while she considered Jamie's suggestion.

Hetty gave her a stern look. "Lady Marsi, ye must not. For once, prithee, heed old Hetty, who kens ye best. And heed the consequences, if ye do such a daft thing. Ye're a noblewoman, my lady, and still a maiden! Ye'd be the talk o' all Scotland when it became known that ye'd run off. No to mention what Albany would do when he found ye, *as* he would. That man believes he has as much right as the King does to order your future, and ye've said your-self that his grace will likely agree with him."

But Marsi rarely heeded consequences. Before her dot-ing parents had died and left her a ward of her aunt, the Queen of Scots, most consequences had been pleasant. And when they were not, they were always soon over.

However, with Annabella dead and no longer able to protect her, the cost of staying to face Albany alone could be even worse than she had imagined.

"I could pose as your assistant, Hetty, and help you look after Jamie."

"And *I* could help ye look after Marsi, Hetty," Jamie said, grinning.

Henrietta looked dourly at Marsi. "What was I thinking to tell ye, ye must *not*?" she muttered. "If ye obey Albany, ye'll face only a marriage ye dinna want, as does many a noble maiden by obeying her father. But a body would think that after knowing ye for most of your eighteen years, I'd ken better than to challenge ye so."

"Is anyone else going with you?" Marsi asked. "Any of Jamie's gentlemen?"

"Nay, for his grace kens fine that some of them be in Albany's pay. And nae one save Albany kens which ones. We'll leave afore they arise, I expect."

"Then there is naught to stop me," Marsi said. "I must collect some of my things, but I'll come right back."

"Ye've nowt that be suitable for a maidservant to wear, my lady! Nor would ye fool anyone for long in any menial guise. Ye were no born to it."

But now that she had made up her mind, Marsi dismissed those objections without hesitation. "I can easily talk as a maidservant would, Hetty. Having often scolded me for doing so, you know that I can. I shall say that I served Annabella and that she gave me some of her cast-off clothing. She did give me some, my fur-lined cloak for one. I can say that, when my position ended with her grace's death, I offered to help you because you and I come from the same part of Scotland."

"I can say that I know Marsi well, too, Hetty, because I do," Jamie said.

"I can also say I just want to go home," Marsi said. "We will likely go north or east from here, so if worse comes to worst, I can ask whoever escorts us to take me to Uncle Malcolm in Perthshire. He wants me to marry his second son. And I vow to you, Hetty, if the choice is between marrying a boot-licker of Albany's and my dull-ard cousin Jack, I'd *prefer* Jack."

Two hours earlier

Striding across the flagstone floor of the royal audience chamber at Turnberry, the tall, broad-shouldered young knight filled the room with crackling energy even as he dropped to a knee before its sole, elderly occupant and bowed his head.

"You sent for me, sire?"

"If ye be the knight that men call Hawk, I did, aye," the King of Scots said, his raspy voice little more than a whisper. "I have need of ye."

"I am Hawk," Sir Ivor Mackintosh said, fighting to conceal his dismay at how much the King had aged since he had last seen him, three years before, and how frail he looked. "How may I serve your grace? Your messenger said it was urgent."

"'Tis Jamie," said the King, who had never sought his exalted role or enjoyed it.

Into the silence, Sir Ivor said gently, "Jamie, my liege? Your younger son?"

A log shifted in the nearby fireplace and sparks leaped before the King said, "Annabella..." Pausing when his voice cracked, he added with tears welling in his pale blue eyes, "My Annabella feared mightily for Jamie's future. The lad be only six months into his eighth year, and she feared that after she was gone, my brother Albany would take charge of him and keep our laddie under his thumb."

"Many people do fear Albany, my liege."

"Aye, perhaps, although few say such things to me, and I canna believe that he would harm a child, his own nephew. It would outrage the country and gain him nowt whilst our Davy, who is years older and wields much power of his own, remains heir to the throne. Albany says only that Jamie would fare better under his eye than under mine, and as frail as I am, he may be right. But 'tis better, I trow, to keep Jamie safe than to weep for him if Annabella should prove to be right."

"What, exactly, do you want me to do, sire?"

"I received word a fortnight ago that Albany would be coming tomorrow or Tuesday to take the lad into his charge. I do not want that, but he is nearly impossible for me to oppose, and he said that if he does *not* take charge of Jamie, other powerful nobles may seek to do so. However, the Bishop of St. Andrews assured me that *he* can keep Jamie safe from them all at St. Andrews, so I sent word to him as soon as I learned of Albany's intent. Ye ken Traill fine, I think, and St. Andrews, too."

"I do, aye. I studied under him there. When he received your message, he sent word for me to hasten here to you. Have you a plan in mind, your grace?"

With a feeble gesture, the King said, "I want to ken nowt of any plans, for I am incapable of lying to my brother. His will has ever been stronger than mine, and as ye must ken, until I named my son Davy to govern in my stead three years ago, Albany had ruled for me. I owe him much. But ye must take Jamie to St. Andrews."

"I can be away in the morning if he can be ready by then," Ivor said.

"Ye need only give the nursery mistress your orders when ye arise," the King said. "Henrietta kens fine that Jamie may be leaving tomorrow and is prepared to accompany him. Her family has long and faithfully served the Drummonds, and she was fiercely loyal to Annabella. I trust her implicitly."

"Then, by your leave, sire, I would sleep now," Ivor said.

"Aye, sure. My own man, Dennison, will take ye to a room near the nursery."

Bowing, Sir Ivor bade him goodnight. Then, following the King's man to a bedchamber and asking him to tell the captain of his fighting tail to be ready to go at dawn, Ivor retired, only to awaken betimes when the lass in his dreams became real.

Afterward, due to years of knightly training and preparing for battle, he soon slept again and woke when the dawn's gray light crept into the room.

His bruised hand and aching cheek reminded him of the lass, but he dressed hastily. Then, deducing which door led to the nursery, he rapped lightly on it.

⁓

Marsi opened the door, having returned to her own room long enough to pack things and don a plain moss-green kirtle, a white apron, and a white cap large enough to conceal her long red hair, lest he whose bed she had invaded recognize it.

After one nervous look at the tall, well-formed, stern-looking man in leather breeks and jack who stood there, she quickly swept him a deep curtsy. Heat flooded her cheeks at the memory of his large hand on her thigh.

Speaking over her shoulder as she rose, she said, "Mistress, methinks 'tis the gentleman ye be expecting, though he ha' come earlier than ye said he would."

"Dinna chatter, lass, but come and help Lord Carrick dress whilst I speak with the man," Hetty said. "I am Henrietta Childs, sir, mistress of the royal nursery," she added in her usual dignified way.

As Marsi moved to help Jamie, she glanced back at them.

Without awaiting further invitation, the man stepped in and shut the door. "I believe you understand the situation, Mistress Childs," he said to Hetty. "We must be away as soon as we can and without more ado than necessary."

"I ken that, aye, sir," Hetty said. "His lordship will be dressed in a trice, and someone should be along soon with food for us to break our fast."

"That is good, but do *not* let his lordship dawdle."

"As to that, sir, his lordship—" Breaking off at the sound of a sharp rap on the door, she added, "Prithee, sir, admit the gillie. He brings our food."

Instead, the tall man stepped to the off side of the door and gestured for Hetty to open it. He had not spared a second look for Marsi.

Hetty opened the door and stepped back to admit Dennison, the King's man.

"I thought you would be here, sir," Dennison said mildly when their visitor emerged from behind the door. "You have a visitor below. I will take you to him."

"One of my men, I expect," the younger man said, nodding.

"I have also arranged for them to serve Lord Carrick's breakfast at once, sir. Therefore, I would respectfully suggest that we go down straightaway." With that, Dennison held the door open for their visitor, and the two men left the chamber.

Hearing their footsteps fade in the distance, Marsi said, "Faith, Dennison whisked that man off without presenting him. We don't even know his name!"

As they walked away, the King's man murmured, "I was sure you would prefer that the men who serve his lordship's breakfast not see you with him, sir."

"You thought aright," Sir Ivor said, wondering if the captain of his fighting tail had encountered trouble. But when Dennison turned right at the end of the corridor instead of left, Ivor stopped him. "This is not the way to the yard."

"No, sir. Your visitor insisted that you meet him at the sea gate."

"Sakes, I did not know that Turnberry boasted a sea gate," Ivor said. "And I'd wager that my men are as unaware of it as I was. Who seeks me there?"

"I know only that he said you would know him, sir. And that he wanted to reveal his presence to as few as possible."

Intrigued, Ivor followed him down a narrow, damp stairway to an enormous, torchlit, water-filled cavern. To his astonishment, it clearly served as a harbor. A fifty-foot Highland galley with *Zee Handelaar* on its stern rested at the main jetty.

As they approached it, a man in deerskin breeks and boots, a loose white shirt, and a leather vest emerged into the torchlight from nearby shadows. Grinning broadly, he strode toward them. Hatless, his soft, moplike, dark curls reflected the torchlight in orange-gold shimmers. His dark eyes gleamed with mischief.

Dennison said, "You will want to talk privately, sir. I'll await you at the landing above this one unless you want me to fetch your charges to you here."

"Nay, I'll fetch them," Ivor said. "I'll take no more time here than I must, and the boy will want to break his fast without me to hurry him." Turning back with a smile to the man from the galley, he said, "Wolf, you devil, what brings you here?"

Shaking hands, the other said, "You do, Hawk, me lad." Nodding toward the galley, he added, "Behold your transport for the first leg of your journey."

"I've been thinking," Jamie said to Marsi when the men who had brought their food had gone. "'Tis good that Dennison paid ye nae heed when he came tae fetch that man. Ye'd ha been finished afore ye'd begun had he addressed ye as 'my lady.' But what will ye do when they return? Ye canna think Dennison will let ye go with us when ye lack his grace my father's leave tae go."

"We'll worry about that if it happens," Marsi said. "But eat now, Jamie. I'd wager that man meant it when he said not to dawdle. And, if he is to get us safely away, we had better not anger him at the outset."

Without commenting on that opinion, Jamie said to Hetty, "Why did *you* not present that man to me, Hetty, afore Dennison arrived?"

"Because I ken nae more about him than you do, sir,"

Hetty said. "Moreover, Lady Marsi is right. We must be ready to go when he returns. I expect gillies will come soon to take our things outside and load them on the sumpter ponies."

"Well, I warrant the reason we do not know his name is that Dennison does not know it either," Marsi said. "And I expect that the two of them will take our things down for us rather than let all of Turnberry know that Jamie is leaving."

"If ye mean to pretend to be my assistant, ye'd better start addressing him as such a minion would," Hetty said mildly. "If ye call him Jamie, that man will ken straightway that ye're no nursery maid. Nobbut what this whole pretense be daft."

"Nay, it is not. But you are wise to remind me of my place, Hetty. It may prove harder than I thought to act as I should, but I *will* do it. Just to think of marrying a man old enough to have sired me, and only because he wants Cargill and has land adjoining mine... I will do anything to avoid that, I promise you."

"Dinna fash yourself, Marsi," James said. "I'll remind ye tae behave when ye need such reminding."

"I don't doubt that," she retorted dryly.

Jamie chuckled, but she had no time to say more, because the door opened without ceremony, and the man who was to escort them walked right in.

"Collect your things," he said. "The fewer people who see us, the better, so I'll help you carry them down to the sea gate."

"The sea gate!" Marsi's exclamation was out before she thought. Trying to conceal her dismay, she glanced at Jamie and saw that his eyes were sparkling with pure delight. Turning back to their visitor, she said, "Where are we going then?"

The man looked at Hetty, who said sharply, "Hold your tongue, lass. Ye've nae call to put yourself forward so. If ye canna behave, I'll leave ye right here."

Quickly bowing her head, Marsi strove to look contrite. But before she could think how to phrase her apology, James said in a tone as stern as Hetty's, "Marsi *must* come with us, for I want her. And if we are to go on a ship, Hetty, I will *need* her. Ye ken fine that boats always make ye sick."

Eyeing their visitor again, Marsi saw that he looked sterner than ever. Before Jamie had stopped speaking, the man's gaze shifted to her. Memories of the night before fired her imagination then. Feeling her cheeks burn, she licked her lips only to feel them curve into a nervous smile.

His expression turned thoughtful. But he said only that Hetty should hurry them along.

The man had forgotten all about *her*, Marsi decided. He could have no suspicion that she was the girl who had fled from his bed the night before.

To be sure, she had donned the plain green kirtle and white apron and had concealed her memorably long, lush, dark-red tresses under the large, frilly white cap. Even so, and although she was relieved that he did not recognize her, she felt an odd sense of disappointment, as if he *should* have.

Chapter 2

Ivor had been about to inform the nursery mistress that he could not take two women on such a journey when he noted that the young maid was still peeping at him from beneath her lashes, clearly not as cowed as she had seemed to be.

Those lashes were long, thick, and dark. Her eyes were the same mossy green as her gown, and her lips were rosy, full, and eminently kissable. Although she was small, her figure was enticingly supple and curvaceous.

Then her cheeks reddened as her lips twitched invitingly.

Faith, but the pawkie minx was flirting with him!

Her father, brother, or other responsible kinsman ought long since to have put her over his knee to teach her the folly of flirting with warriors. A warrior took his pleasure where he found it, albeit *not*, if he was wise, with a maid-servant in the royal nursery. Such a woman likely had some connection to an influential noble family.

Dennison had clearly expected Ivor to take only Mistress Childs and the young Earl of Carrick with him. However, Dennison had not returned with him.

Having found the King's personal attendant on the landing as promised, Ivor had sent him to the stable with new orders for the captain of his fighting tail.

The King had made it plain that he wanted Mistress Childs to go with James. And, in truth, Ivor knew that he'd be wise to take her, if only because she understood the lad's needs. Taking her impertinent assistant along was another matter.

The lass was eyeing him more soberly, her manner more disapproving now than flirtatious. She was a little beauty, though, which could lead to other problems.

However, James's declaration that Mistress Childs would be seasick was something to consider. So Ivor held his tongue, giving himself time to think.

When he saw the pile of baggage they meant to take, he regretted that he had sent Dennison outside. Another set of hands would have allowed his charges to take more of their belongings with them.

But to have sent someone else to his men would have meant another person knowing more than might be safe about his brief visit. As it was, any who had seen him arrive would likely believe that he left with his men. They always led a string of extra horses, so no one was likely to bother counting the horses or the men.

Seeing the small but curvaceous nursery maid trying to lift the largest bundle, Ivor moved to pick it up himself. As he hefted it, he said to Mistress Childs, "You may want to rearrange some of these things, mistress. We will make only one trip down to the sea gate. Leave what you won't need in the first few days here."

Looking surprised, Mistress Childs said, "I packed only necessities, sir."

"There is much more here than any three people should need," Ivor said.

"Mayhap it does *seem* so, sir. But recall that his

lordship is accustomed to his own bedding and his own—"

"He will not be traveling as the Earl of Carrick, mistress. We need to remain as inconspicuous as possible, so the last thing we want is for word to spread that Carrick is a member of our party."

"With respect, sir, I ken fine that we will not stop at noble houses or abbeys where he may be known. But that is the very reason that he will require his own—"

"Nay." Realizing that he had to make himself clear, Ivor said, "We will travel without fanfare, as ordinary folk. But my men will join us in two or three days, and Dennison will arrange for them to carry things that you will want later. But he kens fine what my requirements are. Do not expect to see his lordship's sheets amongst those items or clothing more suited to a prince than to an ordinary lad of his age."

Seeing James bristle, Ivor was taken aback when the nursery maid put a quelling hand on the prince's shoulder. He was more surprised when James obeyed the gesture and kept silent. The last vestige of his reluctance to take the lass along vanished. If she wielded such an influence, she might well prove gey helpful.

"Surely, you do not expect us to travel as ordinary *commoners*, sir," Mistress Childs said. "His lordship will steel himself to accept your guidance, of course, as it is his grace's will that he do so. But he *is* young. And, as second in line to the throne, he is as accustomed to command as you are. Bless us, but behaving as commoners will be hard for us all."

"I expect it will be, aye," he agreed. "I have not forgotten that most royal attendants are members of the nobility. Are you one such, mistress?"

"I can make only a second cousin's claim to nobility, sir. But my family has long served the Drummonds. I looked after several members of that family before taking my position as royal nursery mistress nearly eight years ago."

"I see," Ivor said. "Well, whilst we are on the ship, we can sort out details of any tale we might share with those we meet. His lordship *does* want to avoid falling into his uncle's hands, does he not?"

"He does," James said in the stern tone he had used before. Looking directly at Ivor, he added, "He *would* like to know where you are taking him, though."

"With respect, sir," Ivor said, holding his gaze. "Whilst we are in this room, I will answer your questions as well as I can. I will do that whenever we can speak privily. However, you must otherwise behave as most lads your age do. That is to say, you will obey my orders or suffer the same consequences that an ordinary boy would suffer, especially when others are near. I cannot undertake this task without such an agreement, because I must have your cooperation to keep you safe."

James eyed him measuringly for a long moment and then frowned. "Will everyone we meet treat me as if I am of no account then?"

"No one will behave so," Ivor said. "Nor do I expect you to behave as if you were raised in a byre. You need only treat any adults we meet with civility and those of rank with the respect due to them. Your maidservant, if she accompanies us, may treat you with her customary deference. But I think that you must treat Mistress Childs as you would treat any kinswoman to whom you owe respect. That means that she will not address you as 'sir' or 'my lord.' And you will *not* speak to me again as you just did," Ivor added sternly, "or we *will* fall out."

The boy's eyes widened. But he was silent for a time before he grimaced and said, "I expect our acquaintance will prove a salutary one then . . . sir."

Ivor wondered if the boy meant salutary for himself or Ivor. Deciding that it did not matter, since they would both likely learn a few things, he saw that Mistress Childs had used the time to shift items about from bundle to bundle.

As she finished tying the last one, she looked at James. "If you will carry that blue bundle and your bed pillow, sir, I can take this one and my things. You take yours, Marsi, and that white bundle. We'll let—" Breaking off with a click of her tongue, she said to Ivor, "Pray, sir, we must know what to call you."

"Call me Hawk for now," he said.

"That seems most unusual and rather too familiar, sir. But if you will have it so, and if you will carry that bundle you took from Marsi, we are ready to go."

~

Marsi wondered what the man who called himself Hawk was thinking. She had found it hard to read his expression, except when he'd told Jamie how he was to behave. His stern displeasure then had been plain enough.

As she donned her hooded gray, sable-lined cloak, she realized that the only other person she could recall speaking so to the prince was Albany. However, the thought had only to flit through her mind for her to amend it.

As far as she knew, Albany had never spoken so crisply to anyone. The duke's tone was chilly to the point of freezing one's blood in one's veins. And he spoke so softly that one had to exert oneself to hear what he said.

Hawk had spoken as a man accustomed to obedience from other men did.

But what manner of name was Hawk, for mercy's sake? She'd have liked to ask him. But in her current guise, she dared not question him so. If he expected to command Jamie, he would make short shrift of insolence from a maidservant.

That thought stirred a tingling in her mind as if the notion of such certain dominance challenged her. She had tested most of the adults in her life from early childhood onward and easily recognized the urge to test him for what it was.

She fought the impulse, and it eased. But she knew that once such an urge made itself known, it became hard to ignore. Deciding that she must control it if her pretense, as hard as it would be to maintain at all, was to last long enough to get her away from Turnberry. Catching Hetty's stern eye on her just then, she stepped hastily aside to let the nursery mistress and Jamie lead the way out of the room.

It was not the maid's place to go first. Nor did Marsi want to be right behind Hawk, lest another impulse to question him undo her.

He had already taken a dim view of her asking about their destination. That he would view personal questions in an even dimmer light seemed certain.

In truth, she realized as she hurried down the winding stone stairs after the others, she was beginning to see a vast chasm before her. *Could* she maintain indefinitely this pretense that she had created for herself, or would her temptation to challenge Hawk undo her?

Not only was she dangerously curious about their handsome escort, but she had also failed to consider one important detail—her dislike of waiting on others.

Attending Annabella had been satisfying enough, because the Queen had deeply appreciated all that her attendants did for her. The most Marsi had had to exert herself was to help make the Queen's bed or help look after her clothing. Any more taxing duty fell to ordinary maidservants or menservants, although no males other than the King and Annabella's sons ever entered her grace's bedchamber.

However, some of her other ladies had assumed that Marsi, as the youngest, should wait on them, too. She had been as dutiful as she knew how to be but soon learned that Annabella refused to let the others scold her. She knew she had taken advantage of that fact more than once. But Annabella could not protect her now.

Hetty would not shield her either, because Marsi was one of the Drummond children that she had nursed. Hetty knew her through and through.

In Marsi's present guise, she knew that Hetty would expect her to do things that she had never had to do for anyone before. That did not matter, though.

She could do anything if she made up her mind to it.

Rounding the last turn of the stairs, she looked in astonishment at the cavern before them. She had little time to take it all in, though, because Hetty and Jamie were hurrying after Hawk. Ahead of him, tied to a jetty, was a longboat.

As Hawk neared it, a man jumped to the jetty from the boat and strode to meet him. Taking the bundle Hawk carried, the other man tossed it to a third aboard the boat.

He signed then to someone else to attend to Hetty's and Jamie's bundles.

"I hope you don't need to fetch more things," he said then in a voice that, although quiet enough, carried easily. Marsi realized that although they were right on the water, she could barely hear the sea outside the cavern.

Hawk said, "We've brought all they'll need for now. My lads will carry aught that they've left behind that they may need later."

"Good, because the sooner we're underway, the better. This place is likely to get busier the nearer we come to the turning tide. Who's the lass?"

Hawk glanced at her. "The nursery maid. Hand those bundles to one of these men, lass, and get yourself aboard."

The third man, still aboard the boat, said, "Here, lass, I'll show ye how."

Smiling warmly at him, she said, "My name be Marsi, sir."

"A lovely name it be, too," he said, grinning back. "Come this way now, and see can ye walk up yon plank without tumbling off o' it."

"Will ye no tell me *your* name, sir?" she asked.

"This way," he repeated, glancing warily at Hawk and the man with Hawk.

Noting Hawk's stern eye on her, Marsi caught up her skirt, stepped onto the plank, and walked up it to where her new friend stood ready to hand her aboard.

"Show them to the master's cabin," the man with Hawk said. "The women and lad can stay there. Hawk can share the forecastle cabin with me if need be."

Marsi noted that the ship was a sort of Isles galley with

benches for eight oars on a side. The seaman who had helped her aboard guided her now toward the high stern. There, a door opened into a small cabin with two shelf beds at the rear, one atop the other. A cunning washstand hugged the wall to her right and a small table with flanking benches occupied an alcove to her left.

"This cabin is small for three people," she said to her guide. "That wee table has room for only one adult on each bench."

"The lad can sleep on the floor," her companion said. "Yonder be your bundles, lass. Just shift them about as ye need. There be a small hold under yon trap, too, if ye want tae stow them. Why d'ye look at me so?"

Swallowing her dismay at the familiarity in his tone, she said, "I beg your pardon. I didna mean tae stare. Ye be gey large, is all."

"Aye, sure, I am," he said with a smile. "Sithee, oarsmen need tae be big."

"D'ye ken where we be going?" she asked.

"Now, that would be telling, that would," he said, winking. Then he added soberly, "We're no tae say nowt, lass. So dinna be plaguing me or any o' the other lads if ye dinna want tae suffer the rough edge o' the master's temper."   •

"I thank ye for your kindness," Marsi said, seeing Jamie hurrying toward the cabin with Hetty behind him.

"Right ye are," the man said, turning and striding away.

Hetty looked green, so Marsi said, "Come in, Hetty, and sit down."

"Ye should call her *Mistress* Hetty if not Mistress Henrietta," Jamie muttered behind her. Turning, she saw that he had swung himself onto the top shelf bed. "I like this," he said, patting the thin mat underneath him. "I'll sleep here."

Turning back, she saw that Hetty was eyeing their accommodations with wary disapproval. Her face was paler than it had been a minute before.

"Sit, *Mistress* Hetty," Marsi said, gesturing toward the wee table. "If you want fresh air in here, I think that window above the table may open."

"They call that a porthole, I think," Jamie said. "It has a latch, so I'm sure we can open it. But you should not be climbing about, Marsi. I'll do it."

"Not until we ask if we may, sir," Hetty said. Looking weary, she sat on the bench facing the doorway.

Marsi eyed her helplessly, wondering what she could do to make her feel better. The light in the room dimmed. Turning, she saw Hawk filling the doorway.

"May we know the captain's name, sir?" Hetty asked.

"I call him Wolf," he said.

"Sakes," Marsi exclaimed, "are you in a league of anim—?"

"That will do," Hetty said sharply. "You should be getting our things off the floor and sorted into kists or some such place."

"We'll be getting underway at once, mistress," Hawk said. "When the lass gets a feel for the boat and the movement of the sea, she can attend to all that. Until then, I'd suggest that the three of you stay in one place."

Marsi said, "Sir, the man who brought me in said we might put things in the hold under that trapdoor by your feet. He left when Mistress Henrietta and Jamie—"

"Jamie?"

Feeling fire in her cheeks, Marsi was grateful to hear Jamie say, "I told her she should call me so because ye'd said that she and Hetty should treat me as an ordinary lad. Hetty has a harder time remembering tae do that than Marsi does. *She* still calls me 'sir.' Also, it does occur tae me that if ye dinna want our true names noised about, ye should call Hetty 'Mistress Henrietta' as Marsi does."

Hawk looked from one to the other as if he had recognized Jamie's words as a diversionary tactic and might say so, and more. Instead he nodded, saying, "That is a good notion, lad." To Marsi, he said, "Put anything you like in that hold if it is empty, lass. But they are casting off now, so wait until we are under sail. You don't want to fall into the hold."

"Thank you, sir," Marsi said. She smiled, but he was already turning away.

Had Hetty not been watching her, the temptation to stick out her tongue at the man would have been irresistible.

Ivor shut the door behind him and immediately breathed more easily. He was sorry now that he had let the maid accompany Mistress Childs. Nay, though, the lad was right. He should call her Mistress Henrietta.

That lass, however—being both damnably attractive and impertinent—was bound to draw the attention of every man aboard if she had not already done so.

Wolf had certainly taken note of that infectious smile of hers. And the chap who had handed her aboard had looked *much* too interested in her.

Looking for Wolf now, Ivor saw him a short distance away to his right, talking with his helmsman. The galley was emerging from the cavern harbor, and he saw at once why the water inside remained calm.

The outer rock wall of a long, open-ended tunnel running perpendicular to the entrance broke the force of incoming waves. That wall was far enough from the cavern opening to let the galley turn from harbor into tunnel. Clearly carved by the sea, as the cavern had been, and augmented by a masonry breakwater at each end, the tunnel made for an easy exit, especially for a galley with two men to each oar.

Catching Wolf's eye, Ivor stayed where he was until the other man joined him. Then he said, "Have you somewhere other than the aft cabin where we can talk privately, or should we wait until we are under sail?"

"We'll go to the forecastle. It contains a wee cabin where I keep my rutter. That's the book in which we note details of any coastline we pass and information we glean from other boatmen about other places. My father and I always kept pallets on the floor of that cabin for sleeping. I still keep two in there."

Ivor hadn't thought about sleeping. "How far are we going?"

"As you know, your destination lies on the other side of Scotland, a hundred and fifty miles away," Wolf said. "To save time, we'll take you to a wee place called Milton on the Firth of Clyde between Castle Dunglass and Dumbarton. Dumbarton is the main harbor there and well watched, as is the port of Glasgow on the south side. Milton's charm is that it has a small but comfortable inn that rarely houses folks of the sort who might recognize your charge. Members of the nobility generally prefer accommodations in Dumbarton or Glasgow."

"How long will this journey take?"

The boat had emerged from the tunnel and turned into the waves. Wolf looked musingly at the overcast sky and then turned his face to the chilly breeze.

"'Tis some fifty miles, so ten hours or more if this breeze does not increase or it rains. We barely have wind enough now to fill her sail. But it does blow from the southwest. If it continues so, at least it will not hinder us. Sithee, I'd liefer land you by nightfall than in broad daylight, for although I have legitimate reason to visit Dumbarton, you want to go unnoticed if possible."

"I do," Ivor agreed. "Albany's men likely litter that whole area."

"He keeps a watch at all the ports. You can trust the innkeeper at Milton to house you, but you'd do well not to trust him otherwise. If Albany's men question him, he'll tell them all he knows. Although the duke is no longer Governor of the Realm, his men still act as if he is."

"Aye, sure, because he acts so, himself," Ivor said.

As they talked, they followed the narrow, raised gangway between the rows of oarsmen on their benches. A low, steady beat of the gong marked the strokes of the oars, and Ivor found the rhythm relaxing, as was the gentle salt-laden breeze.

Pulling open the narrow door to the forecastle built into the high stem of the boat, Wolf gestured for Ivor to precede him inside.

The cabin was more spacious than Ivor had expected, but he hoped they would not have to sleep aboard. Although he saw a low shelf for charts and a wee table and benches set into an alcove similar to the one in the aft cabin, he saw no bed. Anyone who slept there slept on the floor.

Shutting the door, Wolf said, "Do I continue to call you Hawk, or may we exchange our true names at last?"

Ivor grinned. "Do you remember our friend Lion from St. Andrews?"

"Our most famous swordsman? Aye, sure, I do. He was as skilled with his sword as you are with your bow, my lad."

"If you know the name Fin of the Battles, you will agree that Lion became even more famous," Ivor said.

"Sakes, Fin of the Battles was the only swordsman save Davy Stewart left standing after the Queen's tourney of champions at Edinburgh Castle. And they say that her grace stopped them only after they had fought for half an hour, and only because she feared that Davy might lose, which would reflect badly on the royal family. No one minded, though, because they had put on such a fine display of skill. That splendid chap was our own Lion from the brotherhood at St. Andrews?"

"The same. And he is now my good-brother. He married my sister, Catriona."

"As I recall," Wolf said thoughtfully, "there was no archery contest at the Queen's tourney. But I did hear of one at Stirling months later, won by an archer who never missed his shot, a Mackintosh. Have you ever missed a bowshot, Hawk?"

"You ken fine that I have. I did not spring from the womb with bow in hand."

Wolf cocked his head to one side, expectantly.

Easily interpreting the look, Ivor said, "Aye, then, my

name is Ivor Mackintosh. My father is Shaw MacGilli-vray, war leader of Clan Chattan."

"Then you must be Sir Ivor by now, I'd wager."

Ivor nodded. "And you?"

"Jake Maxwell, and I have likewise earned my knightly spurs. My father's family lives in Nithsdale. But I spent much of my childhood on his boat and later, on this one. Sithee, my mam died when I was six. After that, I stayed with my da until they sent me to Bishop Traill at St. Andrews. Sithee, when I was eight, Da entered service with the MacLennans of Duncraig. That's on the north-west coast of Kintail. So, we now serve Donald, Lord of the Isles." He glanced out the porthole. "We are beyond sight of Turnberry's ramparts, so we'll hoist Donald's flag now."

Opening the door, he shouted to someone named Mace to take down the Dutch flag and remove the Dutch ship name, as well.

"Then, this must be the MacLennans' boat," Ivor said when Jake had shut the door again. "Do they ken aught of our undertaking?"

"This boat is mine," Jake said. With a mischievous grin, he added, "Years ago, it belonged to the Duke of Albany, whilst he was still the Earl of Fife."

Ivor looked narrowly at his old friend, suspecting a jest.

Jake threw up both hands, palms out. "I swear it!" he said, laughing. "Sakes, I'd forgotten how quick your infamous temper is to leap."

"This boat truly belonged to Albany?"

"Aye, he had it built twenty years ago, thinking that he would like to travel by sea. But he discovered a strong distaste for shipboard life. Since he cannot swim, one hesitates to name him coward—"

"Aye, but physically, he is one," Ivor said. "Last year, he sent men to attack Rothiemurchus, my home in the Highlands. But although he sent two armies, he neither led nor accompanied either. Their leaders wisely turned back when the snow-laden Cairngorms and our forces proved too fierce for them."

"I heard about that," Jake said. "However, Albany rarely risks his own hide or dirties his own hands to get what he wants. Recall that the man has entered his sixty-second year and is still as formidable as ever. It is true that he wants to rule the North. But, sakes, so does Donald of the Isles."

"In troth," Ivor said, "when you told me that you were our transport, I did think that you would take us farther north."

"Not at this season," Jake said. "Winter still owns the landscape and grows fiercer in the north. You surely know what Lochaber, Glen Mór, and the high straths can be like from February through June. At present, in the Isles, the sea can produce thirty-foot waves, which would terrify your passengers. In Dumbartonshire, you'll be closer to St. Andrews and have easier going. You'll find it hard enough crossing from Loch Lomond to Doune through the lower glens. Many are likely still snowbound."

"You may be right. I've just come from Rothiemurchus, in Strathspey. Winter has been mild there this year, but I doubt that our charges would deem it so."

"Not when they are used to weather at Turnberry, Stirling, and Edinburgh," Jake said. "How likely is Albany to come after you?"

Ivor grimaced. "The wicked duke seems to know all. So I'd not be surprised if he already knows that his grace is sending James to a safer place."

"That is my experience of him, too," Jake said.

"Also, if anyone tells him about this ship, he'll know we took to the sea."

"Nay, for he called this boat the *Serpent Royal*. I call it *Sea Wolf.*"

"The name you called yourself at St. Andrews," Ivor said, smiling.

"Aye," Jake said. "This design was new when Albany had it built, but many such boats ply the seas today. He would not recognize it merely from a description. The women will likely pose a greater problem for you. Nobbut what the lass is a pretty thing and flirtatious withal."

"Too flirtatious," Ivor said, remembering her easy smiles and pert manner. "I assume that you can control your men."

"Aye, sure," Jake said. "Although she does look to be a cozy armful."

"Then you will control yourself, too, I trow."

Jake grinned. "Have you an interest there, me lad?"

"I have not. In any event, I've no time for any such interest until James is safe inside St. Andrews Castle and under Traill's watchful eye."

"Aye, well, my long vision is nowt to match yours and the light in that cavern was dim, but I did note that great bruise on your gizz straightaway. So I wondered."

Ivor changed the subject. However, when he went back out on deck, the first thing he saw was the nursery maid. She stood at the stern beside the helmsman, smiling flirtatiously at him in full view of every oarsman.

Thanks doubtless to Jake's having mentioned the bruise on his cheek, his mind shifted abruptly to his dream at Turnberry and the fierce redheaded wench that he had found in his bed. The memory increased his irritation with the nursery maid.

Drawing a deep breath, he let it out slowly as he strode along the gangway.

Chapter 3 _____

Marsi, having accepted Hetty's assurance that she would get Jamie settled sooner *without* her help, had left the two of them to sort their things. Since then, she had been enjoying the fresh sea air and a cheerful conversation with the man at the helm, who was kindly explaining his duties to her.

To talk with such a man, an expert at his job, and have him talk to her with the ease of one conversing with an equal had been an unusual and fascinating experience. Then she saw Hawk step out of the cabin at the front or what her new friend called the stem of the boat. At the same time, Jamie emerged from their cabin.

"Ye'd better come, Marsi," the boy said. "I told ye she'd be sick. Sakes, she got sick once in a wee rowboat on Loch Leven."

"Good lack," Marsi exclaimed, hurrying toward him.

Jamie turned and pushed the door open for her. But as she moved to pass him, she heard Hawk say, "One moment, lass."

Turning back as he stepped down from the central gangway, she was reminded again of his muscular body and height.

Ignoring his frown, she said, "Did you want me, sir?

Hetty is...that is, Mistress Henrietta is sick. So unless you need something impor—"

It *is* important," he said. "You should not be out here alone like this."

"I wanted fresh air. That cabin is tiny. And with three of us inside—"

"Never mind your excuses, lass. It is enough that I tell you not to come out alone. I will tell Mistress Henrietta as well, because—"

"I just told you, Hetty is sick. So it would be better—"

"Do not interrupt me again," Hawk said.

Indignantly, she opened her mouth to point out that he had just as rudely cut her off but shut her mouth again when she remembered her role. "I beg pardon, sir. I be that worried about her that I forgot me place. I ken fine that she would say I must mind my manners, even so. Jamie, do ye get back inside, too, now."

"Nay, then," Jamie said. "It smells bad in there. I was nearly sick, too, so Hetty said tae hie m'self outside."

"You go and look after her," Hawk told Marsi. "I'll look after the lad."

"Is aught amiss here?"

Shifting her gaze past Hawk, Marsi saw the captain at the near end of the gangplank. When he grinned, she grinned back.

Hawk, turning toward him, said, "Mistress Henrietta is sick, Wolf. The lad wants nowt to do with that wee cabin now."

"I don't blame him," the captain said. "If he plays chess, I keep an old set in the forecastle cabin. Or I can show you both more of the boat whilst the lass looks after Mistress Henrietta. How sick is she?"

Jamie said, "She threw up in that pail that sits in the corner."

"Then fetch it out here, lass, and we'll empty and rinse it for you," the captain said. "You won't want to keep it in there. Come to that, if your mistress will not object to my presence, I'll go in and open the portholes to freshen the air."

"I wanted tae do that," Jamie said. "But Hetty said we must wait and ask ye. Nae one did though. Then, after she threw up, I felt too sick tae do it."

"Go on in, lass," the captain said when Marsi hesitated. "Fetch out the pail and ask her if I should open the ports. If she objects, I'll tell you how to do it."

"Aye, sir," Marsi said. Avoiding Hawk's grim gaze, she went into the cabin, only to find that Jamie had been right about the stench. Her stomach roiled in protest, and she had all she could do not to turn and rush back out.

Hetty was leaning against the wall by the washstand, still holding the pail and its odious contents. Her face was ashen.

"Let me take that, Hetty," Marsi said gently. "You must sit down."

"I'm having all I can do to stand still so I don't jar any more loose from inside," Hetty said weakly. "I fear that if I move, this dreadful floor may heave up again and I'll fall."

"I could help you to the lower bed or to the table, where you can sit down."

"Nay, I'm too heavy for ye, my la—"

"Hush, Hetty! What if they should hear you?"

"Ye should tell them who ye be," Hetty said, her voice stronger.

"Aye, perhaps later," Marsi said. "Captain Wolf and Hawk are just outside, and the captain bade me fetch the pail so someone can rinse it out. He also offered to open those windows if you do not object to his presence. Doubtless he or Hawk would also help you to a seat."

"One dislikes imposing on them, especially as I could be sick all over—"

"Don't be daft, Hetty," Marsi said curtly, not wanting to hear where she might be sick. "It will do Hawk good to help you. Sithee, he has just been scolding me for going out on deck alone. As if any of the men would bother me aboard this ship with their captain just a step away."

"Don't expect sympathy from me," Hetty said in much her usual way. "Ye should no be *on* this boat, so dinna be complaining about your lot whilst ye pretend to be someone ye're not."

"But, Hetty, if I had stayed, Albany would have got me. And you ken fine that he will force me to marry Lord Redmyre. I don't like Redmyre, Hetty. He said he looked forward to reforming my character and controlling my estates."

"Even so..." But with a click of her tongue, Hetty paused, then said, "If the captain told ye to fetch this pail, ye'd better do it if ye dinna want to suffer his scolds as well as Hawk's. But, prithee, hurry back with the pail!"

"Aye, sure," Marsi said, gingerly removing it from Hetty's grip. She tried to ignore its contents and hoped Hetty would not be sick again before she could return. Outside, she looked from Hawk to Captain Wolf, wondering what to do with the pail.

Before she had to ask, the captain summoned an oarsman to take it away.

Relieved, she savored a few refreshing breaths of sea air before she said to Wolf, "Hetty does not mind if you go in, sir. In troth, if one of you could help her to the bed or to that wee table, where she can sit, she will be more comfortable."

"You should have helped her before you brought out the pail," Hawk said.

"She wouldna let me, sir," she said, remembering to speak as a maid would and fearing that she had forgotten with Wolf. "She said that did she fall, she'd be gey like tae take me wi' her. 'Twas Hetty herself did say tae ask ye tae do it."

"I'll do it before I open the ports," Wolf said. "I doubt she will thank me for encouraging her to move about, but she'll be fain to have fresh air."

"Take the pail, sir," Marsi said. "She do still be queasy."

He grinned. "Aye, sure, mistress. That floor do be the devil and all tae clean, too. I ken that fine, m'self, for I ha' cleaned it many a time."

His tone, not to mention his sudden use of less than noble accents, startled her, making her fear that her slip, if indeed she had made one, had given her away.

He said no more but took the pail from the man who had emptied it and went inside. Marsi held her breath, listening for sounds from within. She realized only then that she should have taken the pail in to Hetty herself. Aware that she ought never to have suggested that the captain do it, she waited for Hawk to say so.

He stood behind her, and she knew that she could not stand there indefinitely. But neither could she walk away without knowing if Hawk also suspected something.

Unable to think of a better tactic, she turned and said, "Be ye still vexed wi' me, sir? I dinna ken the ways o' this ship, but I'd liefer no vex ye or the captain."

He seemed to study her face until she stopped speaking. Then he said, "I am not vexed with you, nor is it my place to scold or correct you unless your behavior jeopardizes our undertaking. Whether you should have told Wolf to take the pail—"

"I ken fine that I should not," she said. Then, belatedly recalling his stricture against interruptions, she caught her lower lip between her teeth.

Again, he kept silent until she looked at him. Then, with a slight smile, he said, "I see that you do remember *some* of the things I say to you."

"Aye, sure I do," she said, smiling back, albeit warily. "D'ye think *he's* vexed wi' me? It seemed as if he did mock the way I talk."

"Nay, lass, 'tis more likely that he reverted to his own long-ago ways. When I first met him, his accent made him unintelligible to me at times. I come from the Highlands, where we speak the Gaelic. He had learned Gaelic, too, but he'd learned first to speak Scots. Even so, if we tried to speak Scots to each other, it was as if we spoke two different languages. Sakes, but I could understand his *Gaelic* better."

"Where did ye meet, if not at your home? Did ye foster wi' his family?"

"We were schooled together. But we can talk of such things another time. I want you to look after Mistress Henrietta now. I'll keep James with me."

Reminded of Jamie and realizing that he had vanished and was unlikely to have gone back into the cabin, she looked around for him.

Hawk said, "He's by the forecastle cabin, watching the oarsmen."

She saw him then, sitting with his knees hunched up, his arms around them.

"How did you know that? You did not even look!"

Hawk shrugged. "I saw him when he went. You were talking to Wolf."

"Is that really his name... Captain Wolf?"

"Go back inside now, lass. Tend to your duties."

"I'll go, sir," she said, stifling a sigh. "I do have one more question, though."

"What?"

"Do you think that Albany will follow us?"

"I do, but that should not concern you. He takes no interest in maidservants."

Feeling guilty heat fire her cheeks, knowing that Albany would take interest in her as soon as he learned that she was missing, Marsi thanked him and hurried into the cabin. There, she found the air much fresher but noted that Captain Wolf was eyeing her in a speculative and anything but flirtatious way.

Turnberry Castle

"What do you mean, James is away *at present*?"

Robert, Duke of Albany, wearing his usual black velvet with a collar of gold medallions befitting his royal status, fixed a stare as cold as the ice in his tone on his older brother and waited for an answer. They were in the royal audience chamber.

Albany was attended there by a muscular-looking, dark-haired gentleman some ten years his junior, richly dressed in wine-red, silver-laced velvet.

Two minions hovered nearby to attend the King.

His grace, looking frailer than ever, shifted uneasily in his chair. "Now, Robbie," he said. "Dinna be wroth wi' me. Ye ken fine that ye scared Annabella. Sakes, but ye terrified her so on her deathbed that she made me promise I'd no let ye take charge of our Jamie. I have but kept my word to my lass."

"Then you need only have said as much to me, your grace. This…this sneaking about, hiding James, is behavior that should be beneath you."

"I agree, aye," the King said with a sigh. "But ye ken, too, that ye can nearly always persuade me to your way of thinking. Sakes, but when I go against ye, ye cut up all my peace. In the past, ye used your position as Governor of the Realm, pointing out—and rightly, I'd agree—that if I do not rule for myself, I should no gainsay your doings in my stead. But now, 'tis my son Davy who governs for me. So 'tis Davy who must decide if I have done right or wrong by our Jamie."

"Aye, perhaps," Albany said, suppressing his fury. He knew that to vent it would gain him naught. That his grace had named Davy, Duke of Rothesay, to govern the realm three years before was a slight that Albany had not forgiven. Nor would he. Although Davy was heir to the crown, Albany knew himself to be a better ruler. And soon, if all went as planned, he would be Governor again.

To that end, he had come to Turnberry with a purpose of even greater import than seizing custody of the younger prince. Therefore, he would not tax the King further for news of James's whereabouts. He could easily find him on his own. He just needed to do so before any other powerful noble won control of James.

"I have documents for your signature, your grace," he said instead, casually.

With visible relief, the King nodded and said, "Aye, sure, Robbie, I warrant they must pertain to Stirling Castle, since ye do be still our constable there."

Gesturing to the man who had accompanied him to the chamber, Albany said, "Lindsay of Redmyre has them. You've heard me speak of Redmyre, I think."

"I have, aye." Nodding to the duke's companion, the King said, "You are welcome at Turnberry, sir. Forbye, I suspect that you have come to pay your respects to the lady Marsaili Drummond Cargill."

"I have, aye, your grace," the man said, making his bow.

Albany said bluntly, "Redmyre has come to claim his bride, your grace. One must hope that you have not misplaced her as well."

Ivor joined James by the forecastle cabin. When the boy looked up at him, making no move to stand, Ivor sat beside him.

"If the captain should approach you, as I just did," he said, "you must get up, lad. That is what he would expect of any man on his boat, let alone a lad of seven."

"Ye'll have tae remind me of such things," James said, staring over his knees at the backs of the oarsmen as they rowed. Although the air was cold, a number of them had removed the baggy shirts that they called their sarks.

Ivor thought for a moment, then said, "I believe that if you consider how you expect lesser folks to behave toward you, you will ken how to act. People expect a lad your age to make mistakes, but few such lads would get away with behaving as if everyone else must bow to them.

Those who see you behaving so will think that you either are mad or are pretending to be what you are not. Then they will talk. Your uncle has ways of hearing such talk, so you must take care."

"Aye, sure, but I dinna like deception."

"Nor do I," Ivor replied. "I loathe deception and usually punish deceivers. I punish liars most severely when I catch them at it, so I am glad to know that you agree with me on that subject."

"Then why did ye undertake a task that requires such deception?"

"Because his grace, your father, asked me to. This task is not about me or my opinions. It is about the future of Scotland, James. You may well *be* Scotland's future if you manage to survive long enough. Mayhap I should not say such a thing to you at your tender age. I do not want to frighten you, lad. But—"

"You relieve my mind by saying it, sir," James said with a direct look. "I may be gey young, but I have eyes and ears, and I use them. I ken fine that my brother Davy angers many powerful men, including our uncle. And *he* covets his old position as Governor of the Realm and means to steal it back from Davy. I ken, too, that when his grace dies, Davy will be King. And if Davy dies without issue before I die, I will be King. So I hope Davy lives for a hundred years or at least long enough for me to grow up and learn how to *be* a king."

Ivor said, "I hope so, too, lad," and felt a shiver race up his spine.

Shrugging it off, he saw Wolf coming toward them and stood to meet him.

Without urging, James stood, too.

Wolf's grin flashed as usual when he drew near. He said to James, "Would you like to learn how one steers this ship, laddie?"

"Aye, sure," James said, his eyes alight with boyish pleasure.

"Then go and tell Coll, my helmsman yonder, that I said he is to show you how he does it. But if he should tell you to come back here, you come at once and without questioning him or trying to cozen him into letting you stay."

James nodded, glanced at Ivor, and said, "I'll do as ye say, sir."

"Good lad," Jake said, clapping him on the shoulder.

As James turned away, Ivor said to him, "After Wolf and I have talked, you may come back. I'll show you how to play chess then...unless you already know."

"His grace, my father, has shown me how the pieces should move," James replied. "But I do not know how to play well, and I would like to learn."

"Good enough," Ivor said, touching his shoulder. "You may go aft now."

As they watched the boy hurry along the gangway, Jake said, "He already has his sea legs. The lad learns quickly."

"Aye, so quickly that one suspects sometimes that he is seventy rather than half past seven," Ivor said.

"He does display the regal manner. But he is not the one that concerns me, Hawk." When Ivor raised his eyebrows, Jake shrugged. "I do think we should keep to Hawk and Wolf for now. I trust my men to keep mum about aught that I do but not enough to tell them who the lad is—or who you are, come to that."

"Aye, then," Ivor said. "But if the lad does not concern you, who does?"

"The lass, Marsi. I thought at first that she was from the Borders. But she slides in and out of most un-Borders-like accents. D'ye ken aught about her?"

"I don't. Is it important?"

"I doubt it. I just wondered. Likely, she has served members of the royal court long enough to have picked up various manners of speech—even noble ones—and simply tries out a new one now and now. I did that myself as a lad. But I did wonder, because she looked taken aback when I spoke to her earlier."

"She thought you were mocking her manner of speech. I told her that when we met as lads, I could scarcely understand you when you spoke."

Jake grinned. "Sakes, that was the only thing that separated Highlanders from the rest of us at St. Andrews," he said. "Even that wasn't certain, since all of us quickly acquired both tongues. I spent my early life in Galloway but learned the Gaelic from the MacLennans. You spoke both languages well when we met."

"Aye, sure, because my father and grandfather did," Ivor said. "Show me where that chessboard is now. I promised to keep James entertained whilst the lass looks after Mistress Henrietta."

"I don't know how long Mistress Henrietta will let the lass hover over her. She was already muttering when I left. The wind is stronger, though, and the lads have stopped rowing. That should ease what ails her."

Ivor smiled. "I don't like hovering nursemaids, either, when I'm sick. But I told the lass to stay in the cabin. I'd liefer that passersby see no women aboard."

Marsi was at her wits' end. She had never so closely looked after anyone else before, let alone a seasick person. And she had not given a thought to that fact even when Jamie had declared that Hetty would be seasick. She realized now that she had stupidly assumed that Hetty would insist on looking after herself.

But Hetty could not. She had been sick in the pail three more times, making Marsi wonder how much more could come up. The captain had rapped on the door once to give her a jug of water and to tell her where she would find a mug.

"Make her drink some every now and now," he had said.

"Sakes, sir, she will only throw it up again."

"Aye, perhaps," he said. "But it will become more painful for her if she has nowt to bring up."

So Marsi had tried, but Hetty did not want to drink. Nor did she want a pillow or anything else that Marsi suggested for her comfort.

At least, the breeze coming through one porthole and passing through to the other kept the noxious odors at bay. Also, the ship had steadied its motion, and Hetty was lying down on the lower bed with a damp cloth on her forehead.

Marsi had done what she could to tidy the cabin and had washed her own face. She felt better after that. But when she took the cloth from Hetty's forehead to dampen it again, Hetty said, "I'll rest now, my lady. Ye've done enough."

"But you need someone with you. You are too weak—"

"Ye're doing nowt but fretting me," Hetty murmured.

"Sakes, I'm sorry! But I don't know what to do. If you would tell me—"

"I did tell ye. Go away and let me be."

"What if you get sick again?"

"The boat has steadied. I dinna feel the sea so much anymore."

"But what if—"

"Good lack, my lady! Ye've put the pail on the floor by this bed, so I'll do well enough. By my troth, I'll do better without ye."

"Well, I like that!" Marsi pressed her lips together, instantly contrite. "I'm sorry, Hetty," she said. "I know you are sick, and I've no right to be losing my temper. But truly... art sure you don't want—"

"Nay, now, just leave me in peace. If the good Lord be kind, I'll sleep till we make landfall. Try to keep Jamie from annoying the men, and dinna flirt with anyone. I'd wager *that* was what put Hawk at outs with ye afore."

"I was *not* flirting."

"Sakes, dearling, ye flirt as easy as ye breathe when ye speak to any man. Ye be too quick with your smiles. Now, keep to yourself and let me sleep."

Marsi nearly reminded her that Hawk had said she was not to go on deck. But she felt confined, and when Hetty slept, it would be worse. Moreover, she was as sure as she could be that none of the men would take liberties.

Not under their captain's gimlet eye, they wouldn't.

Accordingly, having looked to be sure that all was in order, or as orderly as it could be under the circumstances, she went outside and shut the door.

The sail was up, the oars shipped, and the oarsmen

were resting. The door to the forecastle cabin was shut. Neither Hawk nor Jamie sat before it.

"What d'ye need, lass?" Captain Wolf asked, startling her into whirling about. He leaned against the high stern beside his helmsman.

"Mistress Hetty wants tae sleep, sir, and she said I were a-fidgeting her," Marsi said. "But Hawk bade me stay inside. I think he fears that one o' your men—"

"Nae one will trouble ye." Then, with a twinkle, he added, "Hawk did say he'd liefer we not reveal that we have women aboard. Mayhap it would be better if ye join him and the lad in the forecastle cabin. Hawk is teaching him to play chess."

Tempted to ask if Jamie was teaching Hawk or Hawk teaching Jamie, Marsi restrained herself, recalling his shrewd looks earlier.

She decided she would do better to say as little to Captain Wolf as possible. Accordingly, she nodded submissively and said, "I'll go tae them, then, sir."

"Good lass," he said, nodding.

Without further comment, Marsi headed for the gangway.

Chapter 4 _____

"Do those men ken who I am?" James asked as Ivor moved a pawn forward.

"The captain does; the others do not."

"Would an ordinary lad ask one o' them tae let him sit beside him as he rows, tae see how he does it?"

"He might ask, but I'd wager that the man he asked would tell him that he'd be in the way," Ivor said. "You may ask the captain about that, though. Just mind how you speak and don't be giving him or his men any orders."

"I speak as I speak," James said, moving a pawn and then pulling it back.

"Aye, well, I've often regretted my speech but never my silence," Ivor said.

James eyed him thoughtfully. "*That* is Publius Syrus," he said.

Although Ivor was rapidly growing accustomed to the boy's adultlike conversation, the comment astonished him. "How do you know that?"

James shrugged. "His grace, my father, told me. They do educate me, ye ken. I have learned most of the Roman maxims. As ye, yourself, have said, I may be King one day. I wouldna want anyone tae think they had a dafty on the throne."

"I don't believe that anyone will think that about you," Ivor said dryly.

"I dinna think it either. But I dinna like pretending that I'm no m'self."

"I don't recall offering you a choice about that," Ivor said. "Your royal sire put me in command of this venture. That means you must do as I bid you."

Pushing his lady forward to meet Ivor's pawn, James said without looking up, "I ken that fine. And I ken fine what ye said ye'd do if I fail tae do as ye say. But I think ye ought tae address me as 'sir' when we're privy with each other."

Exerting patience, Ivor said, "I disagree. We should behave in private as we do when others are about, because as Publius Syrus also said, 'Practice is the best of all instructors.' In other words, you, Mistress Henrietta, and Marsi will play your roles better if you continually practice them."

"Aye, perhaps."

"Your king is in peril, lad."

James examined the board. "Ye're going tae win!"

"I think so, aye."

"But my father always lets *me* win. He warns me of my peril, but he also leaves me a way out if I can find it. I dinna think ye've done that."

"Nay, lad, and I won't do that. 'Tis better for you to learn to win on your own. This has been a fast game, so we can replay it, and I will teach you some tactics and strategy to avoid the trap I set. That way, you will learn. Sithee, winning will mean more to you if you do it on your own than if people let you win because you are a child or, later, because you are powerful and they want to win favor."

"Well, I dinna want tae play anymore now." Scowling, James stood up.

"Sit down, control your temper, and finish the game," Ivor said. "In any event, you must not leave here looking like that. You will draw too much attention."

"This game is over," James said, catching the near edge of the board and tilting it to dump the pieces onto the table. Some rolled to the floor.

As Ivor stood up and reached for him, the door opened and the lass entered.

Seeing them, she exclaimed, "Don't you *dare* put your hands on him!"

⟶

Marsi's gaze caught Jamie's. Noting his consternation and evident remorse, she knew that she had made a serious error.

Hawk still gripped Jamie by an arm and looked furious.

But he was not looking at Jamie. He was looking at her.

Hastily, she said, "I . . . I beg your pardon, sir. I do recall that ye said—"

"Be silent," he retorted. "What the devil do you mean by walking in here without warning as you just did? I told you to stay—"

She opened her mouth, remembered about interrupting, and shut it again.

"You do show *some* wisdom, at least," he said, clearly having followed her thinking. "What are you doing out of that cabin?"

"Hetty told me to leave, and Captain Wolf said to come

here. He said ye'd told him that ye'd liefer other ships not see females aboard this one. So I came."

"Dinna be wroth with Marsi, sir," Jamie said quietly and as calmly as if Hawk were not still gripping his upper arm. "I'm the one who was in the wrong, and I do apologize tae ye. I hope ye'll no wreak your vexation wi' me on Marsi."

Marsi held her breath as Hawk looked down into Jamie's sober face and said, "I accept your apology, James. But this is the last time I will warn you. If I see any more of that behavior, you will not sit comfortably afterward. Do I make myself clear?"

"Completely, sir, aye," Jamie said.

"Then you may go and ask the captain your question about rowing. After," Hawk added sternly, "you have put away the chessmen and the board."

Nodding, the boy hastily collected the pieces, including those that had fallen to the floor. After setting them in a wall pocket with the board, he looked quizzically at Marsi, but Hawk said, "She will stay here. I want to talk to her."

Grimacing sympathetically, Jamie went out and shut the door behind him.

Marsi realized that she was holding her breath again and that she had likely given herself away by leaping to Jamie's defense. She could not recall what, exactly, she had said or how she had said it.

"Why did Mistress Henrietta tell you to leave?" Hawk asked.

"She said I was fidgeting her. When I told her I didna ken what to do to make her more comfortable, she said she'd *be* more comfortable if I'd just go away. I—" She did not want to tell him any more. She could see that her words were having no effect on the state of his temper.

"Tell me something, lass. How long have you served as the nursery maid?"

Faith, what demon was stirring him now?

Touching her ring, she said, "Why d'ye ask that, sir?"

"Never mind why. Just answer me."

"N-not long," she said, fearing that he would ask more pointed questions about her duties. For all she knew, he could list them better than she could.

"I thought as much," he said. "Any maid who had served long in a nursery would know how to look after someone in such straits as Mistress Henrietta's. Moreover, any experienced nursery maid would know better than to tell the captain of a ship to take a pail to a sick passenger. So, how did you come to serve in the royal nursery? I should think that his grace, not to mention Mistress Henrietta and James, would want someone more competent."

Irritation stirred within her that anyone, but especially Hawk, might think she was incompetent. But she tamped it down, knowing that the most foolhardy thing she could do would be to let him stir *her* temper again.

"I... I expect that I must *seem* incompetent tae ye, sir. But, in troth, I do learn gey quick, and Mistress Henrietta does ken that fine."

Her brain was working at its normal pace now, and she remembered that she had decided to tell the truth when she could. "See you, sir, I did serve the Queen afore she died and we three did all come from Perthshire. 'Tis why I call Mistress Henrietta 'Hetty,' because her grace did. But I ken that I should not. Nor call Jamie that, either. He did say I should, after ye told us that we must act as ordinary folks do, but..."

She fell silent, aware that she might have already said too much.

"I see," he said, still regarding her in that uncomfortable, measuring way.

She felt then as if she ought to say more. But she did not know what to say.

In any event, she was finding it harder to speak with any semblance of a dialect to Hawk. She found lying to him almost physically painful, even by omission. Also, she still wanted to challenge him, to tell him that he had no right, royal commission or none, to lay hands on any member of the royal family.

"How long did you serve the Queen?" he asked abruptly.

That question, too, caught her off her guard, and an unexpected surge of grief threw her off balance even more before she said, "Un-until she died."

"As I recall, she was sick for several months beforehand. And she died at Scone Abbey. Surely, you did not attend her there."

"But I did, aye," she said. "T-to my s-sorrow, I did."

Her grief threatened to overcome her. Tears welled in her eyes, but she fought them back, forcing herself to meet his gaze.

"I thought that all of her ladies were noblewomen," he said.

She could hear Hetty's voice in the back of her mind, shrieking at her to tell him the truth. But logic said that if she did, he would send her back to Turnberry.

She knew they had traveled up the Firth of Clyde, and there was no other way out of the firth. The ship would be turning back from wherever it put them ashore.

Captain Wolf would therefore surely agree to take her

back with him and would hand her over to whoever met them at the cavern jetty. The next thing she knew, Albany would have her in his clutches and she would find herself married in a blink to the ancient and odious Lord Redmyre.

Desperately, she said, "Queen Annabella *liked* me, sir. She said I made her laugh, and so I did. I did other things for her and for her ladies, too. So they took me with them when she went to Perth last summer to see her son, Davy, whilst he was staying there. Then she fell ill, and they moved her to Scone Abbey so the monks could care for her. We stayed there until..." The rest of what she had meant to say caught in her throat. She could not go on.

Oblivious to her emotions, he said, "Tell me then why you did not just sit quietly whilst Mistress Henrietta rested. Surely, you might have managed to do that, as you must have done if you sat with the Queen whilst she was sick."

"I told you, just my being there fidgeted Hetty, and she *told* me to go away. And when I went outside, I told Captain Wolf what you had said about doing so. He said that I should come here and should fear *no* danger from any man on his ship."

"Did he say that, in troth?" he said softly.

A prickle of alarm shot up her spine at the look in his eyes. But she met it boldly and said, "Aye, he did."

"He was wrong, and if you ever speak to me again as you did when you first came in here, I will show you just how wrong he was. You are in my charge, lass. If you do not want to suffer the same consequences that James will face if he speaks so to me, you would do better never to spit words at me as you did then."

"Would I?" The challenge leaped unbidden to her tongue.

"Aye, and you would likewise be wiser to obey me and not go anywhere on this ship alone," he said.

"Even here, with you, who are charged with my safety?" she murmured.

His gaze locked with hers. "Especially here, alone, with me."

Her lips parted, and an image leaped to her mind of herself in his bed and him touching her, lifting her shift, stroking her bare thigh. Nervously, but with a delicious sense of daring, she continued to look into his eyes, silently.

Faith, but she was flirting with him! She could feel the strength of the attraction between them as easily as she could sense his anger.

He caught her by the shoulders, muttering, "If you want a lesson, lass, I'll teach you one." Pulling her close, he kissed her hard.

She did not resist, because her body leaped so fast in its response to him that it startled her. She could feel the heat of his hands through the sleeves of her kirtle, the warmth of his mouth on hers. But there were other sensations, too, familiar and unfamiliar. The strongest flowed from deep inside her, new and delightful.

She could not recall ever feeling such physical awareness of any man.

The pressure of his lips eased. But to her astonishment, his tongue pressed against her lips as if it would part them and plunge inside.

Just then, she heard a sound at the door, and he released her, stepping hastily away just as the door opened and Captain Wolf looked in.

Marsi fought to keep her composure, taking care not to look at Hawk.

Wolf said without any sign that he saw aught amiss, "The wind is picking up, Hawk, and shifting to hit us from the west. I'm thinking that Mistress Henrietta may soon need the lass again."

As he spoke, the ship rolled so that Marsi reached out to the nearby wall.

Hawk merely shifted one foot to keep his balance.

"You seem to have found your sea legs," Wolf said to him.

"I'll do," Hawk said. "Come along, lass. I'll see you to the aft cabin."

She could still feel the sensation of his lips on hers and felt again the touch of his hand on her inner thigh the previous night. Her body was unnaturally aware of him. It seemed astonishing to her that the man could not tell just by being near her that she had been the girl in his bed.

Not that she wanted him to know that, ever!

~

As Ivor followed her outside and along the gangway, he kept a hand ready to catch her if she missed her step. As they went, he mentally took himself to task for his behavior in the forward cabin. What had he been thinking?

The urge to kiss her had overwhelmed him. But what a thing to do!

She was in his charge, so he deserved smacking as much as she or the lad had.

Wolf would surely have something to say about it. The man was neither blind nor stupid. Nor had he ever hesitated to speak his mind. And he had surely noted her blushes if not Ivor's own guilty reaction to his untimely entrance.

To be sure, the minx deserved the lesson. She had flirted with him now and again since she'd opened the nursery door to him that morning. But that was no excuse for his behavior. She had also flirted with Wolf, with the chap who'd helped her aboard, and with the helmsman. If *one* of them had dared take such advantage...

Mayhap she was just friendly. But something about her had stirred his interest from their first meeting. Then Wolf had described her as a cozy armful, and the next thing Ivor knew, she was deliberately challenging *him*.

He had paid more heed to her manner of speech since Wolf had commented on it, too. And he could easily discern what Wolf had meant. But if she had aped the Queen's speech and that of her noble companions, would that not be enough to...?

He nearly shook his head at the half-formed thought. When she had entered just as he was about to give James a well-deserved rebuke or worse for upsetting the chessboard, she had looked more like an avenging fury than a maidservant.

She had spoken to him curtly then—*and* as an equal.

When he had met her in the royal nursery, he had wondered briefly if she might be the lass who had come to his bed the night before. However, that girl had had magnificent long red hair of so rich a color that surely her eyebrows must be the same shade. Marsi's eyebrows and lashes were so dark as to be almost black. And her cap did not seem large enough to contain so much hair.

Had she been that woman in his bed, she would doubtless be constantly and acutely aware of the fact, to her more notable discomfiture, whenever she saw him.

She was much too calm in his presence to have been that lass.

Also, he had seen a second pallet near the nursery hearth, suggesting that the nursery's maidservant customarily slept there.

As for her flirtation, it seemed friendly rather than intentionally alluring. She reminded him of his sister, Catriona, when she flirted with cousins at clan gatherings, something that Cat had done impulsively, too, before wedding Fin Cameron.

In any event, the lass in his bed was not one he was likely to meet again. Nor was there anything particularly memorable about her that he could recall, other than her long legs, lush hair, and the way she had seemed to change from a fantasy to a real woman while he made love to her. He also remembered the silken nature of her skin. Otherwise, she was no more than a figment of a very odd dream.

Were it not for the bruise on his cheek and two bruised fingers that, from time to time, still reminded him of her, he would not spare her another thought.

The young woman twitching her hips ahead of him as she hurried along the gangway was another matter. He was sure that she had lied to him. He had recognized certain signs that told him so, but he could not be sure which of her comments had been lies and which were true.

When he did catch her in a lie, as he would if she continued the practice, she would quickly learn the danger of lying to him.

She picked up her skirts to step down off the gangway, then went straight to the aft cabin and entered it. Before she could shut the door, Ivor put a hand out to stop it and said, "Is Mistress Henrietta awake?"

"I am, sir, aye," the woman called from inside. "I hope our Marsi has no been a trial to you, nor James either."

Despite the track that his thoughts had taken as he'd followed Marsi along the gangway, he had seen James sitting on a bench between two large oarsmen, holding their oar when he could reach it and bending forward and back as the men did. Knowing that the boy was content, Ivor said confidently as he entered the cabin, "You need not concern yourself, mistress. I'm glad to hear you sounding better."

"I am feeling better, too, sir. But the way this boat be rolling about, I think I should stay where I am if I may."

"Aye, sure. They have shifted the sail to take advantage of the increasing wind. Unless it shifts again, I expect we'll make landfall in good time. Also, when we turn eastward, we'll have the wind behind us, so the ship will not roll so much."

"May we know *where* we are to make landfall, sir?" she asked.

He nodded. "'Tis a clachan called Milton, not far from Dumbarton Castle."

"I ken Milton well," Mistress Henrietta said. "See you, sir, I was raised near the town of Drymen. I expect we'll be traveling through there, will we not?"

He eyed her searchingly. "Why do you say that?"

She smiled. "Good lack, sir, if you were meaning to go east, we'd land at Glasgow and take the Stirling road. If ye'd meant to travel to the upper glens, which to my mind would be unreasonable with winter still upon us, we'd make landfall west of the river Leven. As it is, we'll likely go through the Vale of Leven to the south end of Loch Lomond, northeast to Drymen, Doune, and eastward."

"So you know where we are headed, do you?"

"I believe so," she said. "I suspected it when his grace told me to pack James's things. See you, I ken fine that her grace expressed fear for his safety, and I know who else was present. Mayhap I shouldna say . . ."

Hearing a soft gasp, he glanced at the lass and saw that her lips had parted. She was staring at Mistress Henrietta as if she would control the woman's thoughts.

Ivor said, "We need not mention names, Mistress Henrietta. We must discuss how we will travel, but I'd liefer we not name our destination or openly discuss our route. My lads will take at least a day or two to catch up with us, because they must rest the horses. I was thinking that you might pose as James's aunt. We could say that the lass here is your maidservant and that I am escorting you to visit kinsmen."

Mistress Henrietta looked thoughtful, and the lass had collected herself.

But Ivor had already decided that, much as he wanted to know what game the lass was playing, to demand answers from her while they were aboard the galley would be a mistake. Such a scene was not one to play for a shipload of oarsmen.

Had she represented a threat to James, he might have acted. But as protective of the lad as she was, he doubted that she posed any danger to him.

Turnberry

Albany was furious. Having discovered that no one seemed to know where the lady Marsaili Drummond Cargill was, he had likewise learned that the Queen's other ladies had returned to their homes or had taken service with one or another of his numerous royal siblings. Everyone agreed that the lady Marsaili still resided at Turnberry, but no one could produce her.

Confronted, the King denied knowledge of her whereabouts. "Sakes, but she must be here," he declared, frowning. "I dinna ken where else she could be. She has nae family here, nor any friends save our Jamie."

"Might she have gone with him?"

"She lacked my permission to go. And nae one would take a royal ward from Turnberry without my leave, Robbie. Likely, she is avoiding ye and will turn up when ye leave. 'Tis a big place. But as ye're here, mayhap ye'll explain why ye want me to summon Parliament. 'Tis Davy's right to do that now."

"Davy's three-year provisional term as Governor of the Realm ended on the first of January," Albany said. "It was by your own command that, after he had held the office for that period, the lords of Parliament would decide if his rule should continue. Even you must admit that he has ruled poorly."

"The people love him, Robbie, and he is young yet. He will learn."

"Scotland cannot afford his lessons," Albany retorted. "Almost the first thing he did was agree to marry the Earl of March's daughter. Less than a month later, he accepted a larger dowry from the Earl of Douglas to marry Douglas's daughter instead, thus making a blood enemy of March. Then—"

The King made a gesture of protest, but Albany ignored it, saying, "Then, Douglas died. Since then

Davy has ignored his marriage vows and treated his wife so badly that her brother, the *new* Earl of Douglas, has become another powerful blood enemy. I can provide a detailed list of Davy's *many* illicit liaisons with women other than his wife, if you want one," Albany added. "You cannot be proud of a son from whom no woman, be she maid or married, is safe."

"Davy saved Edinburgh Castle last year from the English," the King said.

"Aye, sure, the lad is a fine warrior but reckless. He may win the day, but he will lose half of his men in the doing. In most cases, diplomacy might have prevented the conflict. But Davy revels in conflict. He is rarely sober, he carries on like a bed-hopping satyr, and he urgently needs bringing to heel. If you wait for *him* to convene Parliament, you will wait in vain, because he kens the risk he runs if he does. Sign the summons I made out for you, sir. If Davy truly wants to learn how to rule Scotland, he can watch and learn from me."

"First the lords of Parliament must agree," the King said.

"They will agree when you suggest it, as you will unless you can name anyone else who would be as capable of ruling this country as I am."

"Ye ken fine that there be nae such man. But few lords of Parliament love ye, Robbie." The King sighed. "'Tis true that they have little love for Davy either. Aye, then, I will summon them. However, as to this other, regarding our Marsi, I—"

"The lady Marsaili is to marry Martin Lindsay of Redmyre," Albany said with chilly patience. "You have agreed to that, I believe. These documents merely set out the marriage settlements that I have negotiated with Redmyre."

"Aye, sure, but sithee, I promised Annabella that I'd no force the lass to marry where she does no want to marry, and Redmyre is much older than she is. Sakes, but he is older than *I* knew him to be. And Marsi has said—"

"Marsaili will do as she is bid, just as any noble maiden must do."

"I fear that the lassie has a mind of her own, Robbie. But I'll think on the matter and give ye my answer when we find her," the King said.

With that, for the moment, Albany had to be satisfied. He had achieved his primary goal—that of summoning Parliament—so he was pleased.

Even so, for putting him to such trouble, he promised himself a few warm minutes with the lady Marsaili when he laid hands on her, as he soon would.

His men were questioning everyone in the castle.

*Chapter 5*_____

Marsi was paying close heed to the discussion between Hetty and Hawk. She did not know Milton, but she knew Drymen, because it was the town from which the Drummonds had taken their name. The first Drummonds had come from there, and her parents lay buried at Inchmahone Priory some ten miles north of Drymen.

It had been years since she had visited Drymen, but if they should travel near the Loch of Menteith, where the priory stood, she might find a way to visit her parents' graves. She would have to think up a good tale, one that...

With a mental bump, her thoughts jumped off that path. She had often made up tales when she had found it useful, and nearly always successfully. Not that she told lies, exactly. If one spoke only the truth but left out inconvenient details, surely that was not the same as lying. Even in her present guise, she had not *really* told any lies. She had never *said* that she was the nursery maid, nor had anyone else. She had simply presented herself as one. She felt uncomfortable about that now, though.

Something about the man...

When Hetty had said that she could guess their route and had mentioned Annabella's having expressed on her deathbed her fears for Jamie's safety, Marsi recalled having told Hawk herself that *she* had been present at the time.

Fixing her gaze on Hetty, Marsi prayed that she would say no more and that Hawk would not mention his knowledge of her presence.

Hawk glanced at her, and although it was a brief look, it was so intense that she felt it to her bones. However, he said only that they should discuss their route.

Hetty said diffidently, "As to pretending to be his lordship's aunt, sir, I would suggest that we might more wisely say that he and I are cousins. See you, I find prevarication difficult, but I *am* a second cousin to his mother and thus..."

"We can discuss that later, mistress," Hawk said. "I understand your reluctance, but we might be wise to ask the lad what he thinks we should say."

Marsi was glad to keep quiet and let them talk. She felt only relief when neither Hetty nor Hawk so much as looked at her, let alone asked for her opinion on that subject or any other. The only time either of them seemed to notice her was when Hetty said that it might be wise to learn when they could expect to eat their midday meal. She did look at Marsi then, but Hawk said he would ask the captain.

When he had gone, Hetty looked shrewdly at Marsi. "I could see that ye were thinking hard, but ye were wise to keep silent. I tell ye, the more I have to remember what to say or not to say, the more likely I am to say what I should not."

"I know, Hetty. It is the same with me. But I cannot tell Hawk the truth until they put us ashore, or he will send me back to Turnberry with the captain."

"I doubt he would send ye back alone with all these men!"

"He would do it in a blink and think it a good lesson for me," Marsi said. "Especially since I told him myself that the captain assured me that I am safe from his men even if I walk about the ship alone."

"Ay-de-mi, surely ye didna say any such impertinent thing to the man!"

"But I did, aye, because I thought it was silly for him to keep me confined to this cabin. Even had I not, since Wolf is Hawk's friend, Hawk must trust him to keep me safe. And if I go back to Turnberry now, after running off, you know what will happen. I'd wager that Albany is already there, and if he gets his hands on me..."

Hetty grimaced and Marsi knew that she need not say any more.

She also knew, however, that her pretense could not continue much longer, and she had witnessed Hawk's volatile temper. She had a temper, too, she reminded herself, but the reminder did little good. Hawk's temper was doubtless a much greater danger to her than hers would ever be to him.

On deck, Ivor found the big square sail up and the tacking spar attached. Oarsmen were still at their posts but had raised their oars, unneeded while the sail stayed full. Jake stood near his helmsman, and James stood between them.

The lad looked as if he enjoyed life on the galley, but Ivor wondered how he would like it if he had to live so day after day.

"All settled?" Jake asked, raising his eyebrows.

"Well enough, aye," Ivor replied. "Mistress Henrietta

is well enough to think of food for others if not yet for herself. She suggested that the lad might be hungry for his midday meal. Can we feed them, or is this wind too strong?"

"We'll eat shortly," Jake said. "It will be cold food, but we have sliced beef, bread, and plenty of apples. If anyone is starving..." He glanced at James.

The boy shrugged. "I'm content," he said.

Jake glanced up at the gray sky and ahead again. "We've some time yet before we enter the narrow part of the firth at Greenock. I'll tell one of my lads to prepare a basket of food for the cabin. Then the lad can eat when he chooses."

"That would suit me, aye," James said, looking at Ivor.

Aware of the helmsman nearby, Ivor said mildly, "I believe that Mistress Henrietta will expect you to join her when that basket arrives."

James gazed steadily at him for a long moment before he said, "I'll remember that, sir, aye. I'll no disappoint her."

"Good lad," Ivor said.

"I can arrange for that food now if you'd like to walk forward with me," Jake said to Ivor. As they turned from James and the helmsman, he added in a lower tone, "That lad kens his worth, I'm thinking. Do you expect difficulties from him?"

"None I cannot handle," Ivor said. "He is used to command and to being obeyed. But I remind myself of how difficult *I* could be... and others of us, come to that, who arrived at St. Andrews with our pride flowing. He is a good lad, Jake."

"Good, because with Albany and his men nipping at your heels, as we both ken fine that they soon will be, you will likely run into trouble enough when you near Stirling. That is Albany's country, after all, as are Fife and Menteith. You'd be wise to avoid the royal burghs and most of Fife by heading north into Perthshire."

"Albany posts men in Perth, too," Ivor said. "He knew last year when Davy Stewart headed north from there, and learned that he had come to Rothiemurchus."

"You should keep clear of the *town* of Perth, aye. But, sithee, I have access to ships on the east coast as well as here in the west."

"How is that possible?"

"D'ye ken aught about the Earl of Orkney?"

"The younger Henry Sinclair? Aye, sure. He owns a great fleet of ships."

"I knew his father," Jake said. "More to our purpose, the Sinclairs know me, and I have access to their ships whenever I need one. They nearly always keep one at Leith harbor near Edinburgh. Sithee, Traill told me to make myself useful to you in any way that I can. So I was thinking that, since my helmsman can take the *Sea Wolf* home after we see to our business here, I might travel to Edinburgh from Glasgow. That way, if you find it safer to sail to St. Andrews from some point along the Firth of Tay, you can send a message to me through the abbot at Lindores Abbey near Newburgh. Any cleric on your way would carry such a message to him."

Jake paused to give orders to a resting oarsman, then motioned toward the forecastle cabin. "I'll show you a map, Hawk, and explain what I have in mind."

Realizing that Jake had had longer than he had to think about any potential trouble they might encounter, Ivor followed willingly.

An oarsman soon brought a basket of food to the aft cabin with Jamie following at his heels. As soon as the man had gone, the boy opened the basket. Surveying its contents, he said, "I think ye'd best tell Hawk who ye are, Marsi."

"I will," she replied. "In good time."

"I think ye should tell him *now*," Jamie said. "Sithee, he's a stern chap and makes his feelings plain. When I said I dislike deception, he said he doesna like it either, that this business of pretending tae be other than what we are goes against his nature. Usually, he said, he punishes deceivers. Forbye, if ye tell him yourself—with me and Hetty by ye as ye do—and explain tae him *why* ye left Turnberry, I think he'll listen. But if ye continue as ye are, and he finds out—"

"I cannot tell him yet," Marsi said, glancing at Hetty but knowing she would find no support there. Hetty had not stirred from the lower bed, although Marsi saw that she did have more color in her cheeks than she'd had earlier.

Although Marsi tried to explain her reasons for keeping her secrets a bit longer, Jamie shook his head at her.

"Ye needna tell me," he said. "I ken fine that ye dinna want to go back. Sakes, anyone o' sense must fear Albany. He makes it plain that he thinks Scotland would be the better had Davy never been born and that a strong king, namely himself, would be better than *any* king my age. Nae one o' sense would argue that, either. The country has had its fill o' governorships. Even my da says so."

His words stirred Marsi's ready sympathy and she moved close enough to touch his shoulder. Her fear of

Albany was real, but as Hetty had said, the worst that she would face was an unhappy marriage. What Jamie faced could be deadly.

Hetty said, "I think that you would both do better now to eat something."

"She is right," Marsi said, giving his shoulder a squeeze. "Hawk will keep us safe, and I will tell him the truth as soon as I know that he cannot send me back."

Taking an apple from the basket, she handed it to Jamie and piled a bread trencher with slices of beef for him.

As he set it on the table, he looked at her from under his brows and said, "D'ye think Hawk would trust ye tae keep quiet at Turnberry if ye've guessed where we be going, Marsi? Because, if he feared that Albany might winkle it out o' ye, belike Hawk would do all he could tae *keep* ye with us."

"But I would never—"

"Enough," Hetty said firmly. "Both of ye will sit down at that table and eat your meal. If I am to pretend to be your aunt, sir," she added with a look at Jamie as direct as any of his own, "I think I had better begin to behave so at once."

He chuckled. "Then ye'll have tae remember tae call me Jamie, I think."

She smiled. "Sit, Jamie, and eat."

"Aye, that's better," he said, sliding onto the nearer bench. Then he added, "Pour Hetty some water, Marsi. The captain said she must keep drinking now and now. Mayhap she can stomach one o' them hard rolls in yon basket, too."

As Marsi moved to obey him, she shot a look at Hetty and was glad to see an appreciative smile on the older woman's pleasant, round face.

Marsi was handing her the mug when Hawk entered after a perfunctory rap.

"We're approaching the Island of Bute," he told them. "This ship will be visible from shore and from passing vessels now, so I want you to stay in the cabin until we make landfall. I brought the chessboard and pieces, James," he added. "Mayhap you can teach Mistress Henrietta or Marsi to play."

Marsi fought to suppress a saucy grin and an equally impertinent urge to inform him that she already played an excellent game of chess.

Handing the chess set to the boy, Hawk looked from one face to the other, his gaze lingering on Marsi longer than on the others.

She gazed silently and, she hoped, solemnly back.

Clearly satisfied that they would obey him, Hawk went out again.

Catching Jamie's quizzical gaze, Marsi said, "Do you want to play?"

"Perhaps later," he said. "Or we can play dames instead. I'm cleverer at that, as ye ken." He hesitated until she cocked her head, then added, "I was just thinking I should tell ye that Hawk doesna approve o' folks letting me win."

"If you think that I've ever *let* you win at dames, my lad, I'll have you know that I have done no such thing. At least, not since you were a wee laddie of six."

He grinned, and they turned their attention to their meal. By the time they had finished eating, Hetty was asleep.

James set up the chessboard to play dames, and he and Marsi played quietly, one game after another, until the light in the cabin grew dim.

Standing on his bench, James announced that he could see a harbor.

"The sun is nearly down," he added, looking to his right.

"That porthole faces south," Marsi said. "Hawk said earlier that we would make landfall on the *north* bank of the firth. Nay, do not go outside," she added quickly when he turned with clear intent to do just that.

He grimaced. "It is too dark out now for anyone ashore to recognize me."

"Try persuading Hawk of that," Marsi retorted.

With a sigh, he got down and began to help her put the game pieces away.

The boat slowed, and they heard noises of increased activity outside the cabin. Hetty awoke then, expressing surprise at how long she must have slept.

"Aye, ye did, but I think we've arrived," Jamie said.

Hawk confirmed that when he entered minutes later, saying, "We have dropped anchor off Milton now. Wolf will send men ashore to see if the inn can put us up for the night. If it cannot, we will consider what other options we have."

"There is a tiny clachan—nae more than a wayside alehouse and a cottage or two—some two miles beyond Milton, sir," Hetty said. "If we go farther, we'll be joining the main road to Stirling, which is heavily traveled."

"The captain mentioned that, too, mistress," Hawk said. "We need to take shelter for the night wherever we can find it. But I'll want to leave early in the morning, before most travelers staying in Dumbarton will have broken their fast."

"What of your own men, sir?" Marsi asked. "Won't they be joining us?"

"Aye, but it will take them another day or two to reach

us. They must take precautions to avoid giving anyone cause to connect them with James's departure."

"But Albany may not even have reached Turnberry yet."

"We'd be wise to assume that he has," he said.

James said casually, "It seems to me that he nearly always does know things, often even before they happen. Also, if he asks his grace, my father..."

Marsi noted that when James paused, Hawk's expression softened.

He said, "His grace does know our eventual destination, lad. But, in troth, your uncle is likely to deduce that for himself. I know that, and so does Captain Wolf, and we will protect you. Moreover, the King does *not* know our route."

"My uncle will fly into a tirrivee when he finds me gone," James said.

"He may, aye. But you cannot stay hidden for long, and he is astute enough to know that few Scots would support his seizing custody of you whilst your father and Rothesay remain alive. Therefore, I doubt that he will pursue us with much vigor. He is more likely to want to see that we go where he expects us to go."

Swallowing hard, Marsi resisted the temptation to look at Jamie.

She knew that although Albany might hesitate to pursue him, the duke would have *no* hesitation about sending his men after her. If their pursuit also yielded him Jamie's small person, Albany would view that event as just an additional gain.

Ivor noted the lass's reaction and added it to a mental list of certain details he wanted to sort out as soon as he could be more private with her. As it was, it would have to wait at least until they were safely ashore. Earlier, she had seemed mischievously amused at something he had said. Now, she was twisting that ring of hers, something she seemed to do when she was worried, nervous, or sad.

He could read her with unusual ease and wondered why that was so.

Reminding the three of them to stay inside, he went back out on deck, where he learned that Jake had sent the towboat ashore. Despite the daylong overcast, rays of the setting sun had found openings between the clouds and the western horizon, where an orange glow shot fiery paths across the water.

It was a splendid sight. But it meant that they had no more than an hour before dusk would fade to darkness.

The towboat returned sooner than expected. One look at the fair, curly-haired man who nimbly climbed the rope ladder told Ivor that the news was not good.

"Six o' Albany's men be staying at Milton's inn, captain," the chap said.

"Art sure they are Albany's, Mace?" Jake asked.

"Aye, sir, all wearing black as they do and bearing his badge. I ambled into the inn, ordered a quaich o' ale, and talked wi' our friend there. He'll tether two horses in them woods east o' the inn—a sumpter pony and one tae carry a woman."

"Good," Jake said. "We'll put you ashore a bit farther along, Hawk. There's a track right from the far end of the beach straight into those woods. Mace will go with you. That way, if you are able to hire horses at the alehouse, he'll bring the two Milton ones back. If you cannot, he'll make all right for you with our man."

Thanking him for all that he had done, Ivor collected the others. He was concerned about Mistress Henrietta. But when he said as much, she replied briskly, "Don't you fret about me, sir. Once my feet are on solid ground again, I'll do."

When they disembarked on the beach, she seemed to recover as swiftly as she had promised. Nevertheless, after they found the horses and loaded all they could onto the sumpter pony, tying the remaining bundles to the second horse's saddle, Ivor said, "You are going to ride, mistress."

"Oh, but, sir, I should not!" she said, looking in dismay from James to Marsi.

"Don't argue," Ivor replied firmly. "Do as I bid you."

"Aye, Hetty," James said. "We *want* tae walk after sitting all day."

With Mace leading the sumpter, and Marsi and James following him, Ivor walked beside Mistress Henrietta's horse. The relief he had felt when James made no objection to walking told him that he was still worried about trouble from that quarter but gave him hope that the boy was settling into his role.

They made their way through chilly hillside woods where a thin layer of snow crunched underfoot until the track met the road again well beyond Milton. To Ivor's relief, Mistress Henrietta proved to be a competent horsewoman and they saw no other travelers on the narrow road.

The alehouse, when they found it, was a squat building with a thatched roof that sat in a clearing near the road, with two smaller outbuildings behind it.

Mace said, "I'll go in first, sir. Doubtless, ye'd liefer

stay tae look after the women and the lad till I see what's what."

Ivor agreed, but ten minutes later, when Mace had not returned and James shot a worried frown at him, Ivor murmured for his own sake as well as the boy's, "We must be patient. There may be men inside whom Mace does not trust."

James nodded, and their wait ended minutes later when five men, all cheerful with drink, strolled out of the house and away down the road.

Mace appeared shortly afterward. "All's well, sir," he said. "The man has only two small rooms, but ye be welcome tae them. He's got good whisky, too, I can tell ye. I asked about horses, but he's none tae spare. So I'll be telling the chap at Milton that ye'll send these two back from Balloch or Drymen."

The lass cleared her throat, and when Ivor looked at her, she gazed back intently, as if she had had the same thought that he had.

To Mace, he said, "I'd liefer you tell no one else our direction."

"I must tell that Milton innkeeper about his horses, sir. And I dinna ken where else along this road ye might go."

"If I may make a suggestion," Mistress Henrietta said, "mayhap you could tell him that we'll send them back from Callander, sir. That would put anyone asking about us on a path well beyond where we'll be leaving the main road."

"That's what we'll say then," Ivor said and saw with a touch of amusement that the lass was nodding her agreement. He reached for his purse to give Mace money for the Milton innkeeper, but Mace refused it with a grin.

"The captain said ye'd offer, sir, but ye're tae keep your gelt. Sithee, he takes good care o' that innkeeper, so he'll oblige us whenever we need him. If the men at Milton hadna been Albany's, our chap would ha' turned them out for ye."

"Aye, well, this place is more discreet and suits us better, I think," Ivor said.

Less than a quarter-hour later, they had settled into two tiny rooms above the taproom, each with a narrow bed and a pallet on the floor. It being clear that neither had room enough for James to share one with Mistress Henrietta and Marsi, Ivor took the lad in with him and soon learned that he was a restless sleeper.

Midway through the night, the boy's fretful muttering woke him. Realizing that James was in the throes of a nightmare, Ivor got up and knelt over him.

Touching the boy's shoulder, he murmured, "You're safe, Jamie."

Squirming, James muttered fretfully, "Where am I?"

"You're with me."

The thin, rigid shoulder under his hand relaxed, and the silence continued until James's breathing sounded normal again. Ivor went back to bed. As he plumped the pillow under his head, he felt a warm sense of accomplishment and realized that he was coming to like Jamie Stewart very much.

It was the last thought he had before he slept. When he awoke Tuesday morning, the first fingers of dawn light were stretching into the room.

Turning onto one side, he saw the boy watching him.

"At last," James said. "I feared I'd wake ye if I got up."

Ivor grinned at him. "Well, you can get up now."

James popped up off his pallet and headed for the night jar in the corner to relieve himself.

"Use that basin and ewer on the washstand to wash your face and hands whilst I pull on my breeks and boots," Ivor told him as he got up and shoved a hand through his hair. "Then we'll go down and see about breakfast."

"What about Marsi and Hetty?"

"We'll bang on their door as we pass it."

He did so, heard a female mutter in response, and paused long enough to say clearly, "We'll break our fast downstairs and be on our way, so don't dawdle." Then he urged James downstairs to see what they could find to eat.

The alewife was bustling about in her kitchen. "Aye, sure," she answered cheerfully to Ivor's question, "I'll have porridge ready in a twink, sir, and eggs and bannocks if ye like, as weel."

Reminding her that there were four of them, he and James moved to take seats on benches flanking a table in the taproom.

They had just sat down when the outer door opened and Marsi walked in.

Ivor's temper flared, bringing him to his feet. "Where the devil have *you* been?" he demanded.

Marsi stopped on the threshold, her heart pounding in response to his evident fury. But when he took a step toward her, her chin came up of its own accord, and she said, "Faith, would you murder me? I promise, I just stepped outside to—"

"I told you to stay *in*side."

"Aye, sure, but when I awoke and needed to..." She

paused, feeling heat flood her cheeks, then added in a rush, "I did not want to wake Hetty."

"I'd wager that the place you sought lies out back and that the alewife directed you to go the shortest way, through the kitchen," he said grimly. "So how is it that you are coming in by the front door?"

Her lips felt dry, and her heart still pounded, but she strove to sound reasonable. "I did ask her, and she showed me the shack out back. The air is so fresh outside that afterward, when I saw only a lad out back feeding chickens and no one on the road—"

"Come in and shut that door," he snapped.

"What are you going to do?"

He took a menacing step toward her, and she hastily shut the door.

"There, I shut it! But I must say—"

"If you are wise, you will be silent."

"For someone who dislikes being interrupted—"

"By heaven, one way or another, I will teach you to obey your—"

"My what? Just what authority *do* you hold over me, sir? In troth, I think you assume too *much* authority," she went on, scarcely aware of what she was saying or that once again he had stirred her to say more in her anger than she had meant to say, or than was wise. The stress of the weeks since Annabella's death was suddenly too much and words spilled from her mouth as if someone else had taken possession of her tongue. "I don't know how you can see danger in taking an early-morning walk from the back door to the front, to breathe some fresh air. But it must always be as *you* say, mustn't it? It can never be as anyone else wants it to be. *No* minion of Albany's can be seeking us here yet, so there cannot *be* any danger in what I did."

"Can there not? I thought I proved to you on the ship that *your* notion of danger may not be the only danger that threatens you," he declared, reaching for her.

As he did, James snapped, "Don't *touch* my cousin!"

Glancing at him in dismay, Marsi looked swiftly back at Hawk and saw that he had frozen in place. Any relief that she felt was short-lived, however, for he was already looking beyond her. Only then did she hear what he had heard.

Horses, a number of them, were approaching—nay, entering—the yard.

"Go upstairs, James, *now*," Hawk said, his tone brooking no argument.

"Marsi must come with me," the boy replied staunchly.

When Hawk nodded for her to go, Marsi fled.

Chapter 6

Ivor sat down again as the alewife bustled in and set a mug and a tall flagon known as a tappet-hen on the table before him.

"Ye'll be wanting tae try this ale, sir," she said, pouring from the tappet-hen into the mug. "I'll bring ye some warm bread tae go with it."

He looked up to thank her. But before he could speak, the door opened and two expressionless men in black with the well-known emblem of the Duke of Albany prominently displayed on their cloaks strode into the room.

"Good morrow, mistress," the taller of the two said to the alewife.

Bobbing a curtsy, she said, "And a good day tae yourself, sir. Will ye and the others yet outside be wanting ale or a meal the noo?"

"Nowt, for we ha' broken our fast. Had ye many guests for the night?"

With a nod toward Ivor, the alewife said, "Just this lad and his auld auntie, wha' still sleeps abovestairs."

"Where be ye headed?" the spokesman asked Ivor.

"My aunt has kinsmen at Callander," Ivor said.

"Aye, then, ye'd best hope ye get there afore it snows,"

the man said. "One can smell it in the air." With a nod to his companion, he led the way outside.

Ivor looked at the alewife. "My auld auntie?"

"Since me business be mine own, sir, I expect that yours be nane o' theirs. *And* that ye'd liefer no answer a lot o' their fool questions. Forbye, they dinna count bairns, so why should we? Now, d'ye like your eggs boiled or spitting wi' butter?"

"Two, boiled hard," he said. "Will those men of Albany's come back?"

"Not them. They spent last night in Milton and will be going back the noo tae Stirling. Sithee, the duke's men come by at odd times each month and stick their noses in wherever they will. 'Tis best tae keep clear o' them when ye can."

"I thank you for your sound advice, mistress," he said, wondering how much she had heard of his angry exchange with Marsi.

She smiled. "Ye'll want tae linger over your meal, sir, tae let them get well ahead o' ye. They'll be eager tae get back home, though, as usual."

She went back to her kitchen, and Ivor sipped his ale, listening until the last sound of the visitors had faded in the distance. Then he went upstairs and rapped on the women's door.

Hearing Mistress Hetty's voice bidding him enter, he did so.

"Those were Albany's men," he told the others. "They've gone now, so we can eat. But before we go down, you should know that the alewife told them that you are my aunt, mistress. She did not mention Jamie or the lass."

"Good lack, sir!" Hetty exclaimed. "Do you think they are looking for us?"

"I don't know how that would be possible," he said. "The alewife said they spent last night in Milton and were heading back to Stirling. Even if Albany reached Turnberry right after we left, it is unlikely that he's had the time or even good reason to send orders out for his men to seek us here."

"That is true, Hetty," the lass said. "Recall that his grace does not know our route and no one at Turnberry except Dennison knows that we left on a ship."

Mistress Henrietta nodded. "We'll go down at once then, sir. We were only awaiting your assurance that the newcomers were harmless or had gone."

"You and Jamie go ahead, *Aunt* Henrietta," Ivor said.

She looked from him to Marsi and back at him. "I expect that if I am to be your aunt, sir, you should call me Aunt Hetty, as Jamie will."

"We'll see," he said, shifting his gaze to Marsi. "Go along now, mistress."

Hetty hesitated. "But, sir—"

"Go," he said without looking away from Marsi. "Since we are apparently to travel as a family, we may as well begin to act like one."

Color flooded Marsi's cheeks, but she did not speak, and a moment later they were alone in the room. Ivor realized then that Hetty had left the door ajar. He shut it with a snap and heard the lass gasp.

~

Marsi eyed him warily. He did not seem as angry as he had been earlier, but alone with him as she was, she felt more vulnerable than she ever had.

In a strange way, she felt as if she had known him all her life. She certainly knew him well enough to know that if he had decided to punish her for her outburst earlier, he would do it. She would be unable to stop him.

His attitude might change when he learned exactly who she was, but she doubted that it would. He was a man who knew himself and not one whom rank or wealth would impress. That the King trusted him enough to entrust Jamie to his care told her that his grace believed Hawk would do whatever he had promised to do.

The tension stretched between them until it was nearly palpable.

At last, he said with unexpected mildness, "Suppose you tell me who you are, my lady, and what demon possessed you to attempt such a deceit. And do *not* spin me more of your lies. My temper won't tolerate them."

"I have told you no lies, sir." Although she said it firmly enough, she felt heat flooding her cheeks again. "I may have left out some details, but—"

"Stop there," he said with a dangerous edge to his voice. "If you are James's cousin, you have left out more than a few details. Not only is your very pretense a lie, but you certainly *told* me one by claiming to have served her grace."

"That was true," she said, striving for calm. If she did not entirely succeed, at least he was controlling his temper. "After my parents died," she went on, "Aunt Annabella invited me to Turnberry to join her other ladies. I...I thought some of them would be near my age, but they were all much older. Even so, they were kind to me. I...I did go with her last summer to Perth, and...and we stayed at Scone Abbey after she fell sick. In December, after she d-died, the King..."

She paused to regain her composure, wishing that he would speak, but he did not. He seemed unaware of the tears welling in her eyes, let alone any other sign of her distress. He seemed only impatient for her to continue.

His attitude steadied her, however. She said, "The King was distraught then. So when he asked me to return to Turnberry with him, to be there when he relayed the dreadful news of her death to Jamie, I . . . I . . ."

Choked by her tears, she could not go on.

"I see," he said quietly.

She nearly explained that she had not *wanted* to return to Turnberry, that she had felt abandoned by everyone until she recalled that Hetty would be with Jamie. Then it had seemed sensible to go. Not that she'd had a choice, since the King was her guardian if only because his Queen had acted in that capacity before her death.

Watching Hawk, she decided that she would be wiser to explain no more just then, lest she stir him to erupt again. With her emotions on edge as they were, she doubted that she could retain what was left of her composure if he did erupt.

"What is your full name?"

"Marsaili Drummond Cargill. They named me for my mother, who was Annabella's youngest sister."

"Very well, Lady Marsaili. We *will* talk more about this, but for now, I'll say only that I will tolerate no more deception. If my own sister had behaved as you have since we met, she'd have earned herself a rare skelping. From now on, you and James will follow my rules, and I will treat you equally if you do not. Think about that before you decide to fly out at me again as you did earlier."

"I do apologize for that, sir," she said, trying to sound remorseful but hearing only exhaustion in her voice. It sounded most unlike her, but then so had the angry virago that she had become when she'd lost her temper earlier. What if he believed that demons really were trying to possess her? And what if they *did*?

To her relief, he nodded, opened the door, and gestured for her to go ahead.

As she passed him, her skin tingled in awareness of how close he was. She felt a nearly irresistible urge to turn to him, apologize again for her actions, and try to soothe away his vexation with her, just as she might have done with Hetty or, before their deaths, with her parents. But instinct warned her that Hawk would not respond as agreeably as any of them would have to such soothing.

Following immediately after that train of thought came the realization that what she had really wanted was a hug from him. Just the thought of those strong arms wrapping around her, holding her tightly...

With a sigh, she pushed the thought away, knowing that he was not finished with her yet. However, he was unlikely to take her to task before Hetty and Jamie, so since just the four of them would be traveling together until his men caught up with them, she should gain a respite. It occurred to her only when she was halfway down the stairs that she ought to have told him that Albany would be almost as eager to get his hands on her as on Jamie, and why.

She could not tell him such a thing right there on the stairs. Nor could she seem to think of another way to tell him straightaway. She would do it later.

If she was being cowardly, so be it.

Ivor followed Marsi, wondering at himself. Her outburst in the taproom had surprised him, but he had reacted as any man of sense in his position would have, with intent to teach her that any time she fought with him, he would win.

With so much at stake, she *needed* to understand who was in charge.

With that purpose in mind, he had meant to give her a tongue-lashing that she would not forget. Instead, the instant he had recognized the depth of her grief, he had wanted to comfort her. He controlled that urge, but by doing so, he had barely even begun to express his opinion of what she had done. Sakes, he had not even demanded all the answers that he wanted from her, chief amongst which was the primary one: What demon had possessed her to pose as a nursery maid?

He could scarcely expect her to believe now that he had meant it when he'd said that he would brook no more deception. Surely, she must think that she had managed to wrap him around her thumb. And, if that *was* what she thought, God alone knew what she might say or do next.

He had to correct the situation, and quickly.

His volatile temper usually alarmed people. His men had deep respect for it.

Recalling even Jake's reaction to a mere frown from him, Ivor wondered what it was about Marsi that had so unmanned him. To be sure, she was much smaller than he was, but so was his sister Catriona. And he had never had any trouble expressing the full range of his temper with Cat when she angered him.

Cat certainly knew better than to lie to him, but Marsi, by her actions and omissions, *had* lied. She would doubt-less continue to insist that she had not, but deception in and of itself *was* a lie, and so he would tell her.

They found Hetty and James tucking into a generous breakfast. At Ivor's place was a bread trencher, a bowl of hot porridge, two boiled eggs in a small basket, a platter of sliced beef, and a large basket of warm bannocks. Bramble jam and a pot of butter sat in the middle of the table beside the tappet-hen.

James eyed Marsi speculatively, and as she took her seat across the table from him, he said, "I'm glad tae see that ye're still in one piece. It got so quiet up there that I feared the man had throttled ye."

Ivor fixed a stern gaze on the boy, but James continued to look at Marsi.

Her cheeks were bright red, but Ivor saw no sign of the tears he had detected earlier. She did not reply to James's comment, though.

Hetty said, "There is fresh cream in that wee pitcher, my la—" Breaking off with a click of her tongue, she looked at Ivor and said quietly, "James told me that he gave her away, sir. Still, I expect we should go on addressing her as Marsi, aye?"

"Aye," he said. "We will also discuss the weather and other such everyday topics whilst we remain in this room, mistress. When we finish eating, I'll go and see that the stable lad is preparing our horses, whilst you three get ready to go."

"It is but ten miles or so from here, I believe, to...to where we are going next," Hetty said. "Unless you mean to travel on from there."

"Nay, we'll wait there for my men," Ivor said. "Wolf told me of an inn at the north end of that town. Before we left Turnberry, on his advice, I gave orders to my men to seek us first in Balloch, at the south end of Loch Lomond.

When they do not find us there, they will go on to that other inn, taking care not to pass us by."

He saw Marsi look at him, and although she pressed her lips together as if determined to keep silent, he understood what she wanted to ask as easily as if she had spoken. "We'll see my men by sundown tomorrow, if not sooner."

Her eyes had lost the merry, often mischievous look that he had begun to watch for, and he missed seeing it. She looked a little sad but not sullen when she nodded and returned her attention to her food. At least, she was not the sort of female who refused to eat whenever she was upset.

James began to stand, saying, "I've finished, so I am going—"

"Excuse yourself properly, lad," Ivor said.

"Aye, sure, but I just want go out and find the pri—"

"Wait for me then," Ivor said. "I don't want you going outside by yourself, James, not here or anywhere else we may go. Not under any circumstance. Nor, when we stay at inns or alehouses, are you to go alone into the common rooms."

"I won't then, sir," James said. "You will be finished shortly, will you not?"

Hearing a small sound from the lass beside him that was surely a bitten-back chuckle, Ivor kept looking at James but smiled. "Art in a hurry, laddie?"

"Ye'll ha' the goodness no tae laugh," James said. Then he shifted his gaze to Marsi. "Ye, too. Nor tae make *me* laugh, either o' ye."

Marsi murmured, "But, Jamie, you said that the reason you wanted me to come was *because* I make you laugh and Hetty does not."

"Aye, sure, but I'm having second thoughts on the matter just now," he said. "If ye're coming, sir, I wish ye'd bestir your behouchie."

"And just where did you hear that dreadful phrase?" Mistress Hetty demanded, her eyebrows arcing high.

"The helmsman, Coll, says it whenever he thinks one o' his lads be dawdling about his work," James replied with his infectious grin. "I like it."

Ivor, still smiling, said, "Doubtless, you should make as little use of it as possible in polite company, lad. What a helmsman says on his ship is not what your father will want to hear in his audience chamber or anywhere else, I'd wager."

"Ye'd be wrong then," James said. "He likes good words and amusing phrases. I heard a number of good ones yesterday tae tell him," he added. "And if I repeat them now and now, I'll be more likely tae remember them for him."

Ivor glanced at Marsi and was glad to see the merry twinkle back in her eyes.

She said, "Mayhap we can compose a list for his grace, Jamie. If we both try to remember as many good ones as we can—"

Clearly aware that she was teasing him, the boy shook his head at her. But when he looked at Ivor again, anxiously, Ivor nodded. "Aye, we'll go now," he said.

To Marsi, he added quietly, "Help Mistress Hetty collect your things. James and I will fetch our bundles when we return, and we'll bring everything down then."

She nodded again, but the merry look had vanished. The change stirred an urge in him to touch her. Abruptly, he turned away to follow James.

Watching them go and aware that Hetty was already getting to her feet, Marsi sighed. She was not looking forward to going back upstairs. She thought Hetty would likely have even more to say to her than Hawk had.

To her surprise, Hetty said nothing about Hawk or about Marsi's being alone with him in the bedchamber. She just bustled about in her usual way, tidying up.

Marsi looked around to be sure that they were not leaving anything behind and then tied up her own bundle. Hetty went into the other bedchamber and soon returned with the things that Jamie had brought with him.

"Hetty, I ken fine that you must be burning to speak to me," Marsi said at last. "I wish you would say what you want to say."

"I've nowt that I need to say, my lady. I ken fine that ye didna tell him that ye were in his bed. And, in troth, I'm thinking ye should keep *that* fact tae yourself."

"Good lack, as if I'd *want* to tell him that! I couldn't, Hetty. Not ever!"

"Did ye tell him that ye be a royal ward?"

"I did not, for why should I? Nor did I tell him that Albany will be after me, but I do know I must tell him that. I should have done it when he and I were alone up here. But, by my troth, Hetty, I never thought of it until I was halfway down the stairs. And, then . . . I *could* not."

"Dinna fret, ye'll get your chance soon enough," Hetty said.

Hearing booted footsteps on the stairs, Marsi knew that she was right.

Hawk and Jamie were upon them by then and gathered

up all the bundles. As the women and Jamie followed Hawk downstairs, the alewife emerged from her kitchen with two sacks in hand.

"I've put up summat for ye tae eat," she said. "Ye'll be glad of it by midday."

Thanking her and giving her a few coins in exchange for the food, Hawk ushered them into the yard, where the stable lad stood with their horses.

Slipping another coin to him, Hawk helped Hetty onto her horse and took the reins of the sumpter pony from the stable lad. Without a word, he led the sumpter out onto the empty road. Following him with Jamie at her side, Marsi realized that, other than Albany's men earlier, she had heard no riders pass by.

The air was cold and crisp, and she could hear the river Leven, just west of them, rushing southward to the Firth of Clyde. Overhead, the sky was still gray but with the kind of mist that thinned quickly after sunrise. Thanks to the hills flanking the vale, the sun had not yet appeared. Low fog still obscured much of the ground and drifted across the road in misty puffs, but her cloak and boots were warm.

Hawk strode ahead of them, leading the sumpter. He still had not spoken or looked back, clearly expecting them to keep up with his long strides easily.

With a wry grimace, Marsi exchanged a look with Jamie and slowed down.

His eyes twinkled. "What d'ye think he'd do if he turned and we'd vanished?"

Behind them, Hetty said, "I think ye'd prefer no tae find out."

He shot a grin at her and then turned back to Marsi. "Shall we? I dare ye."

"Dare away," she said. "Do you think me a fool? Nay, do *not* answer that. Nor do I want to hear that you warned me that he'd be angry when he learned the truth."

"Aye, well, I didna mean tae give ye away as I did," Jamie said gruffly.

"None of it was your fault," Marsi said. "Nor is it over yet," she added when she saw Hawk glance back at last. He slowed until they caught up with him.

"Jamie, you walk beside Mistress Hetty for a time," he said. "And keep your eyes open as we go. If you see aught that seems unusual, tell me straightaway."

"Where will *ye* be, then?" Jamie asked.

"Right in front of you, but I want the lady Marsaili to walk with me now, so that I can talk with her. I'd like you and Mistress Hetty to stay just far enough back to avoid overhearing us and to serve as extra eyes and ears for us whilst we talk."

"Aye, sure," Jamie said with a sympathetic look for Marsi.

She had expected to feel as if she needed sympathy, but the truth was that she did not. For a time, while they had broken their fast, she had dreaded what she knew must lie ahead with Hawk. But now that the time had come, she felt only relief.

As he turned again to move on and she hurried to keep up with him, she told herself that she could accept anything that he might say to her. But when he looked at her, his hazel-green gaze somber beneath his thick, dark-tawny eyebrows, a disconcerting tickle of trepidation slid up her spine.

He faced forward again and remained silent. Then, glancing over a shoulder, he said. "They won't hear us now. So, tell me if what you said to James earlier means that you came with them only because he asked you to come."

Sorely tempted but knowing better, and not having expected him to begin in such a way, Marsi glanced up at his profile, trying to judge his mood.

"Nay, lass," he said, shaking his head. "Just talk to me, and do not try to imagine what will go down best with me. Tell me the truth."

"I mean to," she said. "I was just surprised when you did not start scolding straightaway. I ken fine that I deserve to hear whatever you might say to me, not only for pretending to be what I am not, but also for what I said to you earlier."

"*Did* James ask you to come?"

She thought about that, remembering the way that Jamie had stuck his head out between the bed curtains and surprised her, and Hetty, with his comment.

"Hetty and I thought he was asleep," she said. "I was unhappy that they were leaving, and he did say that I should go, too. He even offered to command me. But I made the decision, sir." She paused, remembering more. "Hetty said I should not."

"Hetty was right," he said.

Marsi fixed her gaze on the road ahead. The dangerous note was in his voice again, and she did not want to see his expression lest it banish the sense of comfort she felt, walking beside him and talking openly at last.

She knew that he must still be angry with her, but she felt no fear of him or how he might punish her. Instead, she wanted to get more of her thoughts out in the open, even if she did provoke him.

When he did not say more, she said, "Hetty said that I was daft to come."

"You were."

"Aye, perhaps. But she also said that, having known me all my life, she should have known better than to tell me I should *not*. I fear she was right about that, too."

She expected him to react, but he kept silent. For a few steps more, she resisted looking at him, waiting, sure that he would say more. Then she could resist no longer. Glancing up, she saw that he was watching her, his lips pressed together.

When her gaze collided with his, his lips twitched.

Relaxing, she said, "Impulsiveness is a dreadful fault, I know."

"It is more than a fault if it tempts you to take such foolhardy actions."

"Perhaps so," she admitted. "But, you see, I did not really know anyone at Turnberry except for Jamie and Hetty. I mean, I know his grace, of course, but not as a friend or companion. Sithee, all of her grace's ladies either returned to their homes or went into service with one of the royal princesses."

The moment of true reckoning had come, and she knew it. Again, the temptation was great to say no more and hope that he would somehow assume that no one at Turnberry would miss her. But she could not do that. Not only did it feel like a betrayal of her promise to him, but also he was very astute and would...

"So you were all alone there," he murmured. "How old are you?"

"Eighteen, but that is not why I left Turnberry."

"Is it not?"

She looked up at him again and saw that he was still watching her closely.

"No, sir, and prithee, do not say more until I have said what I must. I have felt guilty about this ever since you said that Albany was unlikely to pursue Jamie and much more likely to wait until he learns, as he will, where Jamie has gone."

"You fear that he will pursue the lad straightaway, do you?"

"Not Jamie, no. I think you were right about Albany's being more likely to wait and see where Jamie goes. But I'm afraid that he *is* likely to pursue me."

Chapter 7 _____

Instead of expressing his doubt about Marsi's unexpected declaration, Ivor tried to order his thoughts. Uncertain as he was of what game she had been playing, he had nevertheless learned enough to know that he would be wise to go cautiously.

The fact was that he liked her and had felt a strong attraction to her from the start. He therefore wanted to avoid stirring her temper, since his reacted to hers as a flame to tinder. But he did need to find out if she was telling him the truth.

"Why would Albany pursue you?" he asked.

With visible distaste, she said, "He wants me to marry one of his boot-lickers. I know that I should not refer to Lindsay of Redmyre in such a vulgar way, but he is horrid and I *don't* want to marry him. When we learned that Albany would be coming to Turnberry and that Redmyre would likely come with him—"

"How did you hear about that? If you know so few people there..."

"His grace told me. I am not certain how he learned of it, but when he said he was glad that I'd have someone to look after me, I was afraid he might decide the marriage would suit me even though I told him it would not. He is, unfortunately, more likely to heed Albany than to heed me."

"I do not know this Redmyre," Ivor said.

"He is one of the Perthshire Lindsays," she said. "His land abuts the south boundary of the Cargill estates. Aunt Annabella told me that Albany wants to give Redmyre good reason to remain loyal to him. But she promised that I need not marry anyone I dislike. However, Albany wants Redmyre to help him unseat Davy—"

"You mean Rothesay, of course."

"Aye, sure." Her eyes twinkled up at him. "Davy is also my cousin, sir."

Ivor frowned. Of course, Davy Stewart was her cousin, since he and James were brothers. But Ivor knew Davy and did not like thinking of him as her kinsman. He was a charming, likable chap and a fine warrior who would one day be King of Scots, but Davy was untrustworthy around any comely female, be she maiden or married, young, or old enough to be his mother. He might treat a cousin with more respect than others, but the thought that he might easily tease or embarrass her...

Dismissing that thought as no business of his, Ivor said, "You have not told me yet why Albany would pursue you rather than wait to learn where we go."

"Aye, sure I did. 'Tis because of Redmyre. If Albany *does* persuade the King to agree the marriage, he will want us married straightaway before anyone else can persuade his grace to change his mind. He does change it sometimes, you know.

"Moreover," she added with a sigh, "when *any*one crosses Albany, he becomes furious. Although he *will*

likely wait to learn Jamie's destination and is unlikely
to harm him just now in any event, lest such wickedness
draw the ire of the Scottish people, Albany would make
me marry at once if only to punish me for my defiance.
Doubtless, you can understand his desire to do that, sir."

Seeing naught to gain by discussing Albany's tactics
or anyone's desires of any sort with regard to her, Ivor
said, "I do think that, knowing the consequences to yourself, as you do, you ought to have known better than to
cross him."

"Aye, sure, you *would* think that," she retorted. "The
fact is that I do *not* like waiting whilst others decide my
fate. Since I don't want to marry Redmyre, and staying at
Turnberry would mean that I'd have no choice, I decided
to leave."

"To run away," he muttered.

"Aye, then, to run away," she said. "I had hoped to find
an ally in you. In troth, I'd hoped to persuade you—if you
were traveling near Perthshire—to take me to my uncle,
Sir Malcolm Drummond, at Stobhall."

"Even if I could be party to your daft scheme, lass,
what could you hope to gain by going there?"

"When Uncle Malcolm learns of Aunt Annabella's
promise that I need not marry Redmyre, I believe he will
honor that promise and speak for me."

"Speak *for* you?"

"Aye, to the King. Sithee, I doubt that I alone can persuade his grace to go against Albany's wishes, because he
so rarely does. But Uncle Malcolm is a powerful man and
her grace's own brother. The King would listen to him."

Ivor sensed something missing from her reasoning but
could not put his finger on what it was. Frowning, he said,

"I recall that your parents are dead. But surely someone else in your family, your father's heir—"

"I inherited all that my father owned," she interjected. "So the Cargill estates that Redmyre covets are mine. Sithee, I've heard that he called me 'a ripe plum.' I do not want such a man—one, forbye, who is old enough to be my father—daring to call me so. Nor do I want to see my land in his fat hands."

"Are they fat?"

"I don't know," she replied. "I've not seen them, but I'm sure that they must be. In any event, I do not mean to let Albany marry me to the man if I can stop it."

Ivor's hands twitched to catch her by her shoulders, give her a good shake, and scold her well for such fool-hardy thinking against Albany. Also, for keeping so much to herself. As it was, he communicated his feelings only through the lead to the sumpter pony. It tossed its head and gave an indignant snort in response.

He said, "You might have spared a thought for James."

"At the time, I thought only that if you could keep Jamie safe, you could also keep me safe. I did not think about Albany's *not* following you, only that you would keep him from finding us both. I can see that I was foolish to believe that. Even Jamie realizes that his uncle's men are as dangerous to us as his uncle is."

"Why do you say that?"

"Because that is why he insisted I go upstairs with him when they rode into the innyard. Doubtless, you thought he was trying to protect me from you, and I'll admit that I was grateful then to escape your wrath. But, in troth, Jamie feared that if those men *were* Albany's, one of them might recognize me."

"Do you think that was likely?"

"Dressed as I am, I doubt it," she said. "But I spent much time with the Queen, and Albany visited her, especially when we were in Perth. Any number of his men might have seen me there, or at Scone. Albany visited her there, too."

"Even at her deathbed? I had not thought the two of them so friendly."

"Nor were they. But Annabella was gracious, and he *is* the King's brother. Near the end, his presence did disturb her, and Bishop Traill made him leave."

"Traill was there, too?"

"Aye, sure, for as Primate of Scotland, he was her confessor, and his grace's. He administered her last rites at Scone and saw to her funeral at Dunfermline."

She was clearly being truthful, but he still felt a need to test her, although he could almost read her thoughts when she talked with him like this.

Or perhaps that was *why* he still felt a need to test her.

If, after her parents' deaths, the Queen sent for her to join her ladies, and if Sir Malcolm Drummond could do nowt to prevent her marriage to Redmyre but *speak* for her to the King, Ivor suspected that Marsi had left out another significant detail.

~

Eyeing him warily, Marsi said, "Are you still angry, sir?"

"You would know if I was," he said. "I don't deny that I'd like to wring your neck, though, for keeping all of this to yourself."

"You would have sent me back."

"Before our journey ends, you may wish that I had," he retorted.

"You *are* still angry."

"Not as angry as I was earlier."

She was silent, satisfied that she had read him correctly but still feeling something that hovered between them. When they rounded a curve in the narrow road, she said, "I think that must be the main road ahead of us. What do we say if other travelers ask who we are?"

"I doubt that anyone will trouble himself about us," he said. "We look neither like ruffians nor wealthy enough to draw much notice."

"I did wonder why you failed to hire outriders to protect us."

"Our anonymity should protect us, at least until folks hereabouts and Albany's men learn that James is missing," he said. "Or that you are."

"But when your men join us..."

"We will continue to travel as a family party," he said. "We will look more prosperous then but not so much more as to attract robbers. I usually ride with a half-dozen men, and it did not occur to me to take more to Turnberry, because I did not know what his grace meant to ask of me."

"Six is not many," she said dubiously.

"If Albany's men also think that, they will not bother us."

"I hope you are right," she said. Then, aware that he might expect another apology from her, she added contritely, "I'm sorry that I vexed you earlier, sir."

He said nothing until she looked at him. Then, dryly, he said, "Doubtless, that pouty look mixed with a touch of flirtation—which you do gey well—stirs most men to ease your guilt. Does it work on Mistress Hetty?"

She bit her lip, annoyed with herself, but she could not say that his reaction surprised her. Rallying, she said, "I expect you know much about women."

"I told you, I have a sister," he reminded her. "I have seen that look too often for it to impress me. In any event, I will judge your penitence by your future behavior, not by a look or by aught that you might say."

"I shall be the very model of rectitude then," she said, raising her chin.

He laughed, and she grinned at him, delighted to discover that his sense of humor was strong enough that she could stir it even when she had annoyed him.

Turnberry Castle

"'Tis plain now that his grace knew I was coming," Albany said quietly.

The burly Redmyre nodded, saying, "Your movements are generally known, my lord duke, even in such an out of the way place as Turnberry is."

"Not so out of the way as one might think," Albany said. "We are but fifty miles south of Glasgow, no more than a few hours by ship."

"I failed to notice any harbor along this rugged coast and had forgotten that you'd said ships could offload supplies here," Redmyre said, frowning.

"Those ships depart again, too. Evidently, one did so early yestermorn. One of my lads on the ramparts with especially long vision saw that the ship bore a foreign name. But no one seems to ken aught of such a ship or what trading it had done here. Nor did his grace ken aught of it, for so he did tell me."

"One hesitates to suggest that his grace might tell an untruth."

"He never does, for he lacks the ability to produce falsehoods. He is not telling me all he knows about James. But, I vow, he does not know where Marsaili is."

"When two cousins vanish at the same time from the same place…"

"Just so," Albany agreed. "It is no great leap to suspect that they set out together, perhaps aboard that ship."

"Since you will swiftly let it be known that James is missing—"

"Don't be daft!" Albany snapped. "I don't want that news bruited about. Every enemy I have would declare that I must mean James harm. Davy would loudly offer that as reason for him to retain the Governorship and might persuade enough lords of Parliament to agree with him. I dare not risk that."

"But you need only announce James's abduction, my lord. People would understand that duty requires you to lay his abductors by the heels."

"I just want to know where he goes and who takes him there. I have a strong notion as to where, but Marsaili's destination remains a puzzle. She can claim few allies other than his grace and mayhap a few from her own clan."

"Even the Drummonds must be loath to pit themselves against you!"

"I don't want conflict with them over her ladyship or James, nor would I allow it," Albany said. He had less confidence than Redmyre did in his ability to control the Drummonds, especially if they recognized the value of controlling James, who was half Drummond himself. But Albany saw no reason to share that fact with Redmyre.

The man believed him all-powerful, but that would change if he, Albany, failed to produce Marsaili as a wealthy bride for him.

He would find the lass and make her sorry for putting him to such trouble. The arrangement of her marriage settlements would see to that.

Dismissing Redmyre, he sought the King and found him as he all too often did with his chaplain, poring over some religious text or other.

Pointedly, Albany said, "His grace will send for you anon, Father."

Glancing at the King and receiving a nod, the chaplain left the room.

"What is it, Robbie?" the King said. "Have ye found our Marsi?"

"I have not. She must have gone with James and Mistress Henrietta."

"Bless us, are ye sure? I swear to ye, I dinna ken where they can be."

"But you do know where they are going...James and Henrietta."

"Aye, perhaps, but I dinna want tae tell ye."

"You need not, for I will find them. I merely came to take my leave of you."

"So ye dinna mean to follow them?"

"Why should I? I have men all over the country who do my bidding."

"But ye canna want everyone to ken that our laddie be missing!"

"Oh, my men are not looking for James," Albany said softly. "They seek a family party composed of a woman of middle years, a lass of marriageable age, and a boy of seven, all traveling eastward. There cannot be too many such, I think."

Taking his leave after that Parthian shot, he smiled to see the King gaping.

~~~~

As soon as Albany left the chamber, his grace sent for Dennison.

On his arrival, the King said, "Fetch my writing materials, and whilst I write, find a courier we can trust who can be ready to leave as soon as I finish writing."

"I know of many such loyal men, sire," Dennison said. "Have you any more specific requirements with regard to this messenger?"

"He must be willing to guard these documents with his life, he must ken more than one route to St. Andrews, and he must be unable to read."

Dennison nodded and hurried away, returning shortly with writing materials and word that a suitable courier was hastily preparing to ride. At a gesture, he sat, and a few moments later, the King looked up from his task.

"Did Albany question ye, Dennison?"

"He did not, sire, nor would he have gained aught had he done so."

"He was most interested in a ship, a galley that departed yestermorn at dawn."

"Was he, my liege?"

"He was, aye. Might he learn enough about that ship to cause difficulty for its captain or others aboard it?"

"If you refer to possible passengers, I cannot say, sire. Such persons, were there any, would be safe aboard the galley. Its captain and crew will be safe, too. Nowt that anyone saw here can lead to further information about them."

The King nodded. An hour later Dennison left, taking the documents with him.

⌇

Ivor walked with Marsi, conversing idly until they reached the village of Balloch at the south end of Loch Lomond. While the others stayed outside, exploring the contents of the sacks that the alewife had prepared, he entered the inn. There, he learned that he could hire three more horses to take them to Drymen.

"Dinna fret about getting them back to us, sir," the innkeeper said. "If ye'll just leave them at the wee tavern on the common there, I've a son as married the alemaster's daughter. He'll be fain tae bring them home tae me."

"I'll do that," Ivor promised, glad to have one less detail on his mind.

James had been happy to walk for a time, but he had tired an hour since. And after Mistress Hetty had suggested more than once that she let Marsi and James ride the horse or take James up to ride with her, Ivor had compromised. If he could not find horses for them all at Balloch, he'd said, Hetty could have her way.

The boy revived after he had eaten. So, they rode on and arrived at the inn Jake Maxwell had recommended, half a mile north of Drymen, by midafternoon.

Ivor had heard more about the area from Hetty by then than he had wanted to know, and much about the Drummonds. He had known that they'd given Scotland two queens, but he had not known that family members could be buried at Inchmahone Priory, ten or twelve miles north of Drymen, near a place called Aberfoyle.

Since Marsi added nearly as much to the flow of information as Mistress Hetty did, he soon realized that the lass also knew more about Dumbartonshire and Menteith than he did. Her parents, she said, lay buried at Inchmahone.

"If we go to Aberfoyle and then east to Doune," she said as they dismounted in the inn yard, "Hetty says we'll go right by the Loch of Menteith. Since the priory is there, I'd like to see my parents' graves when we do. Sithee, I was not old enough to attend their funeral, let alone to travel all the way from Cargill for their burial, so…"

She paused, eyeing him hopefully.

"That must depend on events," he said. "If it is true that we pass right by and no one has yet taken undue interest in us, I'll likely have no objection. But nowt must interfere with getting James to safety as fast as we can. That *is* my primary task."

"I promise not to take long, sir."

Ivor saw Mistress Hetty press her lips together and shoot him a glance. But motion beyond her diverted his eye to a troop of riders in the distance, fast approaching. Their banner flew proudly, a tawny hawk on a sky-blue background.

"I cannot make that out," the lass said. "Are those your men?"

"Aye, they are," he said. "You and James get inside now with Mistress Hetty. We can talk more later. If you like, I will teach you to play chess."

"Will you, sir?" she asked demurely.

He had already taken two strides toward the oncoming

riders, but the amused note in her voice stopped him. He gave her a searching look.

Her eyes twinkled with the merry, mischievous look he usually liked to see.

"What is it?" he asked. "What is so amusing?"

"Naught of importance, sir. I look forward to learning much from you."

"Cheeky lass," he muttered as he turned away. Then he recalled seeing a similar look when he had suggested that James teach her to play, and it dawned on him that, if Annabella had played chess, it was likely that Marsi did, too.

"Ye willna fool Hawk," Jamie said. "He's a canny one."

"I know," Marsi told him, astonished as she so frequently was at how insightful the boy was. "Did you see him hesitate just then? I'd wager *that* is when he realized how likely it is that I already know how to play."

"He'd have figured it out in a twink when ye do play," Jamie said. "Ye're none too skilled at deceit, Marsi, or at pretending tae be a maidservant. I've seen that for myself. Sakes, but ye have only tae hear him say summat tae ask him about it, as if it were any maidservant's business tae be quizzing the man."

"Is that what I do?" she asked, although she had no doubt that he was right. James had spent his short life primarily in the company of adults and was amazingly observant. "I know that I've spoken out of turn more than once," she added thoughtfully. "I did not think I'd done it as much as that, though."

"I'm telling ye, ye should no do it at all. The plain fact

is that ye ken nowt o' *being* a maidservant and dinna hear or see yourself when ye go amiss. Ye near came tae grief already, and Hawk didna ken ye afore. He does now, though, so likely your efforts willna prosper."

"You may be right," Marsi said. "But over the years, I have found that others, for all they may *say* that they act for my benefit, rarely want what I want for myself. So, when I can see a way to achieve a purpose, I take that path. I should think that Hawk would respect that, because I can see that he is much the same."

"Aye, but he's a man and a warrior. Ye're nowt o' the sort."

She sighed. "I know, Jamie, and I certainly don't mean to defy him again, especially since he has promised to let me visit my parents' graves."

"He made nae such promise," Jamie pointed out. "He said it would depend."

"Aye, sure, but if we are to go right past the Loch of Menteith, he would never be so cruel as to let me see the priory and *not* visit them."

Hetty, however, warned her to be less certain.

"I have heard that it is difficult to gain admittance to Inchmahone," she said gently. "One requires the prior's permission. And it *is* still winter. It may not be possible even to speak with him."

"But we must at least try," Marsi said.

Hetty started to say something more but did not. She nodded instead and suggested that Marsi get ready for supper.

The arrival of Hawk's men shortly after their own had made her wonder if the inn would hold them all. But the innkeeper assured them that Hawk's men could share the

stable loft with the inn's stablemen. So their horses from
Milton and Balloch were led back to the inn on Drymen's
common to be returned to their stables.

At supper, Marsi met the captain of Hawk's tail, a big,
capable-looking man called Aodán, and Sean Dubh, a
younger lad who served as Hawk's squire. She'd seen the
other four men only as they'd headed for the stable, leading a string of the horses they had ridden and several extra
ones, including two more sumpters.

Wednesday morning, they broke their fast and were
ready to mount soon after dawn. Hawk conferred briefly
with Hetty, who advised leaving the main road to take a
track through the nearby forest straight to Aberfoyle.

Despite a few snowdrifts across the track, the journey
through the ancient forest was pleasant. They took their
midday meal in a sunny clearing with a small burn-fed
pond that provided two of Hawk's men with trout that
they cooked on sticks over a small fire for their meal and
willingly shared with James.

They first saw the village of Aberfoyle through the
trees. It lay beyond a swiftly flowing river that, despite
being rather narrow there, Hetty said was the same river
Forth that flowed into the Firth of Forth at Stirling. "Its
headwaters are nearby," Hetty added as they forded the
river.

The inn at Aberfoyle was similar to the others that they
had visited, but a hitch occurred soon after they settled in.

Marsi and Hetty were preparing to take supper when
they heard banging on the door to James's and Hawk's
room, next to theirs.

Marsi opened their door just as Hawk opened his.
"Aye, what's amiss?"

The landlord stood there, wringing his hands. "Beg pardon, sir, but I'll ha' tae ask ye tae move on tae the next clachan for the night."

"What clachan? There is nowt of consequence betwixt here and Doune unless the prior would—"

"Och, nay, they'll no take females at the priory. There be an alehouse a few miles beyond it, though, that ye can get to afore dark if ye hurry. But ye must go, sir. I've a party below demanding all me rooms. I darena turn them away, for they fly the royal banner!"

"Good lack," Marsi exclaimed, "it must be—"

"Silence," Hawk interjected so sharply that she shut her mouth with a snap. "Get back into your room whilst I look into this. Lad," he added over his shoulder, "you go in with Hetty, and do not come out until I say that you may. At once!"

Grabbing Jamie, Marsi urged him inside ahead of her and shut the door, saying, "Oh, how I wish that we were at the front of the house. Then we could see who it is. But it must be Albany," she added. "Who else would dare to turn out everyone at an inn to accommodate himself?"

Jamie's eyes twinkled. "Ye're no thinking right, Marsi. If my uncle was at Turnberry yestermorn, he can hardly be here so soon. I ken fine that he flies the royal banner whenever he chooses, but there be others with more right."

Chapter 8

Giving orders to Aodán to slip out the back way and warn the others in his tail to keep out of sight, Ivor hurried to the main entrance. Nearly certain about whose party he would find outside, he emerged from the inn in time to see Davy Stewart, Duke of Rothesay, Governor of the Realm, and heir to Scotland's throne, dismount from his horse, toss his reins to a stable lad, and turn toward the inn.

Hurrying to intercept him, Ivor said, "My lord duke, may I have a word?"

Davy stopped midstride and peered narrowly at him.

Two of Davy's men who had dismounted moved toward them, reaching for their swords, but Davy waved them back without moving his eyes from Ivor.

"I know you," Davy said to him.

"Aye, sir, you do," Ivor said, pitching his voice low so that it would not carry to anyone but the young duke. "I'd as lief you not mention my name aloud here, sir. But I would speak with you on a matter of some urgency."

At nearly four-and-twenty, Davy possessed more than his share of the Stewart fair-haired good looks and charm. He grinned, saying, "If you are the one I'm turning out of this inn, I imagine that you would think the situation is urgent. But I'm gey hungry and—"

"I pray you, sir, hear me out before you say more," Ivor said quietly. "You know that I am no enemy of yours and that you do have cause to trust me."

The grin faded. Davy turned and said, "Stand back, lads. I would speak privily with this chap. Now, what is this about, Sir Ivor?"

"With respect, sir, it concerns James."

The well-formed Stewart eyebrows knitted together. "What the devil can you mean by that? Jamie is at Turnberry with his grace, our father."

"The King feared that Albany might seize custody of him," Ivor said. "He sent for me and gave the lad into my charge with orders to see him to safety."

"Sent for *you*?" Davy regarded him more narrowly yet. "Methinks that your clan takes more interest in mine than they should, sir."

"With respect, my lord, *you* chose to involve us last summer."

"So I did, but his grace..." He paused. "I begin to suspect that I am not the only one with cause to trust you and yours, Sir Ivor."

"No, sir. And Albany may already be searching for James."

This time the mobile eyebrows shot upward. "My uncle keeps much too busy and would control us all. But you think that he was going south—to Turnberry?"

"His grace expected him on Monday, aye, or yesterday at the latest."

"Yet you are here. Is Jamie with you, then? Because, if he is, Albany will winkle that information out of my father in a trice."

"His grace does not know where we are. Nor does he know exactly who we are. He knows me only as Hawk, sir."

"I see. Then I expect that you would prefer me to avoid a reunion with my little brother just now."

"Aye, sir," Ivor agreed. "'Tis bad enough that I've approached you as I have. But I could scarcely bring him out here into a yard full of your men, most of whom would recognize him and at least one of whom might report his presence here. Also, the lad is tired, and the next alehouse lies some miles beyond Inchmahone."

"I have come from thirty miles north of here, through slush and muck most of the way," Davy said. "I was looking forward to a hot meal and a soft bed."

"Are you so set on staying in Aberfoyle?"

Davy's blue eyes twinkled. "That depends. Are the maids comely?"

Easily concealing his irritation at a question so typical of the man, Ivor said, "I have seen none younger than fifty, sir, but there may be one or two. Drymen, just south of here, has several comfortable-looking inns from which to choose, however."

"If my uncle has gone to Turnberry, he means to make mischief, I think. As I am his favorite target, it may benefit me to visit my father. So, Drymen it shall be."

Ivor started to speak but thought better of it and held his peace.

Davy grinned again. "If anyone asks, I'll tell them that someone here is sick and I don't want to catch whatever it is. I ken fine that I may have at least one spy of my uncle's amongst this lot, for all that they swear fealty only to me."

Ivor nodded, and when Davy put out his hand, he shook it warmly.

"Your family is well, I trust?" Davy said then. "Your sister and Fin Cameron are happy, I expect. Do we look for a wee Cameron to appear soon?"

"Not yet, but they are hopeful. I expect to see them anon. They'll leave home in a day or two to spend a month in Perth with our MacGillivray kinsmen there."

"I may have to visit them there. I miss Fin. Sakes, I miss the man's fine sword arm, and I've a notion that if my uncle is scheming again, I shall need it."

"You know that if you send for him, sir, he will come."

"Aye, he will," Davy said. "Say all that you deem proper for me if you see him before I do. And relay my greetings to Bishop Traill, as well, if you will."

Ivor knew from Davy's expression that he had revealed his astonishment.

"Aye, sure, I guessed," Davy said. "Who but Traill would brave Albany's wrath for Jamie? Albany will guess, too, and he dislikes the bishop but fears that he wields power enough to send him to Hell. So, beware."

With that, he turned on his heel and remounted his horse.

Watching the royal party ride away, Ivor tried to imagine Davy as King of Scots. He'd make a merry king, but he had much to learn before he'd be a wise one.

~

"Where is Davy?" Jamie asked when Hawk returned. "I want to see him."

"Nay, laddie," Hawk said, but Marsi heard the gentle note again. "I ken fine that you'd like to see him. He was disappointed, too. But he understood, as you will, that for him to take notice of us would draw others to do likewise. His

demanding that we give up our rooms to him posed danger
enough. To leave us in possession after doing so might have
increased our jeopardy. But he'll tell his men that someone
here is sick, that they are riding on to avoid catching whatever it is. Had he lingered to visit with you, 'tis gey likely
that one or more of his men would speak of it later."

"Then you told him that Jamie is here," Marsi said.

"Aye, sure, I did," he said. "At present, Jamie is Rothesay's only heir, so Rothesay has a right to know where he
is and under whose protection."

"Did you tell him about me?"

"Nay, lass," he said. Then, just as she was breathing a
sigh of relief for his consideration, he added, "It did not
occur to me to tell him that you had come, although now
that you mention it, I should have. He means to head for
Turnberry, and his grace would be relieved to know that
you are safe."

She had an impulse to ask why it had not occurred to
him that her cousin Davy might like to know that she, too,
was traveling with his little brother. But something told
her that the impulse had little to do with Jamie or Davy
and much to do with the fact that Hawk had forgotten all
about her while he talked to Davy. *And how foolish are
you, to fret about that?* she demanded of herself.

Having no adequate answer, and recalling that she
did not want to aggravate Hawk, lest he refuse to stop at
Inchmahone, she felt only gratitude when Hetty asked if he
meant for them all to take supper in the inn's common room.

He assured her that he did, because he did not want to
stir the innkeeper's curiosity more than they already had.

"I was just pondering that subject, sir," Hetty replied.
"You said that Rothesay would mention an illness here. If

you were to tell the innkeeper that I am feeling poorly and would prefer a light meal here in our chamber..."

"An excellent notion," he said with a smile when she paused. "I should have thought of that myself. But if you stay up here, Lady Marsi should stay with you."

Marsi said, "There is no table or chair in here, sir, and they will bring Hetty her meal on a tray, expecting her to be in bed. Surely, since we are traveling as a family party, no one will think it improper for me to sup with you and Jamie. Unless you would *like* me to stay, Hetty."

"Nae need for that," Hetty said. "I'll do well enow on my own."

Hawk said, "Very well, lass, you may come down with us." Then raising his eyebrows, he said to Hetty, "Just how light do you want your meal to be, mistress?"

"Don't starve me, sir," Hetty said with a smile. "I'll need my strength tomorrow, for I ken fine that you want to be away soon after sunrise."

Marsi feared that if they started too early, Hawk would not want to disturb the prior at Inchmahone, but she held her peace.

She was a little surprised that Hetty had not objected to her supping alone with Hawk. To be sure, Jamie would be there, and the innkeeper, and servants, and perhaps others as well...

Hawk cleared his throat, clearly impatient for her to follow Jamie, who was already clattering down the stairs.

Smiling ruefully at him, Marsi obeyed.

⌒

They found the common room empty except for a maid-servant, who greeted them cheerfully. When she indicated a table, Ivor gestured his charges toward it but asked for the innkeeper. The maidservant speedily produced him from the kitchen.

"How may I aid ye, sir?" the man said. "I dinna ken why me lord Rothesay rode away as he did. I'd already sent me other guests on tae the clachan alehouse."

"Rothesay did fear so, aye, and would offer payment for the inconvenience," Ivor said. Davy had not thought of that, but Dennison had given Ivor more than he could imagine needing for their expenses. "Sithee," he confided, "upon learning that my lady aunt is feeling unwell and should not travel farther tonight, he pressed on to Drymen. He dislikes exposing himself to any sickness, for fear of catching it."

That, at least, was true.

The innkeeper grinned, accepting the coins with a brief, experienced glance at them before slipping them into the purse attached to his belt. "Ye've done me a kindness, sir," he said. "At this season, I'd feared we'd no ha' enough food for so many. As for your lady aunt, me wife brews a whisky posset that will cure any ill."

Ivor smiled. "I think she would prefer whatever it is that smells so good in your kitchen. In troth, she has ridden far today and has suffered enough chatter from my cousins yonder to make her yearn for an hour's peace. If you would be kind enough to send your maid up with a tasty supper on a tray for her..."

The innkeeper agreed, and Ivor joined Marsi and James at the table. Aodán, his captain, came in a short time later to report that the other men had settled in comfortably and that the innkeeper had promised to feed them with his own lads.

"What time d'ye want to depart, sir?" Aodán asked, speaking the Gaelic.

"As soon after dawn as we can," Ivor said in the same language. "But see that our lads get a good breakfast, since the innkeeper is so eager to be of service."

Aodán nodded and left the room, and their food appeared a short time later. After the maidservant had set down a platter of sliced roast beef, a bowl of chopped apples and turnips, a basket of bread trenchers, and another of hot bannocks, she said, "I'll bring in a wee pot o' butter straightaway, sir, and more ale."

As she left, Marsi said casually, "If we leave at dawn, and the priory is just a mile or two from here, won't we arrive too early to rouse the prior?"

"I fear that visiting the priory will take more time than I'd realized or that we can afford," Ivor said. "We must put as much distance between us and the Firth of Clyde as possible, as quickly as possible. Once Albany learns where we landed—"

"I see," she interjected, fighting to conceal her disappointment.

"I told you that I would think about it, and I did." He would have gone on, to explain more clearly, but the maidservant returned with his ale and their butter just then. By the time the maid had refilled his mug and returned to the kitchen, Marsi had regained her composure.

"I do see that your task must come before aught else, sir," she said. "Mayhap you will tell me more about your sister. How much older is Catriona than I am?"

Pleasantly relieved to know that she would not create a scene in the common room, he willingly replied to her questions. When he succeeded in making her laugh by describing one of Catriona's more inventive pranks against him, he decided that she did understand how things would have to be, and why.

Watching Hawk, Marsi hoped she had successfully concealed her emotions. When Jamie had finished his dinner and covered a yawn for the third time in less than a quarter-hour, she suggested that he take himself off to bed.

"Aye, go along, laddie," Hawk said. "I'll be up shortly."

"I thought you might like a game of chess, sir," Marsi said. "I am not sleepy yet, and if I go upstairs, I'll keep Hetty awake unless I go to bed myself. Also, the innkeeper, his wife, and the maidservant will be up and about for some time yet, lest late guests arrive, so there can be no impropriety in our playing a game here."

"I'll see if they keep a chess set," he said.

The innkeeper produced a set with neatly carved and polished wooden pieces that they set up on a parquetry board.

Hawk looked up with a teasing smile when he had set his last piece in place and said, "You are not going to pretend that you do not play, are you?"

Responding easily to his smile, she said, "Had you asked me, sir, I'd have told you that I do. All of Annabella's ladies play, because the King taught her soon after they married, and she likes…liked to play frequently." Ruthlessly, she pushed away the familiar image of her beloved aunt bent thoughtfully over a chessboard.

They talked desultorily while they played, and although he won the game, Marsi knew that she had played well and had nearly trapped him more than once.

Unless his mind had been on other things, they were almost equally skilled. He required less time to make his moves than she did, but he played cautiously, while she loved taking risks. She knew from experience that when a risk succeeded, it often led to victory. In her experience, a cautious player was a predictable one.

⁓

Ivor enjoyed the game. He had never played with a woman before, and although he had assumed that she knew the proper moves, he had doubted that she understood strategy and expected to beat her easily. When he realized that she played as well as he did, he would happily have played a second game. But she pleaded weariness, and he knew that she must be more tired than she had thought she was.

He escorted her to her chamber, looked into his room to find James sound asleep, and then went back downstairs and out to the stable to check on his men. Finding all peaceful there, he returned and sought his bed.

Waking at the approach of Thursday's dawn, he dressed without disturbing the boy and went down to be sure that preparations were in hand for breakfast. Learning that they could eat whenever they liked, he returned upstairs, rapped on the women's door, and then went to wake James.

Answering a rap on his door moments later, he opened it to Hetty, looking distraught. "She's gone," she said. "I had nae notion of it, sir, but she's gone."

"Where?" Ivor demanded.

"I dinna ken," Hetty said. "I woke when ye rapped, and she was gone. Her hooded cloak and good stout boots be gone, as well."

James said from behind Ivor, "Mayhap she just went out to the—"

"Nay," Hetty said. "She kent fine that she was to wake me or you, sir, afore she went anywhere, and she would not chance vexing—" Recognizing the absurdity of what she was saying, she broke off and looked helplessly at Ivor.

"I begin to think that her ladyship rarely heeds the consequences of her actions," Ivor said. "I did think that she understood why we could not—"

"Good lack, sir! Ye didna *tell* her that ye couldna take her to the priory!"

"I reminded her that getting James safely to his destination is my primary—"

"But I warned ye, sir, that whenever one says nay to her ladyship, she will all too likely take the matter into her own hands."

"Well, if that is what she has done, this time she will reap the consequences," Ivor said. "She won't have taken a horse, because she must know that my men are sleeping in the stable loft. And that means that she is walking to the Loch of Menteith. At least we can be grateful that she knows the country hereabouts."

"Och, but I dinna think she has been here since she was a wee bairn," Hetty said. "I ken fine that she never had cause then to visit the priory."

"Sakes, I thought that she knew this area as well as you do."

"Nay, for I was born and raised in Drymen, sir, whereas, Lady Marsi was born at Cargill. She came here only once during her childhood that I know of, to visit cousins. I did tell her how unlikely it was that we could visit the priory in winter, but I did not try to explain the reasons for that. I thought it better for her to see when we reached the Loch of Menteith just how things are arranged there."

"I see," he said, aware of a chilly unease. "Prithee, finish dressing, mistress. James, you get dressed, too. Then escort Mistress Hetty downstairs. I'll send Aodán and Sean Dubh to break their fast with you so you will not be alone in the common room, and when you're ready, Sean Dubh will load the sumpters and Aodán and the other lads will bring you to me. Do you understand all that I am saying to you, lad?"

"Aye, sir, I do. You're going to murder our Marsi is what ye be a-saying."

"I think I can promise not to murder her," Ivor said, ruffling James's curls. "And I expect she'll recover quickly, whatever I do to her."

Returning Hetty's worried look with one that he hoped would reassure her, he hurried out to the stable. Ten minutes later, mounted and riding out of the yard, confident that his men would look after Hetty and James, he urged his horse to the fastest speed that was safe on the rutted and icy track. Twenty minutes after that, as he rounded a curve in the road, he saw her small figure in the distance.

Cloaked and hooded in fur-trimmed gray wool, she stood still, staring southward at the mostly gray-white expanse of the Loch of Menteith.

When he'd caught his first glimpses of the loch through the dense border of trees surrounding it, he'd seen that most if not all of it was frozen. But he still meant to deal sternly with her, so the surge of relief that he felt when he saw her faded quickly. Although she must have heard his horse's hoofbeats, she did not turn her head to look. However, something in her posture—an air of abject defeat—lessened his urge to shake her.

She still had not turned when he dismounted. Looping his reins over a shrub, he walked up to her, took her by the shoulders, and turned her to face him.

Prepared though he was to mete out stern justice, that urge vanished at the sight of the tears streaming silently down her cheeks.

"What is it, lass?" he asked. "Tears will avail you nowt."

When the only answer he got was a shuddering sob, he said more gently than he had intended, "You know that you should not have come here like this."

"How else should I have c-come?" she muttered, twisting her ring. She had taken off her gloves, and her hands were red. "Not that it did me any good," she added. "Everything is covered with ice and snow. I cannot even *see* the graveyard."

"It isn't near here," he said. Pointing, he added, "Look yonder, in the middle of the loch. The priory sits amidst the trees on that island. I thought you knew."

"I haven't been here before. I just know they lie buried at the priory. I-I bade them goodnight one evening, and I never saw them again, because when I woke up, they were b-both dead. Then, they...m-my kinsmen...would not *let* me see them."

"Your parents both died at the same time?"

"Aye, of some horrid sickness that they'd caught in Edinburgh. I...I just wanted to see..." Catching her breath in a near sob, she looked up at him helplessly, clearly fighting to retain her composure. But when he put the hand with which he had pointed to the island back on her shoulder, meaning to offer what comfort he could, she flung herself against him and burst into tears.

Without a second thought, he drew her close and wrapped his arms around her. He did not try to speak to her, but he lowered his chin so that it rested gently atop her head. Then he just held her tight and let her cry.

As he did, his gaze drifted over the landscape, and he became aware of a new, barely discernible tang of smoke in the air. A short way to his right, he spied a thin stream of fresh smoke wafting upward and detected the outline of a tiny cottage in the forest of trees between the road and the loch.

When her storm of weeping ended and she became unnaturally still, Ivor murmured, "The others could be at least a half-hour behind me, and I see a cottage yonder. Likely, someone there can tell us if a safe way exists to get to the island."

She looked up at him, and her hood fell back, leaving only the frilly white cap to frame her face. Although her eyes were puffy and swollen and her face awash in tears, he still thought she was the most beautiful woman he had ever seen.

Quietly, he said, "You'd better dry those tears before we approach the cottage."

"I...I don't have anything to dry them with but my skirt or my cloak."

"Use this," he said, pulling off her cap and handing it to her.

She took it without objection and obediently mopped her face with it.

As Ivor stared at the mass of plaited and coiled tresses

that he had revealed, the sun peeped over the rim of the hills to the east, its golden rays revealing the fiery copper highlights in her lush auburn hair.

Sensual images from his night at Turnberry flashed through his mind. Carefully removing his hand from Marsi's shoulder, Ivor stepped away.

Chapter 9———————————

Marsi used the cap to advantage, even blowing her nose, so she barely noted that Hawk had let go of her. Only as she wadded the cap up to stuff it into the deep pocket stitched inside her cloak did it occur to her that she'd worn the cap for a reason.

Suddenly more aware of him than ever, she concentrated on tucking the cap neatly into the pocket and then paused for another moment to pull her gloves back on before she looked up. When her gaze collided with his, his remained steady, revealing little, but she was nonetheless certain that he had recognized her hair.

As she tried to imagine what she ought to say to him or if there was anything that she *could* say, he said, "Have you got another one of those caps?"

She nodded. "I brought two."

"Then you had better find the second one when the others arrive. Your hair is too easily recognizable for you to be showing it to all and sundry on the main road."

She nibbled her lower lip, certain that he had more to say.

But all he said was, "If you are ready, we'll see who lives in yon cottage."

Drawing a breath, she nearly thanked him for the

respite. But, doubting the wisdom of that, she reminded herself that they might yet be able to visit the graveyard.

It was most unlike her to lose control of herself as she had done twice now with him. But she felt better after the emotional storm and tried to remember if she had ever flung herself at a man before to weep on his chest. She could summon up no such memory. She had loved her father, but if she had suffered any mishap, he had sent someone to fetch Hetty or whoever her replacement was at the time, and had then turned her over to a maidservant to wait for her attendant to come.

Needing to say something, she muttered, "I don't know why I did that."

He said quietly, "The bow too tensely strung is easily broken, lass. You have had much on your mind of late, I think."

Having no reply to that, at least none that she wanted to offer, she said nothing.

As they approached the wee thatched cottage, the door opened and an elderly man stepped onto the low stoop and peered myopically at them. Long, wispy white hair draped down past his shoulders.

"Be ye lost then?" he inquired politely.

"We have kinsmen buried on the isle, good sir," Hawk said. "My lady cousin has never seen her parents' graves and has a powerful yearning to do so."

"As ye should, me lady," the old man said, bobbing a slight bow to her and giving her a toothless smile. "Ye say your parents be there?"

"Aye, sir," Marsi said. "The lady Marsaili and Sir Edward Drummond of Cargill. My grandparents are also buried there."

"There be any number o' Drummonds in yon grave-yard, aye. The grand ones and most Earls o' Menteith lie under the floor in the choir, from Sir William Drummond o' ancient memory tae the last unfortunate Menteith."

"Is there a way that I might pay my respects to my people?" she asked.

"Aye, sure. That lad wi' ye looks strong enough tae break ice if need be. And there still be a path o' sorts where I rowed across yestereve. It shouldna be but a few minutes for me tae take ye across. But mind, ye canna get into the priory."

Hawk said, "I thought we needed the prior's permission to visit the isle."

"Och, nay, ye can visit the kirk betwixt Nones and Vespers or the graveyard any time ye can get there if ye be kin tae them wha' lie buried within it, sir. Sithee, keeping ye out wouldna suit the Almighty *or* the prior. Folks must see tae their kin."

When Hawk volunteered to row, their host laughed. "Better ye should use that ice axe tae good purpose, laddie. I've me rheumatism tae consider, and it be fonder o' the oars than o' the axe."

They soon settled into a tippy rowboat with the old man at the oars. The crossing took only minutes, and when they reached the stone-and-timber dock, Hawk helped Marsi out of the boat.

The old man told them to follow the walk around the near side of the priory and assured them that he would wait as long as they liked.

The sprawling, mossy stone priory scarcely looked occupied, but as they passed a deeply recessed, ornately carved doorway Marsi heard low chanting from within.

The sound was pleasant. Then the path rounded a corner and she saw the hedge-girded graveyard just beyond.

Despite the season, the place was tidy, its low hedge neatly clipped, and its walks clear and dry. Hawk went ahead of Marsi through an opening in the hedge, glancing right and left as he strode along the gravel pathway. Nearing the southwest corner, he paused and said, "Here are your grandfather and grandame, lass."

Their tombstones were not as elaborate as some that she had seen at Scone and Dunfermline, but her grandmother's had a small lamb carved into a lower corner. Crossing herself, Marsi whispered a prayer for them both, but she barely remembered her mother's parents and soon moved on.

Hawk had stopped by two other tombstones. She went to stand beside him and saw that they were her parents' graves. She remembered her recent tears and the absence of any memory that her father had ever held her the way that Hawk had.

Swallowing hard, she told herself that Sir Edward had been no different from most men of his age, who took small notice of their children. But he had loved her and was always kind to her. Drawing a deep breath, she turned to look at her mother's stone, expecting a return of her tears. But she had none left, only a gaping but familiar sense of loneliness mixed with a fresh surge of grief for Annabella.

Her hands felt cold despite her gloves, and without thinking, she slipped one into Hawk's warmer one. He gave it a squeeze, and she squeezed back, wondering at the comfort she took from the presence of a man who was likely still a bit vexed with her. Her earlier anxiety about his having so clearly realized that she had been the woman in his bed at Turnberry had eased, too.

She sensed no impatience in him. He seemed as willing as the old man had been to wait as long as she needed to stay there.

Glancing around, wishing that she had flowers or some other remembrance to place on the graves, she had scarcely formed the thought when he stepped away to a winter-dry bush in the corner of the yard. Breaking off a few stems, he returned and handed them to her.

"Rosemary," he said quietly. "For remembrance."

"How did you know what I was thinking?"

He shrugged. "It is what I would have thought, I suppose."

Quietly, she placed sprigs of rosemary on all four graves. Then, looking up at him, she said, "Thank you, sir. I won't forget this. It means much to me."

In response, he held out his hand, and she slipped hers back into it. They stood so for several moments. Then, deciding that it was time to go, she began to turn away only to turn back impulsively and hug him as hard as she could.

His arms went around her as they had before, and she laid her head against his broad, muscular chest, wishing that she need never let go.

She felt his chin gently against her hair again. Then it shifted, and she felt what seemed to be a gentle brush of his lips there. Without a second thought, she tilted her face up to meet his and kissed him.

He responded at once, and his tongue touched the parting of her lips just as it had the first time. This time she let it ease inside. But when her own tongue darted to meet it, he withdrew his and kissed her again lightly. Then, with a soft smile, he said, "We should go, I think, before we shock the holy residents."

Reluctantly, wondering if he thought her a fool or worse for kissing him, she let him take her hand again, and they went back to the dock.

The return journey across the open path of water seemed shorter than before, and when they reached the road, the others were waiting for them.

~

Ivor saw Hetty give Marsi a look that he easily understood, and although he knew that the lass deserved to hear whatever Hetty wanted to say to her, he still felt protective. It didn't help that his lips still burned from the heat of hers, or that those few minutes in the graveyard had stirred his body in a most irreverent way. As he helped Marsi mount the horse they'd brought for her, he said to Hetty, "I am going to keep her with me for a time, mistress."

Hetty nodded, but James said indignantly, "Sakes, sir, her eyes be all puffy! So ye've already made her cry. What more—?"

"If I want your opinion, I'll ask for it," Ivor interjected. But he spoke mildly. When Marsi had mounted, he returned to the boy and said quietly, "I promised I would not murder her, and I won't. Sithee, she has been visiting her parents' graves, so she is feeling sad, and I think I may be able to ease her grief."

James's somber gaze met his, and the boy relaxed, saying, "Very well then. I thought ye were going tae scold her more for going off alone as she did."

Without further comment, Ivor mounted his horse and reined it near Marsi's.

She eyed him warily. "I expect you still have things to say to me, sir."

"I don't think you need to hear those things, but we do seem to talk easily together," he said with a smile as they urged their mounts forward. "I liked telling you about my sister, and I want to know more about you and your family. You have said little about your uncle, Sir Malcolm Drummond. What manner of man is he?"

She eyed him for a moment longer and then said, "In troth, although he is my mother's brother, he is almost a stranger to me, because he rarely pays me heed. I just hoped he might speak for me now, because I...I was so close to Aunt Annabella."

Ivor had come to know how deeply she'd cared for the late Queen. Knowing now that her parents had died two years before Annabella, he suspected that her storm of tears earlier had stemmed more from her grief over the Queen's recent death. The lass must have felt then as if she had lost everyone who had loved her.

When they had ridden a little ahead of the others, knowing from his own experience that it would help her to talk, he said, "Tell me about your parents."

Marsi searched his expression, wondering why he wanted to know. But he waited patiently, apparently just curious about what she would say.

So she said, "Tell me your real name then."

"I'd prefer that you call me Hawk until we get James to safety," he said.

"I'll do that willingly when others are around, and for as long as you like. But I do think that since I flung myself at you and wept all over your jerkin and brigandine, you might at least tell me who you are. I do not recognize that golden hawk banner. Is it your own or are you just making use of it?"

"It is one that I use from time to time. I belong to Clan Chattan."

"But that is a powerful clan confederation. In fact, it is one of the two that took part in the great clan battle at Perth some years ago, is it not?"

"It is, aye," he said noncommittally.

"Did you fight in it?"

"Thirty champions from each side fought in that battle," he said.

"That is not what I asked you."

"Nay, but I don't want to talk about that now. I'd prefer to talk about you."

She smiled, satisfied that she was right. "You *were* there. And I expect you must have won your fights, because the men of Clan Chattan did win, did they not?"

"It was not a day of glory for anyone," Ivor said bleakly. "It was just one more doing of Albany's that will take him to the devil when his time comes."

She fell silent again, her expressive face showing a mixture of sympathy, curiosity, and acceptance before she said, "My parents enjoyed court life whenever there was any. So they spent more time in Stirling and Edinburgh, or at houses of their friends, than they spent with me. When they were at home, it was wonderful. They brought me presents, and my mother often visited me in my bedchamber before I fell asleep. But mostly I was with Hetty until *she* left to look after Jamie."

"Did no one take her place?" he asked, thinking of his parents. He could not imagine his lady mother voluntarily leaving the upbringing of her sons and daughter to servants. Nor could he imagine his father doing so, warrior though he was.

As those thoughts crossed his mind, Marsi's lips twitched in a near smile.

"What?" he asked.

Chuckling, she said, "You asked me if anyone had taken Hetty's place. I was trying to count them up. Sithee, she left eight years ago. I was ten then, so I know I must have had at least five or six new Hettys, because I had a new one every year. And that first year, I think there were at least three. I don't think they liked me."

"I see," he said, raising his eyebrows.

She twinkled back at him, and he was glad to see the light in her eyes. "I warrant you do, sir," she said. "Aunt Annabella saw how it was when she came to see me after my parents died. I was fifteen, and the woman I had then was an awful scold. She thought I should do whatever she said when she said it and never make a decision for myself. I could do naught to please her."

"I feel for the woman. Did you *try* to please her?"

"I did not. She was horrid. When she began to list my faults for Annabella, Annabella looked down her nose and said, 'That will do, Beatrix. You may go.' And go, she did, because Aunt Annabella left one of her own ladies with me, to advise me about how I should go on as one of the Queen's ladies and help me prepare."

"I have a strong notion that your parents and their

servants spoiled you sadly," Ivor said. "I think you were what my grandame calls 'a limb of the devil.' "

"One of my women did call me that to my face, so I expect your grandame would be right," she said. "Do *you* always do as others say?"

"I'm a warrior, lass. I must do as my commanders bid me. And, growing up, it was my duty to do as my parents and grandparents bade me."

Her eyes widened. "Always?"

"I was a child like any other child, so not always," he said. "But I certainly do as I'm bid whenever it is a matter of duty . . . or honor."

As if the inner voice that served as his conscience took exception to that declaration, an image flashed into his mind of at least one glaring exception to it. As if it were yesterday instead of six years ago, he saw himself standing on the field of the battle near Perth that she had mentioned earlier, facing an exhausted opponent and allowing him—nay, commanding him—to escape.

She said, "I don't understand about some men and their blind sense of duty. No matter how skilled a commander may be, he is bound to be wrong sometimes. Moreover, if one always does what others want, instead of what one wants for oneself, how dreadfully, *tediously* predictable life must become."

"Do you *never* do as you are bid?" he demanded.

She flashed him a smile. "I am not as bad as that."

"In my experience with you, it seems gey close to that."

"I do not seek to defy you, sir. But when people will not even listen . . ."

She looked mischievous now, clearly daring him to react to the provocation.

Deciding that it was time to recall her to order, he said, "What do you suppose her grace would think about your getting into my bed at Turnberry?"

To his surprise, she gave a gurgle of laughter and nearly looked back over her shoulder. But she stopped herself, saying, "I pray you, sir, do *not* tell Hetty you have guessed that it was I. She would be mortified, because, of course, it was *her* bed."

"How did you come to climb into it at all then?"

"It was a horrid night, and I could *not* sleep for worrying about what would happen if Albany took me away. I had no other friends at Turnberry, no one that I could even talk to except Hetty. I had not crawled into bed with her since I was eight, but I'd done it often as a child, and I just longed to be near her, to talk to her if she was awake. But although I could see nothing when I crept into that room, I could hear breathing and decided that she must be asleep. There was room, so I crept in, taking care not to wake her. Only you weren't Hetty. And the next thing I knew...Sakes, do you try to stroke every woman who gets into...No."

She seemed to choke on the last word, and Ivor chuckled. "I won't talk about *any* woman in my bed. That night, I was in the midst of a dream I won't tell you about either. 'Tis enough to say that I thought I was still dreaming when I reached for you."

"Aye, well, Hetty does know what I did, for I told her myself, and it horrified her. She is more comfortable believing that you do not know that I was the woman in your bed, though. So, prithee, do not tell her that I was."

"What if she asks *you* if I know? Will you lie to her?"

"Nay, I cannot. Even if I wanted to, she always knows. Jamie does, too."

"If you made a practice of telling lies when you were younger, someone ought to have skelped you soundly for it," he said.

"They weren't allowed to strike me," Marsi said lightly.

"Ah, much becomes clear to me now," he said, giving her a look.

When she met it, her eyes atwinkle, he felt a strong stirring in his loins.

~

Marsi was enjoying herself, but a thought had occurred to her. "You still have not told me your name, sir. I wish you would. It seems strange to call you Hawk when I ken fine that all of these men know who you really are."

"You are right, lass," he said. "I was just being cautious. Now that we are well away from Turnberry and the Clyde, there is no real reason to conceal it. My name is Ivor Mackintosh. My father is Shaw Mackintosh of Rothiemurchus, war leader of Clan Chattan. My grandfather is the Captain of Clan Chattan."

"You are *Sir* Ivor then, aye?"

"Aye."

"I do not know Rothiemurchus," she said.

They continued to talk about his home in the northern Highlands until it was time to stop for their midday meal. Aodán had arranged for the inn at Aberfoyle to pack food for them so that they could avoid lingering in any town or clachan.

Not long after skirting the village of Thornhill, they found a forest clearing where a sparkling burn provided fresh, icy water to drink. The air was chilly, but the sun shone now and again in a cloudy sky. Although they had met numerous other travelers, including several garbed in black, no one paid them particular heed.

After their meal, they rode on, and a few hours later, in the distance, they saw the castle of Doune on its steep, wooded hill. As they drew nearer, Marsi saw that the hill was a peninsula formed by the confluence of a tumbling burn and the swiftly flowing river Teith, from which the region Menteith had taken its name.

By then, she was riding with Hetty, because Sir Ivor had said that he wanted to confer with Aodán. And, although Jamie had ridden with the women for a time, he had soon urged his horse up by Sir Ivor's, and Ivor had let him stay.

The nearer they drew to Doune village on the river north of the castle, the more Marsi noted Hetty shifting about on her horse and looking nervously around.

"What is disturbing you, Hetty?" she asked at last.

"We are in the heart of Menteith now," Hetty said.

"I do remember this area, aye," Marsi said. "'Tis Drummond country."

"It is also Albany's country. Do not forget that, although he is the Duke of Albany, he is also the Earl of Fife and Menteith, a styling that his son, Murdoch Stewart, has assumed. And Murdoch has made Doune Castle his primary seat."

"But even if one or both of them is there..."

"I do not think it is wise to go right through the middle of town, but I do not know how we can avoid it. The only bridge across the Teith lies just ahead. And, at this season, I doubt that any ford north or south of here would be safe for crossing."

"Then we should tell Sir Ivor," Marsi said.

"Who?"

"That is Hawk's true name," Marsi told her. "Sir Ivor Mackintosh of Clan Chattan. He told me earlier and said that I might tell you. He said we ought not to tell Jamie, because he is so young, but I told him that Jamie is as good as any adult at keeping secrets and that he deserves to know the truth if we do."

"And he agreed?"

"Aye, but if strangers are around, we should still call him Hawk."

"Well, I'm glad he'll let us reveal his identity to Jamie," Hetty said. "But I am more concerned about riding into Doune. Albany's men will be everywhere."

"Surely, they'd be thicker on the ground at Stirling," Marsi said.

"Aye, perhaps, but too many of them know Jamie. Murdoch Stewart is as much his cousin as you are, after all, and kens him fine."

Aware that Hetty knew more about how things stood in Fife and Menteith than she did but was less likely to question Sir Ivor's route, Marsi waited until she could see that he and Aodán were no longer conversing. Then, telling Hetty that she wanted a word with Sir Ivor, she urged her mount up alongside his.

"May I speak with you, sir?" she asked.

"Aye, sure, lass. What is it?"

She looked pointedly at Aodán, who apparently needed only a nod from his master to drop back to ride with Jamie behind them.

"Now, tell me," Sir Ivor said.

"Hetty is nervous about riding into Doune, sir. It is the seat of Albany's son Murdoch, and she fears that Albany's men will be thick on the ground there."

"I ken fine that we are in Albany's territory, lass. But if we do not cross the Teith on that bridge yonder, we will have to go a good distance out of our way. Once we are across, we will do as we have done before and find an alehouse or an inn a mile or so beyond the town on the Dunblane road. Sithee, I want to keep well north of the royal burgh of Stirling as we make for Loch Leven and Falkland."

Marsi bit back an immediate protest, forcing herself to think.

"What is it, lass? You are burning to say something."

"I don't want to vex you again," she said, meeting his gaze.

His lips twitched. "Tell me what you are thinking."

Reassured, she said, "The road to Loch Leven—or any other road or track that leads straight through Fife, come to that—will be watched by now, sir. The first place that Albany will expect Jamie to take sanctuary is St. Andrews, so surely we would be wiser to avoid going anywhere near there."

His eyes narrowed as he said, "I did expect Mistress Hetty to keep our destination to herself."

"Hetty did not tell me. Are we indeed going to St. Andrews?"

"We are, but I would like to know how you guessed as much."

"I wasn't sure, but his grace trusts Bishop Traill, and so did Annabella. Sithee, even Albany respects him and may even fear him a little, or he fears the Holy Kirk. Recall that Traill made him leave when Annabella was dying. So St. Andrews is the most likely refuge for Jamie. But Albany will know that, so you *must* take Jamie elsewhere. In troth, Kincardine Castle may be the perfect place."

He frowned, saying, "I know that Kincardine is a Drummond stronghold southwest of Perth. Might we perhaps expect to find Sir Malcolm there at this season, rather than at Stobhall?"

Her temper flared at the realization that he thought she was subtly trying to influence him, but she realized she had given him reason to question her motives. Moreover, it was possible that Sir Malcolm would be at Kincardine. The castle was one of his many properties.

"I do not know where he is at present, sir. He lives mostly at Stobhall, which as you know, lies north of Perth near Cargill. What I do know, however, is that if we are mad enough to ride right through Albany's own territory of Fife—"

She broke off, hearing a cry behind her from Jamie. They had just passed a group of riders to whom she had paid little heed. Although she did not hear what Jamie had shouted, when she turned back, she saw that he had reined in and turned toward the group of riders, who had also stopped.

Just then Jamie shouted, "Hold there, you! Unhand that lad!" As he did, he flung himself from his saddle and ran toward a man who had apparently pulled a boy of about Jamie's age off his horse and was taking a leather strap to him.

Beside her, Sir Ivor swore, wrenched his horse around, and urged it to a lope.

Chapter 10

Ivor reined in and dismounted beside James just as the chap who had been thrashing another boy tossed aside the strap and reached to grab the prince. Seeing Ivor, the townsman paused, his right hand still outstretched toward James.

Keeping his own hands well clear of the dirk on his left hip, Ivor forced calm into his voice but said nonetheless sternly, "What is amiss here?"

James, clearly angry, looked from the townsman to Ivor. Then, shifting his gaze to the other boy, still clutched by his jerkin in the fellow's left hand, he said, "That chap there knocked that lad off his horse. Then he jumped down tae beat him, as you saw. When I commanded him tae stop, he dared tae threaten *me*."

The man had lowered his outstretched hand as James spoke. Now he glowered at Ivor. "What manner of bairn is this that he dares to interfere with his elders?"

Ivor raised his eyebrows in the way that usually made men back away from him. But the one he faced now stood his ground, wanting an answer.

Ivor said evenly, "You have cause to be wroth with the lad. But you will not put your hands on him unless you want to answer to me. If you would complain of his behavior, complain likewise to me."

"I will then, aye," the other snapped. "This lad is mine own servant, charged with tending my horse's gear. When my rein broke, I spoke sharply to him. He answered insolently and so deserved punishment. Your lad behaved even worse."

"He should not have done so," Ivor said, giving the angry James a look that banished the boy's indignation and brought a flush to his cheeks.

Ivor continued to gaze sternly at him as he added, "I will explain his error to him. Moreover, I will do it in a way to ensure that he never behaves so again, at least not until he is fully grown and it is *his business* to do so. Apologize to this gentleman at once, sir, and show proper humility when you do."

For a long, tense moment, James looked mutinous. But Ivor held his gaze until the boy expelled his inhaled breath and turned to the irate townsman.

"I do apologize for angering you, sir," James said. "Your business is none of mine. I should not have interfered in it."

"Aye, well, that be true enough. If I were your da, though, I'd take good leather to ye, just as I were a-doing wi' this 'un."

Ivor saw James's jaw tighten. Before he could speak again, Ivor put a hand on his shoulder and urged him firmly back to his horse. Then, he picked him up, and as he set him on his saddle, he said curtly, "Not another word or gesture unless you want to feel my hand on your backside here and now. Sit properly on your saddle, and ride back to Aodán. I will have more to say to you anon."

James's jaw remained rigid. But he gave a jerky nod, threw his leg over, and reined his horse around as Ivor had commanded.

Ivor returned to the townsman, saying, "I apologize for his behavior, sir." Remembering Marsi's tale of her own life, he added, "I fear that I have left him in the care of servants too often when I must be away. They have sadly spoiled him. But I will see that he swiftly mends his ways."

"Leather," the other muttered. "'Tis the best teacher." With that, he drew the other lad away. As Ivor remounted, he heard the latter's cries and winced, remembering more than one such painful interlude from his own childhood.

Rejoining Aodán and James, he found the latter unrepentant. "You let him beat that lad unfairly," James said.

"He has every right to punish him," Ivor replied.

"But—"

"You will be silent now and listen to what I say to you, or you will count the cost when we stop for the night. You and I had an agreement."

"Aye, we did. But I never saw such a thing before. I could not just sit by and let it continue."

Noting that Aodán was trying to catch his eye, and seeing the other man raise his eyebrows in query, Ivor said, "Stay where you are, Aodán. I want you to hear what I say to him. If a time should come when I must entrust him to your care, I want him to know that you have my permission to do what you must to see that he obeys your orders as he would mine. He promised me that he would leave his royal ways behind at Turnberry and behave like an ordinary bairn."

"I am *not* a bairn," James said. "I am—"

"For our purpose now, my lad, you are what I say you

are," Ivor interjected. "And I say that, prince or none, you had no right to interfere with that man. The lad cheeked him and deserved punishment for it. I agree with you that the penalty is gey harsh for the crime. But that is no more business of mine than it is of yours. You may *talk* as if you were a man of forty instead of a lad of nearly eight, but you are still a bairn and must act like one. Ordinary lads of your age do *not* order adults about with impunity. That man is going to talk of your behavior to all and sundry, and if you think that your uncle will *not* suspect that the boy who dared accost such a man and order him to desist was you, you are not as smart as I thought you were."

James was facing forward, his chin jutting. But Ivor saw tears in his eyes and knew that he had made his point.

Nodding to Aodán then to drop back, Ivor waited until he had done so before he said quietly, "What did you *think* you were doing, Jamie-lad?"

Still staring ahead, James bit his lower lip. Then, visibly drawing breath, he turned to Ivor and said, "I just wanted to make him stop. You are right, sir. I didn't think. I just acted. I meant to help, but 'tis likely that I only made it worse for him."

"You did show courage," Ivor said. "But you did not show wisdom. And courage without wisdom is nearly always foolhardy. You must learn when to act and when to hold your peace, lad. You are still young, though, and wise for your years."

"Do you really think that that townsman will talk about what I did?"

"I do. I want you to ride with Aodán or with Sean Dubh now, whilst I talk with Mistress Hetty and Lady Marsi. We need to make a change in our plans."

James continued to eye him warily. But Ivor waved him toward Aodán and reined his own horse in near Marsi and Hetty.

~

As Sir Ivor drew in beside her, Marsi said, "I hope you were not too harsh with Jamie, sir. He is unaccustomed to people scolding him. Come to that, he rarely does anything to deserve a scolding."

"As beset with protectors as he usually is, I don't doubt you, lass. But he deserved one then. He should not have drawn attention to himself as he did."

"What did you say to that man to make him go away?"

With a guilty smile, he said, "I used your own tale, or my interpretation of it. I told him that I'd left the lad too long with servants, and they'd spoilt him."

"You lied, in fact."

"Aye, that is exactly what I did."

She shook her head at him, adding, "I doubt that Jamie is spoiled, sir, but there was some truth in your words. Not only have we both had the benefit of Hetty's care but we have also both spent our lives almost solely with adults, rarely having contact with persons of our own age. I think that is one reason that we have become such friends. Although there is a great difference in our ages, we often understand each other better than others understand either one of us."

"Have you ever seen him leap to another child's defense as he did today?"

"I cannot think of a time when he might have had the opportunity. Was it really so bad a thing for him to do?"

"Nay, it is good that he reacted so to mistreatment of a

common lad. I fear, though, that his behavior will stir that merchant to speak of it wherever he goes."

"I see," she said. "Aye, a laddie confronting a grown man like that..."

"Just so," he said. "I think we need to alter our appearance somewhat."

"We must do something," Hetty agreed. "Many of the duke's men have seen James before. And riding right through town as we will..." She grimaced.

"We cannot avoid Doune," Ivor said. "But we'll ride straight on to Dunblane. And if my men and I change into Highland gear, we will look like a different party. We'll change in that thicket yonder and wait until any folks we pass will be new to us and we to them. I've noted that when we don our plaids, folks gape at the garments rather than at those wearing them."

"You'll fly another banner, too, will you not?" Marsi asked.

"We will, aye," he said. "Our Mackintosh banner."

"Not Clan Chattan?"

"Nay, my lads are all Mackintoshes, so Mackintosh will do."

"But won't that help people identify you? We will be the same sort of party, too, with two women and a boy. Many have seen us traveling so."

"No one has paid us much heed," Ivor said. "And no one kens my name."

"With respect, sir, I think you underestimate Albany. He travels swiftly and his men are legion, so he must be back in Stirling by now and will have men on every road. He does that in any event. We have seen them daily since we made landfall."

"Aye, perhaps, although black is a common color, so we should not assume that every man wearing it is Albany's. Also, we've set a good pace. From Dunblane, we will be less than forty miles from St. Andrews, and I know the roads of Fife well. If we avoid the main ones, we'll be safe enough."

"But don't you see that you are thinking only of what you agreed to do, whilst I suspect that no one has stopped and questioned us yet because the men we have seen had received no orders yet to look for us. But, prithee, do not make the mistake of thinking they paid us no heed."

"What makes you so sure that they did?" Sir Ivor asked with a frown.

"Because Albany trains his men to be observant and trains them harshly. Doubtless, as soon as he reached Stirling, he began to collect reports from his men. Sithee, unless one sails from Turnberry round most of Scotland, one must pass through Stirlingshire or Menteith—and Fife—to reach St. Andrews. I expect Albany will assume that you want to get there as directly and quickly as you can."

Ivor was still frowning. To her surprise, though, when she stopped talking, he nodded and said, "You are right about seeking another route from Dunblane, lass. Whilst we shelter in yon woods, we'll talk more. Wolf also suggested considering alternative approaches to St. Andrews."

"Captain Wolf?"

"Aye, but before we talk more, we'll change the look of our party."

When they rode out of the woods a half-hour later, their party looked as if it numbered nine persons instead of ten. Ivor and Aodán led the way, and Hetty and Marsi followed them. Hetty had changed her gray gown to a rose-colored one and wore a formal caul instead of her usual plain white veil.

Marsi had donned a russet-colored kirtle and wore her hair in plaits coiled at her nape with Hetty's veil to cover them. A braided blue band across her forehead secured the veil, concealed her hair, and gave her a young maiden's look.

Both women wore their hooded, fur-lined cloaks and gloves, but Marsi wore hers with the fur lining outward and the gray wool inside.

Although the men had kept their breeks and fur-lined boots on for riding, they wore tunics under their blue-and-green great kilts, or plaids. The voluminous Highland all-purpose garments consisted of long woolen yardage, kilted up and belted, with the remaining length flung over one shoulder to flow behind.

In the Highlands, few men rode because much of the landscape was too rugged for any but the sturdiest, most sure-footed Highland pony. So men wore their plaids every day there and slept in them if they were out over-night, wrapping the garments around them like blankets to sleep.

At present, much of Ivor's excess yardage ballooned behind him as he rode, because he had apparently sat on the end of it when he'd mounted his horse.

The other men in his tail rode behind the women, his squire Sean Dubh first with Ivor's sword slung across his back, Sean having strapped his own weapons to a sumpter pack. The four men-at-arms rode two by two behind him, one of the latter pair leading their three sumpter ponies in a string.

The nine riders had covered half the distance from the

woods to the bridge when a muffled voice behind Ivor muttered, "One dislikes tae complain, but ye ought tae know that it be fearsome hot under all this wool."

"Be glad I did not sling my sword across my back," Ivor retorted.

"Aye, well, it would look gey odd if ye had," James said. "Wi' your plaid billowing out as it does whilst ye ride, I'm no as noticeable as I'd be were your claymore sticking out across me."

"Hush now, riders are approaching us. Keep your head tight against my back and your feet well in, lad. It will not do for a foot to poke out now."

"Aye, sure, they might think ye'd got an extra one, and mayhap a few other extra parts as well. How far do we ha' tae ride like this?"

"Until we go far enough," Ivor said. "Think of your discomfort as penance for drawing so much attention earlier. Now, hush. They're upon us."

As Ivor said the last few words, he glanced at Aodán, so that anyone who could see that he was talking might assume that the two of them were conversing.

Aodán met his gaze with blue eyes atwinkle.

"Did you want to say something to me?" Ivor asked him dourly in Gaelic.

Aodán grinned and replied in the same tongue, "I doubted that wrapping him up in your plaid like that would serve, sir. The lad is a good sport."

"It's his future at stake—if he will face it under Albany's thumb, or not—and he knows it. But keep smiling, Aodán. It appears to be a busy day for travelers, so keep your eyes skinned, and if you see any taking undue notice of us, speak up."

"The lass...that is, I did hear her ladyship suggest we go to Kincardine Castle. I know it lies off the Perth road near Auchterarder. How far is it from Dunblane?"

"Barring trouble, a day's ride through Strathallan. But I don't know Sir Malcolm Drummond, and her ladyship barely does. Also, I must decide if we'll need Wolf's help. He said I could send him a message through the Abbot of Lindores."

"Sir Fin and his lady may be in Perth by now," Aodán said when Ivor paused.

"I may need him, too, before this is done. Let me think now."

⸺

Marsi glanced at Hetty and saw that, although she held her head high and looked as much a Highland noble-woman as any Marsi had met, she also looked tense.

They had heard Sir Ivor talking with Aodán, and she wondered if he assumed that neither she nor Hetty spoke the Gaelic. The Drummonds were a Highland clan, too, after all, albeit not from as far north as Clan Mackintosh.

She knew little about the tribes of Clan Chattan other than that they were scattered through the high country from Strathspey to Strathdearn and paid more heed to the Lord of the North than to the King of Scots or lords of Parliament. They were a fierce clan. The banner flying now showed a Highland wildcat on its back legs with its claws extended. Their motto was "Touch not the cat but with a glove."

Trying to picture Sir Ivor as a cat of any sort strained her imagination. But from the deeply respectful way that his men behaved when his temper was short, she easily believed that he possessed the wildcat's ability to snarl when angry.

The Drummonds were more civilized, or so she had been told, and were much more important, having given Scotland two queens. Even so, men respected the ire of the Drummonds, whose motto—also a warning to others—was "Gang warily."

She smiled at the absurd image of Sir Ivor "ganging warily" in her presence. He was unlike any other man she knew. He was clearly not one to bow before those of higher rank. But she did not think he was uncivilized or of lesser importance than any Drummond. Not in the least.

He had advised her to look straight ahead as if she had no interest in the town or castle of Doune as they passed through. She was not, he had said, to look at any passerby, let alone to smile at anyone. True Highlanders, he said, kept themselves to themselves even in the Highlands and lower glens.

Although she obeyed him as well as she was able, she could not help noticing that people stared at them, and she wondered if any might recognize her. Highlanders were a colorful lot, and she knew by the way that people gaped that they would be unlikely to remember much about her or Hetty. Even so, drawing so much attention after trying to avoid drawing any made her a bit nervous.

They passed through the town of Doune without incident and pressed onward.

The sun had gone down before they reached Dunblane. In the lingering dusk, with no more than a glance back at Hetty and Marsi, Sir Ivor turned northward through the narrow streets of the village.

As they passed Dunblane Cathedral with its tall, square tower overlooking the Allan Water, Marsi breathed a sigh of relief and said quietly to Hetty, "I think he does mean to go through Strathallan rather than heading straight across Fife, don't you?"

"Aye, perhaps," Hetty muttered. More quietly yet, she said, "My lady, ye must not expect too much of Sir Malcolm. He may help ye if he's of a mind to. But he is a man who seeks his own benefit, not that of others. For all that he is our dearest Annabella's brother, he may be unwilling to set himself against Albany."

"But he need not confront Albany, Hetty. He need only speak to his grace and remind him that Annabella promised..." The words dried in her mouth. She had told his grace, the King, what Annabella had promised, and he had replied kindheartedly. Even so, he had said that Albany was determined, as if that were that.

Pushing the dark thought out of her mind, she added firmly, "Uncle Malcolm will understand, Hetty. He cannot want Cargill to go out of the family."

Sir Ivor and Aodán were turning into the yard of an inn at the north edge of the town, and lackeys ran to attend their horses. Marsi watched as Aodán dismounted and went to take James when Sir Ivor handed him down.

If the lads running to help had noted the boy concealed beneath Ivor's plaid, none seemed to think such a thing was odd. Mayhap they thought that Highlanders' bairns always rode that way, or else the lowering clouds and the icy chill in the night air suggested that the lad had ridden so just to keep warm.

She was smiling at the thought when Sir Ivor turned to her. "Art tired, lass?"

"It has been a long day," she said. "But I'm not as tired as I am hungry."

He smiled then and put a hand to her back, steadying her as she deftly shifted her offside leg over and turned so that he could lift her down. "We're all hungry," he said. "Let us see what they can produce quickly for us to eat."

Aodán had relayed their needs to the landlord. So, after the men took their belongings upstairs, Hetty, Jamie, and Marsi saw to their personal needs and settled into the two rooms allotted to them. It occurred to Marsi as she plumped a pillow on the bed she would share with Hetty that she was getting used to staying at inns and alehouses. The amenities were not what she was accustomed to at Cargill, Turnberry, or any place she had stayed when traveling with Annabella. But the hostelries served their purpose, and for the most part she was enjoying herself.

Once again, they took supper in the common room.

Three other men were eating there, too, who seemed to be friends traveling together. But Marsi was not surprised when, the minute Ivor saw them, he said he thought that perhaps she and Hetty would prefer to sup in their room.

Marsi had said reasonably, "We cannot sit in our room, sir, except on the bed, which takes up most of the space there."

Hetty nodded agreement. "The bed is large enough for the two of us, but it *is* a tiny wee room, sir."

"Very well, you may take your supper down here. But we won't dawdle over the meal. Our lad looks as if he may fall asleep at any moment."

"Nay, I'll do," Jamie said, straightening. But Marsi saw him cover a yawn a moment later and knew that he was as tired as the rest of them were.

Glancing at Sir Ivor, she saw that he, too, had noticed the yawn. When he looked at her and smiled, she felt its warmth spread through her, stirring other, less familiar feelings as it did.

Holding Marsi's gaze, Ivor wondered what it was about the lass that kept drawing his attention to her even while James remained his primary concern. The lad was staring at his food as if he wondered what it was. But Ivor knew that James was just tired. It had been a long trip and one fraught with circumstances wholly unfamiliar to a lad who had been cosseted all his life.

The incident with the townsman had upset him, too. Although he had protested against riding under Ivor's plaid, he had soon fallen silent and had slept at least part of the way. Once, Ivor had felt him slip and had clapped a hand over the two linked smaller ones at his waist to hold James if he slid any further. But James had steadied himself, and if he dozed again, Ivor had not noticed.

Conversation was minimal until James said, "I think it is going to snow."

The weather had begun to look threatening shortly before the sun had dropped behind Ben Lomond in the west. Clouds that had hovered above the mountain all day had provided a colorful sunset then. But before the light had gone, the clouds had lowered and darkened. The air was definitely colder, as well.

"You may be right, lad," Ivor said. "We've been fortunate so far, meeting nobbut occasional flurries."

"Will we have to ride on tomorrow even if it does snow?" James asked.

"We'll see," Ivor said, hoping that he'd not have to make such a decision. Bad weather could hold them up for days and give Albany's men more time to find them. The fact was that they had been extraordinarily lucky so far to have avoided the worst that Scotland had to offer. Although it was nearly the first of March, winter might linger for another eight weeks even in the lower glens.

He had *not* liked the look of those fretful, thickening clouds.

Marsi, watching Sir Ivor, could almost hear his thoughts and knew that he was worried about the possibility of snow. But if they did travel through Strathallan toward Kincardine, they would avoid the Ochil Hills to the south-east and others north of Strathallan that were even higher.

If the weather turned bad, those hill routes would be icy, snow-packed, and as good as trackless to anyone who did not know them well. So those routes would be more dangerous than the lower one along the Allan Water.

When they finished supper, Ivor went to be sure his men had settled in while she, Jamie, and Hetty went to their rooms. From her window, Marsi could not see a single star in the sky. The air was so cold that she wished the room had a fireplace.

She performed her evening ablutions quickly. But no sooner had she begun to unlace her kirtle than she heard a burst of hastily stifled, boyish laughter from the next room. Turning to see that Hetty had her head cocked as if she, too, had heard the laughter, Marsi said, "That was Jamie, I think. But I have heard no one else pass our door, have you?"

Hetty shook her head, and since she had taken off all but her shift, in which she customarily slept, Marsi said, "I think I will ask Jamie what was so funny."

"Dinna be long," Hetty said. "Sir Ivor is likely to return at any moment."

Marsi knew that, and she knew, too, that she was rather hoping that he would come up before she returned to Hetty. That thought fled instantly from her mind, however, when she opened Jamie's door with only a perfunctory rap and looked in.

Her gaze alit first on Jamie, who sat on the sole narrow bed, grinning. But his grin vanished when he saw her, and his gaze shifted abruptly, drawing hers with it.

On Jamie's pallet, with his knees up and his arms wrapped around them, sat the boy Jamie had tried to rescue from the irate townsman.

Chapter 11 _____

Looking from one lad to the other, Marsi said, "What is this, then?"

"Will didna like that man he was with, so he's come tae us," Jamie said.

"He has, has he? And what do you think Hawk will say about that?" she asked. Although they had been flying the Mackintosh banner, she thought Ivor would prefer that Will not know his true name and hoped that Jamie had not already provided it.

"I think Hawk will welcome him," Jamie said with confidence that Marsi suspected he did not feel. "He said we ought tae change the look of our group, and I canna think of a better way tae do that than by adding another lad my age."

Marsi turned to the other boy. "Your name is Will?"

"Aye, m'lady. They did call me Fletcher Nat's Will. But, last summer, me da fell out o' a tree a-picking apples for the master and died. Master Lucken called me Dead Nat's Will for a time, but I couldna remember tae answer tae such a thing, even when he clouted me. So now he calls me just Will, which suits me fine."

With hopeful urgency in his voice, Jamie said, "Can we keep him?"

"You know I cannot make that decision," Marsi said. "You must ask Hawk."

"Then I'll go and ask him now."

"Nay, I'll find him and send him to you," Marsi said. Since Sir Ivor could hardly send Will back to the towns-man before morning, she thought he would likely take him out to sleep in the stable loft with Aodán and the other men. "Both of you must stay right here until Hawk tells you what he has decided to do," she added.

They agreed, and she heard them chuckling together as she shut the door. She could not recall another time that she had heard an exchange of such childish laughter between Jamie and another child. His cousins treated him with a much greater degree of formality than Will did.

Pausing to tell Hetty that Will was with Jamie and that she was going to send one of the inn's lackeys to fetch Sir Ivor from the stables, Marsi headed down the wooden stairs. She had reached the half-landing when Sir Ivor appeared below her and stopped with one foot on the first stair to give her a thoughtful look.

She said, "I was about to ask someone to fetch you, sir. Jamie has found a new way to disguise our party, but I thought you would want to discuss it with him."

"I would," he said, holding her gaze as he moved up the stairs toward her. "What is this new idea of his?"

"I doubt that you will be as pleased as Jamie is, but that boy has come here."

"That...Do you mean the lad whose master was leathering him earlier?"

"I do. Evidently, he slipped away and managed to follow us. And he seems to have done so with ease, sir, despite your Highland garb."

"Did he, in troth?" He'd pitched his voice low, and she thought it sounded almost like a cat's purr. The sound seemed to vibrate against nerves deep inside her. He had reached the step below hers and was so close that she had to fight an urge to step back. He said, "You should be with Hetty, lass."

"Aye, perhaps. But I heard two people laughing in your chamber, and I knew you were still outside or below. So I went in to see what was so funny."

"And you found Jamie with his new friend."

"Aye," she said. "Jamie thinks you will welcome Will. He said that adding one more person to our party will make it seem a different one altogether."

"What did *you* think of that reasoning?" he asked in that same purring voice.

"I . . . I think he wants Will to stay with us. He asked me if he could *keep* him."

"You realize that that devilish townsman is unlikely to let him get away so easily." He stepped onto the half-landing with her. "He'll likely search for him."

"Perhaps, but Jamie values him more than the townsman does," Marsi said. Her body was tingling. Ivor was so close that her breasts touched him and seemed to strain toward him, as if they felt an attraction of their own for him.

"I'll talk to the boys," he said. But he was looking at her and made no effort to pass her. Nor had he repeated his suggestion that she return to Hetty.

His eyes seemed to burn into hers, stimulating more reactions deep within. Her lips felt dry but instinct told her that if she licked them, he would kiss her again.

Telling herself that she must resist the urge, she put a

hand on his chest, as if she could hold him off with such a gesture.

He covered her hand warmly with one of his own.

Her breath caught in her throat. Her lips parted.

"Ah, lassie," he said, moving his free hand gently under her veil to the back of her head. "You are as tempting as any woman I've ever met. I believe you'd have tempted Saint Columba, and God kens that I am no such virtuous fellow."

With that, his fingers laced themselves through her hair and he pulled her closer, bending just enough to touch his lips to hers. At first, she thought he would taste them and tease them as he had before. Instead, he pressed his own hard against hers, demanding a response and holding her in place with the hand at the back of her head, as if he feared that she might try to slip free.

She did not. Every fiber of her body responded to his, and eagerly. She could not have pulled away had she wanted to.

When his tongue invaded her mouth, it felt warm and soft and tasted of spices from their supper. Her body sang its desire, and she heard a soft moan.

Her heart was pounding so that a moment or two passed before she realized that the moaning was hers.

The hand that had tangled itself in her hair got free and drifted to the middle of her back, pressing her body closer to his. Her arms had slipped around him, too, although she had no memory of moving them.

Light from the cresset on the half-landing's corner shelf lit his face. When he opened his eyes, she shut hers, wanting him to do as he would and hoping fiercely that none of the other men who were staying at the inn would interrupt them.

Whether the three other guests had retired to their rooms or remained below, she did not know. But, other than an occasional footstep or low voice from servants tending to late evening chores in the kitchen, the inn remained silent.

"What are ye doing there, the two o' ye?"

Jamie's stern voice, coming from above and behind Marsi, startled her. She tried to pull away from Ivor, only to catch her foot on the stair behind her.

Ivor steadied her easily. Looking over a shoulder, she saw the boy peering down at them from the top of the stairs.

"Why are ye kissing our Marsi?" he demanded. "Art going tae marry her?"

"Nay, he is not," Marsi said. She disengaged herself, albeit with difficulty, since Ivor seemed unaware that she was trying to free herself from his grasp. "I told you to wait in your chamber, Jamie," she added firmly.

"Aye, but ye were gone for such a time we feared ye might ha' fallen in the yard. It be blind drifting snow out there—could bury ye in a twink—as ye'd ken fine had ye gone outside tae find him. If ye're no going tae marry her," he added, looking fixedly at Ivor, "why d'ye be a-kissing her? I dinna think ye should."

Evenly, Ivor said, "You mind your tongue and get back to our room. I'll be with you shortly. I think you know that I want to talk to you."

Grimacing, Jamie turned and left without another word.

They stood as they were until they heard the door shut behind him.

Then Marsi said, "What are you going to do?"

"I don't know yet," he admitted. "That townsman may have men out looking for him even in this weather, and the boy is safer here for the night. In troth, now that he *has* escaped, I don't yearn to see him in that man's clutches again. But I must learn how matters stand between them. If the boy is legally bound to him…"

He paused, but Marsi did not need to hear more. If Will's master had legal custody, Ivor would believe that duty demanded that he send the boy back to him.

Ivor had not released her, and she sensed that, given enough time, she might be able to persuade him to keep Will.

As the thought occurred to her, Ivor moved to kiss her again.

Hastily, she said, "His name is Will, sir. And when I found them laughing, I could only stare, because I'd *never* seen Jamie laugh like that, so freely and happily with a friend. I ken fine that they scarcely know each other—"

She stopped when he put a finger to her lips.

"I'll talk to them. That's all I can promise." Then he kissed her lightly and put his hands on her shoulders as he said, "You and I need to talk, too, as you must know. As it is, I have no right to be standing here with you, behaving as we have. But—"

This time, she put a finger to his lips and murmured, "I know. In troth, sir, we *must* talk with my uncle. He will help me. And then, perhaps…"

Reluctant to put the half-formed thought into words yet, she could not finish the sentence. But he just kissed her again and gently turned her on the stair.

"Go now," he said. "You should be grateful that I came in when I did. Our meeting would not have been as pleasant had I found you outside in the snow."

"I wasn't going out," she reminded him, looking back.

His reply was a gesture threatening to smack her backside, so she hurried ahead of him up the stairs. When she glanced back, he was right behind her.

He smiled, and his eyes turned golden in the cresset light.

She went into her room, savoring the warmth of his smile and wondering what it would be like for the woman lucky enough to marry him.

Ivor watched her door shut and wondered at his recklessness. Continuing to his bedchamber, he paused, drew a breath, and let it out before he opened the door.

The boys were sitting on James's pallet in the darkness, so he found a candle and lit it from the cresset on the landing. Then he shut the door and used the candle to light others in the room. Neither James nor Will said a word.

Ivor sat on the bed and looked at them.

"How did you find us, Will?"

Pushing a stray lock of dark hair from his forehead, Will said, "I followed ye, sir. First I asked after a party o' ten wi' a lad me own age, then after one wi' two ladies— one young and pretty and t'other one older, yet comely. When some said a party o' Highlanders had two such females, I followed them. Sithee, I hadna seen any Highlanders m'self, and we'd passed all wha' were heading back toward Doune. But following such colorful chaps were gey easy. When the men here said ye had a lad wi' ye, I kent fine I'd come a-right."

So much for their disguise, Ivor thought. "What did you hope to accomplish by finding us?" he asked.

"I thought mayhap ye'd take me into your service, sir. The lad here, Jamie, be a kind chap, and I hoped ye'd be kind as well. Master Lucken, he's *un*kind and quicker tae take a fist or leather tae a lad than tae speak civil tae him."

"How came you into his employment?"

Will shrugged. "Me da carved arrows for him and looked after me when me mam died a-trying tae birth me a sister. The wee lass died, too, so me da said I should stay wi' him and help by cleaning up shavings and such. That wasna so bad, but after he died, Master Lucken said I was tae do as *he* said. I did try, but he just says do it, and when I dinna ken how, I get the leather. He says the leather will teach me how, but I thought I'd see what I could do for ye instead."

"Your da was a fletcher, was he?"

Will nodded.

"Is Master Lucken also a fletcher?"

"Nay, he trades in leather goods, tanning and selling and such. When me da were looking for work in Doune, Master Lucken said he would pay him tae make his arrows, but we'd ha' tae pay back a part o' the gelt for space tae work and all. He made me da do other things, too, tae earn our keep, till me da fell out o' the apple tree. Now, the master gives me nowt but me sup and the leathering."

James said quietly, "I think Master Lucken is mean, and he treated Will gey badly. Prithee, sir, may we keep Will?"

Ivor's first instinct was to say no. Taking on the added responsibility of a boy the tanner of Doune thought he owned was madness under the circumstances. More-over, unless the miserable weather magically cleared by morning, they would be stuck in Dunblane for at least another day.

On the other hand, he needed to get a message to Jake Maxwell, and Dunblane did boast a cathedral. Accordingly, he said, "Will may stay here with you for the night if you are willing to share your pallet with him."

"Aye, sure. I have never—"

Jamie broke off, looking self-conscious, as if he feared that he might be giving away too much by saying that he had never shared a bed before.

Ivor smiled. "I'll see about getting more blankets. I got cold last night."

"Sir?"

Ivor turned back, touched by the unusual note of childishness in Jamie's voice. "What is it, Jamie-lad?"

"You didn't say about keeping Will, only about tonight."

Shifting his gaze to Will, Ivor said, "What can you do, lad, besides cleaning up after a fletcher and looking after trappings for horses?"

"I can do most anything, sir, if someone shows me what is wanted. I like the horses, and I didna mind tending their gear. 'Twas only that nowt that anyone did pleased Master Lucken. And I were the easiest o' his lads for him tae drub."

"Then you can help out in the stables tomorrow," Ivor said.

"I thought that Will might serve me as Sean Dubh serves you," Jamie said.

"We'll see how he does in the stables first," Ivor said. When James looked as if he would argue, Ivor added quietly, "I'm not of a mind yet to reward you."

Color flooded the boy's cheeks, but he said no more.

And, since Sean Dubh had already been and gone, Ivor went to see about finding more blankets.

He slept well, enjoying pleasant if unseemly dreams of Marsi in his bed, and realized when he awoke that Jamie had slept more soundly than any other night of their journey. The boy had endured no nightmares, nor had he muttered in his sleep.

Both of the boys had slept well.

One look out the window at the still-driving snow told Ivor that they would go nowhere that morning and would likely be staying another night at the inn. He dressed quickly and went to see how his men had fared.

The inn's other three guests were cheerfully breaking their fast in the common room. Outside, the snow still came down in large flakes, but men going back and forth from the stable had tramped a path to it.

Finding Aodán, Ivor learned that the men had eaten and were attending to their usual tasks. The stables seemed well built, warm, and snug.

"I'm thinking that the sky be lighter in the west than it was yestermorn and the snow not so thick, sir," Aodán said. "If this weather lifts, we'll likely still have some time afore we can take to the road safely, and our lads can do with some practice. I'd wager that yon innkeeper would be pleased to have fresh meat."

"Tell me when you are ready to take them out," Ivor said. "If all stays quiet here, I'll go with you."

"We'll no need to go far," Aodán said. "The innkeeper did say there be game aplenty in yon woods above the burn."

Ivor agreed, and when he returned to the common room, the three strangers were preparing to depart. "I hope you need not travel far in such weather," he said.

"Only tae Stirling, sir," one said. "Nobbut five miles. See you, we came from Perth yesterday and decided no tae risk going farther till we saw how the weather would behave. We're gey glad we stopped here."

They were soon gone, so Ivor summoned the rest of his party downstairs to break their fast. James brought Will with him, saying, "The lads in the stable loft must have eaten hours ago. So Will should eat with us."

Ivor made no objection, and Will sat beside James. Ivor was amused to see him ape James's actions and manners as the two talked quietly together.

Looking at Marsi, he saw that she was watching them, too. When she smiled approvingly at him, he smiled back, remembering what she had said about Jamie needing a friend. He wondered then if *she* counted anyone besides Hetty as a friend. She had said herself that her own childhood had been much as Jamie's was.

It was unfortunate, he mused, that he could not take them both to visit Rothiemurchus when his entire family was in residence. A noisier, more boisterous, or more loving crowd, he could not imagine.

Marsi wondered what Ivor was thinking that had put the whimsical smile on his face. She was glad that he had let Will join them, because she had feared he might think that the townsman's lad was too common to eat with Jamie.

However, Ivor could hardly tell Jamie to abandon his royal ways and then refuse to let him associate with commoners. That the young prince looked upon Will more as a friend than as a minion pleased her.

After breakfast, both boys went out to the stable with Sir

Ivor. And, when the snow diminished to scattered flakes, the men bundled up and set off for some woods near the Allan Water with their bows and quivers full of arrows.

Marsi wished that she might have gone with them. Sitting with Hetty, mending a pair of Jamie's breeks while Hetty knitted nearby was not nearly the pleasure that tramping through the snowy woods with the men would be.

With no other guests left, they could at least sit comfortably by the common-room fire. Even so, Hetty insisted that they stay alert for sounds of new arrivals.

"The last thing that any of us wants is for Albany to surprise us," she said.

Marsi grimaced at the thought.

The men returned before the midday meal was ready to serve.

Sir Ivor came in alone, saying, "I've left Jamie and Will to help the cook's lads skin four braces of rabbits."

Hetty's eyebrows went up, and Marsi said in astonishment, "You left *Jamie* to skin rabbits for the cook?"

"Aye, sure. He and Will look upon it as a rare treat, I promise you."

She shook her head in amusement, trying to imagine what his grace would say about setting Jamie to such a task. She suspected that it would have made Annabella smile. But Annabella would never smile again at her beloved little son.

The stab of grief caught Marsi unaware. Tears surged into her eyes, and one spilled down her cheek. She brushed it hastily away and noted thankfully that Hetty had not noticed. The older woman was stuffing her knitting into its bag.

Marsi did not look at Ivor.

Straightening, Hetty said, "You must want to refresh yourself before our midday meal, sir. Marsi, you should come upstairs with me, if you please."

Feeling Ivor's gaze on her, Marsi collected her wits and said, "Aye, sure, straightaway, Hetty. I just need to fold these—"

"You go ahead, mistress," Ivor said. "I'll wait for her."

The ache in Marsi's throat returned with a vengeance, too strong to let her swallow. As she carefully, meticulously folded Jamie's breeks, she was all too conscious of Ivor standing over her.

"Come along now, lass," he said. "They won't fold any smaller."

She sat still, afraid that if she stood up, she would fling herself into his arms again as she had at Inchmahone and cry until she had no tears left. Fighting back the ones that wanted to gush forth, she forced herself to breathe more naturally.

Ivor drew her to her feet, saying quietly, "What is it, Marsi-lass? You cannot be this upset because I let Jamie skin a rabbit."

"N-nay," she said, managing a half-smile. "I just thought about... about how it would make Annabella smile."

"Look at me," he said, putting a gentle hand under her chin and tilting it up until she had to obey him. "I expect you still have nowt to wipe your eyes, and you cannot use your cap here. So collect yourself before anyone else comes in."

His tone was tender, but his words were a command. Strangely, though, it settled her emotions and banished any further urge to cry.

"I beg your pardon," she said. "Despite what you have seen, it is gey rare for me to succumb so easily and unexpectedly to any strong emotion."

"There is nowt amiss in feeling as you do."

"But I should not inflict such feelings on others," she muttered. "I don't know what comes over me that I have inflicted them on you."

"I'll tell you what it is," he said in that same firm tone. "You are grieving, lass, and there is nowt amiss in that. Grief lives long in the hearts of those who lose people they love, and you have lost more than your share. Sakes, you cannot have finished grieving for your parents before her grace, the Queen, died. To have lost her as well must be gey hard. For such heartache to pass takes much time."

"But it is worse for Jamie," she murmured. "She was his mother."

～

Ivor's hands ached to hold her close again, and once more he wondered at the strength of his feelings for someone whom he had known for so short a time.

His temperament had always been volatile, but his relationships had not. His men had deep respect for his temper but were all nonetheless loyal to him. Any women he had known intimately were still friendly, although the few who had experienced his temper *had* shown fear of it at the time.

The truth was that—if one dismissed Bishop Traill, his grace, commanding officers, and the self-important tanner of Doune—until Marsi stepped into his life, the only people who had not trembled before his anger were a few members of his own family. But Marsi had shown undaunted spirit in the face of it and seemed able to deflect it with a word or a look. In truth, she stirred nearly every emotion of which he was capable just as strongly as she could stir him to anger.

Faith, he thought as he gently turned her toward the stairway, he could be wrathful with the lass one moment and deeply sympathetic the next. He had never known anyone else who'd had such an effect on him.

She could stir his sense of humor or his sense of the ridiculous with a twinkle. They often seemed to share the same thoughts, the same reactions. His parents finished each other's sentences. But his mother had once confided that they had *not* done so from the start, and they had been married for decades.

He had often felt as if he could read a thought in Marsi's head from no more than a fleeting expression on her face. However, other times, she was a mystery. He had thought more than once that, like his sister, Catriona, she was stubborn, proud, and determined to have her own way about everything.

She was all of those things. But she was *not* like Cat.

Now, just watching her backside twitch as she went ahead of him up the stairs stirred other thoughts, thoughts that he should not be thinking about a lass in whom the Duke of Albany had taken such a decided interest. The sooner he could deliver her into hands powerful enough to protect her against Albany's political maneuvers, the better it would be for her and for himself. His own liege, the Lord of the North, would *not* thank him for stirring Albany's wrath.

As they reached the top of the stairs, Ivor said quietly, "Have you talked much with Mistress Hetty about your feelings?"

"Nay, for Hetty told me often, when she was still looking after me, that I must not make a gift of my emotions to others. So I ken fine how she feels about that. Forbye, when I joined her at Turnberry after my parents died, I was forever saying the same things to her. So, although she was always kind, I knew she must be tired of hearing them. Aunt Annabella was kind, too. But too often, without warning, something would remind me of my parents, and the tears would come. I soon realized that her other ladies thought I ought to keep my grief to myself."

"So you think the same thing now."

"Aye," she said, visibly drawing breath. At her door, she turned and said rather abruptly, "Shall we wait to hear you go down or go when they ring the bell?"

"You know the answer to that," he said. "I'll go fetch Jamie and see that he is presentable before Mistress Hetty sees him. But we'll all go down together." He put a hand to her cheek and brushed a lingering tearstain dry with his thumb.

Her lips parted invitingly, but he did not mean to let James catch him kissing her again. The lad was right. He should not. He had kissed her too often already, and continuing to give way to the temptation would surely lead to trouble.

"In you go," he said, opening the door for her and fairly pushing her inside.

⁓

Marsi sensed Ivor's desire and was aware of her own. But aside from wishing that they had met in a world without Albany or Redmyre, and weeping on him, she decided that she had generally managed to keep her wits about her.

Hetty handed her a towel when she walked in and suggested that she change her cap and shake out her wrinkled skirts.

Shortly afterward, Marsi heard Ivor and both boys come upstairs and smiled to think that Jamie had persuaded Ivor to let Will dine with them.

Minutes later, when Ivor rapped, Hetty begged them to go ahead. "I've just found a spot on my gown," she explained. "I must change it before I join you."

Downstairs, harmony prevailed until Jamie announced with studied casualness that he had decided he and Will should do everything together. "Sithee, I have never had another lad as a companion," he added earnestly.

"We'll discuss that later," Ivor said. He sat at the stair end of the table with the boys at his right, facing the fireplace. Marsi was on his left, facing the outer door.

Undaunted by Ivor's response, James said, "But I want—"

Cutting him off with a look and one raised finger, Ivor said, "You would do better to discuss the matter with me privately. If you think that Will's presence will persuade me to grant your request, you are wrong."

The outer door of the common room opened, letting in a blast of cold air and four men, who entered shaking snow off their cloaks. From their broad-brimmed hats to their boots, their clothing was black, and each bore a familiar device on both his cloak and his tunic that stirred instant tension in Marsi.

Chapter 12 _____

Noting Marsi's tension, Ivor looked to his right to see the four men enter the common room and recognized them as Albany's men as quickly as Marsi had.

Will glanced over his shoulder. Then he stood, picked up his trencher and a basket of bannocks that a maidservant had just set on the table and, as casually as if the strangers had naught to do with aught, disappeared into the kitchen.

Sitting between Will's place and Ivor, James had his back to the four. With his mind on what he wanted and his gaze fixed on Ivor, he paid no heed to the men or to Will's departure but said tersely, "But *why* can I no have Will—?"

Before he could finish, Ivor surged up and caught him by the shoulders, taking care that James would not face the newcomers.

Giving him a shake, Ivor snapped, "I told you that I did not want to hear another word, my lad. Mayhap, this will help you learn to obey me." Holding James close, he gave him a sound smack on the backside, followed by a second one.

James yelped, whereupon Marsi, sitting across from

him, leaped to her feet. "Let be, sir!" she cried. "He did naught to deserve such brutality."

Catching her eye with his sternest gaze, Ivor said, "You will hold your tongue, too, my lass, especially before *these others*."

Seeing her grimace, he knew that she had recognized the men for what they were and had simply reacted impulsively to his "brutality" toward the boy. His sharp command had swiftly recalled her to the danger.

Even so, she said as curtly as he had, "I *won't* be silent. I have every right to speak my mind, for you are being cruel to him, as these others can see as well as I do." Turning to the four, who had halted at the threshold, she made an elaborate gesture toward Ivor and James, saying, "Just *see* how he treats the poor laddie!"

While she went on in the same way, Ivor leaned nearer James, maintaining an angry expression as he murmured, "I'm going to send you away, lad. Take care *not* to let those men see your face. Now, yell as if I were blistering your backside."

He gave him a few more smacks, and James yelled with gusto.

Hoping the smacks thus seemed harder than they were, especially with Marsi carrying on as if he were the most brutal man in Christendom, Ivor gave James one last spank. Then, urging him toward the stairway with a hand on his shoulder, he said, "Get on upstairs now. And do *not* let me hear your voice or see your face again until you can keep that tongue of yours civilly behind your teeth."

Stomping up the stairs, rubbing his backside dramatically, James obeyed.

Marsi, arms akimbo, said, "I hope you are pleased

with yourself. Doubtless, that poor bairn will not be able to sit a horse again this sennight!"

"I told you to be silent," Ivor said in a near growl. "You would be wise to heed me, lass, unless you want the same lesson I just gave the lad."

Her chin shot into the air. But as she began to reply, the leader of the four men said, "Afore ye attend tae the saucy wench, sir, ye may ha' noted by our garb that we serve their royal lordships, the Duke o' Albany and his son, the Earl o' Fife. Having learned that ye fly the Mackintosh banner, we would ken your name and place o' residence. So, if ye will be so kind as—"

"If he *will*?" Marsi exclaimed with an air of surprise. "Faith, he is so proud of his ancestors that he thinks all the rest of the world lies beneath his feet to be trodden on. Who else should he be but mine own husband and that poor lad his own son by a previous, most contentious marriage. Sithee, the lad has reason to behave as he did, having had such a mother as *that* one! Why, I could tell you tales of that hellicat that would curl your livers. He was much wiser in choosing to wed *me*, for I come from nobler and more respectable kinfolk than that nettlesome slink who went before me."

"What happened tae her?" the leader asked, looking speculatively at Ivor, who was having difficulty maintaining his stern demeanor.

"What *happened* to her?" Marsi's eyes widened. "Why, the very thing that *should* come to such women—a bad end! One *so* bad that I shall not sully my lips to relate the details. Moreover, I warrant my husband would be gey wroth with me if I did," she added, casting a dramatically wary look at Ivor that nearly undid him.

Lowering her voice as she turned back to the men, she added, "You have seen for yourself how the man reacts to the slightest dissension. 'Tis a pity that he did not treat *her* as he treats that poor bairn. But, so it is with men like him."

The leader of the four, whose attention had focused on her as she waxed on about Ivor's supposed previous wife, shifted his gaze again to Ivor. His expression carefully under control, the man said, "I would ken your name, sir."

"His name?" Marsi's eyebrows shot upward. "Good lack, do you not recognize him? By his air of importance and the way his previous lady carried on about his nobility, his gey powerful clan, and his vast skill with weaponry, I should think that every man-at-arms in Scotland would ken him by sight. He is—"

"Enough!" Ivor roared. "Get upstairs now before *you* feel my hand."

"Nay, let her speak," the spokesman said. "In troth— But who is this?"

Ivor and Marsi turned as one to see Hetty halfway down the second flight of stairs. Eminently respectable-looking, as always, she gazed from one person to the next with an air of mild astonishment.

Ivor glanced at Marsi, who turned back to Albany's man and said, "Faith, sir, who do you *suppose* she is? I should think you might stretch your wits enough to do some thinking if you mean to be of service to your royal lords. She is my good-mother and his lady mother, of course, the one person I have seen—besides myself, I need hardly say—whom he treats with the greatest respect. You and your men would be wise to treat her so as well."

The spokesman bowed to Hetty, saying, "I trust that we havena distressed ye, your ladyship. We seek only tae learn what guests be staying here now."

Hetty gently raised her eyebrows as if such an explanation had naught to do with her, which, Ivor thought, was the one thing so far that was true.

Marsi said, "I have been telling these men about your son's first wife, madam. I ken fine that you will agree he is much better off to be married to me than to her."

"Och, aye, to be sure," Hetty murmured. "By my troth, I cannot even bring myself to say that woman's name aloud."

"That is perfectly understandable, madam," Ivor said, straight-faced, albeit with effort, since no one could expect Hetty to know the name of a nonexistent female. To the spokesman, he said, "To answer *your* question, however, *we* are the only guests here at present. Three other men stayed overnight, but they went on to Stirling this morning."

"We did meet them, aye, so we'll trouble ye nae further," the man said. "We'll be going on as soon as the innkeeper produces ale for us."

Marsi opened her mouth as if she might try to add something to speed them on their way, but to Ivor's relief, she closed it again and kept silent.

After the four men had quaffed their ale and departed, shutting the door behind them, she looked warily at him. But when he grinned and shook his head at her, still amused by what she had done, he saw her relax.

James said from the stairway above Ivor, "What were ye about, Marsi, tae say such things tae those men? Ye shouldna have told them such a string o' lies."

"It was just another pretense," Marsi said. "Sithee, they are Albany's men."

"So Sir Ivor said tae me, but ye told them that Hetty is his lady mother. What if my uncle kens *that* lady by sight? What if those men describe Hetty so that he recognizes *her*, too, from their description? Sakes, he'll capture us both in a trice if he does recognize her. And wherever did Will go in such a hurry?"

"Into the kitchen," Marsi said. "But don't fret. We did not tell them Sir Ivor's name, although I had a fine one made up for him. And any description they give of Hetty must fit a hundred other women of her age, figure, and deportment."

"I didna ken that ye were this Highlander's wife, me lady," the innkeeper said as he bustled in from the kitchen, startling them all. "Ye should ha' told us as much yestereve, sir. We could ha' put the two o' ye together in one room."

"Faith," Marsi said, staring at him, "did you hear *all* that we were saying?"

"Not all, me lady. But when I saw them ride into me yard, I came in through the kitchen tae see did they mean mischief or no. Sithee, ye canna tell wi' that lot, and we dinna want trouble. But me wife did hear when ye told them who ye be and who this lady be, as well. So, me wife did hasten tae tell me as soon as I came in. Then, I heard ye say summat about a hundred women—"

"You may be easy," Ivor said to him. "Our chambers are just as I requested. The lad here suffers from nightmares, as many bairns do." Shooting a minatory frown at the indignant James, who looked about to deny it, he added, "Therefore, I keep him with me when we travel.

And although my men do fly my banner, I do not"—he shot Marsi a stern glance—"otherwise generally publicize my identity when I travel, for reasons that doubtless you can imagine."

"Och, aye, sir," the innkeeper said with a sincerity that nearly belied Ivor's certainty that the man had no idea what those reasons might be. "I willna be a-boasting o' your presence tae anyone. And I'll see that me good wife says nowt either. But 'tis as well that ye didna tell them rascals any lies. Now, as ye'll be fain tae eat your dinner, I'll ha' them fetch in the rest o' your food for ye straightaway."

When the man had retreated to the kitchen, Hetty said to Ivor, "Do you know, sir, I doubt that our greatest concern is that Albany may recognize my description."

"He might, though," James said. "He is gey clever."

"I do not think we need worry about that," Ivor said, pulling out the stool that Hetty had occupied the previous evening and gesturing for her to sit down.

As she obeyed him, taking her place next to Marsi, Hetty said, "My concern is that Marsi declared herself married. To you, sir, and before more witnesses than she knew. Not that the four were insufficient, knowing of your banner as they did."

Marsi said, "But, Hetty, I—"

Ivor cut her off without compunction, saying, "Take care now, lass. Say what you need to say, but be circumspect. I hear our host returning."

Biting her lip, she glanced at the empty kitchen doorway, then said, "I don't see why anyone need make a song about it. That tale persuaded them to leave us be."

Ivor, understanding Hetty's concern as Marsi clearly

did not, waited until the innkeeper and a maidservant had hurried in, the one stirring up the fire and the other lighting candles on the table. Both returned to the kitchen before he said, "I doubt that her words matter under these circumstances, mistress. Surely, your presence—"

"My presence had naught to do with her declaration, sir, and its result..." She stopped when the maidservant hurried back in to set two jugs on the table.

Will entered quietly in her wake and slipped into his seat beside James.

"What *are* the two of you talking about?" Marsi demanded as soon as the maid had departed again.

"Aye, I want to ken that, myself," James said, looking from one to another.

To Marsi, Ivor said, "We are talking about your declaration of marriage. You may not realize that, in Scotland, such a declaration from one party without immediate denial from the other can mean that the two are legally married."

Marsi's jaw dropped, but it took her a moment to realize that it had.

"You must be jesting," she said then. "I have heard of such marriages, but surely noblemen do not marry in such a way. Moreover, it is the man who has to declare, is it not? And the maiden who has to agree to his declaration?"

"That is not exactly how the law applies," Ivor said. "Sithee, Bishop Traill warned us about it at St. Andrews. He said attempts have been made to trick men into marrying who had no wish to do so."

Marsi looked at Hetty, whose expression was somber.

Jamie's eyes lit. "But I think this is excellent!" he exclaimed.

Marsi heard noises of incipient arrival from the kitchen as Jamie turned to Ivor and added, "You will make her a gey fine hus—"

Her hand on the boy's knee was enough to silence him just as the innkeeper, his wife, and the maidservant entered and began setting platters of food on the table, along with a fresh basket of bannocks.

"We will postpone the rest of this conversation," Ivor said firmly.

Marsi nodded, but her imagination busied itself with thoughts of what it all could mean. The idea of marrying Ivor certainly did not outrage her, as Albany's command to marry Redmyre had.

She had never met Redmyre but had heard enough about him from Annabella and her ladies to develop an aversion to him that nothing would alter. By contrast, she had known Ivor for just days. Yet she viewed the possibility of marrying him as intriguing, even stimulating... although he would be most unlikely to agree.

Why she should feel about him as she did, as dogmatic as he could be, was another matter. Just then, the memory of him stroking her in his bed that first night sent heat flashing through her body, as such memories had ever since then.

It occurred to her that if she should find herself in that position again, she might readily succumb. She certainly would not clout him again.

The bruise on his cheek was nearly gone, but as her gaze fell on the yellowing mark that remained, she felt a twinge of guilt and something else. She had got away with it once, but she thought that Ivor might well retaliate in kind if she ever dared try such a thing again. The thought made her smile. It also made her wonder at herself for seeing anything in such a thought to stir her sense of humor.

She certainly did not want him to punish her, ever, so why the notion that he might was nearly as stimulating as the thought of being in his bed, she could not explain. Surely, there was something amiss in even *having* such strange thoughts.

However, a brief command from him earlier that day had steadied her as nothing else could have. And there could be nothing wrong in thinking about that.

Glancing at him, she saw that he was watching her and wondered if he might somehow discern her thoughts. Feeling suddenly hot all over, she told herself that the sensible thing was to look away.

Just then, to her surprise, she noted increased color in *his* face.

Jamie spoke, for she heard his voice. But she had no idea what he had said.

Ivor looked away to reach for the platter of sliced roast beef, holding it out to Jamie, who helped himself to more meat. Offering it next to Will, Ivor returned his attention to his own trencher.

Marsi fixed her attention on her food, too. But her mind continued to occupy itself with Sir Ivor, presenting her with fresh images to consider.

First, there was Ivor as he had looked when he'd entered the royal nursery.

He had not wanted her to go with them. She had seen as much for herself, although she had looked at him then only in brief glances. She had feared that if she stared, he would guess that she had been the lass in his bed.

Remembering how irritated she had felt when he had *not* recognized her, she nearly smiled but managed to stop at the first twitch of her lips. She did not want anyone to ask what she found to be so amusing.

⁓

Ivor wondered what had amused her. She had scarcely looked away from her food since they had all stopped talking. A glance at Hetty showed him that she was also eyeing Marsi. Just then, Hetty shifted her gaze to him, speculatively.

He knew that she had to be wondering what would happen next. She clearly knew as well as he did what the consequences of Marsi's declaration *could* be:

Albany would certainly raise a dust. Having planned to marry Marsi to one of his minions, the duke clearly believed that he had the right to do so. There was the fact, too, that Marsi had returned to Turnberry after Annabella's death, instead of to her own home or that of a family member, and had likely done so at the King's command or by his wish, which indicated that his grace felt responsible for her.

Then, she had said that she hoped Sir Malcolm Drummond, the most powerful member of her clan, would *speak* for her to the King rather than simply forbid her marriage to Redmyre. Having suspected then that Marsi might be a royal ward, Ivor remained uncertain of what role Sir Malcolm might yet play. But he was certain that his grace must be her guardian. She had not admitted that he was, but it would explain Albany's belief that he could not only control whom she married but also award her estates to the man. His influence over the King was long established.

Surely, with his grace and Albany doubtless objecting to it, Marsi's impulsive declaration would come to nowt. But Ivor needed to be sure about that.

Noting that Marsi was staring at her trencher and no longer eating, he glanced at James and Will. Both boys had also finished their meals.

"We'll talk more anon," Ivor said. "For now, I think that James and Marsi should go upstairs with you, mistress. Aodán can use Will's help in the stables this afternoon, and I must go out for a while."

"Where will you go?" James asked.

"I thought that I might take a closer look at yon cathedral."

"May I go with you? Now that those men are gone, it must be safe enough."

Ivor shot a look at Hetty, who nodded and said briskly, "You and Marsi can cast dice or some such thing upstairs, James. Recall that others likely heard Sir"—she glanced at Will—"Sir Hawk order you to keep to your room today."

"Only those men heard him. And even so—"

"Come along, Jamie," Marsi said. "He has had enough of us for one day. We'll see if your luck is still in or if the dice decide to be kind to me."

He continued to look at Ivor until Ivor gestured toward the stairway. Then, with a sigh, James followed the women.

With Will at his heels, Ivor went into the yard, grateful to see that the snow had nearly stopped. "Did you recognize those men earlier, Will?" he asked as they approached the stable.

"Aye, sure, laird. The first one o' them in the door serves Lord Fife at Doune Castle and might ken me. When I saw him, I hied m's self tae the kitchen."

"That was wise of you," Ivor said.

"Aye, laird, I thought so," Will said, looking up at him with a grin.

When Aodán greeted them in the stable, Ivor said, "We'll spend at least one more night here, so I thought Will might help you in the stables this afternoon."

Aodán smiled at the lad and said, "Tell Sean Dubh that I said ye should show him what ye can do."

Nodding, Will ran toward Ivor's squire.

As they watched him go, Ivor said in the Gaelic, "I've not decided yet whether we'll go straight to St. Andrews or take a more circumspect route."

"I heard those four men earlier, talking," Aodán replied. "According to them, Albany has men on every road in·Fife. One of them mentioned that they seek a young woman with red hair."

Recalling with relief that Marsi's hair had remained well covered so that the men had seen only her dark eyebrows, Ivor said, "Did they mention the Perth road?"

"They did not. I heard their leader say that those they seek cannot have got this far so fast. However, he also said that the duke reached Stirling yesterday."

"Aye, well, Albany is ever the spider at the center of its web, sending others out to do its stinging. But I don't want to rush off in the wrong direction to evade him *or* them. I mean to walk a bit now," he added. "I want to think about all this."

"Mayhap I should go with ye, sir."

"Do you think I cannot look after myself?"

Aodán grimaced but did not back down. "Ye ken fine that I think only that two men be safer than one, Sir Ivor. I'd warrant that your lord father and Himself would agree with me. They'd say that ye should take a horse, come to that."

"But you answer to me, do you not?" Ivor said softly.

"I do."

"Then ask our lads which of them is yearning for exercise and will not mind a trudge through the snow. I want a look at yon cathedral. I take your meaning, Aodán, but I want you to take charge here."

Nodding, Aodán returned to the stables. Moments later, the youngest of the four men-at-arms, Gib Maclean, strode toward Ivor. He wore his plaid over his breeks and tunic, his sword slung across his back, and his dirk on his belt.

Ivor, although dressed much the same, wore only his dirk.

They made short work of the steep path to the cathedral. When they reached it, Ivor told Gib to look for someone to show him about.

"I'm going to find the sacristan," he said. "I won't need protection here. The Bishop of Dunblane is an ally."

～

Marsi's mind was *not* on casting dice. Her thoughts had followed Ivor up the hill to the cathedral. She understood why he had not taken Jamie. Not only would a bishop of the Kirk be likely to recognize the King's younger son but also, Ivor could not have a frank talk with the bishop if Jamie or she were nearby.

And Ivor would not want to let the boy out of his sight in town, no matter how much he might trust the Bishop of Dunblane.

Were the two men talking yet? What would the bishop say about what she had done? Would he recognize her name? He might. Dunblane could not be more than ten or fifteen miles from Kincardine and was doubtless even closer to other Drummond holdings with which she was less familiar. It would be natural for the bishop to know many Drummonds by name, including any who had served the King or Queen. Heaven knew whom else he might tell if he did know her.

Grimacing, she tried to attend to Jamie's cast of the dice, but he scooped them up, saying, "This game is tiresome. I don't care who wins, and neither do—"

Breaking off at a light double rap on the door, he watched as Hetty moved to answer it and Will came in.

"Aodán said I could come up," Will said. "But if ye dinna want me—"

"Aye, we do though," Jamie said. "I was getting bored, playing games."

"Ye should ha' come out wi' me," Will said. "I like helping Aodán."

"I want to go out now." Jamie looked at Hetty, adding, "If I just go to the stable with Will, Sir Ivor won't mind, because Aodán is there, and Sean Dubh, too, since he has not come upstairs yet to see to his duties before supper."

When Hetty agreed, the boys fled.

Marsi shook her head at them, but Hetty said. "Will is

the first youngster near Jamie's own age that he has seen simply as a friend. I think Will is good for him."

Marsi agreed, and they were still chatting desultorily sometime later when Sir Ivor rapped on the door. When Hetty called to him to enter, he did so, shutting the door behind him instead of leaving it ajar as he usually did.

"James is not with you?" he said as Hetty took her seat again.

"He is out in the stable with Will," Marsi said. "What did you learn, sir?"

He smiled. "So you guessed my intent, did you? Well, put simply, if one party declares before witnesses that he or she has married and the other party hears the declaration and does not deny it—and both parties are beyond the age of consent—the Kirk and the Scottish Crown both recognize that marriage as legal."

Feeling surprisingly calm, Marsi said, "Did the bishop suggest a remedy?"

"If both parties seek to undo the marriage, annulment is the most suitable way, he said. It is also relatively easy unless they have consummated the union. He also said that if property is involved and the two want to *stay* married, they must seek marriage in the Kirk as soon as possible to assure an enduring record of the marriage."

"So the most likely thing to happen is just an annulment, then."

"I expect that Albany will demand one as soon as he learns what has happened. However, he will need clear standing under the law to demand it."

She sighed. "He will have that standing if he unseats

Davy Stewart as Governor. And he will assume it even without that. Albany can control his grace, sir, whether as Governor or simply because he will be determined to do so."

"So, you are the King's ward, then," Ivor said.

Chapter 13————————————

He saw that he had startled her, but she simply nodded.

As he exchanged a look with Hetty, Marsi said, "I expect the bishop told you that I am a royal ward. I should have told you, myself."

"You did, lass, I guessed as much from things that you said. Sithee, I ken fine that you meant only to divert Albany's men today, to keep them from taking undue notice of James. And you did that gey cleverly."

"At your expense," she said. Drawing a breath, she added, "Doubtless everyone here knows that tale by now. I told Jamie not to tell you that he does, but I was wrong to do that."

"Aye, well, I'd wager that Albany's men are having a laugh and felicitating each other on not having married women like either of my fictitious wives."

He expected her to smile, but she caught her lip briefly between her teeth, then said contritely, "I'm sorry to have put *you* in such a position, sir."

"And so you should be," Hetty said.

He dismissed the apology with a gesture, saying, "I was there, lass. And, as I said before, Bishop Traill did warn us about Scotland's unusual marriage laws."

"But you could not speak without calling me a liar," she said. "Then, heaven knows what might have happened. Your primary task is to prevent Albany from capturing Jamie. To have exposed my lie to his men might have endangered us all."

"True," he agreed. "But I confess I did not spare a thought for Jamie or for the danger. I was trying so hard not to laugh at your description of my dreadful first wife that I thought of nowt else. Just the thought that I might somehow have married such a vixen as the one you described was enough to keep me silent."

"So, instead, you are now—evidently—married to me," she said in a small but dignified voice. "You cannot like that any better, sir. Moreover, it could be the death of you if Albany believes that we *have* married without his consent."

"Sakes, he won't murder me," Ivor said.

"Will he not?" She frowned. "Often, if someone fails to do as he bids, the person suffers a fatal accident. I *don't* want that to happen to you."

"I can look after myself."

"Nay, then, you do *not* know him at his worst. Why do you think Annabella was so determined to keep Davy and Jamie away from him? Tell him, Hetty."

But to Ivor's relief, Hetty remained silent with her hands folded in her lap.

"Marsi," he said, "I know that the Queen was afraid for them. But she was their mother. In troth, the Scottish people would rise against Albany if he harmed James. Then Davy would order Albany arrested, and Parliament would try him."

"Mayhap they would. But Albany would have his way. He nearly always does. Sithee, the King shocked him when he let Davy take over as Governor." She stopped to draw breath, but Ivor sensed that she had more to say and held his peace.

She added with a sigh, "I once heard Albany say that if the Scottish chiefs were still choosing the King of Scots, they would have named *him* King long ago."

"Mayhap they would have," Ivor said. "Most Scots prefer a strong King."

"But as things are," Marsi said, "Albany *cannot* become King unless he clears the way for himself."

"I ken fine that the man is devious and untrustworthy, lass. But—"

"If there is *any* way that he can seize the throne, he will do it," she insisted. "Good lack, until three years ago, he'd ruled Scotland for nearly a decade without even *being* King. He can be utterly ruthless, sir. If he gets hold of Jamie, he will arrange for him to die young or terrorize him into doing his every bidding."

Ivor did not want to argue with her, certainly not about Albany. Forcing calm into his voice, he said, "He will find it harder than you think to terrorize James. That lad has an old head on his young shoulders and will, in time, hold his own against men like Albany. But I do agree with you *and* her grace that we cannot trust Albany with physical custody of James. I will do all in my power to prevent that."

"Then we cannot let Albany find out about my declaration, sir."

"It is too late to avoid that," he said. "In my experience, however keenly one watches for pitfalls, one cannot always avoid the worst. You gave Albany's men a good story to tell, lass. They'll repeat it, just as Will's master will talk about Jamie. In troth, I expect to find *that* sour gentleman on our heels soon, too."

Her expressive face revealed her frustration. "Then what are we to do?"

"We know of at least two options, and we can seek counsel from Bishop Traill when we reach St. Andrews to see if he can suggest more. It is likely, though, that he will say what the Bishop of Dunblane said."

"Then what do you think we can do?"

"You must make the choice, lass. I will do as you wish."

"Y-you will?"

"Aye, sure," he said. "If I tried to annul a declaration I did not deny, people would call me a fool or mayhap even a scoundrel for taking advantage of you. Then, they would call you worse names. Such things are always worse for the woman even if the man is *more* at fault. You've done nowt to deserve that. It will be bad enough for you if Albany demands an annulment but worse if I do."

"But why?"

Ivor grimaced. He had wanted to spare her the worst details. But he knew that she would demand them now. And, in truth, she had a right to know.

When she let her impatience show, he said, "To put it plainly, lass, by declaring us married, you created a situation in which most people will assume that we have already consummated our union."

Her mouth dropped open then, so he added gently, "There are ways to prove we have not, but they are unpleasant and would do your reputation no good."

"Mercy, what have I done? I had no idea! I did know

that people could declare themselves married and *be* married if that was what they wanted. But I did *not* know that simply saying that one *is* married could lead to such a muddle."

Hetty shifted position and looked as if she were about to remind Marsi that she had warned her many times not to let her tongue run away with her.

Ivor silenced her with a look.

But he realized that Marsi had seen both the look and Hetty's primly folded lips when she said, "You need not protect me from Hetty, sir. I ken fine what she would say. And, as usual, she would be right. I should have thought *before* I acted. I failed to do that, and it is too late now to do aught about it. Isn't it?"

"Aye, lass, it is," he said.

She sighed again, started to speak, and then pressed her lips together in much the same way that Hetty had after Ivor had looked at her.

"What is it, Marsi-lass?" he asked. "You need fear no consequences from aught that you say to me. I want to know what you are thinking."

Her crimson cheeks told him that her thoughts had to do with him personally. But considering the topic, that went without saying.

To Hetty, he said quietly, "Mayhap James should come back inside now. He can bring Will with him if he likes. I own, I'd be easier of mind if they were both under your eye or mine, rather than out where any visitor might recognize them."

Nodding, Hetty moved to go but paused with a querying look as she began to close the door. Since neither Marsi's reputation nor his would suffer now from being there together unchaperoned, he gestured and Hetty shut the door firmly behind her.

He gave Marsi time to collect her thoughts. Then he said, "Whatever you are thinking, lass, I'll do what I can to help."

"You do not want to be married to me." she said. "I ken that fine. I have made a rare mess of things, sir. I don't *know* what to do."

"Then perhaps I should make a few more things plain to you," he said.

Visibly, she braced herself, but he drew her up to stand before him and put a hand to one soft cheek, then tilted her face up so he could watch her expression.

Looking into her eyes, he said, "I won't let you be the judge of what I want or don't want, Marsi. We created this muddle, as you call it, together. But we do have choices. It is just a matter of discussing them and deciding what to do."

"You make it sound easy, sir. It is not."

"We won't know that until we try. Consider this: We can ignore the whole thing and pray that no one else takes heed of it. I think that is a bad choice, because we would always be wondering if an enemy might use the information against us."

"Albany."

"He is bound to hear about it. If he doesn't guess that you are the one who spun his men that wives' tale, all it will take is for one of them to see you and tell him so. But he will catch up with us eventually in any event."

"His men may not even remember," she said. "They talk to so many others."

"You can believe me when I say that those men *will*

remember you and will remember all that you said to them today."

She grimaced, and he wished he could put his arms around her and promise to protect her. But he wanted her to decide without undue influence from him. He knew that she was attracted to him, but her tendency to flirt with nearly any male she met might, he feared, have deceived him about the strength of that attraction.

He had meant everything he'd said to her. Her allure was undeniable and strong. It had increased tenfold since the night that he'd seen her fleeing down the corridor at Turnberry. Any misgivings he harbored about their sudden need to discuss marriage stemmed from other concerns—his parents and grandparents, especially. But such concerns were of less importance to him than his desire to protect her from the consequences of her actions... and his own.

When he remembered that he had once condemned her pretenses while committing similar sins himself to protect James, it seemed ironic but fitting that their own misdeeds had brought them both to where they were.

One of the things he liked best about her was that she could so easily stir his amusement. And yet that very ability had led to their undoing, in that his delight had blinded him to the significance of what she was saying.

Even so, he would never condemn her for being able to make him laugh.

Just being with her improved any mood. Even when she irritated or angered him, he felt a solid connection to her and understood her more easily than anyone he had known outside his own family.

In truth, now that she had come into his life, he would

resist letting her walk out of it. Come what might, he would do all that he could to prevent Albany, duke or no duke, from using her as his political pawn.

Marsi had been watching Ivor, trying to guess what he was thinking. Gray outside light filtered into the bedchamber through the shutters, making it shadowy but also making her feel as if, just then, they were alone in the world and safe.

She knew that they were not. Albany would seek an annulment whether she requested one or indignantly refused to do so. The duke would not let a little thing like a legally declared marriage sway him from his determination to give her to Redmyre. Nor, she feared, would Redmyre regard such a marriage as an obstacle.

He just wanted Cargill.

Collecting herself, she said, "I do not know what to make of you, sir. You sound as if you want me to accept that we *are* married. I cannot do that so easily."

"Is the notion so distasteful?"

"Nay, it is not. And, if it were, it could *never* be as bad as marriage to Redmyre would be. Just the thought of living with that man is loathsome. To have to marry him just because he wants my land and does not care a whit about me or what I want would be horrid. Sakes, that would be a horrid fate for anyone."

"I agree," he said.

"I believe that you do. But, as bad as marriage to Redmyre would be, if Albany ordered your death because my foolish blethering tricked—nay, *forced*—you into marrying me, I couldn't bear it."

"He may *want* to murder me for that, or for taking Jamie to St. Andrews, but he won't do it. Not the way that you fear. He cannot arrest me for marrying you. The worst that may happen is that he'll find a way to seize control of your land."

"But he *could* arrest you, because Annabella told me of just such a case," Marsi said. "I had forgotten until you mentioned his seizing my land. He called it 'a theft of royal property' when such a thing happened before. And he hanged the man! I do not recall many details, but the girl was also a ward of the Crown."

"Well, Albany is not the Crown yet, much as he might want to be."

"Still, he took that other girl's property under Crown protection, which means, in fact, that he controls it himself. As Royal Chamberlain, he controls *all* Crown property." She sighed. "I do not think that we can defeat him."

"I'm willing to try if you are," he said. "In the eyes of Kirk and Crown, we are married. As to your property, I cannot say. But we won't starve without it."

"I do *not* want to lose Cargill," she said. "You must believe that."

He nodded. "I would *dis*believe you only if you'd said otherwise. But you need decide only about us. The Bishop of Dunblane said our marriage should protect you straightaway from Albany *and* Redmyre and will certainly do so if we consummate the union. Also, although Albany may threaten to seize Cargill, Redmyre cannot get it without marrying you."

She exhaled a long breath, feeling her tension ease. Although she was not sure that she ought to believe what he'd said, her trust in him had grown strong.

"How long will it take us to travel from here to St. Andrews?" she asked.

"Three or four days if the weather does not delay us further," he said. "Wolf has friends hereabouts with ships. He said I need only get a message to the Abbot of Lindores at Newburgh to have one meet us on the Fife coast of the Firth of Tay."

"The *north* coast of the firth would be safer from Albany," she said. "From there, we could also get a message to my uncle, applying for his protection."

"Sakes, lass, Stobhall lies miles out of our way!"

"You do mean for us to go through Strathallan though, do you not?"

He nodded. "We'll avoid the glens by following the Allan Water and then the river Earn through Strathearn to the Fife coast of the Firth of Tay."

"But we'd reach Kincardine long before Lindores Abbey," she said. "In troth, Kincardine would be an excellent place to stop for a night."

"I ken fine that the castle and all of the land around it is Drummond territory, but Albany kens that, too," Ivor said. "The nearby towns will be full of his men."

"But, don't you see, that is *why* we should go to Kincardine. We can avoid the towns by riding up Kincardine Glen right to the gates of the castle."

"How safe is that path after a heavy snowfall?" he asked.

"But the snow stopped hours ago. If we have sunshine tomorrow, by the time we reach the glen..." She hesitated.

"What?"

"Its sides are gey steep," she admitted ruefully. "And

the track along the Ruthven Water is narrow. But our horses are sure-footed."

Ivor frowned. "I'd prefer to avoid the lower glens if we can, because we'd be bound to encounter heavy snow-drifts in any one of them."

"But Albany's men might be less likely to look for us in one," she said.

~

"That is a point to consider," Ivor said. It was, although he knew that Albany would find them easily enough, given time. "How far is it up that glen to the castle?"

"About two miles, I think."

They were ten or eleven miles from the Perth road, he knew, and thirteen miles was not a bad day's travel.

"I'll think about it, lass. But, I'll tell you now that I'd liefer get Jamie to St. Andrews before Albany even catches wind of our trail."

Despite that wishful thinking, he knew that time was running out for them.

~

In the great chamber at Stirling Castle, the Duke of Albany spent a few moments assessing the nervous townsman who stood before him. Then, glancing at Red-myre, a short distance away, picking lint from his maroon doublet while he observed them, Albany shifted his dour gaze to his own son.

In his fortieth year, Murdoch Stewart, now Earl of Fife, was as dark as his sire but shorter and thicker of body. The wariness in his demeanor, which was habitual in his father's presence, rarely failed to irritate the duke.

Without comment, Albany turned back to the townsman and said softly, "Lord Fife tells me you have news for us, sirrah."

"His lordship did say that ye'd be interested, sir. But I canna say about that. I went tae him just tae report me missing lad, is all."

"Tell him about the boy who tried to intercede whilst you were punishing your lad," Fife said impatiently. "*That* is what will interest him, sirrah."

"Aye, sure," the townsman said. "I be Lucken the Tanner o' Doune, m'lord. See you, I were a-taking leather tae the lad responsible for a broken rein when the other ill young rogue flung hisself from his horse and tried tae interfere."

"How old was this young rogue? And why did you tell Fife about him?"

"Sakes, he canna ha' been more than eight... mayhap nine at the most, m'lord. But such a mouth as he had! As voluble as an angry priest, he were."

"You do interest me," Albany said, his tone still soft but now carrying even more chilliness than usual in it. "Describe this arrogant lad to me."

"Aye, arrogant. That be the right word, I'd agree. Why, when he ordered me tae desist..." He paused, clearly noting the duke's increasing impatience. "Aye, sure," the tanner said. "He had auburn hair and were a square-built lad, summat like m'lord Fife. See you, it were his manner what struck me—so odd a bearing in a lad so young. He had a firmer chin than most lads his age, and dark eyes, I think."

"Did you take note of others in his party?"

"Aye, sure, a man grown but not more than five-and-twenty, whose demeanor were as commanding as the lad's. I thought he might be his father, and the lad aping him. I saw two females as well, but I canna tell ye more."

"What color hair had they?"

Lucken shrugged. "Both looked dark-haired wi' fair skin, like cream. But, in troth, a man canna see a woman's hair when she rides hooded and veiled, my lord."

"Any others with them?"

"A half-dozen men-at-arms, I think. Their banner had a hawk flying on it, but none o' this gets me my lad back, m'lord."

"It might, if the young rascal followed them," Albany said. "Do you think he might have done such a thing?"

"There'd be nae telling. He's a stubborn lad, is Will. Sakes, but I'm no so sure I *want* him back. I'll trouble ye no further, any road. But if I do find him—"

"I am more interested in the others you saw." Albany's gaze shifted back to his son. "Did you chance to learn where they went?"

"Nay, my lord," Fife said, flushing. "My men scoured every inn and alehouse to Dunblane and beyond. They did hear about bairns now and now, and females, but none to match our lad's description, nor that of the tanner's lad. They did see one Highland chappie getting his backside well skelped at an inn north of Dunblane, but that *cannot* have been Ja—"

"No names," Albany interjected with more curtness than usual.

"Beg pardon, sir," Fife said. Then with a half-smile, he added, "My lads did tell a good tale about those Highlanders. See you, the one skelping his son caught a devilish scold for it from his lady wife...if she *was* a lady.

They said she is his second wife and that the first was an even rarer vixen. Then his lady mother came downstairs, and... But I'm telling the tale poorly, sir. My lads told it better."

"What did these ladies look like?" Albany asked. "Did they tell you that?"

"Aye, sir. The wife was about twenty, they thought, the mother nearer fifty. If a second lad was there," he said to the townsman, "my men did not mention him."

"Will does keep himself tae himself when he chooses."

Ignoring them, Albany motioned to Redmyre, who stepped forward.

"'Tis little enough we've heard," Albany said to him. "But I'm inclined to take heed of it, Dunblane being central to so many routes. 'Tis Drummond territory, too, and we have discussed your approaching certain persons and establishments in the area. You will be glad to attend to your own interests there, and perhaps you will want to take this fellow along, in the event that he can recognize our party."

Redmyre frowned. "Wi' respect, my lord duke, I doubt he would enjoy the trip, since he has left his tannery untended to bring this information to Stirling. I'll take mine own men and will send news back to you when I have any."

"Good," Albany said. "Be off with you, then. Fife will extend our thanks to Master Lucken and reward him for the information he has provided us."

Redmyre nodded curtly to the visibly bewildered tanner and made a more formal obeisance in the general direction of Albany. Then, without another word, he left the chamber and shouted for his men and horses.

Chapter 14 _____

Although Ivor had not yet said aye or nay to following Kincardine Glen, Marsi took hope from the fact that he had not flatly declared that they would not.

She would have liked to add that her uncle's men-at-arms would keep any strangers out of the glen. But she had taken ample enough measure of Sir Ivor Mackintosh to know that if she pushed him to make a decision before he was ready, he would be as likely as she would be to dig in his heels.

Accordingly, she said, "If it will be days yet before we can talk with Bishop Traill, I think we should go on as we have been, don't you?"

"If that is what you want," he said. "But you ought to consider how you will answer if Albany does catch up with us and asks if we have consummated our marriage. If you say we have not, he is likely to take you in charge immediately. If you can honestly say we have, I should be able to prevent that."

"But you would not be able to keep him from taking Jamie," Marsi said. "So he is *not* going to catch us, and that is all we need say about that." A second thought stirred. "If we are not going to seek shelter with my uncle at Kincardine—"

"*If* Sir Malcolm is even there."

"He does sometimes stay there in winter. But, if we are not to go there, do you think that Bishop Traill can keep Albany from taking me in charge?"

"I cannot answer that, but I doubt it. No women live at St. Andrews Castle, so the bishop cannot offer you sanctuary there. In your behalf, he would be able to exert authority over Albany only as he would over any member of his flock."

"He had enough influence to banish Albany from Annabella's bedchamber at Scone," Marsi said, touching her ring.

"Aye, for the worthy Traill does have a way about him. But recall that Scone Abbey also lies within his purview, as does Lindores, and his authority must always be greater on Kirk ground. Moreover, Albany is a religious man in his own way, so doubtless he fears for his immortal soul if he angers Traill. But whilst he may have bowed to Traill then, the bishop is not your guardian, lass. Your best hope for protection against him must be his grace or a husband of your own."

"Art truly willing to be that husband, sir?"

"More so each day," he said with a look warm enough to stir tremors of heat throughout her body.

Trying to focus on the important matter at hand, she said, "You have not always approved of me, or of my behavior."

"True, but I would have stepped in had anyone else taken exception to it," he said with a gruff note in his voice that stirred sensations stronger than mere warmth, sensations that she had never felt before. "I find myself feeling unnaturally protective of you even when I want to wring your lovely neck," he added dryly.

Despite the depth of her concerns, Marsi could not help smiling at that.

Ivor welcomed her smile, but it did things to him that told him he should not be alone with her much longer. His desire for her was already strong, and the fact that she had legally become his made her even more desirable. But pressing her now for an answer would be unwise, he knew. She had to decide for herself.

A rap at the door preceded Hetty's announcement that the boys were hungry and supper would shortly be ready. The interruption broke the spell between them, if spell it was. "Wash your face and hands, lass," Ivor said as he went to let Hetty in. "I will go and do the same. Then we'll eat our supper and retire early. If this good weather holds, I want to be off as soon as we know the road is safe."

Leaving her in Hetty's capable hands, he went to his chamber and found both boys waiting impatiently to eat.

After supper, when Ivor went outside to confer with Aodán, he noted with satisfaction that the dark sky revealed a blanket of stars. Although the clouds had disappeared, which often meant colder air, it seemed warmer.

Truly, he thought, the gods of weather seemed unable to make up their minds whether to present winter in earnest or pretend that spring was nigh.

"That snow's no sticking to the road, sir," Aodán said when Ivor entered the stable, as if Aodán's thoughts had followed a path similar to his master's.

"I want to be away after we break our fast," Ivor said. "The lads can pack the sumpters whilst those inside are eating. I'll see that their things are ready to go."

Aodán smiled. "Young Will does be a good worker, sir. I'd like to have him about all the time. But our lad seems bent on keeping him by his side. Sakes, but ye could have knocked me down with a broom straw when I saw him mucking out stalls alongside Will before Mistress Hetty came and collected them."

"We'll let their relationship proceed as it will," Ivor said, recalling Marsi's words on the subject. "James has had few friends his own age in his short life."

"And Will's a good lad," Aodán said. "Come to that, both o' them have lost their mams, and Will has lost nigh his whole family. D'ye think that that townsman will come looking for him?"

"I'd expected to see him before now," Ivor said. "Tell our men to wear whatever they like tomorrow. Our Highland gear was a good notion for a short time, but anyone might follow such a colorful group as easily as Will did."

Aodán nodded, and Ivor left, meaning to return to his room. But no sooner did he step back into the yard than the rising moon caught his eye.

The peaceful night was beautiful. Not a breeze stirred. The only sound was that of a nearby stream until one of the horses snorted in the stable. It was a perfect night to be watching the moonrise with a beautiful woman.

He wondered what Marsi was thinking, only to decide that, in fact, he knew. He was also confident that he knew what choice she would make, but the moment that thought crossed his mind, he looked skyward and told himself not to be a fool. Life never went according to one's wishes and rarely according to one's plans.

Suppressing his doubts, telling himself that what came would come, he instantly saw himself trying to explain the situation to his father and grandfather, each as temperamental as he could be himself.

He could hardly tell them that, due to circumstances he would rather not describe, he found himself married to a ward of the Crown. That would *not* go down well. Nor would it help to add that, because of that marriage, he had doubtless made a lifelong enemy of the Duke of Albany.

"Och, aye," he muttered. "That will be a fine talk, that will." Then, sighing, he added silently, *And that's if this business with Marsi goes as I hope it will.*

He decided that at the least, he had better let his sister and Fin know that he was nearing Perth, and alert them to the likelihood that he might need help.

The boys were on their pallet talking when he entered the bedchamber, and he let them chatter until he had got into bed. Then, he hushed them with a single word and fell into deep slumber from which he did not stir until dawn.

An hour later, he and the others were on the road, and by midday, they were nearing the village of Blackford on the south bank of Allan Water. Although they could see its buildings in the distance, it was still a half-hour away.

Ivor called a halt, leading the way to some flat boulders near the burn, where they could eat the food the inn's servants had packed for them. Dismounting, Ivor called Aodán to him and said in Scots, "I want you to see if Blackford is already crawling with Albany's men. "Take Will with you, but do something to disguise him, in the event that any of the tanner's men are seeking him here."

"I dinna need Will, sir. I ken how Albany's men look as well as ye do."

"Aye, sure," Ivor said. "But the tanner's men are just as dangerous to Will, and if Murdoch Stewart's men from Doune are there instead of Albany's, the lad is more likely than you are to recognize them if they are *not* wearing black clothing."

"Aye, for he also comes from Doune," Aodán admitted. "I'd no ken the Duke o' Albany himself if he put off his usual garb."

"Do it as quietly as you can," Ivor said. "The lady Marsaili still wants to go to Kincardine from here. She suggested that we ride up Kincardine Glen, which lies near where this road crosses the Stirling-Perth road, just two miles ahead."

"What d'ye think o' that notion, sir?"

"We'll talk about that after I know what awaits us in Blackford," Ivor said. "Come to that, Aodán, I want to know about *any* large contingent of men in Blackford. Albany has many allies."

Aodán nodded and turned away, shouting for Will to help with the horses, only to hear Will say quietly, "I be here, sir. I thought ye might be wanting me."

Neither man had noticed his approach. But Aodán grinned, patted the boy's shoulder, and told him that he would be glad of his help.

Ivor, noting that Marsi had dismounted and was watching them, handed his reins to Will and went to join her near the water.

Marsi watched Ivor approach, wondering what he had been discussing with Aodán. The way he'd looked at her when the two men parted made her think at first that they might have been talking about her. However, Ivor looked unnaturally wary as he drew near, as if he expected trouble.

Noting that Hetty had kept Jamie from following Will and was supervising him as he washed his hands and face for their meal, Marsi returned her attention to Ivor. Bluntly, she said, "Have you decided yet, sir, which way we will go?"

His eyes narrowed at her tone, but he said evenly, "We will wait here until Aodán and Will have a look at the town. I want to know if Albany's men or the tanner's are there. No one will suspect a horseman with a boy up behind him."

"If the tanner's men are there…"

"I told Aodán to disguise Will a bit. But I doubt they'll run into trouble."

To draw him back to her question regarding their route, she said, "If they do see Albany's men or the tanner's, what will *we* do?"

"We'll avoid the town," he said. "Since we'd have to go into Blackford to cross the Allan Water and continue northeastward, we'd do better then to skirt it by riding into those hills southeast of us if I only knew of a suitable place for us to go."

"Hetty might know," Marsi said. "We'll ask her. I do still think that if we can get to Kincardine, we'll be safe there. The glen itself is guarded, sir, and the people know me well. They will not let harm come to us."

He did not reply, and Hetty, whom Marsi had been eyeing as they talked, quickly responded to a gesture to join them. "What is it, my lady?" she asked.

"Sir Ivor wants to avoid Blackford if Albany's men or others seeking Will are there. Since the Allan Water keeps us from going north without entering the town, we hoped you might know of a place to stay if we must in those hills yonder."

Frowning thoughtfully, Hetty said, "I ken one such place, to be sure. 'Tis a wee alehouse in a clachan not too far this side of the road from Stirling to Perth. If we decide to go to Kincardine, we can follow a fisherman's track much of the way."

Ivor looked at Marsi, and he was frowning. "I've just recalled that you said this Redmyre chap owns land on both sides of the Firth of Tay, lass. If we make for the Fife coast, might we cross his southern estate? Do you ken where it lies?"

"Annabella described it only as a valuable estate with a high tower that overlooks the firth and the river Earn where they meet."

"Then it must lie west of the river," he said. "I mean to keep south and east of that river, so we should avoid trouble with him. I don't recall any way to cross the Earn near its confluence with the firth. It's gey turbulent there, and deep."

"It is not my place to *offer* advice to you, sir," Hetty said. "But…"

Lifting an eyebrow, Ivor said, "I think that you have more than earned the right to do so, mistress. What would you advise?"

"That her ladyship is right to suggest going to Kincardine, sir. It is not only nearby and well guarded but the guards will recognize us or agree to summon someone who will. Also, they will think naught of our having two boys with us."

"What if Sir Malcolm chances to be there? Do you have the same faith that her ladyship does that he will aid her in avoiding Albany's plan for her future?"

"I cannot say that, sir," Hetty said. "But I do believe that Sir Malcolm will honor her declaration of marriage. One of his sisters married in such a way, in the teeth of their father's fury. The old laird let be, asking no more than that they marry properly in the Kirk. I believe that Sir Malcolm will do the same, especially . . ."

She glanced at Marsi, who grimaced, knowing what Hetty was *not* saying.

Looking at Ivor, Marsi found him eyeing her quizzically. She knew then that he had followed Hetty's train of thought as easily as she had.

Bluntly, she said, "Especially if we consummate this mad marriage that I managed to contrive for us. That *is* what you want to say, is it not, Hetty?"

Ivor reacted more strongly to Marsi's words than he had to Hetty's, and in a much more physical way. The thought of a consummation with her had teased his mind ever since the subject had arisen. That she had said the words herself seemed to make the likelihood of its happening much stronger. He possessed better sense, however, than to stick his oar into their discussion.

Meeting the lass's gaze, Hetty said as bluntly as she had, "Aye, that *is* what I'd recommend, my lady. You must know your uncle well enough to realize that if you tell him you are married but cannot look him in the eye and declare that you have consummated the union, he is more likely to lock you in a bedchamber and *send* for Albany than to do aught else. Kincardine sits in Albany's dominion of Fife, after all, not miles away in Perthshire as Cargill and Stobhall do."

"True," Marsi said with a sigh.

"Aye, it is," Hetty said. "And as strong as Albany's authority is in Perthshire, it is stronger here. I doubt that your uncle would willingly draw his ire by aiding you in your consummation or ignoring its lack. There now. I ken fine that you did not want to hear that, but I do believe that is how he would behave."

"And *I* still think he will honor Annabella's wishes," Marsi said. "He will perfectly understand why she opposed Albany's offering me *and* Cargill to Lindsay of Redmyre. My own father held those lands in my mother's name, after all, not his own. And they came to me from my mother. But Albany would hand them over to Redmyre, kittle and kine, just to win Redmyre's vote for the Governorship."

Ivor, noting that her temper was rising, prepared to intercede, if only to keep peace between the two women. But Hetty made that step unnecessary.

"Mayhap you are right," she said calmly. "There is James now, looking for his food. Shall we go and see what the innkeeper's people have provided for us?"

Noting the stunned look on Marsi's face, Ivor had all he could do not to grin at Hetty's tactics. He would remember them.

With a strong sense of hopeful anticipation, he decided

to let the seeds that Hetty had planted have some time to take root.

⌒

Marsi had had other arguments to offer, but Hetty's calm reply had taken the wind from her sails. It did not help that when she looked at Ivor, he gazed steadily back at her... until his lips twitched.

"What?" she demanded.

His eyebrows arced, reminding her that like many men, he did not appreciate curtness unless it was his own.

Moderating her tone, she said, "I expect that you still think I'm wrong."

"I do not know Sir Malcolm," he said. "I do know that I've not heard anyone describe him as a man likely to oppose Albany. Forbye, that does not mean that he will *not* do so on your account. I do think we'd be taking a needless risk. But I won't fratch with you, lass," he added. "If we can go through Blackford safely, we will."

His answer displeased her, but she did not argue. And when Aodán and Will returned, they reported having seen many men in black wearing Albany's device, and others that Will had recognized as minions of Murdoch Stewart in Doune.

"They do seem tae be waiting for summat," Aodán said. "They ha' stabled their horses but only for the day. We saw watchers on the Stirling road, too."

"Did ye see any of your old master's men, Will?" Jamie asked when Aodán paused for breath.

"Nary a one," Will replied. "Mayhap he doesna want me back at all."

"A gey good thing *that* would be," Jamie said.

"Aodán, tell the others that we'll ride to a clachan in the hills that boasts an alehouse," Ivor said. "And send Sean Dubh to me. I have an errand for him."

Aodán hesitated, glancing at Marsi, Jamie, and Will. Then he said in the Gaelic, "Begging your pardon, sir. If you be sending him to Sir Fin, in Perth, do you think it wise to send only the one lad?"

"Sean can look after himself," Ivor replied in the same language. "I want to send two of the other lads to Lindores Abbey at Newburgh so they can arrange for a boat to meet us there or nearby, if need be."

"We have gey few men as it is," Aodán said. "Your lord father—"

"'Tis true that we're a small band, Aodán. But that may aid us in the end, because no one would believe that so few men guard so important a charge. In troth, I can scarcely believe it myself and would feel more secure with an army."

"By your own reckoning, that would just call more attention to us," Aodán said. "Forbye," he added with a sigh, "Albany would just raise a larger one."

"Where are you sending Sean Dubh?" Marsi asked Ivor in Scots.

"I'll tell you later, lass," he said, glancing at the two boys.

Jamie and Will had moved a little away, but Marsi knew that they might well be listening avidly to all that they could hear and understand. Certainly, she would have done so at their age in like circumstances. In fact, by not telling Aodán and Ivor that *she* had understood them, she was doing the same thing now. But it served them right. It was rude to speak a language that they thought others did not speak.

"Does the fact that we're riding to Hetty's wee clachan mean that you have changed your mind about going to Kincardine?" she asked Ivor.

"Not yet," he said. "If we can spend the night safely at that alehouse of hers, I'll send Aodán and one of the others back to town in the morning to see if Albany's men and the tanner's have moved on. Sithee, to go by way of Kincardine Glen, as steep and narrow as you say it is, will take longer than keeping to the lower straths."

She could not argue that point. For all she knew, the glen would be stuffed full of snow. There was little left of the recent snowfall where they were. But the nearby hills still wore lacy caps of the stuff. As sheltered as Kincardine Glen was, all the snow that had fallen might still be just sitting there, blocking their way.

Ivor told Sean Dubh to ride to MacGillivray House in Perth, relay their plans to Fin Cameron, and arrange for him to meet Ivor in three days' time on the south side of the river Earn near a great bridge they knew from their days at St. Andrews.

"Tell Fin to bring as many men as he can," Ivor added. "He will not have traveled with more than his usual tail of six to house in the town of Perth. But he should gather as many others as he can."

He also sent two of their four men-at-arms to Lindores Abbey with a message for the abbot to forward to Jake Maxwell. After that, they had only to pack up the little debris from their meal and find the hill track that Hetty remembered.

The track was little more than a deer trail wending its way up through the thickly forested hills, and Ivor, well aware that their passage would make the trail more noticeable, told Aodán to have one of his two remaining men-at-arms fall back and do what he could to minimize evidence of their passage.

Dusk had fallen by the time they reached their destination. The clachan consisted of four thatched cottages and a barn set amidst a scattering of trees in the otherwise dense forest. Much the largest of the four cottages was the alehouse.

When Ivor wondered aloud how such an establishment could support itself, lying as far as it did from Blackford or any well-traveled road, Hetty explained that the ale-master made his living primarily from late spring through early fall.

"Fishermen stay with him regularly to fish nearby streams more easily," she said. "As I recall, he boasts three wee bedchambers at the top of the house. So, if they have anyone else staying here, we will find ourselves in gey close quarters."

The alewife bustled out to the tiny yard when they rode into it and exclaimed joyfully at the sight of Hetty and Marsi. Professing herself astonished to see the latter, she added that the two boys could not possibly be the lady Marsi's.

Marsi, recognizing the plump, middle-aged woman at once as an erstwhile maidservant at Kincardine, said,

"Nay, Martha, the lads are in Sir Ivor's charge. But it is gey good to see you again! I hope that you and all here are well."

"Aye, sure, m'lady. Sir Ivor must be your husband, then," Martha said.

Noting Hetty's wry smile, Marsi was able to think of only one way to keep all of her own options open. Praying that she could trust Sir Ivor not to take base advantage of what she would say, she cautiously slipped her ring from her middle finger to the next one as she said, "Aye, Martha. He is a Highlander, and we are but newly wed. However, since you have so few bedchambers for guests, you must put Hetty and me together in one and let the boys share another with Sir Ivor. That way, you will still keep your third chamber for anyone else who might come."

"Bless ye, m'lady, I canna do that!" Martha exclaimed, laughing. "We ha' nae one here save our own folk. We'll put Sir Ivor's men in the barn loft wi' our three lads, and them boys in a room by themselves if Hetty thinks they can behave so. Then, she can ha' a room tae herself, whilst ye sleep as ye should wi' your husband."

Marsi wanted to insist that she need do no such thing. But, before she could think of an acceptable way to say so to the beaming alewife, Ivor put an arm around her shoulders and said politely, "You have my thanks, Mistress Martha."

"I'm sure I do, sir," Martha said, twinkling at him. "Folks hereabouts do call me Mistress Muir, though. Me man be Calum Muir."

"Then we shall call you so as well," Ivor said, urging Marsi forward as he did. "If you will just take us to our rooms, I would be privy with my lady."

Shouting for someone named Jem, Martha soon had them settled in rooms they entered from a wooden, railed gallery overlooking the common room. The rooms were small but looked more comfortable than Marsi had expected them to be.

The only one that did not *feel* comfortable was their own bedchamber when Ivor shut the door and turned to face her. He kept both of his hands behind him, as if he did not trust himself to keep from shaking her.

Having not known what to expect from him after her second declaration of their marriage but certain that his reaction must range somewhere between stern censure and outright wrath—more likely leaning nearer the latter than the former—she was astonished when he revealed no expression at all.

Then she heard the bolt on the door snap home behind him.

Tremors shot through her but whether from fear or excitement, she could not tell. Every nerve in her body began to hum as if in preparation to react strongly, one way or the other. Then, despite her warm, fur-lined cloak, a near chill swept over her and spread inward to her bones.

"I...mayhap I should not have..." She paused to lick suddenly dry lips.

"Should not have what?" he said, taking a purposeful step toward her.

She would have stepped back...She was sure that she *wanted* to step back. But her feet had stuck to the floor.

Her skin prickled. She was breathing rapidly, and she could feel her heart pounding in her chest. Sakes, she could hear it!

He gripped her left shoulder, and she felt herself jump. It was as if she stood outside her body, watching him touch her, watching herself react to his touch.

Her heart beat faster, sending fiery heat through her. But her face felt numb.

Chapter 15 _____

Ivor felt Marsi's tension. And sunbeams darting through branches outside and in through the small west-facing window behind her provided light enough to reveal her sudden pallor. Her breathing was unnaturally rapid, too. He had seen that symptom on the battlefield, especially in inexperienced young warriors.

Putting his free hand to her cheek, noting its abnormal coolness, he said, "Easy, lass. I mean you no harm, as you should ken fine by now."

"You are not the one who worries me," she said. "I am."

"Then, come here," he said, opening his arms to her. "Let us see if we can warm you a little. Your skin feels strangely cold."

"Only my face, I promise you," she said, with emphasis, as she let him draw her closer. Apparently hearing the accentuation in her own voice, she reddened as fast as she had paled.

Smiling, he enfolded her in his arms and felt a distinct sense of victory when she not only allowed it but leaned against him. He could feel her inhaling deeply and exhaling, relaxing more as she did.

"That's better," he murmured against her frilly cap.

Reminded thus of its presence, he pulled it off as he had at Inchmahone and cast it aside. "You can stop wearing that absurd thing now," he said. "I prefer to see your beautiful hair."

A dancing sunbeam animated the coppery highlights that had haunted his memory and his dreams since the night she had come to his bed.

She had brushed her hair back from her brow, plaited it, and coiled the plaits at her nape. When he stroked its silken smoothness, she seemed not to notice.

Just as he wondered if he might disturb their sense of comfort by speaking, she muttered, "I thought that if I told Martha we were married, it might help when ... *if* we go to Kincardine. Word travels fast hereabouts."

He had no doubt of that. Word traveled fast throughout all Scotland. "Did you think that your uncle would more easily believe in our marriage if he heard about it first from someone else?"

"Aye. Or, at least, he might *accept* it more easily."

"Mayhap he will; mayhap he will not," Ivor said. "Come to that, he may not believe that we have consummated it even if we do. But I still think—"

He broke off when she put one finger to his lips. "I ken fine what you think," she said. "You and Hetty think alike, and you may be right. I have been wondering long about that. But when I heard you snap that bolt into place just now—"

"I was not locking us in, lass. I was keeping the others out so we can talk."

"Mayhap that was your purpose," she said with a winsome little smile. "But it was as if you *un*locked a door in my mind when you did it."

"How is that?"

She looked up at him, right into his eyes, and deeply, as if she would see to his most hidden thoughts. Then, drawing breath and standing straighter but still so close that he could feel her length against him, she said, "Sithee, I have imagined often since that night... You know the one I mean."

When he nodded, she went on, "I have only to think about that... Sakes, I have only to think about *you* to feel your hands on my thighs again."

He scarcely heard a word after she mentioned "that night." That night and the satin smoothness of her thighs had rarely strayed far from his thoughts since.

His cock stirred as images from his dreams returned full force.

"I felt that," she said.

He smiled. "I warrant you did. My body responds easily to yours, lass, and has ever since *that night*."

"Aye, me, too. That is, I...I realized when I heard that bolt shoot home that I have wanted ever since then to feel your hands again on me...there. Is that not strange? To be thinking so much about such a thing?"

"I don't think so," he said. "In troth, I would think it odd if you did not think often about that incident. I am glad that your thoughts are pleasant, though. At the time," he added ruefully, "I must have frightened you witless."

Color flooded her cheeks. "N-nay. I was astonished, startled, even a bit angry, I think. But—"

"A bit? I wore that bruise for days afterward as you must have seen."

Her eyes twinkled then. "That was the startled part, I trow."

He raised his eyebrows.

A reminiscent smile touched her lips. "Aye, sure, it was also the angry part. I did not know you then, and you were the wrong person in that bed, *and* a man. But the wicked truth is that as I ran down that corridor, I wondered what you might have done next and how it would have felt had I not run away."

"Did you? Then I don't mind admitting that I have remembered that night or dreamed about it every night since. You have tempted me almost beyond my endurance, lass. I nearly succumbed more than once, even though I knew I could not act on my feelings without endangering the task his grace had set for me."

"Then I endangered it just by coming along. Is that what you mean?"

He hugged her. "It is not, but we can discuss why I don't mean that at some other time. What I want to know now, my lass, is if you *are* mine."

"I . . . I think I must be," she said. "I know that I don't want an annulment, certainly not one of Albany's contriving. Nor do I want to marry anyone else. So, if you are sure that you . . ."

"I'm sure," he said, his voice nearly failing him, so badly did he want her.

After a pause, she said, "I don't know what to do next."

"Don't fret about that," he said. "I do."

"I thought you might."

He chuckled and reached for the strings of her cloak.

~

Marsi held her breath, her awareness of him stronger than ever. She could feel energy radiating from his fingertips as he untied her cloak.

He did so swiftly, lifted it off her, and cast it to the floor by her cap.

When his fingers moved to the lacing of her kirtle, so sensitive was she to his touch that it was as if heat radiated from his fingers through the cloth right to her skin. Her nipples pressed against the fabric. When his hand brushed against one, the breath stopped in her throat. She sought his gaze, but he was watching what he was doing.

Glancing up just then, he smiled. "Don't be afraid," he said.

"I'm not," she replied honestly. "I'm curious. I did not know that a man could stir such sensations in a woman by barely touching her."

"It is only fair that he can," Ivor said. "You cannot imagine the sensations that you stir in me with just a smile or a look."

"Tell me," she said. "I want to know what that is like for you."

"Like hunger to a starving man," he said. "Now don't distract me, lass. I want to do this gently. The more you stimulate me, the more likely it is that I will proceed too swiftly for your pleasure."

"It will be pleasurable then."

"Aye, it will. Do you ken nowt of coupling?"

"Gey little," she admitted. She could usually speak her thoughts to him, but to ask him if the act of coupling was similar to what animals did seemed tactless.

"If you have seen animals couple, it is much the same," he said, reinforcing her belief that he often did know what she was thinking. "'Tis not as rough for a man and a woman as it can be for a mare with a stallion—or a doe with stag in rut, come to that," he added. "Men do some-times try to be gentle with their ladies."

"Only sometimes?"

"Sometimes the ladies prefer a little more strength, even some roughness."

"You know much about that, do you?" she said, hearing the edge in her voice and eyeing him to see if her words might have stirred his temper. Not that she cared if they had. She wanted to know how experienced he was.

He grinned. "What I know I will keep to myself, except when I practice what I have learned as *we* couple."

"Aye, perhaps, but before you do couple with me, I would have the answer to one question. Jamie told me that you once named practice as the best instructor, sir. Do you mean to go on practicing with others, as well as with me?"

"Nay, lass, I am not such a fool. Nor am I so cruel. I believe that marriage is forever and that a good hus-band honors his union." His free hand brushed gen-tly across her right breast again, sending a jolt of heat through her.

Her laces parted, her kirtle slipped to the floor, and he untied the strings of her shift, baring her breasts. She heard his quickly indrawn breath, and then he picked her up and carried her to the bed.

"Prithee, sir, my boots!"

Laying her down, he attended swiftly to her boots and to his own jerkin and tunic. Loosening his breeks, he stood for a moment looking down at her.

She stared back at him. The muscles of his broad bare chest rippled when he moved. Those protecting his ribs and stomach looked as hard, if not harder, and well etched. Despite the season, his torso looked as darkly tanned as his face.

His shoulders and arms were well muscled, too, as one would expect in a knight of the realm. His waist and hips were narrow, the powerful thighs under his tight-fitting breeks looking as well toned and muscular as the rest of him.

She felt suddenly small and vulnerable, even more so when he unlaced his breeks. He hesitated, watching her. Then bent and took off his boots.

"I think I will just lie beside you for a time, lass, to let you grow accustomed to being close to me," he said.

Her wariness vanished. Scooting over to make room for him, she watched as he climbed in and lay down beside her. He slipped an arm around her, drawing her closer, until her head rested in the hollow of his shoulder.

It felt as if that hollow existed to hold her head perfectly, and although she had expected to be nervous, she was not. She was only curious, as she had said she was earlier, although—as he might say himself—damnably so now.

She wished that she could think of something clever to say. But her mind was blank unless one counted screaming awareness of his every breath and the energy she felt radiating from him. There was more, too, something deeper that she suspected was his obvious desire for her and her own yearning for him to stroke her.

Impatience stirred. Surely this was not...Then, all thought suspended when he rose up smoothly to lean on his elbow and look down at her with a twinkle in his eyes. "I want to kiss you," he said.

"Do you mean to ask me every time you feel such an urge?"

"Nay, only this time," he said, bending nearer until his lips were an inch from her own. She felt his breath, even tasted it.

He moved slowly, tantalizingly closer, and she knew instinctively that he was exciting his own senses when he excited hers.

Anticipation grew almost unbearable, but at last his lips brushed hers, lightly, then once again before returning to capture them.

The heat she had felt earlier was as nothing to what exploded between them then. Her body leaped to meet his, and his warm hands seemed to touch her all over at once, while his lips devoured hers and his tongue plunged into her mouth.

Her shift vanished, and somehow so did his breeks, although when she tried to remember the details later, she could not. His fingers touched her where she could remember none but her own fingers touching before, and then one of his slipped inside her where none at all had gone before.

She gasped and stiffened, but he murmured, "Take a deep breath, sweetheart, and let it out. Try to relax. I don't want to hurt you."

The endearment caught her off guard, echoing in her mind as he continued to touch her below. He stroked her, used his lips and mouth to tease her nipples, and kissed her, increasing the level of her desire until she yearned in one heartbeat for release and in the next to know how much more intense the feeling could grow.

When he eased himself over her and his cock touched

her entrance, she stiffened again. But again he murmured to her and teased her senses until a single sharp pain, followed by a dull ache and a sensation of fullness told her that he was inside her. She gave an involuntary cry at the pain, but he murmured, "You are a woman now, sweetheart. It won't hurt next time and only a wee bit more now."

He stayed quiet for a time then, letting her body adapt to his. But she sensed his tension and knew that the respite would be brief. Her body stirred, gripping his convulsively. He responded, moving slowly at first, almost gently, even teasingly.

Then his rhythm changed, growing stronger, moving with rapidly increasing speed until he was pounding into her. Just as the sensations threatened to engulf her, just as she began to wonder what could possibly come next, he collapsed atop her.

Breathing heavily but clearly aware of the weight of his body on hers, he eased himself aside while she could still breathe.

She was glad he had not crushed her. But she continued to wonder.

"Ah, lassie," he murmured. "You've unmanned me for sure."

Marsi smiled at his words but stayed as she was, aware of dampness below.

"What happens next?" she asked him.

"We get cleaned up and go downstairs to see if they left us any supper."

Aware of a most unnatural urge to smack him, she rolled up on one side to look at him. "That was the pleasurable part?"

His eyes had closed, but he opened them.

A gleam stirred in their hazel depths. His mouth curved in a near smile.

"I'll admit, lass, I thought more about being gentle than giving you pleasure. I'm told that women rarely do feel pleasure in their first coupling and can even feel great pain. Even so, I do seem to recall some reactions—"

"Aye," she interjected. "But each time I felt pleasure stirring, it seemed to suggest that more lay just beyond my reach, as if even greater delight hovered in the air around me. Good lack, I ken fine that that makes no sense—"

"But it does," he said. "If you enjoy this part of marriage and want to learn more after supper, I will teach you. But, by my troth, I am nigh to starving now."

"You *said* you were starving before," she reminded him.

"Aye, I did," he agreed. "And I was. But fulfilling one appetite can easily stir another. A man must maintain his strength, after all."

Shaking her head at him, she made no further protest but got out of bed and moved to the washstand to clean herself. Only half-aware that he had followed her, she saw with surprise that she had blood on her thighs.

"Is this the way it should be?" she asked.

"Aye," he said. "At the end, I was not as gentle as I'd hoped to be, but you bled less than one might expect. Have you much pain?"

"Nay, only a bit . . . more of an achy feeling."

"That should soon pass."

"Will it hurt more if you teach me more?"

"We'll see, but we'll be careful. I want you to enjoy this part of marriage."

"I think I will," she said. "I'll tell you if I don't."

"I'm sure that you will," he said, grinning again.

Ivor knew then that he had taken the right tack with her. He was pleased with himself and enchanted by her. Her body was all he had expected it to be, her thighs as satiny smooth as he remembered, and her reactions as exciting and arousing as he had imagined they could be. He would never get enough of her.

Dressing, they went downstairs, where they found the others halfway through their supper. The alemaster and his wife quickly provided more food for them, and Ivor noted that Marsi was as hungry as he was.

Hetty seemed pleased with herself and the boys unnaturally quiet.

Jamie gazed steadily at him until Ivor said, "You are gey quiet tonight, lad."

"Aye, sure, because Hetty said we must no ask why ye're late. But I think ye should tell us. Ye'd demand tae know if it were one of us."

Hetty frowned at Jamie, but the boy ignored her and looked sternly at Ivor.

Meeting his gaze, Ivor said, "Lady Marsi and I have married, and married people need private time together. We were just upstairs, James, nowhere else."

"How long are we going tae stay here?"

"Just until morning, I hope. My lads are watching our trail now, and I'll send one or two of them into town in the morning to see if Albany's men have gone."

"Then what?"

"Then we will head for Lindores Abbey at Newburgh, on the Firth of Tay."

"Because that is where ye *said* we'd go or 'cause it be the best thing tae do?"

"Both," Ivor said in a tone that he hoped would end the discussion.

"Marsi and Hetty think it be safer tae go tae Kincardine Castle."

Feeling his temper stir, Ivor quelled it to say, "It may be safe for us to go to Kincardine, but we would be taking a risk. Your uncle controls the region and thus wields strong influence hereabouts. But we are going to St. Andrews, which lies on Fife's easternmost coast. We must pass through some part of Fife to get there."

"But my uncle's men are watching all the roads here. Do *they* not pose a greater risk than a well-guarded glen and my uncle's stronghold?"

Ivor's restless temper urged him to order James to hold his tongue and do as he was bid. But he had trained many a young squire, and James, despite his tender years, might one day be King of Scots. If so, he would have to make decisions even more significant than this one. To squelch him when he was just asking questions would accomplish little and might undermine the very confidence in himself that made the boy seem so much older than his years.

That would not do, especially with Will sitting there beside him.

Accordingly, Ivor said, "Every decision poses a risk, Jamie-lad. Things rarely go according to one's plan."

"But is it not a bad plan that admits of no modification?"

Ivor could not help smiling at that. "Publius Syrus again, lad? How about 'In every enterprise, consider where you want to come out'? By following my plan and returning to flatter ground, we can keep watch in all directions. But once we enter Kincardine Glen, we commit ourselves to its limitations."

"But the glen is safe," Marsi insisted. "Sir Malcolm is *my* uncle as well as Jamie's, sir. We have good reason, therefore, to trust him. Do we not, Jamie?"

Ivor noted James's hesitation but did not think that Marsi did. The boy said rather quickly, "Aye, sure, one should trust those of one's own blood."

"One *should* be able to, aye," Ivor said, catching and holding his gaze.

⁓

Marsi watched the two of them, thinking that it was as if Ivor were trying to send thoughts into Jamie's head.

Jamie shifted his gaze to her and said, "In troth, Marsi, uncles *should* be trustworthy. But we do ken one who is not."

Beside him, Will nodded solemnly.

"Uncle Malcolm is not like Albany, Jamie," Marsi said. "He is Annabella's own brother and has no claim to the throne. Albany does, though. He stands third in line to take it, and that is what drives him to do many of the things he does."

"But Kincardine is in Fife," Jamie said. "So Albany is Uncle Malcolm's liege lord. He cannot defy Albany's commands without consequence. Consider the charters for Auchterarder Castle and Kincardine. Sakes, as Great Chamberlain, Albany could revoke the charter to Stobhall, too. As Governor of the Realm, he—"

"He is *not* Governor of the Realm; Davy is," Marsi said tensely. Feeling Ivor's hand on her knee, she drew a breath but did not look at him. Exhaling slowly and avoiding Hetty's eye, too, she said, "Anyone would agree that Sir Malcolm is more trustworthy than Albany, Jamie. He would not harm his own sister's son."

Jamie's gaze shifted back to Ivor, but Ivor deftly changed the subject.

A few minutes later, Jamie announced that he and Will were going to help in the barn. "With Sean and the other two men gone, Aodán needs us," Jamie said. "But we'll come back in tae sleep. Will Hetty truly have her own room tonight?"

"Aye," Ivor said. "But if I hear much noise from yours, there will be trouble."

Grinning at him then, Jamie pulled Will up, and the two of them ran outside.

Under the table, Ivor's hand moved on Marsi's leg, to her thigh, and higher.

His touch affected her as it always did, and she dared not look at him. She knew that he was no longer thinking about anything that Jamie had said. But neither did Ivor make any further attempt to persuade her that his plan was the right one.

She knew that he had made up his mind and that no argument of Jamie's or hers would change it. Nor should any, she decided. So when Hetty went out later to fetch the boys in, Marsi eagerly accepted Ivor's invitation to return to their own room.

"Now, then," he said, shutting the door and bolting it again. "As I recall, you complained earlier about pleasure that seemed to lie just beyond your reach."

"I did," she agreed.

He pulled her into his arms, and all thought of Sir

Malcolm and Kincardine vanished. So did thoughts of James, Hetty, Will, and everyone else in the world except the man who held her and the passions he stirred in her.

Little instruction was necessary to persuade her not only that coupling with him was more pleasurable than she had ever imagined but also that she could devise ways of her own to delight him in return.

At last, exhausted, they slept, and when Marsi awoke, pale sunlight was making wavering paths on the bed-chamber floor. Ivor still slept beside her.

Getting up cautiously, to let him sleep as long as he could, and moving quietly, she dressed, unbolted the door, and stepped onto the gallery overlooking the common room. Knowing that Hetty was in the next room, with the boys in the one beyond it, she went to Hetty's first. Finding it empty and the next door unlocked, she pushed it open. To her surprise, she found Hetty alone there, half-dressed.

"Ay-de-mi!" Hetty exclaimed. "I thought ye'd be the boys returning at last."

"Where did they go?"

"Jamie told me that Will had slipped out early, saying he wanted to see if the men Aodán had sent to watch our path from Blackford had returned. Will got back soon afterward and said that he'd seen a dozen riders heading this way."

"Mercy! Why didn't he wake us? Who are they? How many?"

"I dinna ken," Hetty said. "That was some time ago, though, and no riders have come. In troth, I'd expected the boys to return straightaway. They *said* they were just going downstairs to tell Sir Ivor."

"But Ivor is asleep," Marsi said. "They must have expected to find him in the barn with Aodán, since Will *didn't* see him downstairs when he returned."

Hetty frowned. "They just said they were going to tell Sir Ivor. I never thought they'd go outside if men were coming. Jamie said he feared they'd be Albany's, and Will said they could as easily be the tanner's. Do you think they told me falsehoods?"

"Jamie doesn't lie," Marsi said, but a chill at the base of her spine shot upward. "Sakes, Hetty, do you think they've run away to evade those riders?"

"I dinna ken, but I'll finish dressing in a twink," Hetty said.

"I'll wake Sir Ivor," Marsi said. "Most likely, the boys *are* with Aodán, but..."

"I remember another thing," Hetty said. "Jamie said he hoped you were right."

"About what?"

"I dinna ken that, either. I didna recall till just now that he'd said it."

Marsi could think of only one thing that Jamie might have meant. "Sakes, I'd wager that he hopes I was right about Uncle Malcolm being willing to aid us. But I swear, Hetty, if they've gone to Kincardine alone, I'll take leather to them myself."

Leaving Hetty and fighting down her own surging sense of guilt, Marsi hurried back to her room, where she found Ivor already stirring.

Hastily, she said, "Jamie and Will are not in their room, and I fear they may have set out by themselves for Kincardine. They told Hetty they were going downstairs to tell you Will had seen riders coming, twelve of them, but Will must have come through the common room, so he'd have known you weren't there."

"Not to mention they could have looked down from the gallery," Ivor said grimly. He was up before she'd stopped talking, and was quickly dressing. "If riders are coming, they ought to have wakened you even if they did think I'd slipped out to the barn. In any event, our gear is packed, so I'll help Aodán with the horses, and you tell Hetty to collect her things and the boys' and meet us at the barn."

"I can do that in a trice, sir," she said as she snatched up her cloak and put it on. "We'll also need food, and mayhap Martha will know where the boys went."

"Aye, she might," he agreed, bending to pull on his boots.

"Also," Marsi said, "apparently Will did not say how far away those men were, if he knew. If they do exist, they'll be even closer by now."

"We won't wait for them in any event," Ivor said as he collected his sword, dirk, and bow. "Can we trust Calum Muir with a message for my other two men?"

"We can trust Martha," she said. "She'd never betray Hetty or me."

"Good, then tell her that we're going to Kincardine but to tell no one except my two men when they return. They can follow us later."

Nodding, Marsi hurried downstairs, sending a prayer aloft as she did.

Chapter 16 _____

Ivor carried his and Marsi's things out to the barn, where he found Aodán brushing one of the horses. Quickly explaining the situation and learning that neither of their other two men had shown his face, let alone reported riders, Ivor handed the bundles to Aodán for the sumpters and began bridling Marsi's horse.

"If Will could see riders," he said, "surely one of our men would have, too."

"Ye'd think so, aye," Aodán said as he shouted for help to ready their other horses. "Mayhap someone surprised them. Should I send someone to have a look?"

"Send one of Muir's lads," Ivor said. "We must warn them that trouble may come. Marsi and Mistress Hetty will come with us, so I want you to look after Hetty, the baggage, and the other horses. I'll take Marsi with me and ride on ahead."

Aodán said, "And if there *be* riders coming—Albany's men, say—"

"Then you abandon the other horses but not Mistress Hetty," Ivor said dryly.

He spoke to Aodán's back, though, because the other

man was already saddling Ivor's horse and issuing orders to the three lads who worked in the barn.

Seeing Marsi hurrying across the yard with a sack in hand, Ivor finished with her horse, accepted the reins of his from Aodán, and led the pair outside to meet her, adjusting his sword as he did. His bow was strapped to his saddle, his dirk at his side.

"What did you learn?" he asked as Marsi handed him the sack that she was carrying, which smelled deliciously of baked oatmeal.

"Those are fresh bannocks," she said. "The boys said naught to Martha, but she said they came downstairs in a hurry, snatched up some bannocks, and ran outside."

"How long ago?" he asked, tucking the free end of the sack under his belt.

"'Nobbut ten or fifteen minutes,' Martha said. I told her what to tell your men and also that we feared that the boys might have gone on ahead of us." She paused there, then added, "Martha said that the woods are boggy and gey dangerous, sir, and...and she hoped they'd have sense enough to follow the fisherman's trail."

"Where is that trail?" he asked, forming a stirrup for her with his hands.

"The track by the barn will take us to it," Marsi said as he helped her mount. "But hurry, sir. Martha also said that with the snow melting so quickly, those woods are nearly *all* bog these days. I'm afraid that something bad may happen and..."

"We'll find them both," he said, mounting his horse. "And something *is* going to happen to them, lass. I'll see to that."

~

Hetty was emerging from the alehouse as they rode out of the yard, and Marsi was glad to see her. She knew that Aodán—with their extra horses, Hetty, and all—would soon be close behind them.

Ivor opened the sack and handed her a bannock, taking another for himself.

They rode as fast as they dared, but although the track to the nearby woods was clear, as the forest thickened around them, they had to take more care. Marsi followed Ivor, munching her bannock and thinking about the boys.

There were patches of snow everywhere, a few drifts on the narrow track and others beneath openings in the canopy. The light was dim, although the sun had been peeking through a dip in the hills to the east as they'd left the yard. They were higher than they had been then, but she saw no sign of sunlight now.

Water gurgled downhill to their left, but they heeded Martha's warning and kept to the mucky path. Sheen on its boggy surroundings was warning enough of the danger that stepping off the path might bring to a human or a horse.

As the horses picked their way through an icy, half-melted snowdrift that sprawled across the path, Marsi listened for sounds of movement or talk ahead, although she knew she was unlikely to hear the boys over the horses' sloshing. She also watched for footprints in the muck and the snow. But everything was watery. Even the horses' hoofprints vanished almost as soon as she looked back at them.

Then they came to a snowy patch that sloped upward

from the path to their right and then downward along a fallen log. Reining in, Ivor gestured to it.

Small footprints followed the log, and Marsi knew he was as certain as she was that they were Jamie's and Will's, and was as relieved as she was to see them.

He picked up the pace, and Marsi urged her mount after his, trusting the two horses to avoid the bog. It grew less boggy as they climbed.

When they crested a hill, despite encroaching shrubbery, the path widened enough on the curving downward slope for her to ease her mount up beside Ivor's.

He glanced at her as she did and smiled reassuringly.

She managed to smile back, and rounding a curve, they almost ran into the boys before they saw them. The two had their backs to them and had hunkered down behind the tall bushes at one side of the path. Beyond them lay a clearing.

The shrubbery was tall and dense, the ground dryer, and hoofbeats approaching from ahead and to the right suggested that they had reached the Stirling road.

Ivor motioned for Marsi to stop, and they saw a pair of horsemen ride by at a trot. Neither man as much as glanced their way.

When the hoofbeats faded away and the boys straightened, preparing to dash across the road, Ivor said, "Stop right there!" When the two startled lads whirled as one to face him, he added, "What the devil do you think you're doing here?"

Straightening and meeting Ivor's gaze, Jamie said, "We're going tae Kincardine, sir. We couldna wait at the inn, because whoever came would want one of us, and we didna—neither of us—want tae go with them. So we thought we'd hie us tae my uncle at Kincardine instead. Now, belike, we can all go together."

The sense of guilt that had plagued Marsi since the moment she had deduced the boys' plan increased tenfold, stirring her temper as it did. Fighting to suppress both emotions, she said in a carefully even tone, "Jamie, did you and Will do this because *I* wanted to go to Kincardine?"

Eyeing her warily, Jamie said, "We did follow your plan, Marsi, but we had tae go somewhere, and we didna ken where else tae go. Ye've said yourself, though, that if one wants a thing and others disagree, one must see tae it oneself. Sithee, we did nae more than ye'd said we *all* should do."

Marsi shut her eyes briefly, then forced herself to look at Ivor. He was watching her, but as their gazes met, he cocked his head slightly, listening.

"Riders," he said then. "Above us on the trail."

"We must cross the road then," Jamie said. "We're too close tae it for safety, and it will be easier tae conceal ourselves in yon glen across the way."

Ivor glanced at Jamie and said, "Wait, lad." Then turning back, he gave the piercing birdcall that he and Aodán often used. When an echo of it came back to him, he said, "It is only Aodán and Hetty with the horses. We'll wait for them."

Marsi said, "What if the other riders are right behind them?"

"Aodán has just come over the crest, lass. He'd have seen or heard them, and if he had, he'd have returned a different signal. We should be safe enough for the moment. However…" He looked at Will. "Tell us about the men you saw, lad."

Will's blue eyes widened at his stern tone, and his cheeks reddened. He glanced at Jamie, but Jamie was watching Ivor.

"Will?" Ivor said. "*Did* you see anyone?"

Redder than ever, Will said, "Aye, sir, and I did go tae look for our two men, but I never saw them." He drew a breath, then added determinedly, "Them others were no pelting along like I told Mistress Hetty, neither. They had stopped, or mayhap even had camped there for the night and were but breaking their fast. I couldna tell what they were a-doing from where I was on me hilltop."

"That doesn't matter, and we won't speculate about what they *might* have been doing," Ivor said. "How many men were there?"

"Nigh a dozen or so, like I said. So I hied me back tae tell Jamie." He paused and then said bluntly, "Are ye going tae leather us for running off as we did?"

"I have not decided what I will do," Ivor said, looking from Will to Jamie. "Both of you knew better than to leave, and if you *believed* that danger was approaching the alehouse, you should have warned the rest of us."

Jamie said hastily, "We were sure that it was Master Lucken coming for Will or Albany coming for me. Sithee, what we believed was that if *we* weren't there, ye could just deny being anyone they might ha' been seeking."

"I see," Ivor said. More sternly, he added, "I am truly to believe that you ran off for *our* benefit and not because *you* want to go to Kincardine. Is that right?"

Jamie flushed. "You do like tae put words in a chappie's mouth," he said.

"What words should I have used?" Ivor asked him.

This time Jamie looked down at his feet. When Ivor just waited, he soon looked up again and said, "You are right, sir. We should have told you."

"Actions have consequences, my lad. If you learn from those consequences, then the actions will not have been in vain."

"I dinna like the sound of that," Jamie muttered.

"I don't suppose you do."

Marsi said, "We can hardly turn back now, sir, not knowing who the men are."

"Agreed, lass. Nor can we take the Perth road. But if my ears do not deceive me, Aodán, Hetty, and the other horses are about to join us."

Moments later, they could see them, Hetty in the lead and Aodán behind her, leading the boys' horses and the sumpters in a string behind him. No one else.

His suspicion that something untoward had happened to his other two men grew to a certainty. Unable to do a thing about it then, he checked the road in both directions to be sure that no one would see them, then hurried the others across.

⁓

Although Marsi had expected to see Sir Malcolm's guards soon after they crossed the road, they saw none. Nor did anyone challenge them as they made their way down the slushy path into the steep-sided depths of Kincardine Glen.

The path ran dangerously close to Ruthven Water,

a burn that had clearly begun as a narrow spring from the hill they had descended to reach the road and, full of snowmelt now, tumbled swiftly over and among icy rocks and boulders. It ran all the way down to the village of Aberuthven, she knew, and beyond to the river Earn.

Trees and shrubbery grew thick on the glen walls despite their increasing steepness, so guards could be anywhere. When they at last rounded a curve, Marsi looked back to see with relief that they were at least out of sight from the road.

Ivor and Marsi led with the boys behind them, then Hetty and Aodán.

The narrow path forbade riding in pairs, and the rushing of water deterred quiet conversation, but Marsi found herself wishing that Ivor would say something. Instead, he was scanning the steep slopes on both sides of the burn.

When the trail flattened out for a time and widened enough for her to move up beside him, she said, "Do you truly have so little trust in my kinsmen, sir, that you keep watch so cautiously as we go?"

"It is not your kinsmen I distrust, lass, just the one who has the honor to have been brother to her grace, the late Queen. Sithee, if Sir Malcolm is trustworthy and so certain to stand with her grace's sons against Albany, then why did his grace send for me and not for Sir Malcolm and a Drummond army to protect Jamie?"

"I cannot answer that," she said, wishing that she could.

"Nor can anyone else," he replied, urging his mount forward when the trail narrowed again.

Ivor kept his eyes on the hillsides, but he knew that such a small party as theirs could do nowt to prevent mischief from anyone concealed there.

His instincts were alive and sending warnings through his body. He had his dirk in its sheath and his sword across his back. His quiver and bow were strapped to his saddle, but neither would be of use to him in a surprise attack.

They were well into the glen with no sign of guards, and turning back was not an option. Ivor reminded himself that Sir Malcolm was unlikely to let harm come to either James or Marsi, especially on Drummond land, so attack was unlikely.

The trail widened again, enough for two, and he glanced back at Marsi. She had been unusually silent, and he saw now that she was brooding about something.

"What is it, lass?" he asked, motioning her forward.

Urging her horse up near his again, she said, with a wry grimace, "It was my idea to come to Kincardine. Jamie and Will acted as they did because of that, and because of what I said about doing things yourself when others say no. They lied to Hetty, too. I did not think that Jamie would ever tell a lie, sir."

Fighting off a sardonic smile as he recalled her previous insistence that she had *not* lied about being a nursery maid, he said gently, "If I understood them correctly, Will told the lie, not Jamie. You should appreciate that subtle difference."

She gave him a look, then said, "Perhaps I should, but that only makes me feel worse. What if they had run into Albany's men? What if whoever is coming from Blackford had arranged for others to approach from the Perth road? Jamie and Will would have run right into them. If harm had come to them because they'd decided that I was right about Kincardine, it would have been my fault, sir. I do see that."

Gently, he said, "It is not your fault that the lads came this way. They may have chosen sides between us in the discussion we had on that subject, but they are the ones at fault, lass. I do believe that they were frightened, and trying to protect themselves and each other. I also think that Jamie wanted to take some control over what was happening to him."

She looked at him then. "But you are gey angry with them."

"Nay, this is mild, believe me, and they should have wakened us."

"Aye, sure, but even if they had, with those men between us and Blackford, and your men not warning us, would we not still be where we are now?"

"'Tis likely we would be," he admitted. "But—"

He got no further, for they rounded a curve just then to find armed riders blocking the trail ahead of them. Others swiftly surrounded them.

"Sir Malcolm Drummond sends his greetings, sir," their leader said to Ivor. "If ye'll follow us, we'll take ye to him."

⁓

Marsi recognized none of them, nor did any speak to her, but she reassured herself with the fact that had they meant anything other than to escort them to her uncle, they would have demanded Ivor's weapons, and Aodán's.

They traveled more swiftly after that and soon reached Kincardine Castle, a formidable quadrangle that crowned what in ancient days had been a promontory jutting into Ruthven Water, which had widened considerably in its journey down the glen. A nearly sheer cliff loomed above the castle.

In time, men had dug a ditch to separate the castle from the cliff and the path through the glen, so that the Ruthven Water forked around it to form a turbulent moat. From the path, Marsi could see that the drawbridge was down.

They crossed it, their horses' hoofbeats muffled by the noisy water, and passed through an arched tunnel into the castle courtyard.

When Ivor helped her dismount, she slid her hand into his and followed the man who had greeted them to the entrance. Jamie and Hetty followed, leaving Aodán and Will to deal with their horses. Marsi did recognize the elderly porter.

"Follow me, if ye please, m'lady," he said, leading them up the narrow, spiral, stone stairway. "Sir Malcolm awaits ye in the great chamber. He told me t' say he be gey pleased t' receive ye"—he cast a swift glance over Sir Ivor, Hetty, and James, who scowled at him—"and your escorts, as weel."

Exchanging a look with Ivor, Marsi followed the old man, only to stop short when he stood aside to let her cross the threshold into the great chamber alone.

Her uncle sat in a two-armed chair near the huge fireplace halfway along the wall to her right. Sir Malcolm was a slender man in his fiftieth year and of average height. His brown hair had grayed at the temples, thinned at the crown, and was longer than fashion decreed. He did not rise when she entered.

The only other man in the room stood by Sir Malcolm's chair. He was solid looking with dark, curly hair, of similar age to that of his host, and richly garbed in a crimson doublet and silk hose. He did not speak, nor did Sir Malcolm present him. But something in the bold way that the stranger gazed at Marsi gave her pause.

Recovering her wits, she curtsied, saying politely, "Good morrow, Uncle. I hope we have not disturbed your peace by coming here unannounced."

"You are welcome here as always, my dear. But I will say I could not credit my ears when I learned of your arrival in such small company. How do you come to be traveling all the way from Turnberry so, my dear, at this season or any other?"

"With good reason, sir," Marsi said, hurrying lightly toward him, smiling in the way that had so often won favor from men in her life...before Ivor. "Sithee, sir," she added, "we act to fulfill a promise that his grace made to Aunt Annabella on her deathbed, and we are traveling so by his grace's own command."

"I do not know what you can be talking about," Sir Malcolm said. "Sakes, but that *is* James with you, is it not, and Henrietta Childs?"

"Jamie is with us by Aunt Annabella's wish and his grace's command," Marsi said. Aware that Ivor had moved to stand beside her, she added, "His grace asked this man to take Jamie to a place of safety, and we require shelter along the way. I assured him that Kincardine is just such a safe place, because I know that, as Aunt Annabella's brother, you will do all that you can to protect her young son."

"Aye, sure, I will," Sir Malcolm said, standing at last. "Indeed, I am glad that I came here, although I did so only because his grace summoned Parliament to meet as soon as possible. I suspect, however, that you've not heard that he means to see if its lords are willing to extend Davy Stewart's provisional term as Governor. The three years that they granted him to prove his ability ended two months ago."

"But Davy remains Governor of the Realm *until* they unseat him," Marsi said. "And they may not. Forbye, should it not be Davy who summons them?"

"His grace is still King, Marsaili. Davy has been ruling in his stead, to be sure. But Davy refuses to summon Parliament. He fears that its lords will return the Governorship to Albany until he—Davy, that is—*inherits* the throne. But there, lass, I should not be boring you with politics." Glancing at the man beside him, he added with a smile, "I am thinking that you do not recognize my guest, Marsaili."

A note in his voice made her focus keenly on his companion as she said, "I do not believe that we have met before, sir."

"Then I have the honor, my dear, to present to you your intended husband. This is Martin Lindsay, Lord of Redmyre."

Tension swept through her. Fighting to conceal her dismay, Marsi nodded to Redmyre as regally as ever Annabella had to anyone. But she did not curtsy.

Redmyre made her a slight bow, saying, "The honor, m'lady, is mine own."

She swallowed hard. Since anything that she had thought about him would be improper to say aloud, she held her tongue.

Ivor stepped nearer, gently touching her back as he said, "You are misinformed, Sir Malcolm. No betrothal exists between Lord Redmyre and her ladyship, nor can one ever exist. The lady Marsaili is *my* wife."

Redmyre bristled angrily. "What is this? Albany promised me—"

Sir Malcolm put a quelling hand on his shoulder and said to Ivor, "You are the one in error, sir. But my niece neglects her duty. She has not presented you to me."

"I am Ivor Mackintosh," Ivor said. "I am a knight of the realm in service to the Lord of the North. My mother's father is Captain of Clan Chattan. My father is Shaw MacGillivray Mackintosh, war leader of our confederation."

"So your grandfather is the Mackintosh himself," Sir Malcolm said, nodding. "Welcome to Kincardine, Sir Ivor. I do not know why you pretend to be Marsaili's husband, though. It sits ill on your knightly honor to act in such a *dis*honorable way."

"By my troth as a knight, sir, we are man and wife in *every* way."

"Not so, I fear. See you, Marsaili is a ward of the Crown, and I know that she did not secure his grace's permission to wed, so we can easily see to its annulment."

"You may *try*," Ivor replied. "However, by law, every Scotswoman reaches the age of consent on her twelfth birthday and can marry the man of her choosing. And she can do that without the consent of her parents or guardian."

"Aye, sure, but my niece is a considerable heiress. Doubtless, *that* is why you continue this charade. But when the lords of Parliament make Albany Governor again, *he* will arrange her marriage settlements. In troth, he wields power enough even now to overturn your marriage."

"Perhaps so. But, even he cannot force her ladyship to marry against her will. Scottish law plainly forbids that."

"Her ladyship will do as Albany bids," Redmyre said gruffly. "And if the Kirk be so misguided as to deny an annulment, he'll not let *you* gain a groat from the Cargill estates. If you think otherwise, you're right daft."

"Her inheritance means nowt to me," Ivor said. "However, it does mean much to her ladyship, so we'll do what we can to settle it suitably. Meantime, we will trouble you no further, Sir Malcolm. You make it plain that we are unwelcome here."

"Nay, now," Sir Malcolm said tranquilly. "I've said nowt about leaving, nor would I have you think me inhospitable. Marsaili is my niece, and my sister loved her like a daughter. Also, James is my own nephew and a prince of this realm."

"Even so, sir—"

"I am no enemy of yours, Sir Ivor. If I have mistaken your character, I will apologize. In troth, my family has had cause more than once to *thank* Clan Chattan, so I would be loath to make enemies there. I doubt that Redmyre wants that, either."

Redmyre grimaced, and Marsi muttered to Ivor, "We should not stay."

Sir Malcolm, evidently overhearing her, said, "My people have already told yours where to put your things, my dear." Then, to James, he said, I hope *you* do not mean to run away, lad. It has been too long since last I saw you."

James did not reply, nor did his uncle press him to speak. Instead, to Ivor, he said, "We won't sup for an hour yet, but mayhap you will honor me by coming down a quarter-hour before the others to take a dram of peace with me."

"I'd willingly take a dram with you, sir," Ivor replied.

Chapter 17 ――――――――――――――

You must *not* do that, sir," Marsi hissed past Hetty and James to Ivor as they followed a gillie upstairs. Again, she led the way with the others following.

"Take a lesson from Jamie, lass," Ivor said. "He has wisely remained silent."

"Aye," Jamie muttered. "I remembered Publius Syrus."

"Who?" Marsi asked.

Ivor replied, "Publius Syrus, an ancient Roman philosopher who said many things, including that he had often regretted his speech but never his silence."

Marsi said with a sigh, " 'Tis a pity he did not say how one is to know ahead of time when one *might* regret one's speech. Then one might gain the wisdom to be silent. Forbye, Uncle Malcolm must have thought Jamie was being rude."

"I won't say what *I* think of *him*," Jamie said. "To talk of Davy as he—"

"That is enough now," Ivor interjected, adding, "I don't want you in a room of your own tonight, lad. You will sleep in Mistress Hetty's room with her."

"Aye, sure," Jamie said. "I'd liefer sleep out with Will and Aodán, though."

At the next landing, the gillie pushed open a door and stepped aside. "Here ye be, sir. Just shout if ye need summat."

"Thank you," Ivor said, moving past Hetty and James to Marsi. "I am sure that my lady and I will be comfortable here."

"Beg pardon, sir. The laird did say I was tae put the women together and—"

"Her ladyship is my wife. She will sleep with me, and the lad with Mistress Childs. Tell me if you need anything, mistress," Ivor added.

"Aye, sir," Hetty said. "I'm thinking James—Lord Carrick, that is—and I would do better to take our meal in our room, though, if someone can arrange that."

"The laird said Lord Carrick was tae have his own chamber," the gillie said.

James, raising his chin, turned to him and said firmly, "I will sleep where *I* decide, sirrah, and that is with Hetty."

"Aye, sir," the gillie said, bowing swiftly. "I'll see to that meal, mistress."

As he turned away to lead Hetty and Jamie to their chamber, Jamie shot Ivor a mischievous look and got a nod of approval at last for his royal ways.

Marsi nearly smiled, but when she and Ivor were alone in their room, she said, "I don't like this, sir. You were right to distrust him. But how could we have known that our own uncle might betray us? You didn't tell me *why* you thought so before."

"I thought it was unnecessary, since I did not intend to come here," he said. "You have little of your family left, lass. I did not want to rob you of your trust in Sir Malcolm unnecessarily."

An ache stirred in her throat, but she ignored it, saying, "Well, I suspect from what he said that he is deep in Albany's pocket. We must leave here straightaway."

"How can we do that?" he asked. "I'll wager that drawbridge is already up. Even if it is not, would you pit us against your uncle's men and Redmyre's?"

"But we must do something! Uncle Malcolm became too welcoming too fast. He was angry to learn of our marriage, too. Art sure it is *completely* legal?"

"I am," he said calmly.

"I wish I'd thought to tell him that Davy already arranged the settlements," she said. "He *is* still Governor, after all. But I didn't think of saying that until now."

"It is as well that you did not," Ivor said. "The *best* liar can get caught in his own lies, and *you*, my lass, are not even a good one. Moreover—"

Knowing that she did not want to hear the rest, Marsi said hastily, "I think they are up to something wicked."

"If they are, we'll soon find out," he said. "I believed Sir Malcolm, though, when he said he does not want trouble between the Drummonds and Clan Chattan. But he is in control now, and with the balance of power against us, it may be best to pretend we are in ignorance of the fact and act as if everything is as it should be."

"I am not sure that I can do that," she said frankly. "Not with Redmyre here."

"Put him out of your mind," Ivor said. "Right here, right now, we are alone with nowt to do for at least a half-hour." After a pause and in a much different tone, he said, "Come here to me, sweetheart. Let us see if we can devise a more enjoyable way to spend that time than to talk of things we cannot alter until we learn more."

The seductive note in his voice seemed to touch her most sensitive places, and the sound of the bolt when he shot it stirred them even more. His hands moved to the lacing of her kirtle, setting nerves alight with every motion as his agile fingers undid her laces with a speed that made her fear for the garment.

"Take care now," she said as thoughts of her uncle and Redmyre faded and she began to concentrate on Ivor. "Recall that I have few clothes with me here."

"I ken that fine, and I like this mossy color on you. So mayhap you could hang this gown to unwrinkle itself before we go down to sup with your uncle."

"Sakes, that garment won't please him, whatever I do."

"You can please me, however," Ivor said, pushing the kirtle off her shoulders and aiding it to fall in a puddle round her feet. When it slid from her hips, he was already untying her shift. Moments later, she was beneath him on the bed, and his clothing was gone, as well. He began kissing her everywhere.

As he laved her nipples with his tongue, his busy hands and fingers occupied themselves by stroking and teasing her belly and lower, heating her body more with each touch and caress. He shifted himself lower then, letting his lips and tongue follow where hands and fingers had gone before until she was nigh screaming for him to possess her. He readily complied.

Afterward, when they lay in each other's arms, gasping, Ivor said with a smile in his voice, "Do you doubt now, lassie, that I am your husband?"

"I do not." She leaned up on an elbow to kiss him. "But if your wife is going to look at all presentable for supper, husband mine, she had better start now."

"Recall that I am to take whisky with him beforehand, so I'll wash first. I'll be quick, though. And, lass, I want you to promise that you will cease trying to persuade him to your way of thinking. Let me see now what I can do."

~

Having donned the blue velvet doublet and hose that he had worn for his audience with the King at Turnberry, Ivor left Marsi dressing and went downstairs.

He found Sir Malcolm and Redmyre again by the fireplace. Sir Malcolm greeted him with a mug of whisky. "'Tis the finest in Scotland, I think," he said. "We distill it at Stobhall. You must tell me what you think."

"Is *your* home near here, Redmyre?" Ivor asked, accepting the whisky.

"I've one this side of the Firth of Tay," Redmyre said. "Another touches the north side of the firth. Me da used to say that we Lindsays owned the land in one piece, long afore the glaciers slashed the firth bit out of it like a slice of pie."

"The Lindsays control much property in Scotland," Ivor said.

"As does Clan Chattan," Redmyre said. "Was not the great battle of Perth fought betwixt your clan and the Camerons over some property?"

"Aye, but we've a truce now. This is a fine whisky, Sir Malcolm. But you will not persuade me to annul my marriage, sir. I love your niece. She is of age and can choose her own husband. 'Tis my good fortune that she chose me."

"Your clansmen will disagree," Redmyre retorted.

"Especially when they learn that they won't get their greedy hands on her inheritance."

"I am my own man, Redmyre," Ivor said. "I make my own decisions, and I have my own land. We won't starve."

"Albany will decide the matter," Sir Malcolm said. "Redmyre told me that the duke is searching for you. One avoids angering him, of course, so I sent a message when I heard that my men had found you. He'll join us here tomorrow, I expect."

Ivor moved to set down his half-empty mug. As he did, the table seemed to heave. Stopping his hand just above it, he thought woozily that he should not take the chance that the table might fling the whisky right back at him.

That thought seemed a strange one. But as he tried to sort it out, his knees buckled, and the great chamber vanished into blackness.

Marsi had felt uneasy since Ivor's departure and wondered what was keeping him. She knew he did not expect her to go downstairs alone. Nor could she go with Hetty, since Hetty had arranged to take her supper with Jamie in their room.

She was not dressed suitably for company, but she could not help that and refused to count Redmyre as such in any event. What, she wondered, if he and her uncle did apply to annul her marriage? Could they persuade the Kirk to agree?

She was still wondering about it all when they came for her.

So swiftly did they subdue her that she voiced only one startled cry of astonishment, not nearly loud enough to reach ears beyond her chamber.

~

Ivor awoke the next morning in a comfortable bed, but when he reached for Marsi, a jolt of pain shot through his head.

His groping hand found only bare sheet and coverlet.

Coming fully awake, he turned onto an elbow, ignoring his throbbing head when he saw what he had already deduced. The space beside him was empty.

The room was, nonetheless, the one to which the gillie had shown them the previous afternoon. Marsi was simply not in it.

He was naked, as usual when he slept. His clothing lay scattered about the room as if he had taken things off and dropped them wherever they might fall.

Such untidiness was rare for him. Like most warriors, his habit was to keep clothing he took off nearby, ready to don in haste if need be. And he never drank himself into the sort of stupor necessary to make him forget his normal habits.

Getting up fast enough to make his head spin, he tried to reassure himself that Marsi had just gone downstairs without waking him.

He poured water from a ewer into the basin on the washstand and scrubbed his face. He was reaching for a towel when his stomach lurched.

His mind regained its usual acuity with a near snap. His last memory was clear. He had been drinking whisky with Sir Malcolm and Redmyre before supper.

Plainly, something other than whisky had been in his mug.

So much for Sir Malcolm's Highland hospitality, the rules of which strictly forbade mistreating one's guests in any way. So much, too, for Sir Malcolm's claim that he did not *want* trouble with Clan Chattan.

Tossing the towel aside, Ivor put on his breeks, boots, tunic, and brigandine.

As he picked up his dirk and its sheath with his belt, he recalled that Aodán had taken his sword, bow, and quiver with him. Hoping he still had them and that neither he nor Will had likewise been mistreated, Ivor drew a breath to calm himself.

Having no idea where the gillie had put Hetty and James, he went down to the great chamber, where he found Sir Malcolm alone at the high table.

Striding onto the dais as though nowt were amiss, and knowing he needed to eat, Ivor told the gillie who came running to bring food and plenty of it.

"So you have wakened at last, have you?" Sir Malcolm said lightly. "You drank gey much of my good whisky yestereve, lad. Why, it took two of my gillies and your lady wife to put you to bed."

The man spoke with assurance, as if saying the thing would make it so.

Wondering how far he would carry such a farce, Ivor said, "Meantime, I seem to have misplaced my lady wife. Do you know where she is?"

"Sakes, I assumed that she was with you. But she has run off before, I'm told. So mayhap she has done so again. She has a mind of her own, does our Marsaili."

Taking a seat but leaving distance between himself

and his host, Ivor said mildly, "I wonder who can have told you that tale."

"I did."

The soft masculine voice came from an archway just beyond Ivor's end of the dais, directly opposite the entrance through which the gillie had gone.

Ivor had to turn his head to see who had spoken.

He had seen the Duke of Albany only at a distance on past occasions. Nevertheless, the tall, lanky figure garbed in black was unmistakable.

Ivor noted that Albany carried himself as if he were thirty instead of twice that age. Men said the duke seemed never to age. But as close as he was, Ivor could see the lines in his face. And his once glossy black hair bore streaks of silver.

Silent now, Albany seemed to wait patiently, even expectantly.

A glance at Sir Malcolm told Ivor that both men expected him to recognize Albany and leap to his feet. But Highlanders did not show respect without cause.

To the duke, he said, "By my troth, sir, I am at a loss. How have *you* gleaned such knowledge of my wife to repeat to our host?"

"Do you not know me, Sir Ivor?" Albany asked, his eyes narrowing. "I remember you. You were one of the last still standing after Clan Chattan defeated the Camerons at Perth. Your swordsmanship impressed me then. And I have learned since that you are even more skilled with a longbow."

"Thank you, my lord duke," Ivor said. He stood then and gave a Highlander's nod of respect. "Entering without due ceremony, as you did, did make me wonder," he added. "I could not be sure that you were indeed yourself."

"I thought you might prefer informality, since you have managed to put me out of temper," Albany said. "I trust that you did not mean to do so. Therefore, I would suggest that you think carefully about what you should do next, to atone."

Albany's voice diminished in volume as he spoke, but Ivor had heard much about this idiosyncrasy from Bishop Traill. He knew that the soft tone was the duke's way of making people listen closely to all that he said...and to unnerve them.

Since Ivor's hearing was nearly as acute as his long vision was, he had no need to exert himself. Nor would he give Albany the satisfaction of intimidating him. He did want to leave Kincardine in one piece, however, and if possible, with his wife.

A rattle of crockery from the other end of the dais diverted his attention to the gillie returning with a tray of food.

Ivor sat again, saying to Albany, "You will not mind if I eat whilst we talk, my lord. I am famished. Our host tells me that I drank much yestereve. But I fear that meantime I must have forgotten to eat. I'd swear I had not eaten since midday."

Sir Malcolm said then, "I hope that you will join us at the table, my lord duke." A gesture brought a second gillie running with an ale jug and two mugs.

Ivor said, "Do you *know* that my lady wife ran off, Sir Malcolm? Or were you merely offering the suggestion as a possibility?"

"Let us cease this useless prattle, sir," Albany said.

"Your wife, as you call her, is quite safe, as is my nephew James. Both are where I will *keep* them safe."

Cold fury swept over Ivor. But he said as softly as ever Albany had spoken, "Do you mean to tell me where this sanctuary lies?"

"I do not. Having created more trouble than I usually tolerate, you should be grateful to ride away with a whole skin and your equerry at your side."

Ivor concealed his surprise at the news that he had acquired an equerry.

Only Aodán and Will had come with him to Kincardine, so he assumed that the "equerry" must be Aodán and wondered what had become of Will. Even as the thought crossed his mind, though, he realized that Will had courage enough to declare that *he* was Ivor's equerry if aught had happened to Aodán.

Nodding to the gillie, who held a platter of sliced meat, and helping himself when the man bent nearer, Ivor looked silently at Albany for a moment or two.

"Was it Redmyre's men who followed us from Blackford?" he asked then.

Icily, Albany said, "Aye, but you are too complacent, sir. Had his grace not summoned Parliament to reinstate me as Governor of the Realm, I'd clap you in irons for daring to marry a ward of the Crown without leave. However, until the lords resolve this matter of the Governorship in my favor, I prefer to avoid angering any of the Highland lords. Therefore, you may leave here without hindrance. You would be wise, though, to return at once to your Highlands."

"Aye, then, I'll go when I've eaten," Ivor said. To Sir Malcolm, he said, "What of Mistress Childs, sir? Is she still here at Kincardine?"

To his surprise, his host flushed deeply, saying only, "Aye, she's here."

Remembering that Hetty had long served the Drummonds, Ivor wondered if she had expressed her feelings to Sir Malcolm or had simply let them show. His certainty that she had done one or the other nearly drew a smile.

Ignoring the urge, he said to Albany, "Do you think it wise, my lord, to separate James from the one person he trusts besides his grace? Mistress Childs accompanied him by royal command, so his grace will not approve that decision."

"I will attend to his grace," Albany retorted. "As for Mistress Childs, since she was party to this outrage, she cannot feel astonished to learn of her dismissal."

"You must think of a better reason to offer his grace," Ivor said. "He will not accept that one. The outrage, as you call it, was by his order to me *and* to Mistress Childs. In troth, the lords of Parliament—*and* the Scottish people— are unlikely to believe that the King *willingly* allowed you to take James into your custody."

"I am a more suitable guardian for him than anyone else could be," Albany said curtly. "However, if you want to stay here to discuss the matter..."

"I have no such intention," Ivor said, knowing he could not afford to press the matter and hoping that Albany would believe he was bowing to superior strength. To Sir Malcolm, he said dulcetly, "Do you mean to *keep* Mistress Childs here, sir?"

The older man's cheeks grew even redder. "I am duty bound to offer her hospitality, naturally. As to whether she *wants* to stay..."

"With your consent, I can take her wherever she wants to go," Ivor said as if he now had nothing more important to do.

"An excellent suggestion," Albany said. "Mistress Childs's people live north of Stobhall, do they not, Drummond? Near Cargill? Doubtless, since Sir Ivor is going home, he will travel that way in any event."

"Aye, sure," Sir Malcolm said. "I'll send a lad to tell her that she should prepare to leave with you straightaway. I'll also send word to the stables for your man to expect your departure."

Nodding, Ivor applied himself to his breakfast. Although he sought to look as if his mind were on his food, his thoughts were all of Marsi. He would get Hetty away from Kincardine and out of Albany's path. But he was not going home.

He was going to find Marsi and Jamie. And, if Albany's men had hurt either one of them, Albany's precious dukedom would soon pass to his worthless son.

Marsi was frightened and furious. At first, she had had no idea what had happened. She knew only that men had invaded the bedchamber she shared with Ivor, overpowered her, and carried her off.

She had fought them and tried to scream, but they subdued her so fast that, as far as she knew, no one in the room or outside it had paid her struggles any heed.

One man bound her hands behind her back, then gagged and blindfolded her. Still ignoring her struggles, two men had carried her downstairs and outside. There, they had put her on a horse without a saddle, given her her fur-lined cloak, and ordered her to make herself comfort-able and ride astride.

One offered to pull her skirts into place for her. When she wrenched away from him, another voice spoke curtly. The man had not tried again.

She knew that they were not in the stableyard and decided they must be some distance from the castle. She could hear water tumbling over rocks to her left, and their route seemed to slope downward. She deduced that they were heading north toward Aberuthven. But she was not even sure of that.

There were a number of men and horses, a dozen each, at least, she thought.

Her hands remained tied behind her. Someone led her horse.

From the start, she assumed that one of Sir Malcolm's men-at-arms was in charge and was taking her to Stobhall. Since her uncle disapproved of her marriage, she thought he just meant to keep her and Ivor apart until Albany or Sir Malcolm himself could arrange an annulment.

Before long, aware that they were definitely riding downhill, she could picture the sides of Kincardine Glen north of the castle. She easily recalled that they sloped lower until they merged with hills near Aberuthven and the confluence of Ruthven Water with the much larger river Earn.

If they were going to Stobhall, she knew they would ford the Earn southwest of Perth, because as the river flowed east to the Firth of Tay, it widened and deepened. Its flow grew much swifter and more turbulent with every mile.

Marsi had hoped to learn more from her captors' conversation as they rode, but the men rode in silence. In time, they rode faster. She was a fine horsewoman, but blindfolded and with her hands tied, she was at a distinct disadvantage. She began to fear that as she tired more, she might fall.

So intently did she have to concentrate on keeping her balance that she did not realize until a strong hand gripped her right elbow and steadied her that one of the men had changed position to ride beside her. He also put up her fur-lined hood for her. She was grateful for that. The night air was cold.

A muttered comment soon afterward resulted in an easing of the pace and then a halt while someone untied her hands and retied them in front of her.

Now, she could grip the horse's mane. But she could do nothing about the blindfold without raising both hands to it. She tried, but at a curt command to leave it be, she quickly lowered her hands. Had she not feared that they would retie them behind her, she might have tried again, even at the risk of falling.

Instead, she listened for sounds that might reveal more about their route.

When she heard a roar of water that could only be the swiftly moving Earn, she realized that they had bypassed Aberuthven, doubtless fearing that someone might ask about their prisoner. Soon afterward, hearing the river loudly to her left, she deduced that they were riding eastward along its south bank. They had therefore turned off the Perth road, which crossed the Earn farther west, where a bridge spanned narrows near the village of Dalreoch.

Marsi had never crossed the Earn anywhere else,

although she knew that another, longer, and more famous bridge existed.

The Bridge of Earn allowed anyone traveling to Perth from Edinburgh, St. Andrews, or Falkland to save miles on their journey. But she could think of no reason for her abductors to use it rather than the bridge at Dalreoch.

So where, she wondered, could they be taking her?

After much wrinkling of her nose and contorting of her face that apparently went unnoticed by her captors, she was able to discern through a space below the edge of her blindfold that darkness had fallen. Perceiving light to her left, she saw that it came from the river. Moonlight glittered there on foamy water.

She had missed her supper. And the men had given her nothing to eat. But they kept riding until at last, exhausted, she leaned forward, resting her head on the pony's neck and dozing, if not sleeping, until a loud clattering startled her awake.

Her blindfold had rubbed up enough for her to see that they were on an arched bridge spanning a broad river. It had to be the Bridge of Earn. Once across, they turned east again to follow a path between the river and what appeared to be imposing cliffs just north of it.

Noting a rider on her right whose horse had moved a little ahead of hers, she saw by tilting her head back that he was a burly man holding a small person, heavily cloaked, in front of him. She could see neither face, but instinct and logic told her that the small person was Jamie. So her uncle *was* in league with Albany.

The thought brought a renewed sense of betrayal.

In time, they turned up a steep path. After what seemed to be hours, they reached the top of a long ridge. From the east shoulder of a hill at the end of it, in bright moonlight, she looked down a wooded slope that descended to a peninsula.

Pushing the blindfold and hood off at last, she saw the landscape more plainly. The Earn lay to her right, where it joined a much broader expanse of water flowing west to east ahead of her. She knew that it must be the Firth of Tay.

A closer look revealed that the area below rose and fell in a series of low hills and shallow pockets. On one promontory near the edge of the firth, a tall, square tower rose sixty or seventy feet above the landscape.

A semicircle of outbuildings framed a sprawling stone building beside the tower that was clearly a noble residence. With a prickling sense of dread, Marsi looked around until her gaze fell upon the burly Redmyre a short distance away.

He was holding Jamie, apparently asleep, before him on his horse.

Although she had not known who had abducted her, Marsi decided that she ought to have guessed and felt no surprise to see him.

"Welcome to Redmyre, m'lady," he said. "My granddad said that when Roman legionaries first saw the view from here, they cried out in a false belief that they were beholding the river Tiber beyond the field of Mars. The prospect from my tower is just as grand. But you will see it, for the tower is where you will stay until Albany arranges your annulment. In sooth, you will remain there until I can be sure that any bairn you carry is mine own."

The smile he gave her sent a surge of revulsion through

her. She wanted to declare that she would drown any brat of his. But her gag prevented speech.

Moreover, she hoped that her experiences with Ivor and Jamie had taught her the wisdom of thinking before she blurted her thoughts and feelings to one and all.

Chapter 18 _____

Having changed to his breeks and plaid for riding, Ivor met his first obstacle when he revealed his plan to Hetty, saying, "Tell me where I can take you, mistress. It should be near here but where you can be with friends."

"With respect, sir," she said, "I could not be easy in my conscience if I were to abandon my lady or our Jamie now. I will go with you."

"In troth, mistress, Aodán and I will ride faster without you and be better able to cope with any difficulty we may meet."

"I will keep up, sir," Hetty said. "I will also try to keep out of your way if we meet trouble. But I will go unless you mean to leave me with Sir Malcolm, who is more likely to hand me over to Albany than protect me."

"I won't abandon you to Sir Malcolm," he said tersely. "Someone ought to have drowned that particular Drummond pup at birth."

"He is a great disappointment to me," Hetty said. "Malcolm and I are much the same age, and cousins. So, until he began training for his knighthood, I saw him often. He was an ordinary boy, but gaining power changed him."

"Power changes most men."

"Aye, but I fear that for him it has become essential. See you, the Drummonds gained most of their vast power through their daughters, not their sons. I think Malcolm resents that and hopes to increase his power through Albany."

Ivor did not mean to discuss Drummonds other than Marsi any further, so he said, "You may come with me, mistress. But I want your word that when I give an order, you will obey it. If I tell you to hide in woodland or elsewhere, I'll expect you to stay there until I return to fetch you."

The sudden twinkle in her eyes told him that her thoughts, like his own, had flashed to Marsi's likely reaction to such an order.

The twinkle faded, and Hetty said, "I am accustomed to following orders, sir. I will do all I can to help you rescue my bairns from those who took them. Men who would do such a thing *must* be ill-doers."

Ruthlessly suppressing thoughts of what Marsi might suffer at the hands of such men, Ivor ordered a hovering gillie to carry Hetty's bundles down for her.

Leading the way to the yard, he found Aodán alone with their horses and wondered if Albany had mistaken the captain of his fighting tail for a mere equerry or had just meant to belittle Aodán. Not that it mattered. He was glad to see him.

"The lady Marsi and James have gone from here, Aodán—taken by Albany's men, I suspect," Ivor said without preamble in Gaelic. "Did you see them go?"

"Nay," Aodán said. "They could have slipped out another way, sir, but only to head north. Until I received the order to ready our horses, I'd watched the track to the south for our missing two lads to come. But I'd have seen anyone in the yard."

"Those were Redmyre's men that Will saw yester-morn," Ivor said. "I fear that they must have ambushed our lads."

Aodán grimaced but said naught as he threw Ivor's bundles and Hetty's on a sumpter pony and tied them down. The horses were ready, and he had Ivor's sword, bow, and quiver. While Ivor arranged his weapons and prepared to ride, Aodán helped Hetty. Then, he gathered the sumpter leads and mounted his own horse.

As they left the yard, Ivor said, "What have you done with young Will?"

"Nowt," Aodán replied. "He vanished overnight. In troth, sir, I had no more than a glimpse of him after he helped me unload our three sumpters and tend the other horses. He seemed gey fidgety then. I had to warn him to take himself in hand lest he pass his nerves on to the beasts."

Ivor frowned. It seemed unlike Will to behave so. The boy had chosen, after all, to follow Aodán to the stables rather than accompany them into the castle.

And Jamie had seemed content with his choice.

Ivor wondered if the boys had had a falling out. But he had neither the time nor reason to ponder that possibility for long. He was eager to get away before Albany changed his mind about letting them go.

They had clear sky above while they followed the track north through the steep-sided glen. But when they emerged from its depths to see the village of Aberuthven in the distance, gray clouds had gathered in the west. And scattered, puffy white ones drifted toward them from the north.

In the cool morning air the clouds suggested rain rather than snow but warned Ivor that they'd be wise to seek shelter by midafternoon. Still, until he knew which way Albany's men had gone with their captives, he could make few decisions.

⁓

Marsi stared bleakly out the south-facing window of Redmyre Tower at the long range of wooded hills jutting behind the flatter area nearby. By daylight, the trees were visibly a mix of evergreens, newly leafing beeches, and other varieties.

She wore her cloak, for the room was chilly. Its three windows lacked glass, and she could not bear to keep them all shuttered. There was no other source of light.

She knew the track from Strathearn led over those hills to Redmyre's estate, because they had followed it the night before. However, from where she stood, looking east or west, she saw no path, only densely growing trees.

Looking west from a second window at gathering storm clouds over an undulating but otherwise tedious landscape of cultivated plots and grassy, snowdrift-dotted pastures, she decided to close that set of shutters against the chilly breeze.

The door leading to the stair landing was in the windowless north wall.

Looking east, she could see where the river Earn flowed into the firth. The view was nice, but she felt as if the river cut her off from the world beyond it. She had seen no roads anywhere, only a few footpaths.

She thought they had traveled less than a mile after crossing the bridge before they had turned and headed up the steep path. But she had dozed after that and did not know how far they had traveled to reach the hilltop. Likewise, her memory of the ride down to the tower was vague, and Redmyre had taken her inside at once. She had been tired and nigh starving by then.

The narrow, winding stone stairway had seemed to go up forever.

When they reached the uppermost landing and entered the room, she had felt weak, dizzy, and disoriented. Her knees had been so wobbly that when Redmyre removed her gag and untied her hands, she sat down at once on a narrow cot with just two quilts and a thin featherbed for a mattress. Only then did she realize that Jamie had not followed them upstairs.

Standing over her as Redmyre did, he seemed even taller and more powerfully built than she remembered. But she refused to let him intimidate her.

"What have you done with James?" she demanded.

"This tower is no fit place for a prince of the realm," he replied. "He will stay in the hall, in rooms suited to his rank, till his uncle takes him in charge."

"Do you mean to starve me until then?"

"You will address me civilly, m'lady," he said harshly. "I do not mean to be a brutal husband. But neither will I tolerate rudeness or defiance."

"Faith, I do not know what to call you."

" 'Sir' will do."

She was silent, as if she were considering that as a suggestion. Then she said, "But 'sir' is a form of address reserved for gentlemen, is it not?"

The bright moonlight beaming into the tower room revealed his darkening cheeks. "You will mind your tongue if you want food, my lass," he snapped.

"Will I? What else will you do if I don't? Beat me? Kill me? I should point out that if I die, you will *not* get the Cargill estates. If Clan Chattan does not claim them for my husband, as I'd expect they will, they will revert to a cousin of mine. The royal charter awarding those lands to Drummonds of Cargill decrees it so."

"As Royal Chamberlain, Albany controls *all* royal charters."

"Only with the consent of Parliament," Marsi said. "Surely, you know that."

"Parliament will do as he bids."

She wrinkled her nose. "I am young yet. But I have forever heard complaints that the lords of Parliament rarely do as *any* particular man hopes they will."

"Albany kens how to make them."

"But, even if he succeeds in annulling my marriage, the Drummonds will not sit idly by whilst Drummond lands go out of the family. I suspect Uncle Malcolm is already queasy about that and agreed to it only to curry favor with Albany. Ah, that hits the mark. I can see it in your face."

Abruptly, Redmyre left the room and pulled the door shut, hard.

If Marsi hoped he would forget to lock it, the thud of a bolt slamming into its socket disappointed her.

~

Ivor, Hetty, and Aodán spent precious time in Aberuthven without learning a thing about their quarry, leaving

Ivor to deduce that the riders they followed had skirted the town without drawing notice.

"Easy enough to do," he said to Aodán. "These heavily forested hills provide many ways to avoid the main road. However, they'll likely return to it before long."

Beyond Aberuthven, they came to a place where the road led eastward from Ruthven Water. Drawing rein, Ivor said, "Much of this path is too pebble strewn to show tracks. But it does look as if a number of horses recently headed east."

"So you do think we are going the right way," Hetty said.

"Aye, for I—" Ivor frowned into the distance. "Do you see that rider, Aodán?" When Aodán shook his head, Ivor pointed. "Yonder, past the dip between the two steep hills to our right, a horseman coming down—looks like Will."

Hetty exclaimed, "Good lack, sir! That dip must be a mile from here. I cannot even discern *signs* of a pathway, let alone a rider."

"He is not following a path," Ivor said. "His pony is picking its way down through the trees. Look straight down from the tallest evergreen at the summit. Midway between the treetop and the road."

"I see him, sir," Aodán said. "That's a rider, aye, and small. But as to its being our Will, I couldna say."

"He has seen us," Ivor interjected. "He is increasing his pace."

On those words, he urged his mount on, letting it stretch its legs. He knew that Aodán, leading their sumpters, would continue to follow at Hetty's pace.

Nearing Will on the flat, he saw that the boy was eyeing him warily.

Greeting him, Ivor said, "I hope you have news, lad."

"Aye, sir, I do. But I feared ye might be vexed wi' me for loping off as I did."

"Why did you go?"

"'Cause them men what caught us in the glen paid me nae heed. So, after we reached Kincardine, I acted as if I was used tae working in the stable there and nae one heeded me save tae toss me an order now and now. I expect the Kincardine lot thought I were wi' them others. But it were plain tae me by suppertime that summat strange were a-going on, 'cause by then I could tell that we had two lots o' men, besides ours and them what belonged tae the Laird o' Kincardine."

"Two lots?"

"Aye, sir. Sithee, they seemed tae be summat together and summat at odds. So I kept me eyes on all o' them and offered tae help yestereve when one lot wanted ponies saddled. Nae one said nowt o' where they were a-going. But just the one lot did set up tae go. Some eight or ten o' them, there were. But they ordered two more ponies besides their own and nobbut *one* sumpter. Forbye, as we saddled each one, a man would lead it away. All o' that stirred me tae think, I can tell ye."

"You showed good sense, Will. I'd wager that the lot that left Kincardine were Albany's men, although he is still—"

"Nay, then, laird," Will said, relaxing. "'Twas the other lot. Their leader be a square-built man in claret-colored velvet wha' behaves as grand as if *he* was the duke. There were men in black, too, though. They may ha' been the duke's, but Lord Fife's men in Doune mostly wear black, too, so I didna ken. Mayhap we should stop talking like this, though, sir. Mistress Hetty and Aodán be almost upon us."

"We'll keep no secrets from them," Ivor said, glancing toward the other two. "You should know, though, that Lady Marsi and Jamie were taken from Kincardine. I suspect they are riding with the men you saw, because unless Albany lied, he ordered them both moved to a place he *said* would be safer for them."

"Aye, well, they'll be with that lot, then," Will said with a nod. "I did think that the lad wi' them looked like James. But the lady wore a blindfold and a gag, so I couldna make out her face. Where be they a-taking them, d'ye think?"

"I don't know," Ivor said. "From your description of their leader, I suspect he is Lindsay of Redmyre. Although he wore crimson, he is Albany's man and has an estate somewhere on Fife's north coast. So we should be able to follow them easily enough. How far ahead are they?"

Will shrugged. "I dinna ken. I thought I'd best hie me back tae tell ye which way they did go. Sithee, I thought ye'd still be at the castle, and I followed them much o' the night. After some hours, when they crossed yon great bridge, I didna ken where I might end up if I went on wi' them. But I kent fine that I could follow that line o' hills yonder back tae Kincardine, so I did."

"That great bridge, was it an arched one of stone across a wide river?"

"Aye, and the river be the one that wends hither and yon through this strath."

"Then the bridge is the Bridge of Earn," Ivor said. "I have crossed it myself more than once, traveling from St.

Andrews to Perth and back. But they would not come so far this way and be heading for Perth."

As he spoke, Aodán and Hetty reined in near them.

"Aodán, you have also traveled to St. Andrews and back from Perth," Ivor said. "Do you recall aught about the area betwixt the Earn and the Firth of Tay?"

"Only that steep hills, even cliffs, line the north side of the strath all the way from the bridge west to Craigend. They extend eastward to the river bend, as well."

"Redmyre bragged that the Lindsays had owned both sides of the firth before the glaciers created it. I'd wager that his southern estate lies on the peninsula that the Earn and the firth form at their confluence."

"Aye, perhaps," Aodán said. "As I recall, sir, the abbey...Lindores...owns the land up *to* the east bank of the river Earn."

"It does," Ivor agreed. "The Bridge of Earn must lie ten miles from here and nearly the same distance from Newburgh and its abbey. So, unless Redmyre keeps a boat near his tower, we'll have no easy path to the abbey from his land. In the message I sent there for Wolf, I said that we'd look for him at Newburgh."

"Wi' respect, sir, we be nobbut two men and a lad against a dozen men-at-arms, plus them wha' Redmyre keeps on his estate. We're heavily outnumbered."

"Aye, so heavily that I'll want you to ride to Newburgh," Ivor said. "Wolf will expect us to approach Lindores by land, as in troth, I did mean to do. He will *not* look for us to be west of the Earn's confluence with the firth."

"But I shouldna leave ye and Will, no to mention Mistress Hetty."

"They can bide with me," Ivor said. "No one will suspect a man traveling with a middle-aged woman and a lad to be any threat to Redmyre. I want to see his estate. His tower likely stands near the water if not right on it."

"Aye, he'd want a clear view o' any boats approaching. He'll likely keep watchers atop some o' the surrounding hills as well, though."

"If I can get a good look from the crest of those hills, I may be able to judge how many men he has. Meantime, Fin needs time to find us and Wolf needs to know where we'll be. Sithee, Aodán, when we find James, I want to get him on a ship as quickly as I can. I doubt that Albany will anticipate that possibility here."

"Likely, he thinks he's outsmarted us," Aodán said, adding, "I can reach Lindores afore nightfall, sir. The abbot will pass on any message, aye?"

"Wolf assured me that he will if you but speak the words 'Sea Wolf,'" Ivor said. "Mention also that Jake should watch for the Mackintosh banner and tell the abbot it's the one with the wildcat facing outward. I don't know what I'll find when I get close, so he should warn Jake that the banner may be flying from a tree or a staff near the water. Wherever he sees it, we'll be nearby."

"What of Sir Fin?" Aodán asked. "He'll likely head for yon Bridge o' Earn. And, since he'll come from Perth..."

"We'll think of a way to get a message to him, too," Ivor said.

Certain now that they were going the right way, he wished that they could ride faster. As it was, he had to spare the horses. So it would be well after midday when they reached the Bridge of Earn, and dusk just hours later.

As he rode, try as he would to consider logistics for

various situations that he might encounter with Redmyre, his thoughts kept flying back to Marsi.

Every time they did, an image flashed into his head of her struggling to fight off Redmyre. His temper stirred each time until a sudden image of Bishop Traill intervened, growling sternly, *A bad temper produces its own punishments.*

That image drew a near smile, because the memory it evoked was both clear and pertinent. Becoming aware that he had mindlessly urged his horse on ahead of the others, he called himself sharply to order and eased its pace.

It would be at least two hours before they reached the bridge. How long it might take Fin to reach the same place was the first issue to consider.

～

The grating thunk of the bolt sliding back startled Marsi from a reverie in which she had been methodically retracing every moment with Ivor, to pass the time. She had heard nothing to warn her of anyone's approach.

Unaccustomed as she was to spending hours by herself, she had slept for a time. But when no one had come by the time she awoke, having nothing to do became more than tedium. Too much solitude, she thought, would drive her mad.

When the door opened and Redmyre entered with a gillie behind him, she got quickly to her feet. "I was beginning to wonder how long you meant to keep me without food or water," she said.

"You would do well to wonder how much longer it will be next time if you are discourteous, my lady."

Deciding that the comment deserved no reply, she made none.

"Good then," he said as if her silence was apology enough. "Someone will bring you food and water shortly." Gesturing to a sumpter basket that the gillie carried, he added, "I've brought you something else, to pass the time."

Concealing what little relief she felt, she said, "I cannot imagine what would interest me more than food or water just now."

"I just hope you are handy with a needle and thread," he said, opening the basket that the gillie held. The latter, carefully expressionless, avoided her eye.

To Marsi's astonishment, the basket held a pile of rose-pink velvet.

Redmyre pulled it out and shook it, revealing a kirtle with long, slim sleeves and small gold buttons from elbow to wrist.

Holding it up to her while she gritted her teeth and stood perfectly still, he said, "Your uncle wanted you to have clothing more suited to your rank. Those three gowns in there were Annabella's. Since she was taller than you, they need altering. But I expect that you attended to such tasks for her grace now and now."

"It was thoughtful of Uncle Malcolm to send them," Marsi said evenly.

"Aye, it was. They are not new or fashionable, since they are clothes that she discarded at Kincardine. But they will look better than that thing you have on."

"Have you needle and thread in that basket?" she asked.

"A needle case, several colors of thread, and a wee pair of scissors, as well."

He seemed proud of himself for thinking of those things, but Marsi wondered only if the needles or scissors might serve her as weapons.

~⌒~

Ivor, Aodán, Hetty, and Will reached the Bridge of Earn an hour or so after midday. Dismounting in a copse a short distance away, they ate the bread and meat that, thanks to a friendly gillie, Ivor had brought from Kincardine.

Will produced two apples from somewhere on his small person, and Ivor cut them into wedges for the four of them.

As he handed wedges to Hetty and Will, he said, "When you've eaten your fill, lad, I want you to gather sticks straight enough to look like arrows. About so long," he added, holding his hands about three feet apart.

"Long as real arrows, then," Will said, nodding. "How many?"

"Five. But you might find a few extra, lest some won't do."

"I'll get them now," Will said, taking another apple wedge and striding off.

"A singularly *un*inquisitive lad," Aodán murmured.

Ivor's lips twitched. He said, "I expect that the ill-willed Master Lucken has taught him the wisdom of questioning his elders only when he requires information to fulfill a task," he said. "Also, Will is practical enough to realize that he will soon *see* what I do with them. As will you," he added, grinning at Aodán.

With a wry look, Aodán turned and reached for another apple wedge.

Marsi stared at the pink velvet fabric lying heavily across her lap and sighed.

"Horrid man," she muttered to the ambient air. "I do wish that he had thought to provide a woman to help me mark the hems of these gowns."

When Redmyre had accompanied the gillie who carried up food and water to her, she had put the suggestion to him. But his lordship said that he could not, as a bachelor, keep female servants. Until he married her, he said, he would have none.

"Meantime," she said tartly, "you destroy my reputation by keeping *me* here."

"Sakes, you did that yourself, lass, by traveling as you did with Mackintosh."

The memory of those words made her shudder. Since Hetty and James, as well as Ivor, had been with her while they traveled, and since they had never given out her name, she could not imagine how *she* had ruined herself. But Marsi had not debated the matter further with Redmyre.

Determinedly returning her thoughts to the task in hand, she decided that without someone else to pin up the hem for her, she could not shorten the gowns.

"I'd never get them straight," she muttered.

She'd wager, too, that the needle or the pins in the needle case, or the small pair of scissors that Redmyre had supplied, would not aid her much against him.

Still stroking the velvet, she closed her eyes. The image of Ivor in the blue velvet doublet that he had worn the previous evening leaped to her mind.

"You *will* find me," she murmured, feeling warmth at the very thought of him. She touched her ring, savoring her knowledge that the fourth finger contained a nerve running directly to her heart. "You will find both of us," she added more firmly. "And, by heaven, I hope you kill the villains who took us from you!"

Experience reared its head then, warning her that she could trust no one, even herself, and especially not people who promised that they would always look after her. People, as she knew, had only to say *that* and they died.

But Ivor had said she could trust him, and she did. He would find them.

A chill stirred then. Would he still *want* her after she had been overnight in Redmyre's hands? She had heard tales of women abandoned by both husband and clan after an enemy had captured and returned them. Would Ivor abandon her, too?

What if, after he rescued her, she found that she was with child? Would he believe that it was his? Or would he, like Redmyre, want proof?

Collecting herself with a shake, she shoved the pink velvet gown aside and got up to look out the south window again at the thickly wooded hills.

Whatever Ivor might do, he had to find them first. After that, when she could look into his eyes, she would know all that she needed to know.

If he loved her even half as much as she knew now that she loved him...

Chapter 19 ─────────────

Having left Will to find his sticks, and Hetty by a stream to wash her hands and face, Ivor and Aodán took a quarter-hour's target practice. Stepping back thirty paces after letting each arrow fly, they shot a quiver's worth at marked saplings. At one point, Aodán said, "I've sent one into the river. D'ye never miss, sir?"

Ivor smiled. "Aye, sure. I just never let anyone else see it when I do."

Will returned soon afterward with five perfectly straight, three-foot-long, arrow-slender rods in hand. "Will these do, sir?" he asked, holding them out to Ivor.

"They will," Ivor said. From his quiver, he took a used bowstring and cut it in two with his dirk. Giving one piece to the boy, he said, "Bind them together at the middle. Then spread them so they'll stand up unaided. I want to see how they look."

Glancing at Aodán, Ivor saw the other man's eyebrows arc inquiringly.

Without responding to the silent query, Ivor said, "We'll want pebbles next, a lot of them. I think we'll find more nearer the river than here. So, if you've finished binding those sticks together, Will, you may fetch Hetty."

The boy darted off, and Ivor and Aodán quickly retrieved their arrows.

Crossing to the north side of the river with Hetty and Will, they found a wealth of river rocks and pebbles of all sizes. Showing the others what he wanted, Ivor gathered a supply to get started. Then he strode west from the bridge along the road until he came to a sizable boulder near enough to the road for his purpose.

Standing Will's bundle of rods atop the boulder, he carefully fanned it to stand up. Realizing that a wind could blow it off, he anchored it with a rock of suitable size set inside its lower half. Then he put smaller rocks around the outside to hold it in place. The message was primitive, but he was sure it would work.

On a flat expanse of hard dirt behind the boulder, not easily visible to riders passing from either direction, he used his pebbles to form letters.

Aodán, Hetty, and Will soon joined him, bringing more pebbles.

Hetty, watching over Ivor's shoulder, quietly corrected his spelling and thus let him know that she could read the Gaelic.

"Does her ladyship speak Gaelic, too?" he asked her, aware that he and Aodán had spoken the language in Marsi's hearing and doubtless in Hetty's as well.

"Aye, sure," she said. "We may have grown up in the lower glens, sir, but we Drummonds are Highlanders as much as you and your kinfolk are."

"You might have told me," he said as he began to form the last word.

"I assumed that you knew we did. Mayhap her ladyship assumed that, too."

Realizing guiltily that he was at fault, Ivor said with a touch of amusement nonetheless, "I suspect that you give her ladyship more credit than she deserves. But it is my fault for not asking you both if you did speak it. In troth, I believed you did *not*. And to speak Gaelic in your presence, under that belief, was wrong of me."

"In fairness, sir, we were nearly always riding behind you when you did. You had no cause to think of aught save your own conversation."

"You are more generous now than *I* deserve," he said.

Finishing his message, he stood to view the result. Aodán moved closer to see what he had written, and Ivor watched him frown as he figured it out. Although Gaelic was Aodán's primary language, he could read only basic words and required concentration to do so.

At last, he murmured, " 'Come here and get meat?' "

When Ivor nodded, Aodán smiled.

"That should do it, don't you think?" Ivor asked him in Scots.

Aodán nodded, but Will said, "Do what, laird? I dinna think it means nowt. We'll ha' nae meat for anyone 'less we kill summat for supper. We ate all we had afore, and since ye and Aodán shot at saplings instead o' rabbits, we still ha' nowt."

Hetty nodded her agreement.

Seeing no reason to deny them the explanation, Ivor said, "The war cry of Clan Cameron is 'Sons of the flesh, come here and get meat.' Also, their clan crest is a bundle of arrows similar to the bundle you've made for us, Will."

"Coo," Will said. "D'ye mean the whole clan will come out tae help us?"

"Nay, but a friend of mine, a Cameron called Fin of the Battles, will come. He'll be watching for a sign from us when he does. He'll bring men with him, too."

"Sithee, Sir Fin willna pass that bundle of 'arrows' without he looks gey close at them," Aodán added. "We can make a pebble arrow, too, pointing the way we go."

Ivor nodded, then said to Will, "When we see where our quarry has gone, I'll send you back to watch for Sir Fin and guide him to us."

"Aye, sure, I can do that. That way, he'll no cross yon bridge by mistake. But how will I know him?"

"His banner will bear that same bundle of arrows but with sharp points."

"Broadhead or bodkin?" the son of Fletcher Nat asked with a grin.

Ivor grinned back. "Broadhead. But your sticks are fine as they are."

"I should be off tae Lindores," Aodán said.

"Trade mounts with the lad," Ivor said. "All the ponies are rested now, but Will is the lightest rider. His wasn't as tired as yours before. Also, I've gelt for you to take," he added, unhooking his purse from his belt. "If necessary, hire or buy another mount. Come to that, since we have our own horses now, trade that one if it becomes necessary. And request a fresh one from the abbey before you return. You must ride fast and get back as soon as you can, Aodán. Watch for our usual signs to follow us, although I doubt that aught will happen before morning."

"What if Albany is close behind us, sir? What if *he* sees these signs?"

"He does not speak or read Gaelic," Ivor said. "Moreover,

he is more likely to ride east than to ride this way from the bridge. He'll know where Redmyre is."

"But Albany *will* come after us."

"In troth, I doubt he's spared *us* a thought. Recall that he thinks I'm taking Mistress Hetty home. Recall, too, that he rarely dirties his own hands. Before he tries to move Jamie elsewhere, he'll want to be sure that nowt has gone amiss. If anything has, he'll blame Redmyre and claim that *he* knew nowt of it."

Nodding, Aodán said, "Then I'm off, sir. Fare ye well."

They watched him ride back across the river and turn eastward.

After aiding Hetty to mount, Ivor gathered the sumpter ponies' leads and mounted his horse. Then the three riders also headed east, nearly keeping pace with Aodán on the other side of the river until he vanished over a hill.

Shortly afterward, Ivor said, "There's a side track yonder."

"I see it, too," Will exclaimed. "A track up into those hills."

"I don't see any such thing," Hetty said.

Although they tried to show her, her long vision was not nearly as keen as Ivor's or Will's. So it was some time before she nodded.

"Men will be watching this path," Ivor said when they reached it and he saw how steep it was. "We'll stay away from the path but nearby, because it likely heads through a pass. I want to find a good vantage point without riding to the very top."

"I'm thinking we've got too many horses," Will said. "Three people wi' six horses canna creep up on anyone."

Ivor said, "I don't want to creep up on the guards, lad.

I want to keep clear of them without having to go too far out of *our* way. If we come to a place where the horses cannot proceed, we'll find water and hobble them so they won't wander far."

"Will yon Fin o' the Battles ken about the watchers?"

"By the time he arrives, they will no longer be a threat," Ivor said mildly.

Will's mouth opened, doubtless to ask another question. But the answer must have occurred to him because, with a glance at Hetty, he shut his mouth.

His eyes were wide when his gaze met Ivor's.

⁓

Marsi passed the late afternoon and early evening by watching for boats.

First, she watched through the west-facing window for one heading east until it vanished behind the windowless north wall of the tower room. Then, crossing the room to watch it appear again on the east side, she waited for one sailing west.

Meantime, her mind kept busy, plotting ways to foil Redmyre's plan. Unfortunately, although she did not lack ideas, most of them seemed likely to require intervention by wee folk or some other magical occurrence.

Locked at the top of that tower, nearly a hundred feet from the ground—for surely, she was at least that high— one either had to grow wings or persuade someone else, preferably someone *with* magical powers, to rescue her.

At that season, boats on the firth were few. When more than a half-hour had passed without one, she lay on the hard bed and pulled her cloak over her for warmth.

She woke abruptly at the sound of the bolt.

From a rocky crag at the top of the ridge, Ivor looked from the east northward over the dusky landscape below and saw that any approach to the tower from the river Earn near its confluence with the firth would have to be uphill. If such an approach were even possible along an unnavigable river overlooked by cliffs, invaders would be visible to Redmyre's guards, and vulnerable to attack.

They would have to approach from the hills here above the tower. The dense woodland stretched to just under a hundred yards from the structure.

He also noted a hook of land that curved into the firth just east of the tower. It hooked around sand now, but the tide was out and there was a jetty. Although no boat lay beached nearby, high water marks indicated that the area inside the hook must provide at least a high-water landing place.

Clouds in the north had piled high and seemed eager to meet the darker ones in the west. The setting sun turned the darker ones pink, orange, and purple.

Some twenty feet below him on the south side, where a spring bubbled from the ground, he heard Hetty murmuring to the horses while Will hobbled them.

A horse snuffled back at Hetty, but Ivor knew the sound would not travel far enough to endanger them. Although he had counted at least thirty men-at-arms, he knew that it was less than a tenth the number Redmyre would need to post guards throughout the forest, and was more worried about rain than about guards.

For Fin, it would be a different matter. While a man, a woman, and a boy looked threatening to no one, the approach of a force as sizable as Ivor hoped Fin would bring would send anyone who saw them sprinting to warn Redmyre.

Studying the landscape and buildings below, Ivor knew that for any plan to be effective, he first had to learn where Redmyre was housing his captives. He suspected they would both be in the tower, which would be easier to secure than the sprawling house west of it could ever be.

However, as cocksure of himself as Redmyre was, he might keep James at least in more suitable quarters.

The thought that Redmyre might keep Marsi close to himself stirred such a rush of fury that Ivor firmly squelched both the image and the thought.

Will, coming to stand beside him just then, gazed downward in somber silence before he said quietly, "I'm thinking that a place like that 'un yonder must ha' duna-many rooms tae search."

Resting a hand on the boy's near shoulder, Ivor said, "You must not concern yourself about that, lad, for to do two things at once is to do neither. If we are going to rescue them, you must think only of doing your part well and safely. You need to go back to the road and hide near our signs so that you can see Sir Fin coming."

"Aye, sure. But if he comes in the night, he willna see nowt."

"There should be a moon from time to time even if those clouds dump rain on us," Ivor said. "I don't expect him to arrive before morning, but you should go now. Find a place that will shelter you as much as possible if we do get a storm."

"A bit o' rain willna trouble me."

"Then even if you go gey carefully, you should make

good time. I have seen that you have a knack for making yourself invisible in company. Tonight we will learn how skilled you are at doing so in the woods. It occurs to me, though, that you may not be quite comfortable in such unknown woodland all by yourself."

Will shrugged. "I'm no afeard, sir. I ken fine where I'll be a-going and how tae get back. Be there summat I ought tae say tae Sir Fin, so he'll ken I'm a friend?"

Ivor suppressed a chuckle. "I doubt that he will take you for aught else, lad. But if you like, or just to show him that I *am* the one who sent you, you may tell him that you ken him for the one man who can touch our Cat without a glove."

Repeating the words, Will said doubtfully, "He'll ken what that means?"

"He will, aye. Recall that we were speaking earlier about mottoes. Ours for Clan Chattan is 'Touch not the cat but *with* a glove.'"

"I could just tell him I ken your motto."

"Many people know it, including the Duke of Albany."

"Aye, then, I'll say it just as ye did."

Putting both hands on his shoulders, Ivor said, "I'm depending on you to know yourself, Will, and not to promise more than you can do. Art sure, lad?"

Will met his gaze easily. "I am, aye, sir. Sithee, I made it tae yon bridge and back tae find ye. I can find yon bundle o' sticks again just as easily, I trow."

"Very well then. Off with you."

When the boy had gone, Ivor checked with Hetty to make sure that she was as comfortable as possible under the circumstances.

"I'm going to leave you for a time later, mistress,"

he said. "I want to make sure that the way is clear for Fin Cameron and his men. But I'll wait until Redmyre changes his guard. I should be able to see from here when he does."

"Aye, sir, 'Tis a gey unlikely place for anyone to seek us, so I'll fare well enow. I have my cloak, and I found a dry patch of ground amidst some boulders yonder, where I warrant I can doze."

"If you sleep, mistress, and you do not snore, you will be safe. I'm going to get some rest myself before I leave you."

"Shall I stay awake until then and wake you?"

"Nay, I've a good clock in my head. I'll waken."

He returned then to his vantage point. There was still light enough below to see that all of the visible tower windows were shuttered except the two that he could see at the top, the south-facing one and the one that faced east.

As he watched the latter window, he saw fleeting movement as if someone walked past it. Focusing on that window but maintaining peripheral awareness of the darker, south-facing one as well, Ivor waited.

Marsi stopped her pacing and stared again at the closed door. Although the sound of the bolt had wakened her, no one had come in. Wondering if someone (or magic) had unlocked the door for her, she lifted the latch and tried to open it.

It didn't budge.

A second, more disturbing thought stirred. What if Redmyre had quietly unbolted it and eased it open to stare at her while she slept?

What if someone else had? She had no way to protect herself. The only furniture in the room besides the bed was a spindly washstand with a cracked ewer and a basin, a pail in the corner, and a low table more spindly than the washstand.

She could drag the cot across the door, but she held no illusions about the result. A child could push the door hard enough to move that narrow cot, and Redmyre was no child. Nor did she want to make him angry. So she had paced.

An odd feeling touched her, as if even now someone stood on the other side of that door. She felt an uneasy sense of being watched. But, having earlier examined the door to be sure that Redmyre had not drilled a squint in it to watch her, she knew there was no way to see through it.

Turning back to the east window, she made herself smile at the absurdity of her thoughts. It would do her no good to let her ever fertile imagination terrify her.

Doubtless Jamie was frightened, too. But he would know as well as she did that he had naught to fear from Redmyre. Albany would kill the man himself if he harmed Jamie. The duke might eventually want Jamie out of his way, in order to take the throne. But he'd take good care to avoid any hint that he or anyone who answered to him had had a part in whatever might befall the young prince then.

She wondered then if Sir Malcolm and Redmyre had arranged on their own for their abduction, hoping to please Albany, or if Albany had ordered it. Either way, he would know where she and Jamie were and would soon be on his way to fetch Jamie.

The last light from the setting sun had faded, taking all

color from clouds and landscape. Everything except the dark woods to the south was gray.

~

Albany and his men had ridden from Kincardine to the Castle of Falkland, his seat in Fife for more than thirty years.

As he took his supper alone in Falkland's great hall, the duke wondered if he had made the right decision by riding to Falkland rather than to Redmyre Tower. It was rare for him to second-guess himself. But at present, with many irons in the fire, he knew that even a shrewder strategist might err.

He was trusting Redmyre not to harm the pesky lass, although she deserved to have a tawse taken to her backside for defying *him* as she had. Someone, long ago, ought to have taught her to obey those in authority over her.

His intent was to put the fear of God into her. Surely, when she feared the ruin of her reputation and banishment from the royal court, she would do as he bade her. But he thought it best to let her simmer in the tower for a time, so she would let him quietly annul her marriage to Mackintosh and arrange one to Redmyre.

Redmyre would keep her in the tower and house James more suitably.

In any event, he would have her marriage to Sir Ivor Mackintosh annulled. He had learned enough to tell him that the lass had simply declared them married, but the marriage was evidently legal enough. The first thing he had done after arriving at Falkland was to summon his chaplain and put the question to him.

The old man's gray eyebrows had shot upward. "A *woman* declaring herself married, my lord? 'Tis gey odd, to be sure! But a true marriage as long as she be of age, her declared husband was present, and he did not deny her statement."

"Even if she is a ward of the Crown?"

"Aye, sure, my lord," the priest replied. "As ye ken, in a previous such instance, the man was guilty of an attempt to steal Crown property. But at the time, ye controlled the lady's estates as Governor. Forbye, the man was the declarer then. The Crown does control her settlements, but it canna seize her property without an annulment first. If the lady inherited the property and *she* is the declarer, the lords o' Parliament may take her part in—"

"Thank you, that will suffice," Albany said in his usual soft voice.

Reddening, the chaplain nodded, bowed, and took his leave. Doubtless the fellow felt misused and would lick his wounds privately. But he'd hold his peace.

One thing was irritatingly clear. To get an annulment, he'd have to approach the Kirk. And that meant treating with the Primate of Scotland, his old nemesis, Bishop Traill. Traill would doubtless have much to say. And others would listen.

To ensure that his reverence would comply with *his* wishes, Albany decided to visit him next. Not only would he make his demands clear with regard to James's welfare, but he would also make sure that his own version of what had happened at Kincardine reached the bishop's ears before Marsaili's did.

If he left in the morning, he would make St. Andrews by midday.

Ivor watched the darkening tower for a few more minutes, imagining that he could discern a figure there, looking back at him. He could sense her presence, but the light was nearly gone and the south window too much in shadow to see her.

Only because the east window had faced the sunset's fading glow on the northeastern clouds earlier had he been able to discern movement through it then.

Nevertheless, he believed that he had seen Marsi pacing and tried to imagine her emotional state. Her anger with Redmyre would be uppermost, he thought, since he doubted that she knew of Albany's fine hand in the matter. However, if she knew that Jamie had also been taken and he was housed elsewhere, she would likely be too concerned about his welfare to worry about her own.

But James was safe enough with Redmyre. Of that Ivor was nearly certain.

Aware that he could do nowt for them until he had reinforcements and knew more, he wrapped himself in his plaid and found a place dry enough to sleep. Wondering if he would awaken to rain but otherwise clearing his mind, he slept.

When he did wake around midnight, he saw stars through the bare branches of the tree above him. Although clouds still hid many stars and drifted across the moon now and again, the brewing storm had moved on.

Standing, he soon saw four men below in the moonlight, crossing the open space from the woods toward the tower. Redmyre had changed his guard.

Keeping his plaid for warmth, he kilted it up with his

belt. Then, leaving his bow and arrows behind, and his sword, he moved silently away through the woods.

He had seen only the four men, which probably meant that Redmyre's guards were widely spaced along the path. They'd been afoot, too, which made sense. Unless they could keep their horses well away from the trail, the beasts might make noises that would warn anyone coming that the guards were there.

Deciding to clear the path from south to north, in the event that Fin arrived earlier than expected, Ivor wended his way quietly but swiftly southward, staying nearer the trail than he, Hetty, and Will had done. Wanting to ascertain the location of each guard as he went, he found himself silently cursing the moon one minute, if it disappeared behind a cloud, and blessing it the next for revealing an obstacle or an easier way ahead.

Redmyre's guards had done little to conceal themselves, likely believing that anyone coming at such an hour would make noise enough to warn them.

Having located three, and finding the fourth at a point from which he was high enough to see approaching riders in Strathearn, had there been any, Ivor dealt with him first. He moved swiftly then to deal with the second.

A short time after that, he heard sounds of the next one ahead of him.

Creeping closer, he saw the man pacing the trail, clapping his hands against his arms and chest as if he were cold. Timing his movements to match the clapping of the other man, Ivor crept up behind him, clapped an arm around the fellow's upper torso, and put his dirk to his throat.

"Not a sound," he said.

Instead of obeying the fellow cried out, "Tae me, Alf! Back tae me!"

The fellow was strong and managed to snatch his own dirk from its sheath. But Ivor dispatched him and stepped lightly off the trail.

The echo of the fellow's shouts still reverberated through the woods.

As they faded, a sharp point of cold steel touched the back of Ivor's neck.

When he stiffened, a harsh voice said, "Dinna move now, man, except tae toss that pig-sticker into them bushes. I'd liefer take ye prisoner for the laird than kill ye. But I'll kill ye where ye stand an ye dinna do just as I say."

Chapter 20 _____

Tensing, Ivor gripped his dirk tighter. The cold steel point against his nape was too small and too sharp to be that of a sword. Moreover, the woodland in which they stood was too dense to allow effective swordplay.

Redmyre's man-at-arms doubtless carried a great sword, because each of the other three had carried one slung across his back in a leather sling or baldric.

"I tell ye, man, drop that dirk. If ye dinna drop it at once—"

An eldritch screech rang through the woods, startling both of them.

Feeling the point against his neck shift, Ivor ducked away and turned, thrusting his dirk upward as he did. The other man, recovering almost as swiftly, parried with the edge of his blade to deflect Ivor's weapon.

Enough pale moonlight pierced the canopy to let each man see the shadowy figure of his opponent. However, littered as the forest floor was with rocks, dead branches of various sizes, shrubbery, and logs, the footing was uncertain.

For several moments, the two slashed and thrust at each other. But both were agile, experienced warriors.

Knowing that he must end the battle quickly or risk

defeat, Ivor pressed his opponent hard until his own foot came down on a rock that rolled beneath it. As he lurched precariously to retain his footing, the other man's weapon slashed upward.

A rock flying from a density of trees at Ivor's right smacked his opponent's left shoulder. Diverted, the man glanced to his left for the source.

In a blink, Ivor grabbed the hilt of the other's dirk with his free hand and, with a swift kick to the back of the fellow's right knee, brought him down hard on his back, ending the fight.

Redmyre's man lay where he was, gasping, and Ivor held both dirks.

He saw that his opponent was younger than his voice and tone had suggested. But he was also fit, strong, and admirably skilled.

"Ye did it, sir!" Will exclaimed, thrusting his way through nearby shrubbery. "I kent fine that ye could take him if he didn't kill ye first, so—"

"Thanks, lad, but hush now. There may be more of them nearby."

"Aye, well, if there be, I've no seen nowt o' them," Will said. "Just two dead ones wha' I near tripped over as I came up yon path. Aodán sent me tae tell ye—"

"Be silent, Will, and stand back," Ivor interjected as he hauled his erstwhile opponent to his feet. Looking the other man in the eye, he said, "How came you to be close enough to attack me? I saw earlier where you stood your post."

The other man grimaced. "'Cause I were daft enow tae let Kai there take m' supper wi' him when he and the others left me. I came tae get it and had just stepped in tae the woods yonder when he shouted."

"I see," Ivor said "Well, I don't know if you *could* have killed me outright, because you'd have had to move faster and thrust harder to do so. But I believe you did mean just to take me prisoner. So I will give you a similar chance now. If you will tell me your name, swear fealty to me, and agree to leave Redmyre's service for my own, I will accept your parole."

Without looking away, the other man drew a breath and let it out. Then, he said, "Aye, then, I'll do those things. They do call me Fip Mingus, sir. And I'll swear tae God above and by me own life tae serve ye faithfully and right readily."

Will said with a sneer in his voice, "But so *any* man might swear when his choice be instant death, laird. Can we trust this villain tae keep his word?"

"A good question," Ivor said. To Fip Mingus, he said, "Can you tell me why I *should* trust your word?"

"Because I dinna hold wi' abducting females and bairns, sir," the other said without hesitation. "I ha' served the laird here well for two years. But he cares for nowt save what will please the Duke of Albany. And I owe nowt tae Albany."

"What has Redmyre done with the lad and the lady?" Ivor asked.

"Her ladyship be locked in the room at the top o' the tower," Fip replied. "The lad stays wi' Redmyre in the house."

Ivor frowned. His first duty was to rescue James, but he worried more about Marsi's safety. He did not believe that Redmyre would let James die on his estate, because too many people knew or would guess that the boy was there. Certainly, Sir Malcolm would blame Albany *and*

Redmyre as soon as anyone mentioned that James and Marsi had visited Kincardine. And someone would.

Will was fairly dancing beside him. Even in the dim moonlight, Ivor could see that he'd pressed his lips tightly together, as if to keep himself silent.

"What is it, lad?"

"Aodán said tae tell ye—"

"Aodán is back then from—"

"Aye, sure. How else could he ha' tellt me?"

Ivor kept his gaze on his erstwhile opponent but let his tone express his irritation. "Just tell me what he said, Will."

"Aye, well...He did say he'd delivered your message and brought back the two lads that rode tae the abbey afore. He said, too, that he'd ride on tae meet the others wha' be coming. Sithee, I saw them from yonder hillside all a-coming. Ye did say that ye'd clear the way, so when I found the first dead one, I kent—"

"Will, slow down. Do you mean to say that you could see men...riders...coming? Art sure they were ours?"

"Aye, 'cause they came from where ye said they'd come and stopped at the place where ye set the stick arrows I made, tae read wha' was there. *And* I could see Aodán wi' them. Sithee, I didna ken the others, but I could see that he did. And it willna take them long tae get here, sir."

Ivor was watching his captive carefully.

Fip had looked toward Will as he listened but met Ivor's gaze now. Quietly, he said, "If the laird has warning, sir, he'll be a-waiting for ye."

"Has he other watchers up here? More than the four of you?"

"He sent just us tae watch the trail. I dinna ken about

others, but I think he thought only the duke might come. To keep him from coming unbeknownst upon the laird, we was tae tak' word back, one man tae the next, as fast as we could run."

"So he does not trust Albany. How many men does Redmyre keep here?"

"None so many as he keeps on his Perthshire estates."

"*How* many?"

"Mayhap forty, armed. There be others, but this area ha' been at peace for years, so most o' them others be farmers. They'll fight if they must, but..."

He started to spread his hands but stopped, shooting Ivor a wary look.

"What will Redmyre do if he gets warning of an approaching army?"

"Sakes, the man will hie hisself tae his tower. That tower's solid stone, sir, wi' nine-foot-thick walls at the bottom. "Ye might breech that door, given time enow and a good ram. But one man can defend against many on its wicked stairway, and ye'd gain nowt if ye got in by trying tae burn the insides, save mayhap some o' the lower floor. But ye'd no want tae do that wi' her ladyship at the top."

"What about the boy?" Ivor demanded, fighting off the distraction of *her ladyship*. "What would Redmyre do about him if he hears that an army is coming?"

Fip thought briefly, then said, "I warrant he'd try tae hold that lad for ransom o' some sort. Likely, he'd move him tae the tower, as well."

"Then you are going to warn him," Ivor said.

"Eh?" The other man gaped at him. "I dinna tak' your meaning, sir."

"I would test your fealty," Ivor said amiably as he

restored his dirk to its sheath. "Do you have family here, Fip?"

"I ha' nae wife nor bairn. What kin I do ha' be in west Perthshire or beyond."

"So your people are Highlanders."

"As ye are, yourself, I'd wager. Lowlanders dinna wear the plaid."

"Good then," Ivor said. "It will be dawn in a few hours, so here is what you must do. Say nowt of your dead comrades, just that an army approaches..."

When Ivor had finished giving his instructions, returned Fip's dirk, and the man had vanished into the night, Will muttered doubtfully, "D'ye trust that chap, sir? What is tae keep him from telling yon Redmyre all he kens o' us?"

"It won't matter if he does," Ivor said. "Unless you are mistaken about the riders you saw, Sir Fin and Aodán will soon be here with our army. Redmyre can think what he likes about its size or aught else. He may think that Albany is coming from Kincardine to collect the lady Marsi and James, or he may believe it is someone he ought to fear. In either event, he'll take steps to protect his charges."

"Even from the duke? I thought ye said he were Albany's man."

"He is, but he will protect them nonetheless. And if our new man persuades him that it is *not* Albany, he will definitely take such precautions."

As he fell silent, he heard noises of approaching riders.

"It's them," Will said. "Now we'll do. D'ye think Jamie kens we'll come?"

Ivor nodded reassuringly. But he was thinking of

Marsi, knowing that he had most likely just put her in much more danger.

⤙⤚

He was touching her thighs with one hand, stroking them while he teased her nipples with his tongue. Flower petals drifted down in the sunlight, touching her bare skin, tickling it. One caught in his hair when he raised his head to look at her.

She smiled at him and reached for him, but when she did, her hand grasped naught but icy cloth and . . .

Marsi stirred, recognized briefly where she was and that her cloak had slipped off her. She reached for it, pulled it up, and then . . .

⤙⤚

Ivor greeted his good-brother, Fin Cameron, in the Gaelic and with a hearty clap on the back when the latter dismounted. The two were much the same height and build, but Fin's hair was dark, and he wore leather breeks and a brigandine under his plaid. He also wore his sword across his back in its sling.

Fin was not only one of Scotland's finest swordsmen. He was also Ivor's best friend and had been since their boyhood days at St. Andrews, despite a longtime feud between their clans at the time and years of separation since.

" 'Tis good to see you," Ivor said.

"Where have you hidden your horse?" Fin asked.

"I left him atop the ridge whilst I saw to Redmyre's guards."

"How far have we to go?"

"For a bird, less than two miles. But this trail wends

through the hills. It took us more than two hours to get to the top of the ridge, trying to go quietly."

"But we'll ride," Fin said.

"Aye, and the trail is clear. So it should take us no more than an hour."

"Then we'll have plenty of time left before dawn to get some sleep."

"Aye, sure, but I'll want a horse."

Grinning, Fin agreed to lend him one of the extra horses that he and his company of thirty men led in a string behind them.

Turning to Aodán, Ivor said, "You made good time. I trust that the Abbot of Lindores will get our message to Wolf."

"Better than that, sir," Aodán said. "I spoke to Captain Wolf myself. He said he'd borrowed a ship and docked it at the Newburgh jetty, because you might need him gey quick. He was to leave Lindores soon after I did and said he would sail along the north shore of the firth to avoid alarming Redmyre. He promised to keep a good watch and said to tell you that the tide will ebb at dawn. Unless you object, I'm to meet him at the water, so he can help if we need him."

"Good," Ivor said. Turning back to Fin, he said quietly. "Captain Wolf is our own Sea Wolf from the brotherhood at St. Andrews. His real name is Jake Maxwell."

"I look forward to seeing that scoundrel again," Fin said, gesturing to one of the other men, who led a horse forward from their string.

As Ivor mounted, he said teasingly, "I half-expected to see our Cat riding at your side, Fin. How did you succeed in leaving her behind?"

Fin laughed. "Do you think I let my wife ride with me when I *know* that a battle is forthcoming?"

"As I recall, my unpredictable sister has a mind of her own," Ivor said. "We do not call her 'Wildcat' for nowt."

"*We* have an agreement," Fin said loftily. "When I must attend to business of my own, she obeys. And, too, I threatened to lock her up in her cousin's attic until I returned if she did not give me her solemn word that she would stay put."

Ivor grinned, but Fin's words sent his thoughts flying to Marsi. Drawing breath, he said, "I, too, am married now."

"In troth?"

"Aye, and my lass *is* locked up. Redmyre has her captive in his tower."

"Aodán said only that Redmyre had captured James and one of the two women traveling with him," Fin said. "He also said that Redmyre is Albany's man."

"Aodán is prudent when it comes to discussing my personal business. Sithee, Albany needs Redmyre's vote to unseat Davy Stewart, but the crux of that matter is that Albany promised Redmyre the lady Marsaili Drummond in return."

"I see," Fin said. "I foretell a short life for Redmyre if he does not come to his senses right speedily."

"Mayhap even if he does," Ivor said grimly.

⌒

Marsi woke from another pleasant dream, in which she had been laughing at something that Ivor had said, to find narrow rays of sunlight, full of dust motes, beaming into the chilly tower room through cracks in the east window's shutters.

Renewed awareness of where she was banished any amusement lingering from her dream. With a sigh, she got up and opened the shutters wide, all of them.

The previous day's storm clouds were gone, leaving only a few tattered white ones to drift through an azure sky. Although a chilly breeze drifted in when she opened the western shutters, it was not the chill of incipient snow. It was, she thought idly, only the first day of March. But she could feel spring in the air.

She washed her face and hands and tidied her hair as well as she could without a comb or brush and was wondering how long she would have to wait for food when she heard a noise from the landing.

The door opened as she turned, and Redmyre entered alone, carrying a stout, wooden bar. "Good morrow," he said, shutting the door and putting the bar across it in two iron hooks to which she had paid no heed. "I've come to break fast with you."

The look in his eyes stirred a prickle of warning. She stepped back.

He continued toward her until she backed up against the south window.

Irked, she put up her left hand, saying, "Stop where you are. I would remind you that I am his grace's ward and a married woman."

Catching hold of her hand, he looked at her ring. "*That* means nowt."

Terrified that he would try to take it off, she wrenched her hand away and said, "If you think that the King will not act when I tell him what you've done, you are mistaken. He does retain *all* of his power, no matter who may be Governor."

"We will see about that," he said as his gaze drifted to her breasts. "You would be wise to admit that I will soon be your husband, lass. I did say I'd nae wish to be a brutal one, but by the time his grace hears aught of this, I will have taught you a few lessons, I trow. Come here to me now. I would see more of you—aye, and touch more of you, come to that."

He reached for her, and when she tried to elude him, she failed, earning a rough shake. Trying to push him away, she realized too late that he enjoyed her struggles. Chuckling, he clapped a large hand to her left breast and squeezed hard.

Recalling some long-ago words of advice from her cousin Davy that she had never expected to think about again, let alone to follow, she twisted enough to bring a knee up sharply between Redmyre's legs.

He pushed hard against her breast with that hand and turned a hip to counter her intent, showing that he had half-expected such a move.

With a stinging slap across her cheek, he released her and backed away. His face was red, though, and his eyes flashed, making her wish that she had kept her scissors nearer at hand. Small though they were, they had sharp points.

Glowering, he stepped toward her again. "By heaven, you will pay—"

A loud knock on the door stopped him.

"What?" he shouted, still eyeing her angrily.

"Laird, Fip Mingus be below. He says an army be a-coming over yon hills."

"'Tis nobbut Albany," Redmyre retorted.

"Nay, m'lord. It be Highlanders, Fip says, dunamany o' them!"

Ivor and Fin stood atop the hill overlooking Redmyre's estate. They had watched as Fip Mingus ran from the hillside and another man dashed to meet him.

After conferring, Fip and the other man both hurried toward the tower.

Movement in the tower room's south window diverted Ivor's gaze.

"There," he said to Fin. "Top window, this side. See her?"

"I do," Fin said. "I also see that someone is with her and that that tower will resist any effort we make to get inside it without a key. Moreover, your plan to force Redmyre to turn the lady Marsi and James over to you seems to lack detail."

"I needed to see the place by daylight," Ivor said. "But I want Redmyre out in the open so I can see what he does. Mostly, I want him to move James to the tower as Fip said he would. We cannot risk aught happening to the lad amidst all this."

"What if Redmyre just threatens to kill him if we don't leave?"

"Then I'll shoot Redmyre, and your men will defeat his," Ivor said bluntly. "I mean to find a vantage point lower on this hillside, whilst you take our men down there. Sithee, I told Fip to say that Highlanders were coming, so Redmyre might expect to see me. You will come as a surprise to him."

"Dare I mention that Albany may arrive to put a damper on any plan of ours?"

"He may, of course. But he has no reason to move swiftly

and every reason to look busy elsewhere if aught goes amiss here. I warrant he will lie low at least until he learns how much support he will have when Parliament meets."

"And until he has persuaded enough reluctant lords to join in that support."

"That, too, aye," Ivor said. "Meantime, I see two men pulling a coble ashore."

"Wolf?"

"Aye, for there is Aodán, going to meet them as arranged. Sithee, this may take only a show of strength. Redmyre is full of bluster, but I think he is inept."

"An inept man who would appear powerful can be gey dangerous."

"He can, aye," Ivor said. "Hence my decision to stay on the hill with my bow. Forbye, if you can spare archers competent enough to hit where they aim at such a distance, that would increase the threat we pose to those below."

"I have two such. I'll tell them to move about, but you'll ride down with us."

"At least halfway," Ivor said. "I'll start looking for my vantage point there, so Mistress Hetty and Will can stay with me. It won't do to leave them here if Albany comes or sends someone else with an army."

"Nay," Fin said absently. He was gazing at the tower, frowning. "Anyone near that tower will be at least a hundred yards from the edge of these woods," he said. "Being halfway up this hillside will add another sixty."

Ivor nodded, his thoughts already shifting to consider various tactics.

"How much accuracy do you expect from my lads at that distance?"

Ivor looked at him. "They can take their positions where they will. Do you think that *I* cannot hit my mark at a hundred and sixty yards?"

"I have seen you do so at nearly twice that distance. But I also know that few men are as skilled as you are with a longbow at *any* distance."

"Few have had the training that you and I had."

"Aye, so what about Wolf?" Fin asked.

"His men will stay with the ship, because we'll want to be away as soon as we can collect Jamie and Marsi. You will stay here to tidy things up, so don't forget to take our horses back to Perth with you. Aye, and take Fip Mingus, too."

"I'm returning to Perth then? You don't want us to ride on to St. Andrews? You may need more men there, my lad."

"If I do, it will mean that Albany is already there with a real army. And if he is, Traill will find a way to warn us off. He is deep in this, Fin. He sent Wolf to me, just as he sent me to his grace."

"Aye, well, mayhap the worthy bishop has raised his own army then, from the rest of our old St. Andrews brotherhood," Fin said. "So, let's move."

Ivor nodded, and they went to collect the others and their horses.

Halfway down the hill, they reined in so that Ivor could talk to Fin's archers before turning off the trail with Hetty and Will to seek his vantage point. Just before they and the two archers parted from Fin and the other men, they all saw Redmyre in a claret-colored cloak crossing from the house to the tower with James.

"Go on, Fin," Ivor said. "Remember, I want Redmyre *out* of that tower."

"I'll do what I can, aye, because whatever he does, you can't shoot him if he stays in that room with your lady and Jamie. No one could make *that* shot."

Ivor eyed the south tower window speculatively.

⁓

When Redmyre had gone with his man, Marsi hurried to the south window, hoping to see the army. If they were Highlanders, Ivor must surely be with them.

Unable to see any horsemen below or on the forested hill, she fought back a surge of disappointment and continued to watch the hillside.

Remembering a bit later that Ivor had said something about getting a message to friends of Wolf's who had boats, she moved to the east window, praying that she would see a ship full of men-at-arms nearing the tower. The tide was in, but she saw no boat in the harbor. Farther along the coast, perhaps a quarter-mile, she saw that someone had pulled one lone coble ashore, but she saw no men and no ship.

With a sigh, she returned to the south window. As a flash of movement through trees halfway down the hillside suggested that she might be seeing a horseman or two, she heard the bolt and turned back toward the door.

Redmyre came in, dragging the wooden bar with one hand and gripping a visibly furious Jamie by an arm with the other. Redmyre kicked the door shut.

"Marsi!" the boy exclaimed, jerking away when Redmyre turned to set the bar across the door. "They wouldna tell me where ye were!"

"I'm here, Jamie, and our rescue is nigh. Sir Ivor is coming with an army."

"You'd better hope that is untrue," Redmyre said. "Because if it's true, you should know that Albany will be close behind him and will hang him by day's end."

"First, he would have tae come here...Albany, himself," Jamie said. "Forbye, ye must ken fine that he rarely puts himself at risk. Also, he'd have tae win."

"You sit down and keep quiet," Redmyre growled.

Marsi turned back to the south window.

~

Ivor saw her standing at the window, and the sudden tension in his chest made him feel as if his heart had turned over. He had positioned himself higher on the hillside than he'd first intended, to give himself a direct view of the window.

She was looking at him as if she could see him, although he was sure that she could not. He felt as if he could hear her thoughts and sent his own back to her: *I'm here, my love. I'll get you out of there, one way or another.*

A thickset man appeared behind her, Redmyre. He pushed her aside and peered out toward the hillside. His claret-colored cloak stood out clearly.

"If I thought you'd stand still long enough, you scurrilous blackguard, I'd end this now," Ivor muttered.

"What's that ye say, laird?" Will asked.

"What the devil are you doing here? I told you to stay with Mistress Hetty."

"She told me tae see could I help ye. She's safe enow. None can see her from the path, or our horses, neither. Sithee, I thought I could hand ye arrows if need be. Save ye from having tae pull them from yon quiver each time.

Also," Will added in a burst of candor, "I wanted tae see wha' happens."

"Well, I'd liefer you—"

"Ay-de-mi, laird, look! Sir Fin be a-riding on tae yon tower alone!"

Ivor saw that Fin was carrying on some sort of parley with Redmyre, who leaned out the window and shouted back at him.

In the still morning air, by shutting his eyes, he could almost hear their words. Fin's voice was calm; Redmyre's was not.

"Hand me my bow, lad," he said without looking away.

As he strung the bow, still watching Redmyre, Ivor prayed to God to keep Jamie and Marsi well away from that window.

Chapter 21 ⎯⎯⎯⎯⎯⎯⎯⎯⎯⎯⎯

Marsi and Jamie exchanged a look as they listened to Redmyre shouting to the horseman who had reined in below.

Jamie glanced at the barred door, but Marsi shook her head. The bar was too heavy to lift quietly, and for all they knew, a guard stood on the other side. She might have risked the attempt had she been alone, but she dared not risk Jamie's safety.

She had not seen Ivor, but the man leading the Highlanders was much like him in build and demeanor, and was likely his good-brother. When he rode forward alone, two of Redmyre's men ran to meet him, but both backed away after only a word or two. The rider wore a great sword diagonally across his back in a sling and doubtless had other weapons, as well. But he did not seem to have threatened the men on foot.

When Redmyre had pushed her aside, she moved away from him to Jamie. "Did they hurt you?" she asked him.

"Nay, nor will they," he murmured. "At least, so that lout Redmyre did say. I warrant my uncle would be wroth wi' him if he *did* harm me. He may want tae clear his path tae the throne, but he'd no get there by killing me afore he kills Davy."

"True," Marsi agreed. "His grace would condemn such a vile act. Sakes, he'd condemn him if he hurt Davy, too. But if aught happened to you at Albany's hands, his grace would order his arrest, and Parliament would condemn him."

Redmyre snapped, "Did you *hear* that fellow? I'm to send you both down to him by his grace's command, he says. Well, I've an answer for him."

Before Marsi recognized his intent, he caught her by an arm and jerked her forward. Pulling his dirk from its sheath, he spun her in front of him, facing the window, and put the blade against her throat.

"Here's your answer!" he shouted to the horseman below. "Try to break into this tower and the lass dies. Then the lad. By my troth, if you do not turn round and leave this estate with all your men, I'll cut her now."

"Don't hurt Marsi!" James shouted, grabbing Redmyre's arm.

Redmyre shook him off easily, and Marsi said sharply, "Jamie, stand back. He won't harm me, because the King would be almost as angry about that as he would be if he hurts you. So would Davy. But if you *anger* him—"

"Sakes, lass, I'm angry already," Redmyre growled in her ear as he pressed her even closer to the window. Its lower ledge cut into her waist.

The thought that he could easily fling her right out of that window to the ground sent a shudder through her. Telling herself that she should *not* look down, she noted nonetheless that the rider below was reining his horse around.

"He is leaving," she murmured, fighting for calm.

The man she had decided must be Ivor's good-brother, Fin Cameron, was riding away but *very* slowly, as if he dared Redmyre to order action against him or feared that any quicker movement might stir *him* to act. Redmyre's men fell in behind him, clearly meaning to see him and his entire army off Redmyre's estate.

Her heightened senses told her that James had moved to the east window.

Looking straight out the south one, she sensed Ivor's presence although she could not see him. Then, she felt the edge of Redmyre's blade press at her throat.

"You are hurting me," she said. "If you don't *mean* to kill me…"

He took the blade away and slipped it into its sheath but continued to watch as Fin Cameron—if it was indeed Fin—continued to ride slowly away.

She saw colorfully garbed Highlanders emerging now from the woods, two by two, but only to form a line at the forest edge, apparently waiting for Fin.

Having relaxed when Redmyre lowered the dirk, she realized that he was paying her no heed and wondered what he would do if she just walked away from him. She did not want him to put his hands on her again if she could avoid it, so she slowly eased aside just far enough that she need not feel his body against hers.

Fin halted his horse, still some distance from the line of mounted Highlanders.

Redmyre growled, "What the devil is he doing n—?"

The word ended in an odd sort of gurgling noise. His hands flew up and clawed briefly at the arrow stuck through his neck as he collapsed to the floor.

Marsi stared at him and then looked swiftly at James.

He'd turned from the east window, his eyes widening when he saw that Redmyre had fallen. His mouth fell agape at the sight of the arrow.

"Where did *that* come from?" he exclaimed.

"From Sir Ivor, I'll wager," she said, wanting to cheer but aware that God might disapprove of her delight in such a case. Still, Redmyre had ceased his clawing and—from all she could tell—his breathing. He showed no sign of life at all.

Jamie had no difficulty expressing his feelings. Grinning, he said, "Marsi, I saw a galley turning into that harbor yonder, much like the one that Captain Wolf has. I ken fine that he could no ha' got round all of Scotland so quick, but—"

"He has friends hereabouts with ships," Marsi said. "Ivor told me so. He said we had only to send a message to Lindores Abbey, by any clergyman, to arrange for one. I'd wager that is why he visited Dunblane Cathedral. One reason, anyway," she added conscientiously, recalling that he had also asked the Bishop of Dunblane about the legality of her marriage declaration.

James turned toward the door. "Let's ha' that bar off and get out o' here."

"Wait," she said. "There may yet be a guard out there, and the Highlanders must attend to Redmyre's men before they can come for us."

"But how can they get in if we dinna *let* them in? He locked the outer door."

"Did he bar it, too?"

"Nay, he said it does no require a bar because that door is so stout."

"What did he do with the key?"

James looked at Redmyre's body. "He stuck it in a wee pouch under his belt, in front, inside his hose."

Redmyre lay curled on one side where he had collapsed. The thought of poking around to find the key turned her stomach. Jamie, too, looked doubtful.

Marsi swallowed hard. For all that Jamie acted as if he were as old as she was, he was not. And she could not ask him to do what she abhorred to do herself.

From the hillside, seeing Fin rein his horse back toward the tower and the other Highlanders emerge from the woods to follow him, Ivor grabbed his quiver and snapped, "Will, come quickly. I must fetch my horse, and I want you to stay with Hetty. You will ride down with her when Sir Fin waves to you. But first, do you see that harbor yonder and the galley with its oars up, gliding into the landing?"

"Aye, sure, laird. But I want—"

"Never mind what you want. What you will do is escort Mistress Hetty down to that boat. And you will stay with her until I come. Do you understand me?"

"I do, aye, but Jamie—I dinna ken how ye shot that arrow through that wee window, but I saw it fly there m'self. What if Jamie were there wi' the lady Marsi?"

"He likely *is* there," Ivor said. "But even so, he is safe. Now, run."

They both ran. And when they reached Hetty and the horses, Ivor said as he flung himself onto his saddle, "They are both safe, I think, mistress. Will knows what I want you to do, but I must get down there at once."

"Aye, sure, sir," Hetty said calmly. "The lad will take good care of me."

Needing to hear no more, he urged his mount to the trail and down the hill. When he reached the bottom, he saw that Fin had the situation in hand.

Redmyre's people had surrendered quickly, many of them having seen their laird fall. Others, realizing that although their numbers seemed 'greater they would be no match for the fierce Highlanders, put down their weapons.

Fin rode to meet Ivor and said, "We have a problem." A chap who was inside the tower earlier told me that Redmyre locked and bolted the door himself from the inside and sent the man out to join these others. If Redmyre is not dead…"

Ivor grimaced. "I cannot be sure that he is. But I'm certain I hit him."

"If he was wearing steel plate under that doublet and cloak of his—"

"At that distance, the arrow might pierce chain mail but not plate," Ivor admitted. Shifting his gaze back to the window to see Marsi waving with one hand and pointing at the other, he added, "Redmyre *is* dead, I trow, and she has the key."

Fin said, "I'm sorry I missed seeing that shot. But I knew you would try if I could just keep him at that window long enough. If you did kill him, my lad, most folks would agree with me that you've done the impossible."

"She was right beside him, Fin. I was sure that Jamie was somewhere in that room, too. I could not afford to miss. But Jake is waiting. Let's go get them."

Marsi barely had time to meet Fin before Ivor bundled her aboard the galley with Jamie. To her astonishment, Captain Wolf was there to meet them.

"Where did you spring from?" she demanded.

"Did Ivor not tell you, my lady?" he asked, glancing at Ivor. "I arranged to meet him near here, although he may not have expected me to arrive so swiftly."

"He said only that you had friends with ships."

"Aye, well, that's true. But I can use one of theirs whenever I need it. Get you into yon cabin now. We'd liefer you stay inside today, lest Albany's spies be watching and find a way to inform him that you are both free."

"Am I ever to know your true name, sir?"

Grinning, he bowed. "Jake Maxwell, my lady, entirely at your disposal."

"Sir Jacob," Ivor muttered.

"Nay, I'm Jake to my friends."

"I'm starving, Jake," she said. "Have you food aboard?"

He laughed, but Ivor said, "Move along, lass. You, too, lad," he added to Jamie. "Hetty is already aboard with Will, and Aodán is waiting for our horses."

Marsi looked at Ivor again then, trying to gauge his mood. He had scarcely spoken to her since the tower, except to tell her to come, go, or just to follow him.

After she had thrown the key down to him, he had run around to the door, opened it, and by the time she had wrestled the bar from their door and pulled it open, he was there, and she'd flung herself into his arms. He held her tightly but only until Jamie spoke, telling them dryly that they were blocking the way.

Then Ivor had told them both to follow him and led the way down the stone stairway and outside, where Fin had horses waiting.

The ride to the ship took only a short time, but Fin had stayed behind. The ship was another galley, high in the stem and stern, like the one that had taken them to Dumbarton from Turnberry.

Giving their horses into Aodán's care, Ivor ushered Marsi and Jamie into the aft cabin and waited until they had exchanged greetings with Hetty and Will. Then, telling them all to keep out of sight, he went back out on deck.

Jamie said happily, "This be gey fine, Marsi. Will's been worried that his old master may still come for him. But old Master Lucken won't find him now."

"It be good thing, too," Will said. "That man has nowt about him for a chappie tae love, so I reckon he'll come tae a bad end like the laird's first wife did."

"The laird?" Marsi said, shooting an accusatory look at Jamie.

He gazed blandly back at her. "Ye should ken that Will often calls Sir Ivor so," he said. "Sithee, we'd told him he was Hawk. But I kept forgetting, so I told him the truth and explained that we must not say 'Sir Ivor' where strangers might hear us."

"So I dinna say it at all," Will said.

"I see. I also see that James has been telling tales that he ought *not* to tell. Will had left the table, sir, before..." She paused, regarding Jamie sternly.

"Sithee, *I* didna tell that tale first," he said virtuously. "Ye're the one as said about Sir Ivor having two wives when he'd no got one yet." Then, eyes twinkling, he added, "I *can* keep Will now, though, can I not?"

"I don't know about that, but we'll see," Marsi said. "Forbye, I'd advise you to take care that Will does not reveal his knowledge of that wives' tale to Sir Ivor—or to anyone else, come to that."

Jamie chuckled and then informed Will that he would teach him to play chess.

Their journey to St. Andrews occupied the rest of the day, for although they departed with the outgoing tide, the winds were capricious and aided them little.

Darkness fell an hour before they entered St. Andrews Bay. But the boats moored there were easy to discern through the cabin porthole. Their own oarsmen easily maneuvered the galley to a sheltered spot, where they dropped anchor.

Ivor came back in then. "The coble will take us ashore," he said. "You'll come down the ladder with me, lass. Jake will help Hetty. Will, you stay here."

"Nay, then," Jamie said. "Will must come with us. I missed him, and I am not fain tae bid him farewell. Also, neither of us needs help down any ladder."

Ivor hesitated, words of denial clearly on his tongue.

When he nodded instead, Marsi smiled at the boys' mutual sighs of relief. She hoped that Jamie's obvious plan to keep Will would succeed.

Descending to the smaller boat on a rope ladder seemed perilous to her, but with Ivor below to steady her and her skirts kilted up, she managed easily. She disliked the walk up to the town more, for the trail up the cliff was steep.

"The place seems quiet enough," Ivor said to Jake at the top.

"It does, aye," Jake said. "And Traill would have left

some sign if there were danger. Sakes, that wily old man would have sent someone out to meet us at sea."

⁓

Ivor agreed that Traill would have warned them, but his instinct for danger remained on high alert. Albany had practically herded them through Kincardine Glen to the castle and had certainly arranged for the abduction of Marsi and James.

Yet he had not followed them to Redmyre's tower.

His thoughts continued so while they made their way to St. Andrews Castle, perched high on the cliffs overlooking the sea. Ivor led the way to the main entrance, his thoughts still on Albany. To be sure, the man avoided risk. Nevertheless—

The main door was open with Father Porter at the threshold to greet them.

"Sir Ivor, Sir Jacob, my lord Carrick," that worthy murmured with a nod to the two men and Jamie. "We ha' been watching from the tower for your arrival. My lord bishop would see you at once, afore we sup."

"Is there trouble here, Father?" Ivor asked him bluntly.

Orange-gold light from candles and cressets in the spacious entryway revealed fleeting doubt on the old man's otherwise cherubic face. "Not to say 'trouble,' my son, but Bishop Traill did suggest that Sir Jacob might stay in the porter's room down here. We must just trust his reverence... *their* reverences, come to that," he added.

Ivor would have questioned him more, but the priest turned away. Gesturing toward the porter's room for Jake, he led the way up a few stairs into the great hall.

Marsi, Hetty, Jamie, and Will silently followed Ivor.

The hall was empty, and the priest hurried across it diagonally, ignoring the dais and high table to approach a door in the far corner. Thrusting it open with just a single rap beforehand, he stood aside and motioned for Ivor to enter first.

Directly opposite the doorway, Bishop Traill, looking older and frailer than the last time Ivor had seen him, sat in a high-backed chair at a wide table that he clearly used as a desk. A pair of rolled and sealed documents lay at his right.

So astonished was Ivor to see how much the formidable Traill had aged that a moment or two passed before he perceived the others in the room.

Behind Traill to his right, near the corner of the room, stood another cleric, a stouter, younger, stoic-looking man. Then, but only when Ivor stepped further into the room, did he see Albany standing in a window embrasure well to Traill's left.

The duke had clearly meant to conceal himself until then.

"Good evening, Mackintosh," he said. "As you see, I preceded you here. I have already explained the need for an annulment of your illicit marriage, and I am sure that their reverences must agree that one is necessary."

Ivor turned back to Bishop Traill, who said with a slight smile, "The Duke of Albany has indeed told us a tale, my son. But before we continue, I must present you to Sir Henry Wardlaw, Bishop of Glasgow, who comes to St. Andrews at the behest of His Holiness the Pope. Sir Ivor Mackintosh is one of my former students, Henry."

Albany said, "You did not come by road, Mackintosh. Who brought you?"

"We'll leave that question for now, my son," Traill said gently. "Your other matter is more important, as I am sure you agree. Set stools for her ladyship and her friend, Sir Ivor. James, my lad, it is a great pleasure to see you again and a greater one to know we shall have the honor of your company here for some time to come."

"We will discuss that further, too," Albany said.

Traill looked at him, and Ivor was glad to see that the old man's ability to stare an unruly student to silence was as well-honed as ever. Traill said, "We will talk more, Robert. Meantime, James, prithee present your companion."

"This is Will, sir. He...he is my squire."

"That lad can be no such thing," Albany snapped.

"One needs to win knighthood before employing a squire," Traill said gently.

Ivor said, "This lady is Henrietta Childs, sir. She is mistress of the royal nursery. His grace asked that she accompany James here."

"It was kind of her to do so," Bishop Traill said, nodding to Hetty. "But this is a male establishment, as you know." Shifting his gaze to James, whose face had fallen ludicrously at learning that Will could not be his squire, he added, "Forbye, my son, we can find another place here for Will if that would please you."

Jamie's face cleared in an instant. "I'd like that fine, sir. I'd hoped ye might."

When the women had taken seats near the wall at Traill's right, he turned his gaze back to Ivor. "Art then married, lad, as Albany says?"

"I am, aye, sir, to the lady Marsaili Drummond Cargill."

Traill's lips twitched as he shifted his gaze to Marsi. "Is that true, my lady?"

"It is, my lord," she said calmly.

Traill smiled. "It is also a pleasure for me to see you again, my daughter."

"Pleasure or none," Albany interjected icily, "if Mackintosh has taken her to wife, he has broken the law."

"What law, my son?" Bishop Wardlaw asked.

Albany was silent for a moment—collecting his wits, Ivor thought. The duke had not expected Wardlaw to interfere.

Then Albany said in his usual soft tone, "Marsaili is a ward of the Crown. She therefore requires royal permission to marry. Since he married her without that, he is guilty of attempted theft of Crown property...in essence, her estates."

Bishop Traill had been watching Marsi. Now he said, "Is that true, my lady? *Did* Sir Ivor marry you without your permission?"

"Not *hers*," Albany said impatiently. "His grace's consent is required."

"But she does not require even his grace's permission to marry of her own free will," Wardlaw said. "Any maiden past the age of consent can do that."

"Forbye, her ladyship has not answered my question," Traill said.

With a droll look, Marsi said, "If anyone married anyone without permission, Father, it was I who married Sir Ivor without his. See you, I declared us wed before witnesses, and my declaration stunned him so that he did not think to deny it."

"Do you wish to remain married to him, my daughter?"

Marsi looked at Ivor, her expression turning solemn.

He tensed, wondering if she might hesitate to declare her feelings so publicly, or be too afraid of displeasing the Kirk or the King to do so.

Then she smiled at him, and her smile seemed to warm the entire room. He smiled back. Even the stoic Wardlaw smiled as he watched them.

Albany did not, but Ivor did not count Albany.

⁓

"I do want to stay with him, Father," Marsi said without looking away from Ivor. "With all my heart, I do. Prithee, do not say that the Kirk will forbid it."

"On the contrary," Traill said. "The Kirk must allow it."

Turning back to him, she saw that behind him, Wardlaw was nodding.

Albany said with audible annoyance, "The Kirk may allow it, but it can do naught about her estates. Those remain under the Crown's control and under mine, aye, as Royal Chancellor. And, by my troth, they will remain so."

The fact that she would have to sacrifice her inheritance to marry Ivor was a hard one to swallow. But Marsi said calmly to the duke, "If that must be, then it must. I love him, and I will *not* change my mind."

"Nor need you do so to keep your estates," Bishop Traill said as matter-of-factly as if the statement were of no moment.

She stared at him and saw that he had rested his right hand on one of the documents beside him on the table.

"I received this from his grace two days ago by courier," he said, lifting it and carefully unrolling it.

Marsi glanced at Ivor and saw that he was watching her. She turned back to Bishop Traill, who had only been waiting for her to do so.

"This document," he said to her, "grants you royal permission to wed whomever you choose and specifies Sir Ivor Mackintosh by name if you should choose him. It came to me under royal seal and signed by his grace. I will testify, if necessary, that his grace wrote the document with his own hand. I know it well."

Albany said grimly, "I fear that the marriage settlements will not be—"

"*This* document," Traill interjected in a firmer voice than Marsi had yet heard from him, as he touched the second document, "is a charter granting the Drummond Cargill estates directly to the lady Marsaili Drummond Cargill, her heirs and assigns. The document is likewise written and signed by his grace's own hand."

"Still, as Royal Chamberlain—"

"Even the Royal Chamberlain cannot revoke charters granted directly by the King without his royal consent, as you should ken fine, my son."

Anger stirred on Albany's face, but he swiftly controlled it. "That may be so," he acknowledged. "However, I shall soon be Governor again—"

"Nor," Traill interposed calmly, "can anyone acting as regent for the King of Scots do so. His grace has commanded it so herein, directly, and by his own hand."

His fury plain now, Albany took a step toward Traill. "By God, you old—"

Marsi glanced again at Ivor, expecting him to intervene.

He stood where he was, relaxed.

Traill had not spoken, nor had Bishop Wardlaw. Albany had simply stopped speaking. She saw that he had also stopped in his tracks, glowering impotently, much as he had done in Annabella's death chamber when Traill had ordered him out.

The duke glanced at Wardlaw but found no comfort there. In fact, while she had looked briefly at Ivor, Wardlaw seemed to have moved closer to Traill.

The silence lengthened so that when Hetty cleared her throat, Marsi jumped.

The slight sound seemed to startle Albany, too.

Visibly collecting himself, he nodded to the two bishops and took his leave without another word, shooting an evil look at Ivor as he passed.

Marsi shivered. Everyone else seemed to be listening to the duke's footsteps as he crossed the hall. But the silence lingered even after they faded away.

It did so until Father Porter entered with Jake Maxwell.

~

Ivor smiled at Jake as Traill said to the porter, "Albany has gone?"

"He has left the keep, sir, and I bolted the door behind him. His men are just finishing their supper in the refectory, so I offered to order their horses prepared. But he snapped out—rudely, I thought—that he'd see to that himself."

"Excellent," Traill said. Glancing at Wardlaw, he said, "This is Sir Jacob Maxwell, Henry. I believe I have told you that, to avoid clan wars erupting in my halls, the lads I invite to come here and study with me take names from the animal kingdom. Ivor and Jake were Hawk and Sea

Wolf. See you, Albany has met Jake before, so although I doubt that he would know him now, I thought it safer to have Jake wait in the porter's room during our discussion. Likewise did I stop Albany before he could question Ivor too closely about how he got here."

"I see," Wardlaw said. "Then mayhap we should curtail this visit."

Nodding, Traill held out the two documents to Marsi. "These are yours to keep, my daughter." To Ivor, he added, "I think it best that you leave tonight rather than waiting until morning, lad. Wait only until we know that Albany has indeed left the town. Father Porter will attend to that whilst you sup."

Less than an hour later, the porter came to assure them that the duke had gone. "I had my lads follow them, Sir Ivor. He did send one to the harbor, but the chap took one look at all the ships moored there and returned without going down."

Since Ivor's party had brought no gear up the hill with them, their leave-taking was brief. He felt suddenly reluctant to part with Jamie and realized that he had come to care deeply for the boy. Jamie himself seemed content to be staying at St. Andrews as long as Will would stay, too, but he hugged Marsi hard and made her promise that she and Ivor would visit them often.

Somewhat to Ivor's surprise, Traill went with them to the entryway, leaning heavily on Father Porter's arm as they descended the few steps from the hall.

At the door, the bishop looked from Ivor to Jake and said, "I should tell you lads both before you go that Sir Henry is here at the Pope's command and will soon take my place as Primate of Scotland."

"Why?" The word flew out before Ivor had known he would speak.

Traill looked at him sadly, his frailty so visible then that the answer was plain. Feeling tears leap to his eyes, Ivor said gruffly. "It won't be the same."

"Things never stay the same, my son. But Henry approves of *all* that we have done and means to create a proper school here. That should please you."

Jake said, "He approves even of our brotherhood?"

Traill nodded and said more briskly, "Now, get you both well away from here and guard those documents well. Davy Stewart sent word that he means to see that Wardlaw and James are safe here. I assured him this castle is impregnable and warned him that if he comes, Albany may follow. But . . . well, you both ken Davy."

Ivor and Jake exchanged glances. But it being more than plain that Traill's energy was fast waning, they took their leave without further discussion.

When they reached the ship, Jake said to Ivor with a mischievous grin, "Anticipating your . . . uh . . . desire, I took the liberty of having my lads make up a bed in our hold for you whilst we were away. I thought you'd be using it tomorrow, but it should be ready by now. The hold is gey clean. We've only our own stores down there, and one can enter it from the deck. However, if you're afraid of the dark . . ."

Marsi gave a little gasp of laughter, and Ivor's cock stirred hard. He made no objection and neither did she. Arm in arm, they followed Jake to their bedchamber.

Epilogue

His naked thigh felt rough and hairy to her stroking palm until she slid it to the smoother skin of his inner thigh. When her knuckles brushed lightly against his cods, she smiled to hear his quickly indrawn breath. His cock stood stiff and eager for her touch. It was heady to know that she could stir his lust so easily.

Their bedchamber lay just across the landing from that of Fin and his wife, Catriona. She liked Cat. She savored the fact that Cat had immediately accepted her as a sister. In a way, Marsi thought, that was nearly as heady as having sex with Ivor.

The strength of her astonishment at Cat's ready acceptance would ease quickly as they became better acquainted, she knew. But she doubted that the strength of her love for stirring Ivor's lust would ever wane.

He was an impatient man, though, and she knew that he would not lie quietly for long. Already he had begun teasing her right nipple. As the thought occurred to her, he rose up on an elbow, pushed her gently back, and positioned himself for taking her. As she spread her legs for him, she continued to caress him in all the ways that he had taught her, delighting in his lustful response.

His hand moved to her mound, and he slipped a finger inside her. She knew he would try to restrain himself, to be gentle. He had apologized once when he'd thought that he might have been too aggressive, but she had hushed him. She loved knowing that he could not resist her, that he wanted to dominate her in bed.

She trusted him and knew that he would not hurt her.

He took her swiftly, powerfully, and left her gasping in her culmination. His own release followed swiftly. When they both lay back, sated, she sighed and snuggled against him, resting her head on his chest.

"*Now* do you believe we are truly married?" he murmured, stroking her hair.

"I do," she said. "I believed it in that pitch-black hold of Jake's. But that was *not* my ideal bedchamber. I would not have wanted to be down there without you."

"I'd liefer you not be anywhere without me, sweetheart." But he could scarcely blame her for disliking the dark hold.

Jake had stood in the entry to light their way down into it but had refused to leave a flame burning there while the ship was moving. He had offered to leave the entrance open instead. A look from Ivor had elicited another of Jake's mischievous, flashing grins, but the door had shut softly a moment later.

Ivor smiled at the memory and at the knowledge that Jake was going to spend a few more days with them at MacGillivray House.

"I love you," she murmured.

"So you told their reverences the other night. And me, too, come to that."

"I did, aye."

She sounded drowsy, but she did not fool him. He knew what she wanted to hear, and he would say the words as often as she wanted to hear them. "I love you, too, sweetheart, more than life. I didn't know that I *could* love anyone so much."

Her sigh expressed her contentment. Then, still drowsily, she said, "I hope Jake finds someone to love, too, don't you? I think he admires your cousin Alyson."

"I hope not," Ivor said. "Alyson is betrothed and will marry in June."

"Do you think a wee detail like that would defeat Jake?"

"If he values his hide, it will," Ivor said, putting sternness in his voice.

"You are gey fierce, sir, but I doubt that you would murder Jake. Forbye, but you will be too busy looking after Cargill. I want to see Rothiemurchus, too."

"When Fin and Catriona return to Loch-an-Eilein, we'll go with them. My family will want to see us married by a priest, I'm thinking, documents or none."

"Life is going to be much more interesting with you than it was at Turnberry."

Knowing that he had made a powerful enemy in Albany, Ivor hoped that his future would be delightfully tame.

A fortnight later, he received a message from Bishop Wardlaw.

Bishop William Traill, Primate of Scotland, had died at St. Andrews, and the Duke of Albany had arrested Davy Stewart, heir to Scotland's throne.

Dear Reader,

I hope you enjoyed *Highland Hero*. For those who like more information about certain details, I include the following:

If you have visited the Lake of Menteith (the only "lake" in Scotland), you may wonder why it is the Loch of Menteith in this book. The reason is that until the end of the nineteenth century, most maps including the *Gazetteer of Scotland* called it so. Therefore, I figured that folks at the beginning of the fifteenth century probably also did. So I did, too.

Those of you who noted that Robert III, King of Scots, and his younger brother Robert, Duke of Albany, seem to have had the same given name, Robert Stewart, will be interested to know that the King's given name was not Robert but John, Earl of Carrick. John of Carrick became Robert III because, had he kept the name John, he would have become John II. This name was deemed unacceptable, even likely to undermine the Stewart kingship, because John Baliol (with English assistance) had "usurped" the throne as John I before Robert the Bruce, progenitor of the Stewart line, defeated him (and the English) to become King of Scots. So Robert III took his royal name from his own father, Robert II, and from the Bruce, who was Robert I. The man who persuaded John to do so was none other than his younger brother Robert.

Information about archery at the time comes from various sources, but most are listed in the bibliography of the (for once) excellent article about the subject on Wikipedia.com. Detailed information about lengths of longbows (yes, used at the time throughout Britain), and how far a good archer could shoot an arrow, comes from what scholars learned when bows and arrows were found on the *Mary Rose* in sufficient quantity that they could be tested for distance and accuracy.

The custom of wearing a betrothal or wedding ring on the "third finger," (counting the index finger as "one") or "fourth finger," if one counts the thumb first, seems to have stemmed from a belief that a nerve in that finger ran right to the heart. Ecclesiastical rituals from the eleventh to the fifteenth centuries in France prove that with few exceptions the nuptial ring was worn on the bride's right hand. However, a gold ring found in an ancient burial place near Salisbury was on the left one and twice encircled the "fourth" finger. Also, the Holy Kirk's marriage ceremony of nearly the same period in Britain ordains that the man put the ring on the "third finger" of the bride's *left* hand. The very ritual was elaborate: The ring was first given by the man to the woman, then taken from the woman by the priest, who after blessing it returns it to the man, who then puts it to her thumb while saying "In the name of the Father," then to her first finger when he says, "and of the Son," then to the second finger for "and of the Holy Ghost." Then, he slips it onto her "third finger" as he says, "Amen."

I also received help from unexpected sources. A fan sent email from Scotland to offer a suggestion and tell me how realistic my settings seemed to her. I explained that I did a lot of research and mentioned that I was just then trying to figure out how I should spell Loch-an-Eilein in this book. My favorite source of all things Scottish had said that Eilean was the correct Gaelic spelling (and the aforementioned *Gazetteer* had likewise spelled it so). My correspondent said, "I have a friend who lives there. Shall

I ask her?" So, the residents of Rothiemurchus got to call that tune, deeming that it should be Loch-an-Eilein, as it is spelled today.

My sources for *Highland Hero* include *The Confederation of Clan Chattan, Its Kith and Kin* by Charles Fraser-Mackintosh of Drummond, Glasgow, 1898; *The House and Clan of Mackintosh and of the Clan Chattan* by Alexander Mackintosh Shaw, Moy Hall, n.d.; *Rings for the Finger*, by George Frederick Kuntz, New York, 1917; and of course, the always impressive Donald MacRae.

Again, I also thank my wonderful agents, Lucy Childs and Aaron Priest, my terrific editor Frances Jalet-Miller, Senior Editor Selina McLemore, my publicist Nick Small, Production Manager Anna Maria Piluso, copyeditor Sean Devlin, Art Director Diane Luger, Cover Artist Claire Brown, Editorial Director Amy Pierpont, Vice President and Editor in Chief Beth de Guzman, and everyone else at Hachette Book Group's Grand Central Publishing/Forever who contributed to this book.

If you enjoyed *Highland Master* and *Highland Hero*, please look for the third book of the Scottish Knights Trilogy, *Highland Lover*, at your favorite bookstore in April 2012.

In the meantime, *Suas Alba!*

Sincerely,

Amanda Scott

www.amandascottauthor.com

When she set sail for France,
Lady Alyson MacGillivray
never dreamed her ship would
be attacked—or that her rescuer
would be a man like no other...

Please turn this page
for a preview of

Highland Lover

Available in mass market

in April 2012.

Chapter 1 ─────────────

The Firth of Forth, Scotland, late March 1403

Nineteen-year-old Lady Alyson MacGillivray grasped the urgent fingers clutching her arm and tried to pry them loose as she said, "Prithee, calm yourself, Ciara.* If this ship sinks, clinging to me will avail you naught."

"Mayhap it will not, m'lady," her middle-aged attire woman said, still clinging hard enough to leave bruises. "But if this ship drops down off another o' these giant waves as it did afore, mayhap neither of us will go flying into yon wall again."

Alyson did not reply at once, having noted that, although the huge vessel still rocked on the heaving waters of the firth, the noises she could hear had changed. The wind still howled. However, the awful creaks and screeches that had made Ciara fear aloud—and Alyson silently—that the ship would soon shake itself apart had eased.

"We're slowing," Alyson said.

─────────
* Pronounced Shara.

The cabin door opened without warning, and Niall*
Clyne, Alyson's husband of two months, filled the opening. He was a handsome, fair-haired, blue-eyed man of
mild temperament, and she had known him most of her
life. He ducked his head as he entered, to avoid banging it
against the low lintel.

Alyson saw at once that Niall looked wary.

"Put that lantern out, Allie," he said. "We must show
no light aboard now."

"Who would see it?" Alyson asked reasonably. "That
tiny window—"

"Porthole," Niall said.

"—is shuttered," she continued. "Little light would show
through it in any event. Surely, on such a dark night—"

"Just put it out," he said. "It isn't safe to keep a flame
here in such weather."

Ciara protested, "Sir, please, it be scarifying enough
with it in this place! Forbye, *in such weather*, we ought
never tae ha' left Leith Harbor! Men did say—"

"An overturned lantern would quickly start a fire,"
Niall said. "And a fire at sea would be even more terrify-
ing than one on land. We'd have no place to go."

"But—"

"Hush, Ciara," Alyson said, watching Niall. Although
the order he'd given was sensible, she was as sure as she
could be that he was relaying it from someone else. Without moving to put out the lantern, and relieved that Ciara
had let go of her arm when the door opened, she said to
Niall, "We have stopped, have we not?"

"Aye, or nearly, for we have dropped two of our

---

* Pronounced Neal.

anchors," he said. "But you must put out that light, lass. Even the storm lights on deck are dark now."

"So we do not want to be seen," Alyson said. "But who would see us?"

"That is not for you to know," Niall said.

"Do you know?" she asked. "Or is your friend Sir Mungo keeping secrets from you as well as from us?"

With audible strain in his voice, he said, "You must call Mungo 'Sir Kentigern,' Alyson. His friends call him Mungo, because that is what friends often do call a man with that name. But he is not *Sir* Mungo to anyone."

"I keep forgetting that," she said calmly. "Sir Kentigern is such a lot to say. But you do not answer my question, Niall. Do you know why we have stopped?"

"I ken only that they have sent a boat ashore with six oarsmen," he said. "Now, that must be enough. Will you put out that light, or shall I?"

"I'll do it," she said. "Good night, Niall."

"Good night, my lady." Evidently, he trusted her word, because he went out and shut the door without saying more.

Ciara waited only until he had shut it to say with panic in her voice, "Ye'll no put that light out, m'lady, I prithee! 'Twould be dark as a tomb in here!"

"Do you want Sir Kentigern to come down to us?" Alyson asked her.

"Nay, I do not," Ciara said. "For all that he may be the master's friend, I dinna like the man."

"Nor do I," Alyson said, careful not to reveal the understatement of those three short words in her tone. "You should lie down on yon shelf bed now and try to go to sleep when I put out the light. I shan't need you to undress me."

"I ken fine that I shouldna sleep in your bed, m'lady," Ciara said. "But I'll take it and thank ye for letting me have it, because get in that hammock and let this storm-tossed ship fling me about with every motion, I *will not*!"

"Hush now, Ciara. Take advantage of this respite, and try to sleep."

Why, though, Alyson wondered, *were* they stopping so soon? They had left Edinburgh's Leith Harbor at dusk, Sir Kentigern "Mungo" Lyle having insisted they could wait no longer. Mungo was secretary to the Earl of Orkney, whom Niall served as well, and it was on business of Orkney's that the two men were traveling to France.

Alyson had met the earl. He was only a few years her senior and knew his worth, but he was not nearly as puffed up in his own esteem as Mungo was.

They had had to wait in the harbor too long as it was, Mungo insisted. Earlier storms had delayed and battered their ship, the *Maryenknyght,* on her voyage from France to Edinburgh with a cargo of French wines. Then they'd had to load the return cargo and spare two more days for hasty repairs.

But now, whatever was happening on deck...

"I'm going to go up and see what's going on," Alyson told Ciara. "Prithee, do not argue or fling yourself into a fret, because you will not dissuade me. We are where we are. But I want to know where that is and what they are doing."

"Prithee, m'lady—"

"We can judge our danger better if we have information, Ciara, so you must be patient. Occupy yourself with trying to sleep. I will hold this lantern until you are safe on that bed but no longer, lest Mungo should come down to look in on us."

If he did, he would more likely run right into *her* on her way up. But Alyson doubted that Ciara would think of that. Ciara was concerned with her own safety, which was reasonable but immaterial when one could do naught to increase it.

Ciara eyed her mistress measuringly. Although she had served Alyson for only the two months since Alyson's wedding, Ciara evidently knew her well enough to realize that further debate would be useless, because she swiftly unlaced her kirtle and pulled it off. Then, in her flannel shift, with a thick quilt over her, she lay on the narrow bed with its thin pallet, visibly gritted her teeth, shut her eyes tight, and nodded for Alyson to put out the light.

Alyson donned her warm, hooded cloak first, then blew out the lantern and felt for its hook on the wall. Hanging the lantern carefully, she felt her way to the door latch and raised it, hoping that she would not be so unfortunate as to meet anyone before she had seen whatever there was to see.

The cabin door opened onto a narrow, damp passageway that led to a ladder up to the deck. The ship's hold lay below her, no longer full of wine casks but of roped piles of hides and wool on their way to France. That cargo was already noisome enough to fill the passageway with pungent odors.

Wrinkling her nose but grateful for the faint light coming through the open hatchway, she raised her skirts with one hand, touched the wooden wall with the other for balance, and hurried toward the ladder.

Its rungs were flat on top and the ladder no more than five or six feet to the hatchway, but the process of climbing it in skirts was awkward. The shipmaster's forecastle cabin and a smaller second one flanked the open hatchway. A wooden rail aided Alyson when she climbed high enough to grasp it.

The wind sounded thunderous, but the hatchway, recessed between the two forecastle cabins as it was, sheltered her somewhat. The hatch cover itself was strapped against the portside cabin. She wondered if it had been so all along or if Niall had opened the hatch and left it so. Surely, it ought to stay shut to keep the angry sea from sloshing into the passageway, the two tiny lower cabins, and the vast hold below.

Overhead, black clouds scudded across the night sky. Gaps between them briefly revealed twinkling stars, and as she emerged onto the wet deck, she saw a crescent moon rising over the open sea to her right amidst those flying clouds. They seemed to whip above, below, around, and across the moon in a wild, erratic dance. Since Edinburgh lay behind them, she knew she must be facing east. The prow of the boat therefore pointed south, so they were at the mouth of the Firth of Forth.

From where she stood, looking aft and to her right as she did, she saw only the moon and glossy black mountains of ocean. To her left, she easily made out the land mass of the firth's south coast. Dots of light twinkled in the southwestern distance—perhaps the lights of North Berwick.

Moving forward a few feet to look directly south, beyond the master's cabin, she had to hold her hood against the whipping wind. But the view was astonishing.

At no great distance beyond the ship's rail, sporadic moonlight revealed a huge, precipitous rock formation looming above angry, thunderous waves that broke around it in a frothy skirt turned to silvery lace wherever the moonlight touched it.

She could hear the noise of that crashing surf over the howl of the wind.

Surely, Alyson thought, no boat could land there. But, stepping back into the dark shadows of the space between the two cabins, she kept still and watched.

Although shadowy figures moved about on deck, none challenged her.

Not long after that, through the darkness, she saw a boat, a coble, plunging toward them through the waves. When the moonlight touched it, she saw that it was full of people, at least two of whom were small enough to be children.

Not far away, unbeknownst to anyone aboard the *Maryenknyght*, another ship more nearly akin to a Highland galley than to the merchantman rode the heaving seas. Sir Jacob Maxwell, the *Sea Wolf*'s captain, kept his gaze fixed on the much larger ship. When its sail had come down as it passed North Berwick, he had strongly suspected that it was the ship he sought. When it dropped anchors off the massive, formidable, nearly unapproachable formation known as the Bass Rock, he was sure of it.

The wind came from the northeast quarter, and the merchantman had stopped well away from the Bass Rock and anchored so that its prow faced southeastward. Thus its length had somewhat sheltered its steerboard side earlier as it lowered a boat.

"Be that our quarry, sir?" his helmsman, Coll, asked him quietly in the Gaelic.

"It must be, aye," Jake replied in the same language.

Although he'd been born in Nithsdale, in the Borders, he had spent two-thirds of his life on shipboard, much of it in the Isles, and considered himself nearly as much a Highlander as his helmsman was. Moreover, few of the men aboard spoke Scots or any language except Gaelic, so most conversation aboard was in that language.

"I canna make out her flag in this darkness," Coll said.

"She is the *Maryenknyght* out of Danzig," Jake said. "She was flying a French flag when she entered Leith Harbor, though, and I'd wager that she flew that same flag when she departed. However, it could be a Norse one by now."

He did not add that the *Maryenknyght* belonged to young Henry Sinclair, second Earl of Orkney, or that Henry had sent orders bringing the ship to Edinburgh for this particular, albeit hopefully secret, purpose. Orkney owned more ships than anyone else in Scotland but had not wanted to use one that would be too easily recognizable as his. Hence the *Maryenknyght*'s making what Jake understood to be her first voyage to Scotland.

Since, for a fortnight, he had kept a man posted at the harbor to watch for the right ship (harboring the *Sea Wolf* at a smaller, less frequented site on the firth's north coast), he had not learned the *Maryenknyght*'s name or its intended time of departure until that afternoon. He glanced at his helmsman, knowing that Coll must be bursting with curiosity, but Coll's face had resumed its usual stoic expression.

Shifting his gaze back to the *Maryenknyght*, Jake said, "There's the boat returning now."

"I don't envy anyone trying to climb that great ship in these seas," Coll muttered.

The merchantman's broad side did at least offer some protection as the first of the coble's passengers prepared to climb a rope ladder to the deck of the ship.

Jake realized that he was holding his breath as he watched the man, clearly the coble's rudder man, begin to climb.

One of the six oarsmen had caught the ladder's end while his two comrades on that side were doing their best to keep the coble from banging against the ship. Meanwhile, the fierce winds and incoming waves were trying to push ship and coble back to Edinburgh.

"By my soul," Coll muttered when the first man had reached the deck and a second, much smaller passenger moved to the ladder. "That be a bairn, Captain Jake! Whatever mad business goes forward here?"

Jake did not answer him. His full attention was on the lad, and he could feel the pulse hammering in his neck, as if his heart had leaped into his throat.

"Sakes now, look at him," Coll breathed admiringly. "He's going up that ladder as deftly as ever ye might yourself, sir."

"I suspect that after being lowered in a basket from halfway up the sheerest face of Bass Rock to that boat, as I was told they would be—because the rock boasts only that one place on this side sheltered enough for any boat to approach—climbing a rope ladder on his own must seem easy," Jake said.

"On a night like this one?" Coll exclaimed. "Who the devil was crazy enough to order such a thing?"

"His grace, the King," Jake replied.

Aware of Coll's stunned silence, Jake watched the

second lad climb the ladder almost as lithely as the first one had. Returning his gaze to the coble to see a tall, slender man grab the rope ladder, he felt his jaw tighten. He had counted the men in the boat and knew that this had to be Henry of Orkney. Jake had known him almost from Henry's birth and liked him. He did not want the wicked weather to send the young earl into the ice-cold sea, where he might drown before the others could get to him. But Henry could swim, and Henry was not Jake's first priority.

"Am I to know who those lads be, sir?" Coll asked bluntly.

Jake hesitated, but he had known Coll for over a decade and trusted him. Moreover, they'd be following the *Mary-enknyght* to her destination, and accidents did happen, even to men like himself who had lived on ships most of their lives. If aught did happen to him, his men should understand the exact nature of their mission.

Knowing that the wind would blow his words away before they reached ears other than Coll's and that, with the *Sea Wolf*'s sails down as they were, the other men were focused on their oars, Jake leaned nearer and said, "Wardlaw said nowt about any second lad to me when we were in St. Andrews, Coll. But one of them is now heir to the Scottish Crown."

In the uncertain moonlight, he saw Coll's eyes widen. "Jamie Stewart?"

"Aye, sure, for since Davy Stewart's death—"

"Sakes, sir, that were a year ago!"

"It was, aye, but whilst the news of Davy's death was still new, James was safe at St. Andrews Castle under Bishop Wardlaw's guardianship. Forbye, after Parliament proclaimed that Davy's death was accidental instead of the murder we all ken fine that it must have been, his grace did begin to fear for Jamie's life, too."

"That would explain why the lad has been missing these two months past and more," Coll said. "But how could he have lived on that rock for so long?"

"There is an ancient castle built right into the rock about halfway up."

"Ye be jesting, sir. Nae one could build a castle there."

"Believe it," Jake said. "The plain fact is, Coll, that because after Davy's death his grace did recognize the threat to Jamie's life, he arranged to send Jamie to our greatest ally, the King of France, for safekeeping."

"Aye, well, ye need not tell me who his grace fears would do the lad harm," Coll said with a grunt. "Only one man would be sure to benefit from it, and that be the one next in line for the throne. But if aught happened to the wee lad, would not the country rise in anger against his murderous uncle, the Duke of Albany?"

"Most likely they would have, had Jamie's death occurred soon after Davy's," Jake agreed. "But it did not. Recall, too, that folks expected Parliament to understand that Albany was responsible for Davy's death. Instead, thanks to an earlier winter this year than last and the inability of many Highland lords to reach Perth, Albany's allies in Parliament prevailed. Not only did they declare Davy's death an accident. They also named Albany Governor of the Realm again."

Coll nodded. "'Tis true that once the wicked duke held the reins of power again, even his grace would have had to acknowledge that Jamie was no longer safe here in Scotland. But what be our place in all this, sir?"

"We are merely to see that Jamie gets safely to France,"

Jake said. "And mayhap to do what we can to aid him if aught goes amiss."

∼

After watching men rush to aid the first child aboard and wrap him in warm blankets, Alyson went back down the ladder to her own tiny cabin. Since the country had speculated on the fate of their eight-year-old crown prince for months, she immediately suspected who at least one of the children might be.

The presence of Mungo and her husband on that ship—and thus her own—likewise suddenly grew more understandable. Did Niall and Mungo not serve Henry of Orkney, chief member of the wealthy and powerful Sinclair family, which had long supported kings of Scots even when they disagreed with them?

Indeed, she had wondered why they were sailing on such a wretched ship, on Henry's business, when Henry owned dozens if not hundreds of ships of his own. But well aware now that if she was right and Jamie Stewart *was* their primary passenger, she dared not wait there to see who else was with him.

Better to proceed cautiously until she learned more.

The winds seemed to ease for a time after they raised anchor and headed southward, and the following day dawned overcast with rain clearly threatening.

Alyson wasted no time after waking before showing herself on deck, where one of the first men she saw was Henry Sinclair. He clearly was neither astonished nor delighted to see her, but he greeted her cordially enough.

"Good morrow, my lord," Alyson replied.

"In troth, 'tis a dismal day, my lady," he said with a

slight smile. "Forbye, I must tell you how sorry I was to miss your wedding to our Niall."

"And are likewise sorry to see me here," she said. " 'Tis true, is it not, sir?"

With a rueful look, he said, "It is, aye, though in courtesy I should not say it."

"With respect, sir, you may always speak the truth to me, for I prefer candor. What others call tact or cosseting nearly always results in misunderstandings of one sort or another. Do not you agree?"

His blue eyes twinkled. "I might, but many would disagree with you, madam. Most people, in my experience, do not appreciate bluntness."

She smiled but said with her usual frankness, "That was Jamie Stewart I saw come aboard from your coble last night, was it not?"

He glanced swiftly around before saying in a lower tone than before, "The captain of this ship is French, Lady Alyson, and so is his crew. So, although we call both boys by their given names, we will say little about them during the voyage."

"Doubtless an excellent notion, sir, but I trust that you will not keep them cooped up in that wee cabin opposite mine below."

With a wry smile, he said, "In troth, they slept on pallets in the master's cabin last night, with me. I had meant to turn Mungo and your husband out of the smaller forecastle cabin and order them into the cabin opposite yours. I did not do so last night, though, for fear of waking you and your woman."

"I see," she said. "But if you want no undue attention drawn to the boys..."

"Sakes, I do take your meaning," Henry said. "I had been thinking that as Jamie has been living rough these past months, I could at least give him the more comfortable cabin. But I cannot. Still, one dislikes..." He paused, clearly thinking.

"In troth, sir, I was trying to imagine how Ciara and I might earn our place on this ship, since you are unhappy to have found us aboard."

"Not unhappy, certainly, nor is it of use to repine now..."

"Prithee, sir, we can certainly help to look after the boys whilst we travel."

His relief was plain. "I'll accept that offer," he said. "After more than two months on that rock, my ability to devise new entertainments has long fled me."

Well satisfied, Alyson went to inform Ciara that their voyage would no longer be nearly as tedious as it had already begun to seem. What Niall or Mungo might say to it all, she did not trouble her head to consider.

~

The uncertain weather continued. By the second day, the winds had picked up strongly again, and Jake thought that the merchantman allowed them to push it dangerously near to the English north coast. Although England, France, and Scotland were enjoying a rare truce, he had little faith in truces. Moreover, he had heard that pirates often prowled that coast.

On the third afternoon, a squadron of five ships emerged from behind a great outcropping and sailed toward the *Maryenknyght*. Hearing cannon fire and seeing the merchantman begin to heave to, Jake watched in dismay as the English ships surrounded it and two of the larger ones, using grappling irons, flanked it.

He could do naught. The *Sea Wolf* carried no artillery and was heavily outnumbered. Nor had it been anyone's intent that Jake should do aught but witness the prince's safe arrival in France and report it to the bishop. However, if the pirates took captives, he would follow them and mayhap render aid to the captives then.

Sometime later, when the five other ships left the *Maryenknyght* to plunge about, apparently uncontrolled in the angry seas, Jake ordered the *Sea Wolf* closer, wondering why the pirates had not sailed the merchantman into harbor.

When the *Maryenknyght* began to list, he realized that it was sinking. Only then did he see that at least one person, a young woman by the look of her, remained aboard.

THE DISH

Where authors give you the inside scoop!

From the desk of Bella Riley

Dear Reader,

The first time I ever saw an Adirondack lake I was twenty-three years old and madly in love. My boyfriend's grandparents had built their "camp" in the 1940s, and he'd often told me that it was his favorite place in the world. ("Camp" is Adirondack lingo for a house on a lake. If it's really big, like the Vanderbilts' summer home on Raquette Lake, people sometimes throw the word "great" in front of it.)

I can still remember my first glimpse of the blue lake, the sandy beach, the wooden docks jutting into it, the colorful sails of the boats that floated by. It was love at first sight. My mind was blown by the beauty all around me.

Of course, since I'm a writer, my brain immediately began spinning off into storyland. What if two kids grew up together in this small lake town and were high-school sweethearts? What if one of them left the other behind for bright lights/big city? And what would their reunion look like ten years later?

Fast-forward fifteen years from that first sight of an Adirondack lake, and I couldn't be more thrilled to introduce my Emerald Lake series to you! After thinking she had left the small town—and the girl she had once been—behind forever, Andi Powell must return to help run Lake Yarns, her family's knitting store on Main Street. Of course everyone in town gets involved in a love story that she's convinced herself is better left forgotten. But with the help of the Monday Night Knitting Group, Nate's sister, Andi's mother and grandmother, and an old circus carousel in the middle of the town green, Andi just might find the love she's always deserved in the arms of the one man who has waited his entire life for her.

I hope you fall as much in love with the beauty and people of Emerald Lake as I did.

Happy reading,

Bella Riley

www.BellaRiley.com

P.S. That boyfriend is now my husband (Guess where we honeymooned? Yes, the lake!), and four years ago we bit the bullet and became the proud owners of our very own Adirondack camp. Now, just in case you're tempted to throw the word "great" around, you should know that our log cabin is a hundred years old...and pretty much original. Except for the plumbing. Thankfully, we have that!

♥ ♥ ♥ ♥ ♥ ♥ ♥ ♥ ♥ ♥ ♥ ♥ ♥ ♥

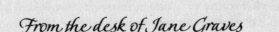

From the desk of Jane Graves

Dear Reader,

In HEARTSTRINGS AND DIAMOND RINGS (on sale now), Alison Carter has been stuck in the dating world for years, and she's getting a little disillusioned. In personal ads, she's discovered that "athletic" means the guy has a highly developed right bicep from opening and closing the refrigerator door; and that a man is "tall, dark, and handsome" only in a room full of ugly albino dwarves. But what about those other descriptions in personal ads? What do they *really* mean?

"Aspiring actor": Uses Aussie accent to pick up chicks

"Educated": Watches *Jeopardy!*

"Emotionally sound": Or so his latest psychiatrist says

"Enjoys fine dining": Goes inside instead of using the drive-through

"Friendship first": As long as "friendship" includes sex

"Good listener": Has nothing intelligent to say

"Likes to cuddle": Mommy issues

"Looking for soulmate": Or just someone to have sex with

"Loyal": Stalker

"Old fashioned": Wants you barefoot and pregnant

"Passionate": About beer, football, and Hooters waitresses

"Romantic": Isn't nearly as ugly by candlelight

"Spiritual": Drives by a church on his way to happy hour

"Stable": Heavily medicated

"Young at heart": And one foot in the grave

"Witty": Quotes dialogue from *Animal House*

Alison finally decides enough is enough. She's going to hire a matchmaker, who will find out the truth about a man *before* she goes out with him. What she doesn't expect to find is a matchmaking *man*—one who really *is* tall, dark, and handsome! And suddenly Mr. Right just might be right under her nose...

I hope you'll enjoy HEARTSTRINGS AND DIAMOND RINGS!

Happy reading!

Jane Graves

www.janegraves.com

From the desk of Eileen Dreyer

Dear Reader,

I love to write the love story of two people who have known each other a long time. I love it even more when they're now enemies. First of all, I don't have to spend time introducing them to each other. They already have a history, and common experiences. They speak in a kind of shorthand that sets them apart from the people around them. Emotions are already more complex. And then I get to mix in the added spice that comes from two people who spit and claw each time they see each other. Well, if you've read the first two books in my Drake's Rakes series, you know that Lady Kate Seaton and Major Sir Harry Lidge are definitely spitting and clawing. In ALWAYS A TEMPTRESS, we finally find out why. And we get to see if they will ever resolve their differences and finally admit that they still passionately love each other.

Happy Reading!

Eileen Dreyer

www.eileendreyer.com

♥ ♥ ♥ ♥ ♥ ♥ ♥ ♥ ♥ ♥ ♥ ♥ ♥ ♥ ♥

From the desk of Amanda Scott

Dear Reader,

St. Andrews University, alma mater of Prince William and Princess Kate, was Scotland's first university, and it figures significantly in HIGHLAND HERO, the second book in my Scottish Knights trilogy, as well as in its predecessor, HIGHLAND MASTER (Forever, February 2011). The heroes of all three books in the trilogy met as students of Walter Traill, Bishop of St. Andrews, in the late fourteenth century. All three are skilled warriors and knights of the realm.

Sir Ivor Mackintosh of HIGHLAND HERO—besides being handsome, daring, and a man of legendary temper—is Scotland's finest archer, just as Fin Cameron of HIGHLAND MASTER is one of the country's finest swordsmen. Both men are also survivors of the Great Clan Battle of Perth, in which the Mackintoshes of Clan Chattan fought champions of Clan Cameron. In other words, these two heroes fought on opposing sides of that great trial by combat.

Nevertheless, thanks to Bishop Traill, they are closer than most brothers.

Because Traill's students came from noble families all over Scotland, any number of whom might be feuding or actively engaged in clan warfare, the peace-loving Traill insisted that his students keep their identities secret and use simple names within the St. Andrews community. They were on their honor to not probe into each other's antecedents, so they knew little if anything about their friends' backgrounds while studying academics and knightly skills together. Despite that constraint, Traill also taught them the value of trust and close friendships.

. The St. Andrews Brotherhood in my Scottish Knights series is fictional but plausible, in that the historic Bishop Traill strongly supported King Robert III and Queen Annabella Drummond while the King's younger brother, the Duke of Albany, was actively trying to seize control of the country. Traill also provided protection at St. Andrews for the King's younger son, James (later James I of Scotland), conveyed him there in secrecy, and wielded sufficient power to curb Albany when necessary.

We don't know how Traill and the King arranged for the prince, age seven in 1402, to travel across Scotland from the west coast to St. Andrews Castle. But that sort of mystery stimulates any author's gray cells.

So, in HIGHLAND HERO, when the villainous Albany makes clear his determination to rule Scotland no matter what, Traill sends for Sir Ivor to transport young Jamie to St. Andrews. Sir Ivor's able if sometimes trying assistant in this endeavor is the Queen's niece, Lady Marsaili Drummond-Cargill, who has reasons of her own to elude Albany's clutches but does not approve of temperamental men or men who assume she will do their bidding without at least *some* discussion.

Traill's successor, Bishop Henry Wardlaw (also in HIGHLAND HERO), founded William's and Kate's university in 1410, expanding on Traill's long tradition of education, believing as Traill had that education was one of the Church's primary duties. Besides being Scotland's first university, St. Andrews was also the first university in Scotland to admit women (1892)—and it admitted them on exactly the same terms as men. Lady Marsaili would have approved of that!

Suas Alba!

Amanda Scott

www.amandascottauthor.com

Find out more about Forever Romance!

Visit us at
www.hachettebookgroup.com/publishing_forever.aspx

Find us on Facebook
http://www.facebook.com/ForeverRomance

Follow us on Twitter
http://twitter.com/ForeverRomance

NEW AND UPCOMING TITLES

Each month we feature our new titles
and reader favorites.

CONTESTS AND GIVEAWAYS

We give away galleys, autographed copies,
and all kinds of exclusive items.

AUTHOR INFO

You'll find bios, articles, and links to personal websites
for all your favorite authors—and so much more.

GET SOCIAL

Connect with your favorite authors, editors, and
other Forever fans, and share what's important to you.

THE BUZZ

Sign up for our monthly romance newsletter,
and be the first to read all about it.